ANYWHERE BUT SCHUYLKILL

By Michael Dunn

If you wish to enjoy God's bounty,
Go anywhere but Schuylkill County.

HISTORIUM BOOKS

Cover design by White Rabbit Arts

Follow the author at
www.thehistoricalfictioncompany.com/hp-authors/michael-dunn

www.michaeldunnauthor.com

EBOOK ISBN: 978-1-962465-04-5
PAPERBACK ISBN: 978-1-962465-45-8

Published by Historium Press 2024
New York, NY / Macon, GA USA

For my father, Fredric G. Dunn, who always rooted for the underdog, and who instilled in me, at a very young age, a passion for labor history, poetry and music.

May this be his pie in the sky.

TABLE OF CONTENTS

Chapter 1
Avondale, Pennsylvania
Monday, September 6, 1871

Mike Doyle knew it was going to be a bad day as soon as he saw the platoon of cops, with their bell-shaped helmets and Winchester rifles, and the miners slouching past them with their picks dragging in the dirt. He moved closer to Da, who continued marching forward, with his chin up, as if everything was fine, toward the headframe and cage that would take him down into the bowels of the earth. That damned headframe always gave Mike the shakes. It looked like a giant wooden gallows towering over the mineshaft, only eviler, with its cables and hoist, and the illusion of security. A gallows, at least, was honest. With a gallows, you knew exactly when you would die.

"Can't we go home? Come back tomorrow?"

"Ye know we can't." Da stopped and gazed down with concern. His eyes were deep blue, with golden halos around them that made him seem both powerful and forgiving at the same time. "Ye aren't gonna win every scrap, Mikey. But if ye fight with honor, like we did, then ye gotta accept your losses with honor, too. Can't go around with a chip on your shoulder. Does nobody any good. Now let's walk past those cops with our heads high."

As they walked, Mike couldn't stop thinking how much more they could have gotten if they had held out a little longer, like a school, so Tara and Li'l Bill wouldn't have to go to work when they got to be his age.

"Why'd Schuylkill County get the minimum wage and not us?"

"Hmm." Da stroked his beard. "I reckon the union's stronger down there. Up here, the coll'ries're all owned by big railroads, with expensive lawyers. They can afford to starve us."

"We can move to Shenandoah!" The words rushed out so fast, Mike's voice cracked. "With Aunt Mary and Uncle Sean. That's Schuylkill County, ain't it?"

"'Tis. But we can't go running like rabbits each time there's trouble. Besides, ye really want to live with Uncle Sean? Remember the thrashing ye got last time we were there?"

Mike didn't want to live with Uncle Sean or leave his friends in Avondale. But how would they ever get ahead? The Company owned everything in town. The dingy clapboard houses. The streetlamps and outhouses. Even the Pluck Me, where they bought their groceries. Shenandoah at least had its own schools and stores. And the possibility of rising wages.

He glanced at the breaker. Its long, sloping roof looked like a wolf's snout jutting from the hillside. Boys were lining up outside, innocent young mice marching right into its maw. And Oswald was at the door, with his cigar and rats-nest sideburns, smacking his switch against his hand, like he couldn't wait to use it on them.

"Da, I'm sick of being a breaker boy."

"Really? Ye sick of supporting your family? Protecting 'em from hunger? Being a man? That's what cleaning coal does."

"Um." Mike softened his voice. "Couldn't I support 'em more with a better job?"

"You're thirteen." Da gave him a playful nudge. "You'll be a nipper soon enough. Then a muleboy. Guaranteed. Those jobs are based on age. That's how it works."

Mike wished he could speed up time, but with his luck, he'd speed it up too much. Wind up in a coffin. "Hey, why ain't ye going to the wake today with the other Irishmen?"

"Wanted to, but Evans needs me to help timber the new manway. We don't do that today, there'll be a lot more wakes tomorrow. Anyhow, we'll get paid sooner. And, God willing, we'll start living like humans again."

"You can say that again, Doyle."

Mike looked over his shoulder. It was Mr. Evans, with Methusalem and his two brothers.

"Guess it's time," Da said, shaking Mike's hand. "Gonna be a darn fine day, son. Too bad we won't get to see it."

Mike smiled, remembering the day he started in the breaker, when Da first made this joke. How scared he'd been. How this silly little joke had given him the confidence to get in line and face

Oswald. Heck, today would be fine. Easier than that first day. He started to wave goodbye, but when the entire Evans family followed Da into the cage, including Methusalem, his vision clouded and his hand dropped back to his side. What was *he* doing in there? He was barely ten!

"I'm a nipper," Methusalem called, with his tiny girl's voice, waving, as the cage descended.

Mike's head started to throb. Any harder, it would explode. He wanted to punch the little pissdapants in the nose. Why'd he get to spend the day underground, whittling sticks and killing rats? No aching back. No burning knuckles. And no Oswald. It was Mike's turn to get that job. He was older, *and* he'd been there longer. Methusalem was just a little boy. Looked it, too, with those thin wisps of yellowy-white hair peeking out from under his cap like the tail of a baby duck, and skin so pink and clean-smelling. Da was wrong. He got that job because he's Welsh!

"Doy-le!"

Mike slowly raised his head. Oswald was standing right in front of him.

"Ye here to work, or shirk?"

"W-work, sir."

"Then move it." His breath smelled like a latrine.

Suppressing a gag, Mike marched across the Bloomsburg tracks to the breaker, past three footmen, with black arms and racoon faces, their clanging spades barely audible under the sputtering engines. He tried not to sneer, since he figured he'd be one of 'em someday. Bottom of the heap. Lowest paid. Ridiculed as half-men. Real miners had to descend the mineshaft each day, three hundred feet down, something a jellylegs like him would never be able to do. Just the thought of it gave him vertigo. He always imagined the headframe cracking, or the hoist breaking free, and the cage plummeting to the bottom in an explosion of shattered wood and body parts.

Probably just as well he didn't get that nipper's job.

He stepped into the breaker, with Oswald close behind. It was as loud as an avalanche inside. The gnashing iron teeth of the crusher. Whirling sorting screens. Rivers of coal thundering down steel chutes in great black torrents. Dust so thick you could barely see. It burned the eyes and throat. Got stuck between the teeth. Smelled like rotten eggs.

Pulling his shirt over his nose, he proceeded through the diagonal maze of chutes that crisscrossed the room. Each had ascending rows of boys sitting side by side above them on thin planks, as if they were on bleachers at a ballgame, except instead of facing home plate and enjoying the game, they all faced uphill, hunched over, their arms and legs darting in and out, like cockroaches rummaging for food.

Seamus was sitting right in the middle of their plank. He refused to budge until Oswald slapped it with his switch, and then he only scooted a few inches, his lip curling. You'd think he was being asked to sit next to a corpse.

Oswald smacked it again with his switch. "You girlies play nice."

Mike sat down, swinging one leg into the chute, and then the other. He began kicking back and forth to slow the flow. He reached for a piece of slate. Nabbed it. Tossed it aside. Seamus's body moved stiffly against his. Four months off the job and he'd gotten fat and lazy. Four months with a stupid grudge. The big baby should be treating him like a hero. He had taken the worst licking any of them had ever seen, standing up for Methusalem when Oswald abused him.

"Glad to be back?" Paddy called to Seamus from the next chute over, as if Mike wasn't there.

"Hell, yeh," Seamus yelled. "Beats bein' stuck at home with the girls and babies."

"Or bein' a tramp."

Shit, being at home with the girls and babies would beat being here with these two knuckleheads. Even being a tramp sounded better. Sleeping in the woods. Plucking what he needed from orchards. Hopping freights. Seeing a bit of the country. No one bossing him around.

He reached for another piece of slate, imagining what Mamai would cook for supper. With him and Da back at work, maybe she'd serve meat. He closed his eyes and conjured the smell of a smoky roast. But then the emergency whistle shrilled, jarring him from his dream. Louder and louder. Pulsing. Desperate. An infant shrieking in his ears.

He jumped down and ran from the building, Seamus close behind, zigzagging past the patchy fires that were sprouting up everywhere, to the front gate, where he fell to his knees panting.

The air was thick, like breathing hot soup. Mike started to choke. His eyes watered and his ears throbbed as if he was being sucked into a tornado. Probably that terrible howling, he thought, looking up. Flames roared from the mineshaft one hundred feet into the air, swirling around and around. They were devouring the headframe. Pullies and cables crashed into the shaft. Blocking the only exit. Filling the mine with blackdamp. Suffocating the men. And Seamus, standing there with his fat chipmunk cheeks and stupid grin.

"What's the big deal? Just a bunch of Welshmen down there."

Mike pulled back his fist and smashed him in the nose.

"My da's down there!"

Chapter 2

Mike staggered back; his legs so wobbly he could barely stand. He grabbed the coll'ry gate for support and scanned the area, wondering what to do. The crackling air stank of burnt wood and creosote. Everything was yellow, hazy, except for his knuckles, which were bloody. Up the hill, men and boys were passing buckets down from the water tower. Must've been thirty of 'em.

He stepped over Seamus and ran to the line. Someone handed him a bucket. He passed it forward in exchange for an empty one. Then came another, and another. Full buckets sloshing forward. Empty ones ratcheting back up the hill. A well-lubricated machine. Efficient. Unerring. They'd have the blaze out in no time. Send a rescue team. Have Da home in time for supper.

An ember popped near his ear. He jerked his head up.

Fire was still gushing from the mineshaft as if they were doing nothing. Each bucket of water they tossed at it evaporated instantly. No more effective than spitting into Hell. It was devouring the storehouse and metal shop, punching through windows, shattering glass, spreading up the hillside, advancing toward the breaker. If they didn't extinguish it soon, it would take down the water tower, sweep into town, destroy their homes.

"It's useless. We need a flood. A downpour!"

"That's up to God," said the man behind him. "This is all we got till the fire engines arrive."

Of course, a fire crew would put it out.

Mike looked heavenward. Black clouds. Hurray! God was listening.

"Keep going," said the man, handing him another bucket.

Passing it forward, Mike could see the road into town. No fire engines. Just a lot of wild-eyed people, mostly women and children, running toward the pit, screaming and crying. Behind them, the sun was rising over Curry Hill. The sky above it was the color of robins' eggs.

The bucket dropped from his hands.

Those weren't rainclouds. It was smoke!

He wanted to run home, bury his head in Mamai's bosom, like he was still a little boy, her soothing voice whispering that everything would be alright. But how could he? If he came home without Da, she'd never let him in the house. Li'l Bill would scrunch up his eyes, kick him in the shins. Tara might never speak to him again.

There had to be something else he could do, something more effective.

To his right, the stable boss was driving the mules onto the road, bucking and kicking in terror. At the water tower, he saw Mr. O'Neil, Da's best friend, digging a trench with six other men. Mike dropped the bucket ran as fast as he could, grabbed a shovel, and thrust it at the ground, but the earth was so dry it barely pierced the surface.

"Back in line!" yelled Engineer Weir. "Leave the digging to the men."

The shovel grew heavy and fell from his hands. Everyone was staring at him. In the background, he heard wailing and sobbing from down by the pit. The entire patch was probably there, searching for their fathers and husbands. And here he was, wasting everyone's time, getting in their way. Weir was right. He was useless.

"Let him dig," said Mr. O'Neil. "His da's down there."

"Yeh," said the others.

Mr. O'Neil handed Mike a pick. His underarms were damp and smelled like onions. "Use this first. It'll loosen it up."

Mike wiped his eyes with his sleeve, then took a swing, wedging the blade in the earth.

"Like this." Mr. O'Neil crouched low and pried the pick loose. He took several short, shallow jabs, sending dust and pebbles flying. Standing up again, he handed it back to Mike. "We'll save your da. There's enough clean air to last at least twelve hours. Maybe twenty-four."

Squatting, Mike took a few quick stabs at the dry earth, keenly aware of the men watching him. A visible groove was forming. Then a furrow. If he got it deep enough, they could get all the water they needed from the tower to the fire engine. He grabbed the shovel and thrust it into the ground, standing on the blade with both feet, working it deeper into the earth. Levering it back, he pulled out a large clod, tossed it aside. Bouncing slightly on his toes, he shoved it in again and removed another. He continued without letup, even as the blisters on his hands popped and bled. It was not until he heard a cheer from below that he paused to catch his breath.

A fire crew had arrived with a small, red hand tub the size of a coal wagon. They connected the hose to the side of the engine, while the bucket brigade filled the tub. A fireman screwed a long copper nozzle to the end of the hose and dragged it toward the fire. Another pumped the brake handle up and down. The hose swelled. Water came out, first as a sputter, then in small pulses, but it was no more effective than the bucket brigade. The crowd saw it was hopeless. Their sobbing and shrieking intensified. They wrung their hands and beat the ground. "God help us!" someone cried. "Who'll feed my babies?" A woman in brown calico fainted and was dragged away by two men, as her sausage-fingered child toddled after her, bawling.

Pushing up his sleeves, Mike returned to his excavating, even more determined than before. His shirt clung to his moist torso, like a snakeskin that was partway off. He wanted to rip it to shreds, but that would waste time, so he ignored it and kept digging, his shoulders and back aching worse than they did after his first day in the breaker, when he was ten and wanted to quit. The only reason he didn't was Da's strong fingers, kneading his shoulders and back, his soothing voice explaining that a feller got used to it, that he had to keep working, even when sore, to keep his family fed. And the realization that Da had never missed a day of work, even when he hurt his back. Never complained, either. And his job, shoveling coal all day at the bottom of the pit, in water up to his knees, was way harder and more dangerous than picking coal in the breaker, or digging a trench.

Leaping back into motion, Mike jammed the shovel into the ground. He stomped on it, wedged it deeper, scooped out a pile, then did it again. Each time his back spasmed, he pushed himself harder, reminding himself it was for Da. Each twinge in his shoulders, just a minor sacrifice. Nothing compared with the sacrifices Da had made for them, like spending a week in jail after the Citizens' Committee bashed his head during the strike.

He continued digging for an hour, until Weir said it was time to open the valve.

"Your da's gonna be proud," said Mr. O'Neil, as the water rushed down the hill.

Mike tossed the shovel to the ground and surveyed their work. Weir was wrong. He could dig as well as the men. And Mr. O'Neil had said "gonna," not "woulda." That meant Da was still alive and really would be home for supper. He had to find Mamai, tell her the news. But how? It was bedlam down there, at least a thousand people, pushing, shoving, struggling to get closer, as if they'd be able to see their loved ones through the flames and debris. There was no room for the firemen to work. Cops were pulling people out of the way, trying to make a corridor, but as soon as one person was gone, another took their place.

"See your family?" Mr. O'Neil asked.

Mike shook his head.

A second engine pulled up, a horse-drawn rig. It was so big, it took twelve men to pump the brake handles. They folded and unfolded like jackknives, rocking the engine so hard its bell began to toll. But they couldn't get near the fire, the crowd was so thick. So they aimed at the people to disperse them. The water came out in a powerful jet. It knocked people over and sent them skidding in the mud. Mothers pulled children down with them. A preacher's hat flew off. It blew past the remains of the storeroom, landing near Mamai, who was sprawled on her back.

Mike ran down the hill and knelt beside her, cradling her head.

Her hair, which was normally plush like an auburn ball of yarn, was matted and dense. Her blouse, usually immaculate, was smeared with mud. And her fists were uncharacteristically balled at her sides. She looked up, bewildered, as if she was just now recognizing it was him.

"You're alive!"

Before he could reply, Tara emerged from the crowd, with Deirdre screeching in her arms. She squatted beside him and stared at the fire, with the confused, haunted look of a person awaking from a bad dream. Usually, Mike thought she resembled a school teacher, even though she was almost two years younger than he was, dignified, with porcelain cheeks and curious brown eyes, and her hair always arranged in two tight, perfect braids. But right now her appearance was unsettling. Her face was smudged with tears and soot, and her braids were coming undone, like a teacher who had met her match in an unruly student.

Li'l Bill, who followed behind her, was in no better shape. He was shaking so hard that his freckles seemed to be ducking for cover beneath his fiery orange mop, as it flailed against his forehead, and Johnny clung desperately to his leg, sobbing, trying not to get flung off.

"Why don't ye pick him up?" Tara said, pressing Deirdre's face to her shoulder. "Can't you see he's scared?"

Bill looked around, as if trying to determine who she was talking to.

"W-what about your father?" Mamai asked.

Mike started to shrug, but caught himself.

"Fire'll be out soon. Rescue crew will have him out in no time."

"Thank God."

"He's gonna die!" Tara cried, pointing at the fire.

Mike grabbed Deirdre from her arms, just as Tara's body heaved and vomit spewed out.

Bill jumped back, his face blanching. "Disgusting."

Mamai got up and wiped Tara's lips with the hem of her dress. Leaning in closer, like she was going to embrace her, she grabbed her chin and held it firmly, her eyes boring into her. "Ye listen to your brother. He knows what he's talking about. If he says your da's gonna be fine, he's gonna be fine. Right, Mighael?"

"Right."

He put Deirdre down next to Johnny, hoping Tara would snuggle them both. Instead, she shrank closer to Mamai, twisting a lock of brown hair between her fingers, while Bill stared at the ground and chewed on a twig.

"They've got enough air to last a day or two," Mike added. "And miles of tunnels. Plenty of places to escape th-."

"Yeh," Bill interrupted, with that devilish twinkle in his eye that always made him look like he was planning some sort of mischief. "He's probably already made it to the next coll'ry over."

"That's right." Mamai wrapped her arms around Mike's brothers and sisters, a mother swan shielding her babies from the rain, as she worked her rosary between her fingers. "The darker the moment, the more hope brightens your future."

Usually Mike cringed at Mamai's sayings, but this time he was grateful she had regained her composure and was back to her old self. He wanted to move closer, squeeze in under her wings, too, but hesitated when he saw Mr. O'Neil approaching.

"Oh, Francis," Mamai said. "Tell me he's gonna be alright."

"Of course, he is, Siobhan. Look, fire's almost out. Best thing right now would be to take everyone back to my place. Help Mrs. O'Neil fix some grub. None of us have eaten all day. By the time you're back, we'll have the derrick up. Send down a rescue team."

"I'll be more use here," said Li'l Bill. "Than stuck at home with Tara and the babies."

"Are ye kidding?" Tara said. "Ye can't even tie your own shoes."

"At least I didn't puke."

"Enough!" Mamai pushed them apart. "Both of yiz."

Bill reminded Mike of himself when he was nine, how frustrated he'd been that he still wasn't working in the breaker, along with other boys his age. But then one night, Da came home with a miner's cap and an extra pair of boots and told him he was all grown up. He still didn't believe it until he felt the cool black leather in his hands, and smelled their earthy odor, like dry oak leaves at the end of summer, and then he didn't take them off for days. It's what Bill needed right now, to feel grown up, useful; not someone else's burden.

Mike grasped him by the shoulders. "Da's counting on ye. Find his tools. And bring 'em back here. Mamai and Tara won't know which ones."

"He's right," said Mr. O'Neil. "When ye return, ye can help us with the derrick."

"Yeh," Bill said. "Da's counting on me."

Chapter 3

By sunset, they had cleared enough debris to send down two men. Mr. Wilcox, the hoist operator, carefully lowered them down in a bucket attached to a winch drawn by two mules. Hundreds of people encircled the derrick and watched in silence. Mike sat wedged between Tara and Mr. O'Neil. But he couldn't sit still, fidgeting at the long, drawn-out groan of the pully, the mist droplets suspended in the lamplight, the steamy snorts of the mules, Tara's foot jittering anxiously against his leg.

Mamai sat in front of them, suckling Johnny beneath her shawl, while Deirdre sat droopy-eyed on her thigh. Li'l Bill, who was chewing on a twig, nuzzled closer. There were scabs on his elbows, as usual. Mike wondered where they came from this time.

As the mules approached the derrick, their nostrils twitched, like they smelled something bad. They tried to back away.

The signal line jiggled.

"Pull," Spade yelled. "Pull!"

Wilcox cracked his whip. The mules broke into a trot. The crowd became frantic. They rocked side to side. Children shrieked. The twins started to sob. An old man threw his cap on the ground in frustration. The air had the strange odor of doused bonfire mixed with skunk.

When the bucket reached the top, only one of the rescue workers was visible. With effort, he bent down to retrieve something, which he hoisted over the rim of the bucket. It looked like a filthy burlap sack filled with rubble, except for the crisp hair, and the lips caked with black froth.

The crowd gasped.

Mike got a sick, dizzy sensation. His arm stung from Tara's nails digging into it.

The rescue worker wiped the sweat from his forehead, then squatted down and hoisted another corpse over the rim. Neither had beards.

Not Da!

A tall, horse-toothed woman burst through the crowd.

"My Palmer!"

Four girls trailed behind her, sobbing pitifully. The biggest, no older than Tara, carried a squalling infant in her arms. The other two little girls clung tightly to their big sister's dress, as if they were afraid they'd get sucked down the shaft and disappear forever if they let go.

"Ain't that Mr. Steele, the stable boss?" Mike asked. "And his muleboy, Slocum?"

"They look terrible," Li'l Bill said. "What's that crust around their mouths?"

"Dried blood," said Mr. O'Neil.

"No," Mamai cried. "Please, no."

Mr. O'Neil grabbed her hand and pressed it between his. "Stable's right next to the furnace, Siobhan. Would've filled instantly with blackdamp. Those fellers hadn't a chance. Everyone else would've had time to run for cover. Bill's safe behind a brattice somewhere deeper in the mine."

Tara stopped sobbing. "Really?"

Li'l Bill's lips formed a quivering smile. "Yeh, Da's no fool."

The rest of the day, men went down and brought up more debris, which Mike, Bill and Tara helped load into coal-carts. Deeper and deeper they went without recovering any of the men. Sometime after dark, a heavy rain began to fall. When lightning struck near the derrick, Spade sent everyone home.

Li'l Bill fell asleep quickly and started to snore, which seemed remarkable considering that Tara was tossing and turning right next to him, whimpering and moaning as if she was in mortal agony. Mike lay on his back on the other side of the bed, eyes wide open. Nothing left to do now except rest up for tomorrow. But how could he sleep with Da still trapped? He might not make it till tomorrow.

Jumping out of bed, he dressed and snuck downstairs. He knocked on Mr. O'Neil's door.

"What in blazes?" Mr. O'Neil rubbed his brow, like his head

hurt. 'Tis three in the morning."

"We can't wait." Mike's voice cracked. "What if he's still alive?"

Mr. O'Neil stared past Mike, out into the darkness, as if weighing his options. "Reckon you've never been down there. Wouldn't know where to look."

Mike shook his head.

"Alright, but if Spade's there, let me do the talking. And when we're underground, you'll do exactly as I say."

"Yes, sir. Anything ye say."

"We'll need someone to drive the mules."

"How 'bout Bill?"

"With our lives at stake?"

"You're right. I'll get Tara."

He ran back upstairs. Tara was already awake, sitting up, with the blanket held to her chin. "What's going on?" she whispered.

"Tell ye outside. Get dressed."

Mr. O'Neil gave them each a headlamp. It had stopped raining and the atmosphere was warm and slippery. A dog-sized raccoon glared at them from the side of a house. The faint pee-like odor of spruce wafted up from the banks of the Susquehanna and hung momentarily over the gummy path, which snatched at their boots like the hands of ghosts reaching up from their graves. They sloshed through Welshtown, which was full of puddles and completely dark, except for the lamp in front of the Pluck Me, left on by mistake, or perhaps it was the Company's attempt to get folks shopping again.

When they reached the bend in the road, Mr. O'Neil told them to wait. He snuck up to the derrick, looked around and hurried back.

"Think ye can drive the mules?" he asked Tara. "Like Wilcox did?"

"Absolutely! I wouldn't let anything happen to either of ye."

"What if they start going too fast?"

She grinned, as if it was obvious. "I'll shout, 'Whoa!'"

"Thatta girl." He pointed to the bucket. "Ready, Mikey?"

"Guess so."

In reality, he was far from ready. His heart was racing and he could barely breathe. He felt as if he was going to swoon. The derrick and bucket looked like a miniature headframe, only ricketier and more dangerous. Instead of a steel cable, it had a thin rope. And everyone knew that mules were stubborn. What if they decided to quit in the middle of the trip down?

Mr. O'Neil held the bucket steady for him. He forced himself to climb in.

There was a snap and the bucket jerked downward.

His stomach dropped. He grabbed the rim of the bucket, as if that would stop him from plummeting to his death. His underarms were slimy with sweat. There was a foul, sour taste in his mouth. He closed his eyes and prayed.

"Shifting timbers," Mr. O'Neil said as he climbed in.

Again, the rope jerked. Another flash of panic. But when he opened his eyes, he could still see Tara. They hadn't dropped more than an inch.

"Ready?" she called.

"Slow and steady," Mr. O'Neil called back. He turned toward Mike. "Keep your lamp on and your hands inside."

Tara whistled and the mules started walking toward the derrick. As they descended, sparkling black walls slid past them, spiked with rusty nails and burnt shards, a nightmare sky spinning out of control. The air got warmer, heavier, the deeper they went. Stale, deathly. Difficult to breathe. The odor of scorched, wet wood. Melted iron. Burnt grease. Shit and piss, worse than a latrine. His hands trembled. His skin was clammy. He thought he would puke.

But then the bucket hit the ground and everything went still.

He looked around and realized they were still alive. He made the sign of the cross and then grinned. That wasn't so bad.

"Keep your headlamp low," Mr. O'Neil said as he climbed out. All kinds of hazards down here. Most of 'em under the water."

Two roads branched away from the shaft. Mr. O'Neil went to the left, the west gangway, beckoning Mike to follow.

"Why this way?" Mike whispered.

"Rescue crews already went the other way. Goes to the airway and furnace, where they found Slocum and Steele."

Mike stepped into a deep puddle. Water overflowed the tops of his boots, soaking his socks. Each subsequent step squished and squeaked, making his toes slimy and cold.

A rat got up on its haunches and hissed, sending a shiver down Mike's back.

"Normally this place is crawlin' with 'em." Mr. O'Neil chucked a rock after it. "Fire must've scared 'em all off."

"But it's a good sign, right? Means plenty of clean air."

O'Neil wiped the back of his neck. "Reckon so." He turned his head away from Mike. "Could ye keep your headlamp down. Damned thing's blindin' me."

"Sorry." Mike tilted his head downward and watched Mr. O'Neil from the corner of his eye, suspicious there was something he wasn't saying.

They turned a corner and the gangway narrowed. The ceiling became so low they had to walk like they were praying, with their knees bent and their upper bodies bowed so acutely it seemed as if they'd topple over. Mr. O'Neil clasped his hands behind his back as he waddled awkwardly forward, holding his head erect to see what was coming. "Duckwalking," he chuckled. "Not bad for short trips, but it's a hundred yards more to the rear breasts. Where your da probably is. Furthest point from the fire."

Mike anticipated the enormous hug he'd give Da. He tried to speed up, but accidentally kicked Mr. O'Neil, who abruptly stopped. Twisting his headlamp to the side, he looked Mike in the eye.

"Remember how Slocum and Steele looked? Your da could look like that."

Mike's hands clenched into fists. Why did he say that? The whole point of coming down here was to bring Da back, alive. Why come at three a.m. to recover a corpse? Why tell them everything was gonna be fine? That there was plenty of clean air and places to hide from the blackdamp?

"Wait. The rat proves there's enough clean air!"

Mr. O'Neil gently tapped his arm, nodding. "Sorry, Mikey." His headlamp washed up and down the foot of the wall, illuminating a trail of bloated rat carcasses.

Mike shuddered. He took a step backward, with his hand covering his mouth.

Disgusting, but not proof. Da was smarter than a rat. He'd know where to hide.

"C'mon!" he cried, duckwalking as quickly as he could to the end of the tunnel.

It opened into a large chamber, where they found a barricade made from a coal-cart and powder kegs. Every crack and crevice had been stuffed with socks, shirts, chunks of coal. As airtight as they could've made it.

Mr. O'Neil pulled away a powder keg and they crawled inside.

Another barricade within it. And a corpse sentry.

Mike grabbed Mr. O'Neil's arm.

"It's Bowen," Mr. O'Neil said. "From Hyde Park. Decent feller, bless his soul."

They dragged Bowen into the gangway and began dismantling the barricade. Mike sweated profusely, trembling with the effort. Each sock he yanked away from the barricade, he prayed was not Da's, begging and pleading that the next shirt, kerchief or scarf belonged to someone else.

Mr. O'Neil grabbed a pick. Two swings opened a hole the size of a small window.

"Brace yourself. It ain't pretty."

Mike peered through the hole and shuddered violently. There were bodies were everywhere. More than sixty. Many were naked, having given up their shirts to plug the cracks. Some were sitting up, looking as though they had simply fallen asleep in the middle of a card game. Some had scarves or shirts over their faces in a feeble attempt to ward off the blackdamp. Others were contorted in agony, with hideous, frothy black grimaces. And Da, naked except for his trousers, sitting against the back wall, his blue eyes open, but dim and empty. The skin around his underarms and waist was purple. His beard was hard and crusty.

Mike vomited. He rocked back and forth. His temples throbbed. The bridge of his nose, his cheeks, the back of his throat, ached as if they were holding back the Susquehanna. He rubbed his eyes. Smacked his temples. Stomped his foot. But got no relief.

Mr. O'Neil pulled him gently toward the gangway. "Why don't ye have a wee rest outside. I'll bring him out. We can wheel him back in the coal-cart."

He flung Mr. O'Neil's hand away. *He* was the one who should bring Da home.

Climbing into the chamber, he made it halfway to Da, before something made him freeze. Laying at his feet was Mr. Evans, with Methusalem sprawled across his chest in a final embrace. His brothers, Lewis and Thomas, were on either side, each held snugly in their father's arms. Their entire family, dead. Everyone except their mother. But instead of seeing Mrs. Evans, whom he had never met, Mike pictured Mamai. That's when the tears really started to flow. Everything poured out of him at once. Tears of sorrow and self-pity. Loneliness and despair. Tears that had been sitting in the back of his skull for years because he was too old to cry. Tears for tragedies that hadn't yet happened. That might never happen. Tears of uncertainty and fear. How would he support his family? Protect them? Stay alive in the pit?

What if he got home and Mamai was dead, too?

What if he never made it back home?

Chapter 4
Tuesday, September 14, 1871

Mike gazed down from the landing at Uncle Sean, asleep on the bench of a muddy buckboard wagon, partially covered with a gray horse blanket, feet propped up and head tilted back like his throat was slit. Periodically he jolted upright, as if his snores were seizing him by the collar to yank him awake. Each time he slumped drowsily back into that same twisted-up position, as his two oxen nibbled weeds and swatted flies with their tails.

It was so peaceful with everyone still in bed. Nobody marching to work. No droning donkey engines or sputtering pumps. The air was sweet. Slightly minty. Clean.

A fresh, clean start in Shenandoah.

A tear trickled down Mike's cheek. Better a lifetime here, with all its stink and black phlegm, without any minimum wage, than one without Da. If he had only lived, he would have found a job on the reconstruction crew despite being Irish. Probably would've found Mike one, too. If not, they would've spent their days together, setting rabbit snares in the Shawnee Flats, beneath a buttery half-moon, and the smell of cows and moist alfalfa. Maybe a little fishing, an afternoon swim, same as when he was little, when Da would come out of the water, sopping wet, and wring his long, ruddy beard over his head, like a sopping dishrag. For a moment, Mike thought he smelled river grass steaming on the exposed rocks, but then he realized it was an illusion. Just like the idea that an Irishmen could get a job on the reconstruction crew, when everyone was blaming them for the fire. Yesterday, Paddy's da was found by the river with a bullet in his thigh. At least Mike's family had somewhere to go, somewhere better than Avondale. Aunt Mary was Da's big sister. She wouldn't let anything happen to them.

He went inside. Mamai was kneeling in front of the stove, blowing on the embers.

"Uncle Sean's here."

She looked up, blinking, her eyes red and vacant, as if she was lost in a foggy forest without any hope of ever escaping.

Mike bit his lip, as he fought back more tears. He just wanted it to end. The grief and mourning. Mr. O'Neil said his wife sobbed for days after her father's wake, but then everything went back to normal once she had gotten it out of her system. Mamai never had the chance. The Company sent all the bodies away as soon as they were recovered. Whisked away to the Darling Street Cemetery, in Wilkes-Barre, before anyone but Mike got the chance to say goodbye.

"It'll get better," he said, wrapping an arm around her waist and guiding her to the table. "Let's have a wake for 'im when we get to Shenandoah."

Her cheeks looked like wrinkled pillows beneath her drooping eyes. When Mike was four or five, he thought of her as girl, not a woman, because she only came up to Da's chest and had such a youthful complexion. Yet, even after five kids, (six, if you include Ciara, who died when Mike was a baby), she still looked young, except for her plump, creamy arms, which were quivering with sorrow.

He sat her down across from Tara, who was dunking a crust of bread into a cup of hot water as she bounced Deirdre on her knee. She held the wet dough in front of her, as if trying to decide whether it would be more satisfying to eat it all at once, or in nibbles. But when Deirdre cried, "Bwead, bwead!" she handed it to her instead, covered her face, and wept.

"This always happens," Mamai said.

"What does?" Mike asked, rubbing her shoulders.

"When ye raise a stink, trouble always follows."

Tara nodded.

"The strike?" Mike's voice rose in pitch. "It was an accident! No one set that fire."

"Ye really are like your father," she said, gazing up at him with a soft expression. "My father, too. Beautiful men, both of 'em. They'd do anything for their families. Neither was ever satisfied with how things were. Always fighting to make 'em better."

"That's a good thing," Mike said, remembering that night six months ago, when he had stayed up late with his ear pressed to the door and heard Da tell her how they didn't have a choice, with so many men and boys dying, and wages dropping every year since the war. How John Siney had united all the miners into a new union, the WBA, including the Welsh and the Dutch. How they would shut down every coll'ry in Pennsylvania. Drive up prices. Force the coal barons to give 'em a raise. And Mamai had still worried. Said people died in strikes, went to prison. That it sounded just like Tipperary all over again.

Was she going to use that against him too, someday? Stop him from joining the next strike?

"What happened in Tipperary?"

She reached for Deirdre, who had started crying, lifted her blouse, and pressed her to her bosom. "I had two sisters," she said, wincing. "Both younger than her. Died on the passage over."

Tara's chin trembled. "I-I didn't know."

"There was an uprising at the McCormacks'. They were gonna send your grandda to Van Diemen's Land. We never would've seen him again. So we fled in the middle of the night, just like we're doing today." She glanced down at Deirdre, a tear running down her face.

"Trouble always follows," Tara said, sniffling.

"It ain't the middle of the night!" Mike said. "And it's a much shorter, safer trip."

He went to the bedroom with his jaws clenched, suppressing the urge to scream. It was like they were blaming Da for his own death—a betrayal of everything he stood for. He always said that a man who let himself get treated like a dog was no better than a dog. That sometimes a feller had to take risks, push back, to be treated like a man. And when the Welsh from Hyde Park cut a deal with the bosses and went back to work, Da didn't call 'em cowards, like the rest of the Irishmen did. "How can ye call anyone a coward who risks his life in that dreadful pit, day after day, just to feed his family? Nah, Mikey. They were starvin', same as us."

Mike remembered nodding, even though it made no sense.

"It's the job structure," Da said, apparently sensing Mike's confusion. "Most of those Hyde Park fellers are contract miners. We work for 'em as laborers. Get paid outa their wages. So, there's already a lotta mistrust. The bosses just exploited that. Offered 'em just enough to abandon the strike. Drove a wedge between us. Ye wanna win the next strike, Mikey? Convince 'em their success depends on ours."

Mike folded up Mamai's mattress with Johnny wedged inside. Bill watched blearily from the other bed, as Mike dragged their giggling brother into the front room. He was still just a baby, innocent and carefree. But soon enough he'd be a breaker boy, lucky to make it to manhood with all his limbs intact, never getting a chance to go to school or drink milk every day.

He dropped the mattress by the table and scrubbed a hand over his face. Mamai was right. He was like Da. But he'd finish what his father never accomplished. He'd get a contract job, earn some real money. That's how he'd avenge Da's death. And it would start in Shenandoah.

"Sooner we're outa here, the better," he said, picking Johnny up and placing him at the table next to Tara.

"Maybe you're right," Tara said. "But—"

"But what?" He opened the front door and lugged the mattress onto the landing. "Ye know we can't stay here."

She followed him outside. "I won't know anyone."

"You'll know Uncle Sean and Aunt Mary."

She peered over the banister. "He looks like a troll. Probably eats children." She tugged at the collar of her dress, which was buttoned up to her neck. "What do ye think it's like to be dead?"

"Um." Mike turned sharply away from her, as he struggled for a response. From the corner of his eye, he could see Uncle Sean, still asleep in the wagon. There was something unsettling about him, with all that wispy hair on his long, pointy chin. It reminded Mike of a recurring dream he used to have, where he was walking with Da, hand-in-hand, but when he looked up, instead of Da, Death was glaring down at him. Shuddering, he turned back toward Tara, and tried to calm her. "We'll be fine. Aunt Mary's always been kind to us. Besides, remember what Da used to say about Shendo? All the grocery stores, hotels, and restaurants? Bet you'll even get to go to school."

"Really?" She brushed a lock of hair from her eye and started to smile.

"Heck, yeh. You'll make tons of friends. Now, let's get this into the wagon."

They dragged the mattress down the stairs and heaved it into the wagon, causing it to jerk.

"Wha? What?" Uncle Sean sat bolt upright. "Goddamn, Billy. Don't ye know not to sneak up on a sleepin' man?"

"I ain't Billy."

"Ye ain't?"

"I'm Mike. I'm thirteen now. I've been working in the breaker two years." He flexed his biceps. "Whad'ya think?"

"I think the strike must've hit really hard up here. You're nothin' but skin and bone."

Mike gripped his biceps. His fingers went all the way around.

He looked down to avoid his uncle's gaze.

"Ask him about Shenandoah," Tara whispered, clinging to the back of his shirt.

"Um."

"Stop stammering and get over here. And bring that little mouse with ye."

They took a few steps forward, but were interrupted by Li'l Bill, bounding down the stairs with Johnny in his arms. "Can we feed the cows, Uncle Sean? Can we?" He put Johnny down beside the wagon and tilted his head, squinting at the pink blotches on his uncle's cheeks.

Uncle Sean's ears reddened. "They're not cows, ye ninny. They're oxen."

Bill looked like he was going to cry. "I nu-knew that."

Mamai came out, with Deirdre in one arm, and a cup of tea. She approached the wagon.

"Oh, Sean. What am I going to do with five children and no husband?"

"You'll come live with us," he said, offering a weak smile. He climbed down and reached for the tea, but her hand went limp and the cup fell to the ground and cracked, splattering his ankles.

Mike braced himself for a loud curse. His uncle twitched, but said nothing, then started walking toward the house. "I'll just, uh, go get the rest of the bedding."

He returned moments later with a mattress on his head. The veins in his neck bulged, like fat, green worms, and the blotches on his cheeks seemed bigger and redder, perhaps from the strain. Aunt Mary called them tetters. Said they came from drinking milk with his fish as a boy.

"Told ye it wouldn't take but a minute." He tossed the mattress into the wagon and brushed his hands together with a satisfied sniff. "If we leave now, might make Shendo by sunset."

Mike and Tara went back inside for the rest of their things. When they returned, Li'l Bill was sitting gloomily in the back of the wagon, with his chin pressed against his chest and his eyes wide with fear and uncertainty. Tara got in beside him, looking just as miserable. Mike lifted Deirdre over the rim, then Johnny. His brothers and sisters huddled together in the middle of the mattresses, as he packed the rest of their worldly possessions around them. A couple sets of clothes. A few cookpots. The large wooden crucifix with the shiny brass Jesus that used to hang by the front door. And Da's tools. Thirty-two years on this Earth, more than half of it working for the Company, and this was all they had to show for his efforts?

Mike snatched the chisel he ruined last year and examined the twisted blade. Only got the screw halfway in before it bent. Da always said, "Use the right tool for the right job." Mike knew it was the wrong tool. Knew they didn't have enough money for a new one, either. He tried straightening the blade against the side of the wagon, but it wouldn't budge, so he chucked it at the house. Thoroughly ruined. No more stupid kid mistakes like that.

He climbed into the wagon, between Uncle Sean and Mamai. Neither of them spoke. He twisted his head and watched Tara folding Deirdre's fingers and singing *This little piggy went to market*. Avondale was fading behind them, the little patch houses growing smaller and smaller, the hills giving way to golden pastures and lazy cows. *This little piggy had roast beef*. Maybe they'd pass through a forest, thick with pine trees and deer. Maybe they'd see a bear or a wolf.

When Tara got to the piggy that had no roast beef, Mike couldn't bear it any longer and turned to looked straight ahead again. They were approaching Nanticoke. It looked the same as Avondale. Hills pockmarked with mine pits. Tall, rumbling breakers, farting out smoke as they lapped up hunks of coal with their long black tongues. Their bellies filled with boys, like Mike and Bill. Some missing fingers or hands. All doubled over like hunchbacks with consumption. At least that wasn't his job anymore. And with him and Mamai and Uncle Sean all working, maybe Li'l Bill could go to school with Tara.

Mamai started to fidget. "What kind of mother am I? Runnin' away like a thief in the night?"

Uncle Sean slapped his thigh. "Well, Siobhan, what else could ye do without any money or husband? Ye couldn't very well keep your laddies safe, now, could ye? They wanted blood an' they didn't care if they squeezed it out of a Molly Maguire or an innocent widow."

"They don't have Molly Maguires in America."

"Course, they do. They meet in secret. In back rooms of taverns. Threaten mine owners and anyone who doesn't agree with 'em. They're the ones that started that draft riot in Cass a few years ago. Killed that coll'ry owner in Audenreid, too."

"My Bill was no Molly Maguire!"

"Holy cripes!" Sean pulled a small bottle of whiskey from his pocket. "I know ye don't drink, but have a dram anyway, in his memory. It'll chirk ye up a bit and help the trip pass more quickly. An' trust me. There's nothin' to worry about. Shendo may not be Philly, but you'll be taken care of. We'll make sure of it. Nothing more important than family."

Mike watched in disbelief as Mamai took a swig.

"Ye too." Sean passed him the bottle. "Just a wee dram in your poor father's memory."

Unsure what constituted a wee dram, Mike took a tiny sip, but it burned and he choked, spraying it all over his lap.

Uncle Sean roared with laughter.

"Sha-awnn," Mamai whined.

He snatched the bottle back. "Er, I forgot he's still just a lad."

Still just a lad? Mike wanted another try, but Mamai was giving him a sideways stare, so he closed his eyes and slumped down between them and pretended to sleep.

The wagon bumped and lurched over roots and potholes, at times pitching so heavily it seemed like they'd get thrown into the ditch. He refused to open his eyes, unable to bear another breaker or smokestack. Besides, the oxen were strong. They wouldn't let anything happen. He could hear Tara playing patty-cake with the twins, and Bill snoring, and Uncle Sean grumbling about a nickel for the turnpike. After that, the road became a washboard. An even, steady rattling that made Mike's knees knock together and his muscles jiggle loosely until they were warm and relaxed and his thoughts started to drift.

When he opened his eyes again, he was in a strange bed, in a dark, musty room. Bill was asleep beside him, with one leg wrapped over his. And Tara's fluttery breaths.

Shenandoah?

Chapter 5
Shenandoah, Pennsylvania
Wednesday, September 15, 1871

Mike awoke to the smoky, sweet smell of sausage and biscuits. He quickly got dressed and followed the scent downstairs to the front room, where Mamai and Aunt Mary were whispering over a pan of gravy. Uncle Sean sat at the table sipping tea.

Aunt Mary called it the "best room," which must have been a reference to the wonderful aromas she conjured from it, because it bore no resemblance to a parlor, which was what Mike imagined when he thought of a "best room." There was no fireplace, rug, or sofa. No cabinet filled with fancy dishes. The walls were unadorned, and the ceiling was so low Uncle Sean had to hunch when he stood, making it seem even smaller. But it perfectly suited Aunt Mary, who was also petite, with skinny ankles that didn't seem strong enough to hold her upright, and a thin gray stripe down the middle of her hair, like a trail of ashes that would scatter in the gentlest breeze. Yet, despite her apparent frailty, she moved about the "best room" as gracefully as a dancer, with her dress rippling and her tiny lips pressed into a contented smile.

Uncle Sean nodded as he watched her, as if everything, for once, was right with the world.

Mike sat down, enjoying the warmth of the crackling stove, wishing things could stay peaceful and quiet like this forever, or at least until Li'l Bill woke up. But after a few minutes, Uncle Sean suddenly stood up, shoving the table into his guts.

"'Scuse me," he said with a laugh.

Tara was in the doorway, wearing her white church dress, bouncing on the balls of her feet, as if particularly eager to start her day. Li'l Bill was behind her, barefoot, in tattered trousers.

"Ready to fetch the coal," she said.

Uncle Sean pounded a fist on the table. "Shoulda been up an

hour ago. Billy can do it after breakfast. Starting tomorrow, ye best have it done before I'm up or expect a lickin'."

Mamai stopped stirring. "Fetch the twins, Billy, before ye get in trouble."

Sitting back down, Uncle Sean took another sip of tea.

"Guess that's his job," Tara said. "Now that I'm going to school."

Uncle Sean choked, spraying tea across the table. "Think we're runnin' a charity here?"

"*Tá brón orm*," said Mamai. "We have to work today."

Tara's face went pale. She looked as though she might to faint.

"The twins?" Mamai repeated.

"I gotta stay home with the babies," Bill said. "And Aunt Mary?"

"Shut your mout'!" Uncle Sean bellowed. "You'll do as you're asked. Now get over here!"

Bill slowly scooted around the table, without taking his eyes off Uncle Sean.

"Hand me my rod."

There was a broomstick in the corner of the room, thick enough to bust a boy's bones.

Bill handed him the stick and leaned against the wall, legs spread wide, fingers splayed like a frog's toes. Uncle Sean stood behind him and swung it across his bottom with a loud thwack.

He screamed. His legs looked ready to buckle.

"I'll teach ye not to talk back!"

Tara ducked behind Mamai, who clutched her apron.

Aunt Mary covered her eyes, her lips moving like she was counting to ten.

Bill shrieked. Tears streamed down his cheeks. His hands started to slide. He crumpled to the ground, knees pressed to his chin, sobbing convulsively. The seam of his trousers was split.

Tara peeked from behind Mamai.

Sean glared back at her, his face red and glistening with sweat.

"I'll tolerate no haughtiness from ye, neither."

She stepped backward, her eyes wild, like a rabbit with nowhere to run. Her head shook back and forth, as if to say, "I didn't mean it."

Maybe that was it. A stern warning and they'd all leave for work. But then Mike noticed the vein pulsing in Sean's forehead. The spittle in the corners of his mouth. His glinting eyes. His long, leathery index finger, beckoning, like the Grim Reaper.

Mike heard Tara whimper, then a trickling sound, as if someone had spilled a spilled glass water. He forced himself to look. There was a puddle at Tara's feet. Her face was red and her hands were covering her privates.

Mamai glanced at Sean, then draped an arm around Tara and scooted her toward the staircase. "Come, sweetie. Let's get ready for work."

"Wait for me," Bill cried, crawling after them on his hands and knees.

For a moment, Uncle Sean did nothing. But then he wrinkled his nose and stepped over the puddle, grabbing his coat and cap from the wall. Aunt Mary ran to the door and waited, with two lunch pails. Her neck scrunched up, as if she didn't want to be noticed.

"Be safe." Her voice was soft and sweet, like a mewing kitten.

"Ye know I will." He kissed her on the forehead, as delicately as if she was a dandelion seedpod. "I'd never do anything to worry the one who truly loves me, tetters and all." He glanced over his shoulder at Mike, his expression suddenly hardening. "Let's go."

Grabbing his lunch pail, Mike squeezed Mary's wrist and left.

Sean was waiting across the street for him, at the coll'ry entrance, staring at a knot in the rough-hewn gate, smiling as if he had completely forgotten the morning's earlier conflicts.

"Beautiful, ain't it?"

"I guess." All Mike could see was a darkened oval that didn't match the rest of the wood.

Sean crossed his arms. "You just see a mistake, don't you? A deformity? But there's color and texture and beauty in it." He raised his palms to indicate the vast, barren hillside behind the breaker. "Just like Locust Mountain. Another of God's marvels.

Kehley's Creek runs right behind the stable, where you'll be working. Our own little Eden."

It seemed no different than Avondale. Similar hillside, blackened by years of tailings. Same clattering pumps and engines. Identical stench of rotten eggs.

"This here's the east end of Line Street. Eden. Everyone here's a loyal Company man. Pious an' patriotic. Not a bad bone among 'em. Mr. Thomas treats us square. Keeps food on our table."

Mike ran a hand through his hair, even more confused than before. Da always said the Company made its profits by ripping off the working man. Was Mr. Thomas so different?

"West end's a whole different story." Sean thrust his finger over Mike's shoulder. "Those Kohinoor Boys are nothing but trouble. Drinking. Whoremongering. Striking over the slightest grievance. Caught there on a dark night? You're jammy if ye don't get your throat slit."

"But I thought Shenandoah was an Irish town."

"Hah! Kohinoor Boys are as Irish as ye and me. Pure Cat'lic thugs. Every one of 'em. Want Welsh thugs? Go to the southside. Plenty of 'em there. Call 'emselves Modocs. They'll stick a knife in ye, too." He swatted a hand through the air. "One more thing." His voice deepened. "You're only here 'cause of your Aunt Mary. And she's a delicate woman. So, ye best do as I say, and never upset her. I didn't even like your da, the shifty sonofabitch. But he was her baby brother. So, I guess it's my job now to keep all yiz safe."

He spat and started to leave.

Mike glanced back at the house, shaking his head, wondering what Da could have done to make Sean so mad. Whatever it was, there was nothing he could do about it out here, and getting fired on his first day wouldn't help. He turned and took a step toward the stable, nearly colliding with a man passing by with a girl.

"Pardon me," Mike said, pretending to button his coat.

Her eyelashes were like feathers and her ears were as round as a baby bear's. She smelled of lavender, fresh and unsullied, as if she'd never been near a coal mine and was only passing through town on her way to bigger and better things. Perhaps a big house in

Philadelphia, with flowers and trees, and plenty of good food. She smiled, then looked away.

His chest fluttered and he quickly looked away, too, wishing he could move closer and stare into her dark eyes, breath in her sweetness, feel her curly brown locks tickling against his skin. He slowly raised his chin, hoping for another glimpse, but she was already gone.

He kicked the fence, then trudged up the path, convinced he was worthless, that he'd never get a girlfriend. When he finally looked up again, he could see a man at the stable door.

"Excuse me," he said. "Are ye Mr. Miller?"

The man stepped away from the door. "You the new stableboy?" His face was round, same as his torso. His spectacles, which clung to his nose like a clothespin, bobbed up and down as he spoke. His eyes darted from the water barrel, to the stable, then back to Mike. "See a bucket?"

Mike scanned the area. "No sir."

"I'm a busy man, Doyle. I've twenty-four men under my watch. I expect independence and initiative." He paused to adjust his glasses. "And personal responsibility. Understand?"

"Yes, sir," Mike replied without thinking.

"The most important rule is to water the mules before the drivers arrive. A well-watered mule is a happy mule. Efficient, sure-footed. Gets the coal quickly to the breaker. Understand?"

"Water's the most important thing for mules."

"Well?" Miller stood stiffly, clicking his fingernails against the stable.

Mike squirmed, unsure what he wanted.

"The drivers, Doyle. They'll be here any minute!"

He gave Miller a nod, then ran inside. It smelled of dung and damp hay. There were eight stalls, but no bucket to be seen. Several mules stuck their snouts over their gates and curiously sniffed the air.

"Where would I leave it?" he muttered.

The water barrel!

Racing over, he peered inside. It was sunk at the bottom. He pulled off his coat and shirt, tossed them in the grass, and dunked his head in. It was ice cold, but it only took a second.

"Well done," Miller said, clapping, as Mike came back up, shaking like a dog.

He quickly dressed, but continued shaking for the next five minutes as he filled the troughs.

All the mules began to drink, except for one. "What wrong with that one?"

Miller removed his spectacles, blinked twice, then put them back on.

"That's Betz. She's just moody. You'll figure it out. Be firm, but compassionate. And remember, Mr. Thomas says it costs a hundred bucks to replace a mule, but muleboys are a dime a dozen. So, any mule acts odd, you let me know at once."

"Yes, sir. Any sick mules, you'll be the first to know."

"Independence and initiative," Miller said, as he walked away. "They'll pay off in the end."

A few minutes later, a skinny boy in in overalls entered the stable. He had pale blue eyes and a faint mustache, and wore a miner's cap, tilted slightly to the side, as if he didn't care what others thought about him. He walked right up to the mule next to Betz, fed him a carrot, and began stroking his muzzle. "Here ye go, Jonesy. This'll cure what ails ye." He spat a gob of brown tobacco juice into the stall and the mule promptly slurped it up. He spat another at Betz, who licked hers up, then started drinking from the trough.

The boy looked at Mike and extended his hand. "Tom Hurley, best driver in Shendo. Anyone tells ye otherwise, ye let me know. I'll *show* him!"

Hesitating, Mike shook his hand. "I'm Mike Doyle. Best stableboy in Shendo. At least I intend to be."

"Nothin' to it. Just gotta treat 'em right. The trick with these mules is tobacco." He reached in his pocket and handed Mike a chunk. "In case ye get into trouble with 'em later."

He pulled a collar and blanket from the wall, tossed them over Jonesy's back and led him outside. Mike followed with a bridle.

"People think they're stubborn," Tom said. "But they're as smart as can be. They'll pull three coal-carts, no problem, but soon as ye hook up a fourth, they'll stop. Might even kick ye. They know when you're makin' 'em do somethin' dangerous. But they're faithful, too. Once saw a mule drag a man out of the rubble after the overburden collapsed on him."

"You've worked in the pit?"

"Sure. Inside stable at Rainbow Coll'ry, in Saint Clair. Think Betz is skittish? Ye oughta see the inside mules. Poor bastards spend their entire lives underground. Never get to see the sunshine or nibble fresh grass. Once saw a pack of rats devour everything in their trough before they even poked their noses in." He shuddered forcefully before continuing. "But if ye bring one of 'em out in the sunshine, might as well take it home. Give it a pillow by the fire. It'll never do another lick of work. Inside or out."

Mike handed him a bridle, but he just rolled his eyes and pushed it away.

"But how're ye gonna steer?"

Tom laughed. "Didn't I say I was the best driver in Shendo?"

"Sorry, your honor."

"Relax. Only grudge I bear is against someone who mistreats the animals, like Allen."

"Who's Allen?"

"Gregory Allen. Welsh boy. Always shows up last and gets stuck with Betz 'cause no one else wants her. Has no idea how to handle a mule. Look."

He went back inside. Betz walked up to the gate and nuzzled him. When he ran his hand along her neck, she stiffened and shook her head violently. He pulled his hand away. There was a bloody wound on her neck. "That sonofabitch!" He spat a gob of tobacco at her feet which calmed her down. "That's how he got the last stableboy fired."

"Please, Tom. I don't wanna get fired. Can't ye take Betz today? Give her a chance to heal?"

"Not a chance, Doyle. Me and Jonesy are a team." He pressed his face against Jonesy's. They had the same silly smile, as if they were brothers. "Why don't ye get Johnny Morris to take her. He's good with females."

"Take who?" said another boy, stepping into the stable. "A

pretty new girl in town?"

"Now you've done it," Tom whispered, jabbing Mike in the ribs with his elbow.

"Not a new girl?" The new boy wore a black vest and a felt derby. He was taller than Mike and Tom and looked like a grown man, except for the softness of his cheeks. "Someone's taken Jack an' left me with Betz?" He shot Mike a glance. "Who's this guy?"

"That's Doyle," Tom said. "New stableboy. And Jack's still here."

"Really?" The boy's eyes brightened. He walked up to Jack's stall and stroked his sleek buckskin fur. "That's a good boy."

"Johnny Morris," Tom whispered, wiggling his eyebrows. "Notice how his vest and hat match Jack's fur?"

Mike nodded. "But what about Betz? How do I get Allen to stop whipping her?"

Morris yanked back his hand and thrust out his chest. "He uses a whip?"

"I don't wanna get fired." Mike pleaded. "Couldn't ye take her today?

"Sorry, Doyle. What would the girls think if they saw me on that beat-up nag? But I'll straighten that little bastard out for ye. There's no excuse for whipping a mule. In the meantime, there's liniment in here somewhere. Rub it on her twice a day. That'll doctor her up quick."

Tom walked toward the door. "Time's a-wastin', boys."

"Wait," Mike followed him outside. "If Miller sees you without reins, he'll have a fit. Lemme put a halter on him. At least then we're doing things according to Hoyle."

"Rules are for suckers," Tom said, as he hitched a cart to Jonesy. "Besides, what the hell'd Hoyle ever do for me?"

Mike clutched the halter to his body. "Kept ye employed, I reckon."

"You sound like my wife." Tom climbed onto the bumper of his cart, like a trick rider at a wild west show, and blew Mike a kiss. "Home by supper, dear." Then he drove away.

Mike threw the halter on the ground. If Tom Hurley really cared about mules, he woulda taken Betz. And if he really was the best driver, he could handle her, too.

Johnny Morris led Jack out of the stable, pausing next to Mike. He removed his derby and held it to his chest, frowning at the halter laying in the dirt, as if it pained him that anyone could think so little of him. "That ain't for me, is it?"

Mike stared back, speechless, not only at Morris's haughtiness, but also because he *did* look like his mule. Same rueful brown eyes. Same black mane. Only difference was that the mule didn't care how it looked, whereas Morris was constantly straightening his vest and hat.

Morris attached the cart and climbed up.

"Reckon it'll do more good there than on this fine feller."

Mike kicked the halter, as Morris drove off, but it gave him no satisfaction. He'd still have to confront Allen and he had no idea how old he was, or how big. What if Allen punched him in the nose? He couldn't go to Mr. Miller. That'd just prove he lacked independence and initiative. And Tom Hurley and Johnny Morris would think he was a sissy.

He picked up the halter and went inside. The liniment was near the bridles. When he tried to smear some on Betz's neck, she brayed and rattled her head. On his third attempt, she bared her teeth and screeched.

Now what? If he forced her, one of them could get hurt. If he did nothing, she'd never heal. Damn, stumped by a stubborn old mule. But then he remembered the tobacco. He pulled it out of his pocket and bit off a piece. Saliva filled his mouth. It dribbled out the corners and down his chin. Some trickled down his throat, causing him to retch. Most of it flew out, landing at her feet. As she licked it up, he smeared liniment on her neck, but a wave of nausea overtook him. He dropped the liniment and ran to the water barrel. He took a drink, but the sweat and saliva just kept flowing. Sitting down, he closed his eyes, vowing to kill Gregory Allen.

Chapter 6
Wednesday, September 15, 1871

As Mike closed the stable door, a gust of warm, moist air flushed past him. It smelled strongly of milkweed, which grew in patches along the path home, and reminded him of steamy Halloween barmbrack, fresh from the oven; of costumes, candy, innocence, and joy. His skin tingled from the waning sunlight, like had just bathed. For a moment, it seemed as if Uncle Sean was right. This *was* paradise. He had a boss who trusted him to run the stable on his own. He'd made two new friends. His shoulders didn't ache and there weren't layers of coal dust caked to his face. And best of all, Gregory Allen never showed up.

He ran up his front steps, eager to tell everyone about his day. But when he opened the door, instead of cheerful banter and wonderful aromas, it was eerily quiet. Aunt Mary was at the table, with her face buried in her hands, looking as frail as a burnt piece of paper.

Mamai stood behind her, running her fingers through the gray skunk stripe on the back of Aunt Mary's head. She gave Mike a little nod. "Billy's gone."

"Whadya mean, *gone*?"

Aunt Mary lifted her head. "I didn't mean to yell at him."

"He'll be back." Mamai smoothed down her hair. "And it's not your fault. He knows better than to get brought home by the Coal and Iron Police. At least I've one boy who can do a job correctly." She reached for Mike's hand and squeezed it. "You'll find him, right? Before your uncle gets home?"

The compliment gave him no pride. He was sick of bailing his brother out of trouble. Besides, Bill could be anywhere and Mike barely knew this town. Maybe if he did nothing, let him come home on his own and take his lickings, he'd learn not to provoke people. But what if this wasn't about protecting Bill at all? Mamai knew he would continue causing trouble. Maybe she just wanted to make Aunt Mary happy. And didn't she deserve a friend?

"Alright. But lemme get Tara to help."

He raced upstairs and found her hunched on the floor near Mamai's bed, rocking back and forth, sobbing softly, as the twins napped. A narrow beam of sunlight shone directly on her, like a cat, curled up in the one sunny patch in the house. Her clothes were soaked and her brown hair was matted against her slender neck, with a single curled wisp lapping at her milky cheek. It seemed odd that she could be so unsettled, until Mike remembered that she was only eleven. It reminded him of how she use to play with Li'l Bill like he was her ragdoll, grabbing his finger and moving it in the air to count the coal cars on the train outside their window in Avondale. "One-uh. Two-uh. Three-uh." But then he blinked and noticed the bright red scalds on her arms.

"Uncle Sean do this to ye?"

Shuddering, she hugged her knees to her bosom and wept even harder.

He wrapped his coat around her, wishing she'd just tell him what was wrong. But maybe this was one of those things that couldn't get fixed, that you just had to live with, like a cruel boss. He tried to think of what Da would've said, but *Stand tall* didn't seem right.

After a long, uncomfortable silence, he said, "Rough day?"

She brushed away a damp strand of hair that clung to her cheek. "I must look awful."

"No worse than I did after my first day in the breaker, I reckon."

"Oh, Mike." She grabbed his arm. "I miss Da so much."

A lump formed in his throat. He pulled her against his shoulder so she couldn't see his moist eyes. He struggled to remember how Da could always make 'em feel better. When Granny died and they couldn't sleep, he told them to close their eyes and think of their favorite memories. Mike remembered how Granny called Da her little boy even though he was a foot taller than her. How Da would hug them when they were scared, matching his breathing with theirs, until they calmed down, even when it was right after work, and he was still wet and smelly from the pit.

Mike's skin got clammy just thinking about it. Or was that Tara's soggy dress?

"Think of your favorite memories," he said, as he tried to match her surging breaths.

After a while, she relaxed and sat back on her knees.

"Oh, Mike. We must've carried a hundred pounds of coal today. Forty gallons of water for each boil. Plus, another ten for each rinse. And we did twenty loads! The whole time, hot water splashing our arms and faces, and so much steam ye couldn't see your hands."

"Sounds way harder than my job."

"Probably is. My shoulders feel like lead."

"She nice?"

"Mrs. McGill? Guess so. Didn't scold me." Her eyes twinkled. "But she's the funniest-looking woman you've ever seen. Hips so wide she could barely squeeze into the washhouse. And arms like a bull's. Bet she could beat Uncle Sean wrestling."

"I'd like to see that."

"And one night, her husband nearly strangled himself on the clothesline, even though he's the one that strung it up." She started to giggle. "He's C&I."

"A Coal and Iron cop strangling himself?" Mike laughed. "*That* I'd really like to see!"

"Guess what?" She reached for Mike's hand. "I made a friend."

"Really?"

"Her name's Hannah. Moved here a month ago. Helps Mrs. McGill coupla times a week. Really clever, too. Knows as much about the union as Da did. Her da's a WBA organizer."

Mike's posture perked up. "What's their name?"

"Lawler?"

"Know which coll'ry he works at?"

"Gosh, Mike. I don't even know which street I work on. We musta crossed five or six streets to get there. But I know where Main Street is. On our way home, we stopped at Vandussen's for groceries. You shoulda seen it! Barrels of spuds and apples. Peaches. Tinned beans and fruits. An entire glass case filled with candy." She clasped her hands to her bosom. "You were right."

"Huh?"

"About making friends. Hannah's about the best friend I've ever met."

"How do ye know? It's only been one day."

"She knew all about Avondale. They helped raise the money for the burials. Her da stood outside the inquest and signed up a hundred men to join the union."

Mike figured he'd have to meet this guy. If there was ever any trouble at work, he'd be able to fix it. But then his thoughts shifted back to Hannah. He wondered if she was pretty. Maybe she could become his girlfriend. Much easier getting to know Tara's friend than a stranger.

Just then, Mamai walked in with a jar of lard and an old rag.

"We were just about to go look for Bill," Mike said.

"He's back." Mamai smeared lard on his sister's arm. "Your uncle, too. He's not happy."

"Because of Bill?" Tara asked, her voice rising in alarm.

"C&I caught him stealing from the culm heap."

Tara jerked her arm away from Mamai and flopped onto her belly. "He hates us!"

The twins woke up and started to cry.

"He doesn't hate ye." Mamai switched beds. She plopped Johnny on her left knee and Deirdre on her right, spread her shawl over their heads, and unbuttoned her dress. "He's just not used to kids. And he's worried about money. Ain't easy feeding this many —"

"He called Da 'shifty,'" Mike interrupted, trying to control his tone. "Said he hated him."

Mamai's eyes widened. "How could anyone hate your da?"

There was a thump from downstairs, like a chair being flung. The twins' hands shot in the air. Tara curled into a ball and yanked the covers over her. "I'm never goin' down there again."

"Ye gotta eat. We gotta work tomorrow."

"I'd rather starve. What if someone dies because of him? I couldn't bear any more death."

Mamai offered a deep sigh. "It'll be over soon. Then we'll creep down there quiet as church mice. He'll be too spent to bother us."

Mike lingered near the door, praying that Mamai was right. He could be a church mouse if he had to, but what if Sean spoke to any of them? He might fly into a rage. And what about tomorrow and the next day? They couldn't spend the rest of their lives walking on eggshells.

"This is all my fault." He moved back toward the beds. "I knew something terrible was gonna happen. Shoulda trusted my gut. Made Da turn around and come home with me."

"Better the trouble that follows death than the trouble that follows shame." Mamai placed her rosary in his hand and squeezed it shut. "Ye couldn't have stopped him. He hadn't worked in months. We were starving. Ye both would've been fired."

Tara sat up with the covers around her shoulders, like a cape. Mike fiddled with the rosary.

"I know it's sad without Da and hard living with Sean. But we'll get past it. Better get past the shame, too, Mighael. Otherwise, it'll follow ye around forever." She leaned closer to him. "This house might be Sean's, but you're the man of this family. Don't ye forget that!"

Chapter 7
Thursday, September 16, 1871

The rain came down like handfuls of gravel, thrumming against rooftops and pinging the back of Mike's neck. It smelled earthy, of worms and mulch. He glanced around, hoping to see the girl from yesterday, but only saw a delivery man, shivering in front of his wagon, and some miners hustling toward the coll'ry to avoid getting soaked. He'd probably never see her again. Probably never get a girlfriend at all.

Lowering his head, he pulled his coat over his neck and ran across the muddy street, anxious for the warm tranquility of the stable, the sweet odor of moist hay, steamy mule breaths against his cheek. Instead, he found a stranger lurking at Betz's stall, a tall boy with stringy, blond hair and tattered overalls. A small, black and white bulldog sat in the corner beside a pile of hay, eyeing the boy suspiciously.

"Allen?" Mike asked, though it couldn't be anyone else.

The boy's back arched. He dropped his bridle and whip and slowly turned. His complexion was pale. His eye socket was purple, like maybe Betz had kicked him.

Mike stepped closer and extended a shaky hand. "I'm Doyle, the new stableboy."

Allen abruptly withdrew his hand. "I- I gotta go."

He picked up the bridle and whip and slowly approached Betz, with his arms up, like he was going to wrestle her. But then she bared her teeth and brayed so loudly he fell back on his rump.

Mike had the urge to kick him, but reached down to help him up, instead. "Um, what happened to your eye?"

"Base ball," he muttered, fiddling with a button.

Mike figured he got beat by his da. Probably got yelled at every day, smacked around worse than Li'l Bill. Hopefully, he wasn't as stubborn as Bill and was willing to learn.

He handed Allen a carrot, but the fool just took a bite, frowned, and tossed it into the hay.

"It was for her," Mike said through gritted teeth, leading Betz outside.

Allen's chin dipped. He quickly climbed onto his cart, driving off with both hands on the reins, eyes straight ahead, shoulders hunched over as if that would keep him dry.

Good riddance, Mike thought, returning to the stable just as Tom and Johnny Morris arrived.

"Was that Allen?" Tom asked. "Why come early after all these months?"

"To avoid me." Morris sneered.

Mike's brows narrowed. "You're the one that blackened his eye?"

"Told ye I'd straighten him out, didn't I?"

"How's a black eye gonna teach him?"

"Did he whip her?"

"Nah, but he did crack it over her head."

"Give him time," Morris said. "He'll learn." He fastened Jack's harness and left.

Mike slumped against the wall, only slightly reassured. Allen couldn't even get Betz out of her stall without bullying her. Fear of Morris wouldn't solve that. "Got any more chew?"

Tom reached into his pocket, pulled out a plug, and tossed it to Mike. "Getting a taste for it?" He grabbed a harness and slung it over his shoulder.

"Nah. Gotta teach Allen how to control a mule."

"So, you're one of them reformers, eh? Choirboy, too?"

Mike's ears flushed. "No-uh."

"Noah? So, ye are a choirboy!"

Wincing, Mike stuffed the tobacco into his pocket. Why'd Tom have to be that way? Every helpful word followed by something mean. One minute acting like a friend; the next, like a rival.

"What's wrong with reform, anyway? Don't ye like the minimum wage?"

"Relax, Doyle." He slapped Mike on the back. "It was a joke. Of course, I'm for reform. My da's a WBA man. I was on the line with him every day of the strike."

"Really?" Mike rubbed his hands together. "Heard of a feller named Lawler?"

"Course I have. Lives right up the street from me. One of the toughest fellers you'll ever meet. Really good boxer, too. Only seventeen. Already won ten fights."

"My sister just met a girl. Says her old man's Lawler. A top WBA man."

Tom slapped his thigh and laughed. "That's Eddie's uncle, Michael. Moved here a coupla weeks ago. My da says he's the best organizer in Pennsylvania. Works at Kohinoor. Soon as he got to town, they stopped under-weighing the coal. Finally getting paid for every ton they haul."

"Ain't the Kohinoor dangerous? My uncle says the Kohinoor Boys'll slit your throat."

"They just might," Tom laughed. "If you're Republican. Or Welsh. Who's your uncle?"

Mike ran his hand through his scalp. "Sean Campbell."

"I wouldn't say that too loud."

He wished he hadn't said it at all.

"But it figures. They probably *would* slit his throat, the damned blackleg. Tried to work through the strike. But the Kohinoor Boys stopped him."

"Stopped him? H- how?"

"Had a *word* with him, I reckon. With their reputation, that's all it woulda taken."

"Know any of 'em?"

Tom pulled back his shoulders and grinned as though he'd been waiting all day for that question. "I know all of 'em! Eddie Lawler. His buddies, John Gibbons, Ned Monaghan. Junior members, actually. But the real Boys, Frank McAndrew, Fenton Cooney, Ed Cosgrove—they all live nearby. See 'em every day."

"Ye ain't scared of 'em?"

"Scared?" Tom led Jonesy outside. "Truth is, I'll be one of 'em someday."

"But why?" Mike asked, following after him. "They're murderers."

"They've always treated me square. Eddie and Gibbons let me

play ball with 'em. And during the strike, the Kohinoor Boys fought the hardest. If a blackleg got hurt, well, he got what he deserved, right?"

Tom climbed onto his cart. "Without the Kohinoor Boys, Modocs would run this town." He gave Jonesy's haunches a pat and drove off toward a mist-shrouded Locust Mountain.

Mike returned to the stable, his forehead wrinkling as he considered what Tom had said. Maybe the Kohinoor Boys really weren't so bad. Wasn't loyalty to strikers better than loyalty to the Company? And what was worse, beating up blacklegs for stealing your job, or beating up your own family members? Tom *was* right. Uncle Sean couldn't be trusted. Not to tell the truth about Shenandoah, nor to treat his family right. But why?

All day long he thought about this, but none of his answers made sense. Meanness would explain Sean's anger and violence, but not his love of the Company, nor his fear of the Kohinoor Boys. And why be loyal to the Company if they weren't giving him special treatment? And what could he possibly have against Da?

By the time the drivers had gone home for the evening, he realized he wouldn't solve the mystery today. He just didn't have enough information. He knew next to nothing about Sean, and even less about his relationship to Da. But he vowed to find out. The way Tom talked, nearly everyone in town had a grudge against Sean. Someone would know something.

Mike picked up a harness and hung it on the wall. It was so peaceful with the mules back in their stalls, tired and smelling of sweat, rustling softly as they munched on hay. Jack propped his neck on his gate and yawned, his fur glistening in the lantern light. He nuzzled closer, as Mike stroked his neck. Such a beautiful animal. No wonder Morris wouldn't part with him.

He reached for another harness, but was startled by a loud snap. Turning, he saw Betz with her mouth wide open, tongue flailing back and forth, and Allen right behind her with a whip.

Stiffening, Mike dropped the harness. "No!"

He ran to the doorway, yanked the tobacco from his pocket, bit off a wad, and spat.

Allen jumped back with a look of disgust.

Mike ran for the liniment, as Betz licked it up, determined to punch Allen in the nose if he said anything. He smeared some on her neck, then he led her into her stall.

"How 'n blazes ye able to do that? I can't get her to move without cracking the whip."

"Gotta give her something she wants." Mike wondered why he was being helpful instead of cussing him out.

"Oh." He tittered nervously. "I just thought they were stupid."

"Stupid?" Mike crossed his arms, frowning. "Why, they're smarter than some people. Loyal, too! Just give 'em a little food or tobacco. Ye can get 'em to do most anything."

Just then, Mr. Miller, his boss, arrived. "What's this, Doyle?" He picked up the liniment.

Allen stepped back, his eyes wide, like a cornered mouse.

Mr. Miller ran an index finger along the side of Betz's neck, his spectacles bobbing on his nose. "Hmm. Not bridle chafing." He turned toward Allen. "You striking this animal?"

Allen blinked several times.

"You know how Mr. Thomas feels about his mules?"

Nodding, Allen's lips parted, but nothing came out.

"That what you use on her?" Miller peered at the whip on the floor. "I fired the last stable boy because of the mysterious injuries on this animal. But they weren't his fault, were they?"

Allen gnawed his fingers like they were a corncob.

Mr. Miller picked up the whip. "What do you think, Doyle? Should I fire him?"

Mike shook his head, certain Allen wouldn't hurt a fly after today. But then he started to sweat. Had he just sentenced him to a whipping? But Miller just walked across the room with the whip and returned it to the shelf.

"Well, Mr. Allen. Thanks to Mr. Doyle, you'll work another day."

As Mike walked home, he decided Mr. Miller must be the nicest boss in the world. Oswald would have whipped Allen. And Uncle Sean flew into a rage over the tiniest things. Last night, he gave Bill three days' worth of lickings. One for the fine the Company charged him. Another for getting his bucket smashed by the C&I. And one more for coming home without any coal. He was supposed to take care of them, like a father, but he was worse than a cruel boss. Even Oswald you could get away from at the end of the day. But Sean was there from supper till bedtime, and all-day Sunday. If only he had a fraction of Mr. Miller's compassion. But Uncle Sean was no Gregory Allen. He was a grown man, set in his ways. No teaching him anything, especially not compassion. Yet, if Mike didn't do something, one of them could really get hurt. He had to find a way to move his family out, but how? Uncle Sean knew exactly how much they earned and expected every penny of it. He controlled every aspect of their lives. Every detail.

Chapter 8
Monday, November 18, 1872

"I saw that." Tom threw an arm over Mike's shoulder. "I saw that sparkle in your eye." He bit off some chew he was holding in his other hand, and stuffed the rest into Mike's breast pocket. "Found youself some nice diddies, eh? Get a pogue outa her yet?"

"Nah." Mike cringed, then jabbed Tom in the ribs. "No girl. Just happy for all the work. Should have enough to rent our own house by summer."

"Should already have your own place!" Tom let go of his shoulder and spit a wad of tobacco juice into the snow. "You're a driver now. Buck seventy-five a day. All thanks to Michael Lawler. Wherever he goes, the bosses get scared."

Mike let out a booming laugh. He knew his promotion was due to his own initiative and hard work. "Let's go."

Ice crunched beneath their boots. The naked birch trees along the path glimmered like candlesticks in the moonlight. Patches of snow clung to their quivering branches, occasionally breaking free and falling to the ground in puffs of white dust. The air was crisp, with a faint whiff of fatback and frying onions. A warmth flushed through Mike's body.

"I'm the one who healed Betz. Taught Allen how to handle a mule, too. No more whips or bridles for him."

Tom chuckled. "Ye turned him into a dude. Got him dressing like Morris, now. Not that it matters. Still looks like an undertaker. Girls still think he's a creep."

A mangy dog shivered beneath a hack carriage parked at the end of the trail, near the streetlamp. Across the street, Mike could see his house. The window was fogged up and smoke was billowing from the chimbly. His stomach grumbled. He spat a ribbon of brown saliva, then grabbed Tom's hand and shook it, as they did each night, with their pinkies hooked. Tom said he learned it from Eddie Lawler. "We'll make a Kohinoor Boy out of ye yet, Mikey-Boy."

Mike ran across the street and up the steps, flung the door open. Everyone was already seated. Aunt Mary and Uncle Sean, Mamai, the twins, Li'l Bill, Tara, and some girl he didn't know. Two candles flickered at the ends of the table.

"Evening," he said, hanging his coat on the wall. "Smells great!"

He was trying to stuff his scarf into his coat pocket when Tara said, "Mike, this is my friend, Hannah. The one I told ye about."

"How do ye do?" he replied, glancing over his shoulder.

Her eyelashes fluttered, then she quickly looked into her lap. She had curly, raven-colored hair, tied back with a pink ribbon, and cute little bear ears.

His scarf fell from his hands. It was the girl he saw outside the coll'ry his first day at work!

"Hurry up," said Uncle Sean. "We're starvin' here. And you, slow as molasses in January."

Hannah giggled.

Mike's ears got hot. He walked quickly to the table, too embarrassed to go back for his scarf, praying Sean wouldn't embarrass him further in front of this remarkable creature, whose big brown eyes and soft complexion, so unblemished and pure, filled him with a hope and desire he had never before experienced.

"Alright, then." Uncle Sean made the sign of the cross and dipped his head. "Bless us, O Lord, and these Thy gifts."

Mike stared into his plate. When he looked up again, Sean was already shoveling beans onto his plate. "Better enjoy His bounty while ye can." He gulped down two mouthfuls before reaching for the meat. "Coal combination's cuttin' wages thirty percent."

"What's that mean?" Tara asked.

Mike ran a hand through his hair. It meant he wouldn't be able to save any more money. It would be years before they could move out.

Li'l Bill reached for a biscuit, but Sean slapped his hand away. "Mind your manners. Workin' men first. Then adults and guests." He turned toward Tara, waving his biscuit like a weapon. "It means Billy's goin' to work in the breaker tomorrow."

Bill rose up out of his seat with a big grin.

Mamai flinched. "B- but he's only ten!"

"That's how old Mike was." Bill settled back in his chair with a sneer.

"But he knew how to follow directions." She flashed him a fake smile. "I'll talk to Mrs. McGill. Maybe she'll let me bring home extra laundry to do after supper."

Uncle Sean rolled his eyes.

"I'll be more use in the breaker," Bill muttered, "than stuck at home with Aunt Mary."

"Watch your mouth!" Uncle Sean leaned across the table and slapped him.

The twins started to cry. Aunt Mary slid down in her chair with her hands over her face. The skin bunched up beneath Hannah's beautiful eyes. She grabbed Tara's arm.

Mike's fists opened and closed. That sonofabitch!

Mamai stood up, reached for Deirdre, and placed her on Tara's lap, then lifted Johnny and held him against her bosom, gently patting his back until he calmed down.

Li'l Bill sat rigidly upright, quiet and motionless.

Uncle Sean finished his biscuit in one bite and washed it down with a gulp of whiskey. He leaned back in his chair with a nasty grin. The stringy ends of his beard bobbed on his Adam's apple, like a loose feather flittering in the wind. He looked content, satisfied he'd made his point.

Mike reached for a biscuit, then passed the tray to Hannah, who gave him a pained, watery stare, as if terrified of what might happen next. His throat ached to see her suffer. He tried to comfort her with a smile, but was so nervous, his lips kept twitching. His body froze with his hand still on the plate. Sweat pooled in his armpits. After several awkward seconds, he jerked his hand back into his lap, where it remained, trembling, until Aunt Mary suddenly sat up.

"So, Hannah Lawler. What brought your family to Shenandoah?"

Hannah's eyes brightened. She moistened her lips, which were the color of blush, underripe strawberries. Her cheeks were as smooth as a baby's. Mike wanted to touch them, to run his fingers against her skin. He leaned forward, stroking his own neck, wishing he could get closer.

"My da got a job at the Kohinoor," she said in a bubbly voice. "Contract job. Better pay than his old job, back in Ashland."

"Good for him. And your mother?"

"Stays home." Her expression hardened; her tone grew deeper. "Takes care of my brothers and sisters."

"Her da's a WBA organizer!" Tara said, reaching across Deirdre to touch Hannah's arm. "Helped raise money after the fire in Avondale."

"I went with him every day," Hannah said, smiling in a way that made her teeth and her eyes sparkle. "He liked having me there."

Aunt Mary clapped her hands together. "How wonderful!"

"The Kohinoor?" Uncle Sean glared at her.

Mike's throat dried up. He slowly shook his head. *Great! He thinks her da's a Kohinoor Boy. He'll never let Tara near her again.*

"Ye listen to your brother," Mamai whispered to Bill. "I don't want ye losin' any limbs."

Bill gave her a dismissive nod.

Mike dropped his spoon. *How could he keep Bill safe when he never listened to anyone?*

"I still wanna know what that word means," Tara said, bouncing Deirdre on her knee. "Coal combination?"

"Ye kiddin'?" Sean's eyes bulged out. "They're the ones trying to starve us!"

Tara stared blankly.

"Coal barons! Railroad presidents! Live in castles in New York and Philadelphia. Never worked a day of their lives! All ruled over by Franklin Benjamin Gowen. A greedier, viler man you've never seen. Runs the Reading Railroad. Blocks every effort to make the mines safe. Over 500 men and boys killed these past few years. Just in Schuylkill County." He poured himself another drink. "Now, everyone shut up and eat."

Mike bit into a biscuit, but couldn't swallow. His saliva had vanished. Were they really going to strike again? Another six months of pickets, beatings, and jail? Just to get sold out again by the Welsh? He took a sip of water, forced down the mouthful.

"Wait. I thought we had the minimum wage. Doesn't that protect us from a wage cut?"

Sean pounded the table with his fists. The candles flickered and nearly went out. "Didn't I just tell everyone to shut up and eat? Now ye can go to bed without any supper."

Heat flushed across Mike's cheeks. His thoughts were cloudy and jumbled. If he resisted, Sean might sock him, which would be humiliating and painful. But if he left without a fight, he'd look weak, and Hannah would never respect him. So, he raised his chin and glared back.

Sean stood up, waving his fork. "Ye best get going, if ye don't wanna foot in your arse!"

Mike flashed him a cold, hard smile and slowly got up. He tried to leave, but his muscles had gone limp. His chin dipped and he shuffled forward, eyes on the floor. But as he passed Hannah, he couldn't resist a quick peek. He expected a disappointed frown. Instead, she was smiling. Her eyes followed him as he moved toward the counter and lit a candle. She gave him a sly wink.

He held her gaze for a moment, then flipped back his hair and laughed, even as wax burned his fingers. She was on his side! His fingers tingled as he walked toward the staircase. Perhaps tomorrow, he could take her for a stroll in Heckscher's Grove after supper. But halfway up the stairs, his smile wavered. That wink could've meant anything. Why indicate she liked him right after he got scolded? That made no sense. More likely, it was a sign of pity, telling him she knew Uncle Sean was a beast. Then again, everyone in Shendo knew that. Maybe she was trying to say that he shouldn't worry about the minimum wage because her da would straighten things out. Besides, she was Tara's best friend. He couldn't get in the way of that. And why would she be interested in him anyway? He wasn't handsome, like Johnny Morris,or funny, like Tom.

Entering his room, he put the candle down beside the washbowl. He stared at the yellow teardrop flame reflected in the rippling water, before dunking his face, hoping the light would penetrate his forehead and bring him clarity. But all he got was an intense shiver and a headache.

He scrubbed his face with his shirt, then threw himself on the bed, burying his face in his pillow. So many questions and nobody to answer them. If Da was here, he would've explained the wage cut. He would've known what the WBA was gonna do about it, too. Probably could've even told him what Hannah's expression meant and how to find out if she liked him.

Rolling onto his back, he opened his eyes and watched a spider crawl up the wall. Da wasn't going to help him now. Neither was Uncle Sean. But tomorrow he could ask Tom about the wage cut. His da must've spoken about it. And maybe he could swallow his pride and talk to Johnny Morris. He'd probably have something useful to tell him about girls.

Chapter 9
Tuesday, November 19, 1872

Snowflakes twinkled like falling stars beneath the hazy streetlamp at the coll'ry entrance. Li'l Bill leaned back and caught one on his tongue. As he grinned, his freckles bunched up around his nose. He wore Mike's old boots, which were still too large for him. His feet were wrapped in rags so they wouldn't slip off, and bailing wire was tied around them to keep the soles attached.

Uncle Sean spat, then kicked him in the rump. "Best start acting like a man, 'cause you're getting a man-sized licking if ye get fired."

Three men with picks marched past, muttering about the wage cut. They smelled of stale sweat and mud. Mike swallowed several times. Sean's threats from last night were still fresh in his mind, but he couldn't stand the suspense. He tightened his scarf and mustered his courage.

"Uncle Sean? How come the minimum wage ain't protecting us?"

Lowering an eyebrow, his uncle glared down at him. "It's that bastard Gowen!" He kicked a snowdrift and nearly stumbled into a horse and wagon that was clomping by.

Li'l Bill started to giggle, but Mike jabbed him with his elbow.

"Got all the owners to ignore the contract. Thinks he can walk all over us."

"Why ain't the WBA stopping 'em?"

"The Whiny Bunch of Arses? Hah! John Siney'd bloody sleep with the bosses than defend us hardworkin' miners. Truth is, he's just a worthless Souper, no better than the Welsh!"

"What's a Super?" asked Li'l Bill.

"Oh, that's a grand one!" He placed a hand on Li'l Bill's shoulder and looked him dead in the eye. "A Souper's a Cat'lic who drank the soup."

"What soup?" Bill asked with alarm.

"The *free* soup, ye ignorant moron! The poison the Protestant missionaries were handin' out durin' the Hunger. If ye took it, it made ye one of 'em."

"The Hunger?"

"Bejasus damn, Billy. Ye really that dumb? Ye henny heard of the Hunger? When the spud crops got away? Cripes almighty, I've had enough of your foolishness!" He smacked Bill on the back of the head. "My little brother Timmy died from it. May his soul rest in peace."

"Jeez," Mike said. "That's awful. How old was he?"

Uncle Sean turned toward Locust Mountain without responding. His shoulders curled forward and his arms hung limp, like a sickly old man with miner's asthma. He stared bleakly at the breaker, which rested on a step-shaped mound at the base of the mountain, as if the answers to his troubles were hidden inside its frosty windows. The area surrounding it, normally black with tailings, was dusted with fresh snow and resembled a coal-cart splattered with bird shit.

Li'l Bill edged closer to Uncle Sean, blinking rapidly. "How'd he die?"

"It was a famine," Mike whispered, squinting at his brother, praying he'd shut up. "He—"

"Broke his neck," Uncle Sean said, with his back still toward them. "Fell from an apple tree." He continued staring off at nothing, uncharacteristically quiet.

Bill's eyebrows squished together. He tugged on his earlobe.

Mike shrugged, not knowing what to do.

Uncle Sean suddenly turned around. His cheeks were hollow, as if he was sucking on a pipe, and his eyes were red around the rims. "Think I'm hard on yiz? My da kept a shillelagh by the door. Told folks it was for thieves. But he used it on us. If he'd been there, woulda used it on Timmy before he was halfway up that tree. Woulda fractured his arse, too. But at least he'd still be alive. Instead, I got the licking of my life. Far worse than anything either of yiz have had. Couldn't walk for a week. Every day, reminded how irresponsible I was. Sonofabitch didn't care about the dozens of times I brought him home safely. Or the time I saved him from a mad dog."

He scrubbed a hand over his face, then drew himself to his full height.

"So, when I tell yiz to do something, best do it quickly!"

"Yes, sir," Mike said, his voice cracking. Despite the chill air, his body was uncomfortably hot under his coat.

Uncle Sean glanced at the headframe. "I gotta go."

Bill tried to follow, but Mike grabbed him by the collar.

"What's the hurry?"

"It's my first day."

"So? Ye prefer *he* took ye to work? When he's acting crazy like this?"

"Um." Bill shook his head. "Ain't that how he always acts?"

Mike rubbed his forehead. "What about his brother? And his da? He's never talked about them before. And didn't he act kinda odd about it? Like he was sad? Maybe even ashamed?"

"He ain't 'shamed of nothing!" Bill's fists were balled up. He started walking away. "Only feelings he's got are anger and rage."

"Wait." Mike ran to catch up. "Don't ye wanna know how to avoid a licking in there?"

"Haven't ye already told me a hundred times?" He smirked like he was hiding sweet cherries in his cheeks, savoring the syrup as it trickled down his throat.

Mike wanted to hit him, but figured Uncle Sean smacked him around enough and that didn't change his behavior.

"Alright, Bill. I guess you're ready. Just remember to keep away from the gears and belts and don't volunteer to unclog the screens. Breaker boss always tries to get the new boys to do it."

"Yes, Mommy."

Mike's vision clouded over. He pressed his elbows to his sides, fists clenched, trying to remain calm. He wished he was already in the stable, saddling his mule. Away from all this nonsense. If he hit Bill, it would only make him late for work, get him fired on his first day. They'd both get beaten silly.

"Forget it. Let's get going."

Bill rocked back on his heels with a snicker, then proceeded up the path with his chin jutting out like a ship's captain. Mike said nothing the rest of the way, even though Bill kept bumping into him and forcing him into the snow. He couldn't risk any more conflicts. Just get him to work before the starting whistle.

Mr. Dewees was at the breaker entrance, leaning on his walking stick. He was a short, bristly man, with a strange, sickly smile that made Mike's teeth ache. Bill started to walk past him, as if he'd worked there for months.

"Wait," Mike said. "Excuse my brother, sir. He's just anxious to start. Our uncle told us there was work for him."

"What's your name?" Dewees asked.

"Bill Doyle." He didn't even bother looking up. "And my da died in Avondale."

Dewees went very still, then cleared his throat. "Er, how old are ye, Doyle?"

"Ten. And I know the difference between chestnut, pea, and buckwheat."

Dewees stroked his walking stick, as he looked Bill up and down. His nose wrinkled like a rabbit's. "I have only one rule, Doyle: You're paid to *gob*, not *gab*." His thin lips parted slightly and emitted a raspy little cackle. "Know how to *gob the bone*?"

Bill didn't respond, even though Mike had explained it to him a hundred times: remove all the bone, slate, anything that wasn't coal.

Dewees slapped his cane against the breaker.

"If ye don't want to experience this on your hindquarters, you'll clean your coal efficiently."

"Y-yes, sir."

Dewees turned toward Mike. "Make sure your brother knows what to do. I'm good friends with Mr. Miller. Wouldn't want 'Doyle' to become a bad word around here."

The entire rest of the day was a blur, as thoughts of blacklisting filled Mike's head. He drove back and forth from the headframe to the breaker, through cold white fog, loading and unloading coal, with no memory of Tom, or Johnny Morris, or even Mr. Miller. Only thing he could remember were the words *Bill listens to no one*, playing over and over in his head, but in Dewees's screechy voice. By the end of the day, he wanted to shove that cane straight down Dewees's throat. He'd prove that sonofabitch wrong. Bill would be an excellent breaker boy. He'd make sure of it.

When he got home, Li'l Bill was sitting on the front steps with his elbows on his knees and his head hanging low. His cheeks were black and droopy, like those of a hound. There was a twig between his lips and a new scab on his forehead. Mike remembered that feeling well, the achy shoulders, the cracked and bleeding knuckles, the stinging hindquarters from the breaker boss's switch, more exhausted than he'd been after two weeks of scarlet fever. Maybe this was a good sign. Maybe he was humbled.

He sat down next to his brother. "Pretty beat, eh?"

The window was all fogged up. He could hear the muffled chatter of Mamai and Aunt Mary inside. A pan clanging on the stovetop. The thick, buttery aroma of steamy, hot beans.

"Looks like ye survived all your lickings."

Bill nodded.

"You're smart, Bill. Bet ye have it all figured out by the end of tomorrow."

Bill leaned back with a laugh. "I've already figured it out! I'll be a muleboy in a year and a nipper by the time I'm twelve."

"How in blazes ye gonna do that? They don't let eleven-year-olds care for the mules."

"They'll let *me*. Shoulda seen me, Mike. I was the fastest boy there!"

"Jeez, Bill, that's nothing to be proud of."

"I was faster than boys two, three years older 'n me. All thanks to ye."

"I never told ye to go fast! That's just risking your life for nothing. The boss is the only one who benefits from that."

"I *was* the fastest. And the only one with the grit to climb up top and unclog the screens."

"Goddamn it, Bill! That's the quickest way to lose a limb!"

"But I wanna be a nipper. I know a thousand ways to kill rats."

Mike shook his head. "Those jobs are based on age. Nothing

you can do to speed up time. Except maybe change your name to Evans or Thomas. Besides, it's a fine line between impressing the boss and enraging him. Remember what Da used to say? 'Ye can curse the boss, shirk, quit. But never let 'im catch you getting hurt!'"

"Dewees don't care if we get hurt."

"He cares if your body's clogging up the gears, preventing them from makin' money."

Bill crossed his arms. "I ain't a sissy! And I ain't workin' the breaker till I'm as old as you!"

"You little shit!"

He plunged his fist into his brother's stomach.

Bill yowled in pain.

The door swung open. Uncle Sean rushed toward them. He yanked Mike by the collar and held him against the wall with his feet dangling. "Think this is a game?"

Mike knew it wasn't. He couldn't breathe.

"When I bailed your da outa jail, he was treated like a hero. For what? Goin' to jail and putting the rest of yiz at risk of starvation? Then he died a martyr. And I barely got a nod!"

He slugged Mike in the guts so hard that everything went black.

When he awoke, Mamai was crouched beside him, wiping his forehead with a damp rag. She had a soothing look that reminded him of when he was a boy, when tiny little cuts were life or death disasters, and a soft kiss made everything better. For a moment, he forgot about his numb fingers, and the knives stabbing into his chest each time he inhaled.

"He nearly killed him!" Bill said, shivering from the cold.

"No one's gonna die." She wrapped an arm around his shoulder, snuggling him closer. "How're ye feelin', Mighael?"

"Bad." He wished Sean was dead.

"Ye were only out a coupla seconds." She stroked his forearm. "Guess ye got the wind knocked outa ye."

"Was Da in jail during the war?" Li'l Bill asked.

"Jail?" She shook her head, as if it wasn't true. "Uncle Sean say something?"

Mike propped himself up with his elbows. "Said Da was a hero."

Mamai's eyes moistened.

He squeezed her hand. "It's alright."

"No. It's time yiz knew." She rubbed a hand against her heart and her eyes brightened a bit. "Remember when we lived in Audenreid, during the war? That weekend Da didn't come home?"

"Just barely."

"Ye were only four. Billy wasn't a year old."

Mike nodded. "I thought he was visiting Aunt Mary."

"A little white lie." Mamai's hand brushed his face. "Ye were scared. Wouldn't stop crying."

"What happened?" Bill asked.

"It was July 4th, 1862. The war recruiters were in town. Your da and a coupla friends went to protest, drive 'em out. Your uncle thought Da was a hero for refusing to help free the negroes. Thought they'd take all their jobs. But he was wrong. Your father hated slavery. Said it drove down wages for everyone. How could a feller compete against men who weren't paid a penny? Who couldn't form unions and fight for their rights? What he opposed was being used as fodder in a war that only benefited the bosses."

The door flung open and slammed into the wall. Uncle Sean stood in the doorway.

"Get the hell inside. All of yiz! It's suppertime. Wanna stay out here and get frostbite, yiz can go find somewhere else to live. I ain't supporting a bunch of invalids."

He stepped back inside and closed the door.

Mamai shook her head and sighed.

"Times like these, I've a mind to steal a wagon and drive us all out of Schuylkill Country forever."

Chapter 10
Thursday, January 16, 1873

Mike glanced uneasily at the men marching up and down Line Street in their long coats and woolen caps, chanting for fair pay, their picket signs bobbing in the air. Others huddled around a rubbish fire, poking it with sticks, stirring up a miasma of smoldering horse shit, cabbage leaves, and moldy leather. Near the coll'ry gate, half-buried in the snow, was an overturned coal wagon, black, with "Thomas Colliery" painted in red on its side. Three boys, Bill's age, were jumping on it, trying to smash it to pieces. One of its wheels was spinning.

Bill's hands spasmed at his hips. He gave Mike a pained look.

"It ain't right," Mike muttered. "Everyone's on strike but us."

Uncle Sean smacked him in the back of the head.

"Shut up an' don't start any trouble! This here's a Welsh strike!"

Snorting, Mike started to walk off, but Uncle Sean grabbed him by the shoulder.

"Forget how those taffy bastards sold us out last time? Attacked Irish homes? Drove yiz outa Avondale?" He wagged a finger. "It's middle of winter, goddamn it. Completely arseways. Strike now, we'll starve."

Li'l Bill clutched the collar of his coat with both hands. "Th-that'll make us blacklegs!"

"Don't be a scut!" Uncle Sean kicked him in the seat of his pants. "Family first. A man's gotta make sacrifices."

He led them across the street and up an embankment, through frozen thickets that crunched beneath their boots. Mike's gaze darted back to the men by the rubbish heap. One of them had holes in his trousers and his unmentionables showed through. He was shivering as if he had a fever.

"Shame on you, Sean Campbell!" yelled an old man. "Corrupting your nephews."

Uncle Sean's fists opened and closed. "We're just tryin' not to starve, ye scoundrels!"

"Us, too!" yelled the shivering man. "But we ain't doin' it on your back!"

Mike angled away from the strikers, but found himself staring right at Uncle Sean, whose lips were pressed tight, like he was trying to hold back the squirts. It was disgusting and he wanted to get as far away from him as possible. He wanted to run to the strikers, tell 'em he was with them.

He pulled his cap lower, praying they'd start walking again before his friends saw him.

"Blacklegs!" the men yelled.

A rock whizzed past Mike's ear. He tried to cover up with his arms, but the next one hit him anyway. Church bells rang in his head. He fell to the ground.

"Get up!" Uncle Sean tugged his sleeve. "Run, Billy, run!"

Rolling onto his hands and knees, Mike watched his uncle and brother scamper up the path. He tried to stand, but was too dizzy and fell back on his face. The snow was soothing against his throbbing head. He wanted to lie there until the pain and wooziness went away, but then he heard footsteps. His heart thumped against the cold earth. Hot breath blew across his neck. He braced himself for a boot in the gut, but instead was pulled to his feet.

Johnny Morris was holding him steady.

Tom was on his other side, grinning. "Took one to the noggin, eh, Mikey?"

"Guess so." He rubbed his temple. When he saw blood on his fingers, his legs weakened.

They guided him to the log outside the front gate. "Have a seat, till ye feel better."

Morris took off his scarf and wrapped it around Mike's head.

"I'm no blackleg. And neither's my brother. Uncle Sean made us go."

"We know." Tom shook his head. "He's the blackleg, the pigeon-livered bastard."

Morris eyed the breaker. "Bill might be the only one in there today."

"And Dewees," Tom added.

Mike rubbed his head. "That ain't good."

"Forget it," said Tom. "Can't do nothin' 'bout it now. But those boys over there, destroying Company property?" He raised an eyebrow. "We sure can do something about that."

He ran to the wagon, leapt on top, and stomped his foot until it punched right through. Winking, he raised his fists over his head. "That's how it's done, lads."

Mike fiddled with the scarf on his head, then chased after him. He jumped up beside Tom and pulled off a slat. Laughing, he pulled off another and tossed it to the ground. If Uncle Sean could see him now: on strike *and* destroying Company property. It would drive him nuts!

Standing tall, he watched the younger boys whack each other with discarded slats.

"That's how we do blacklegs! That's how we do blacklegs!"

One of them pried off a wheel and rolled it down the road, chasing after it with a stick. He nearly trampled Johnny Morris's shiny black boots.

"Watch it, kid!" Morris shook his fist.

A tall, broad-shouldered miner with a bright red scar down the side of his neck approached them. Mike thought he was going to tell them to stop letting the younger boys hurt each other. Instead, he walked up to Tom. "These your buddies?"

"Yup," Tom murmured, jumping down from the wagon. "Mike Doyle and Johnny Morris. Best buddies in the world." He raised his chin high. "And this is my da. Best WBA man in Shendo."

"Pleased to meet yiz." Mr. Hurley tipped his cap. He had a thick, lampshade mustache, and the same playful, blue eyes as Tom, except his were guileless, like Da's. "But remember what I told ye, son. A union's only as strong as its membership. And Shendo's got the best team in the league. With fellers like Coyne and Lawler, we can't b—"

The emergency whistle shrilled.

Mike's body stiffened. He knew it was Bill. He jumped down and ran as fast as he could. Past discarded wagon parts. Wide-eyed breaker boys. The stable and headframe. A striker who'd slipped on the ice. A pale-faced boy crouched in the doorway, cringing at each bloodcurdling shriek.

It was completely dark inside, still as a cave, except for Bill's agonizing screams. Dewees was slumped in a corner, his chest heaving as if he'd just fought a bear. Past him, an empty sorting table. Overflowing hoppers. Chutes without boys. Mounds of coal. And between them, a quivering, groaning lump.

Dewees cleared his throat. "I've sent for the doctor."

Mike rushed to Bill's side. He took off his jacket, draped it over his shivering brother. His right foot was a bloody tangle of sinew and flesh.

"You're gonna be alright, Bill."

"I-I slipped, Mike. I swear I wasn't showing off."

"I know." He clasped his brother's hand. His pulse was racing. His skin was ghostly and cold. "You've got a lot of grit, Bill."

Mike peeked at the door, wondering what was taking the doctor so long, when Uncle Sean burst inside. He shoved his way past Mr. Hurley and several other miners, nearly knocking Tom and Johnny Morris over. He rushed across the room, squatting near Bill's head, with a pained look in his eyes and his hands floundering in front of him.

"Oh, Billy."

"It hurts so much, Uncle Sean."

"Doctor'll be here soon. Get ye fixed up."

It looked like Uncle Sean was going to reach down and scoop Bill up, but then he suddenly tucked his hands into his armpits with a grimace.

"Any idea what this'll cost us? I told ye to be careful in here!"

"Sean Campbell!"

His eyes narrowed. He slowly turned his head.

Eight miners were marching toward him. Including Mr. Hurley. Tom and Johnny Morris remained near the doorway, mouths agape.

"He's your own kin," said Mr. Hurley. "If you're here to help 'im, we'll let ye be. But if you're gonna torment him, then ye best leave before your face looks like his foot."

Uncle Sean's gaze bounced from one man to the next. He

rubbed his forehead, as if it ached. His other hand was squeezed into a fist.

"You're right. He is my kin. And it's none of your damned business, ye feckin' gowls."

A big miner, who looked like he could tie Sean into a knot, leapt at him and pulled him away from Bill. Another two grabbed his flailing legs and dragged him outside, cursing.

"Thank God," Bill grunted.

Mike closed his eyes and exhaled. Yeh, much less bad with him gone. But now what? How would he get Bill home? How would he explain it to Mamai? Cripes, how would he get him through the surgery? He glanced at Bill's foot, what was left of it, and shuddered. He hadn't noticed how cold he was until now. His fingers were numb, his arms half-frozen, his throat cracking with dryness. It musta been twenty degrees in there. He wanted his coat, but Bill needed it more. He needed a drink of water, but didn't dare leave Bill's side.

"Your brother?"

He looked up. It was Mr. Hurley. His gentle gaze never wavered from Mike's. Tom stood behind him, nodding at his every word.

"I'll help ye get your brother through this, if that's alright with ye."

He placed a hand on Mike's shoulder, which relaxed a bit.

"Hear that, Bill?" Mike whispered. "You're gonna be fine."

When they left the infirmary, it was dark and snowing heavily. Bill was unconscious from the medicine. Mr. Hurley carried him from Miller's wagon to the house. Tom ran ahead to get the door. Mike walked slowly behind them, his limbs heavy, as if he had been picking coal all day in the breaker. He wished he could go straight to bed without supper. Everyone had probably already eaten anyway.

Mamai was waiting inside, clutching her rosary, crying. She looked like she was going to faint. "My baby!"

Aunt Mary stood behind her, rubbing her hands together.

Tara was rocking side to side. "What happened?"

"Accident," Mike said, pausing when he noticed Tom staring at her, standing perfectly still, like an egret waiting for its chance to pluck a fish from a pond. "Um, lost his foot under a belt."

She tugged at her braid. "He-he won't be able to walk?"

"No!" Mamai screamed, crying all the more.

Tara leaned closer, until her eyes were only a few inches from Bill's foot, her head twisting as she followed the bandages, which were crusty with dried blood, from his ankle down to his stump. Her nosed scrunched. She lifted her head. "What's that strange smell?"

"Carbolic," said Mr. Hurley. "To clean the wounds."

Mary glared at Tom, and Mr. Hurley, as if they were the ones who'd caused Bill's injury. But then Mike figured it was probably just that she didn't know them. None of them did. And on top of that, Tom was being a fool.

"Um, that's my friend Tom," Mike said, hoping that hearing his name would bring him back to his senses. "And his da, Mr. Hurley. He was with us the whole time."

Mr. Hurley nodded, producing a small smile. "Where shall I put 'im?"

"One of those chairs?" Mike said, squinting. The room seemed brighter than usual. And hot. He slipped off his scarf and coat and draped them over a chair.

Bill groaned.

"Nah." Mamai dabbed her eyes. "More comfortable in his own bed. Down here he'll just annoy his uncle." She scooted around the table to the stairwell and opened the door. "Tara, show him the way. Careful not to wake the twins."

Tom bowed as Tara walked past.

Tara rolled her eyes. "Why don't ye make yourself useful?"

A flush crept across Tom's cheeks. He shoved his hands into his pockets and sat down at the table, quieter than Mike had ever heard him.

Aunt Mary collapsed onto the chair beside him, rubbing the back of her neck. "I suppose your uncle's at the tavern. Rather get drunk with his friends than take care of his own nephew." Her hands danced around in her lap, like she couldn't remember what they were for.

Mike didn't know how to respond. Those men could've done anything to him. He really could be at the tavern right now, licking his wounds. If that was the case, he'd be home soon. No point in worrying her over nothing. But what if those men had killed him? She'd be devastated. And when she found out, she'd think Mike was a coward for not telling her.

"I-I can look for him."

"Don't." Mamai reached for his hand. She was trembling. "It's late. I need ye here."

Aunt Mary glanced at the door, then at her feet.

Fidgeting, Mike cleared his throat. Sean could be anywhere. There were two dozen taverns in Shendo, if that's where he was. And a hundred nooks and crannies to dump a corpse.

He yanked his hand free from Mamai.

"I'll go with Mr. Hurley. It'll be quick with him and the wagon."

They found Uncle Sean in a snowdrift, behind Shoemaker's Slaughterhouse, barely moving except for occasional shaking. His nose was bent sideways, with a puddle of frozen blood below it. His left eye was swollen shut. All around him, more blood, as if someone had sprayed the snow with red paint.

Mike couldn't understand how men could work here, day after day. The smell was awful. Rotting flesh. Rancid fat. Manure.

Tom looked like he was going to vomit.

Mike pinched his nose. "Uncle Sean! Wake up."

Mr. Hurley poked him with his boot.

"Bloody hell, ye sonofabitch! Come to finish me off?"

"It's me, Uncle Sean." Mike leaned down. "We're here to take ye home."

"What about him?" Strands of bloody drool dangled from Sean's mouth. "Ain't he one of 'em?"

"One of who?" Tom's eyebrows squished together. "It's just my da."

"He's a Kohinoor Boy!"

Mr. Hurley shook his head. "Look, Campbell, I'm just tryin' to help."

"It's true, Uncle Sean. They were with us through the surgery. Helped get Bill home."

Uncle Sean sat up and stared.

Mr. Hurley reached down and picked up a card that had fallen from Uncle Sean's coat pocket. There was writing on it. A casket. Two pistols. "Know what this is?"

"What's it say?" Mike asked.

"Can't read it," Mr. Hurley replied, shaking his head. "But it's a coffin notice."

Uncle Sean's eyes narrowed. "So?"

"Ye know damned well. Means a bullet in the head if ye try to work again during the strike."

Uncle Sean's face tightened. He wrinkled his nose.

"How're we gonna pay the doctor if we don't work? How're we gonna eat?"

"No way!" Mike's fists clenched at his sides. "Bill lost his foot for bein' a blackleg. And you nearly got killed. I ain't doin' it no more. You're always saying real men make sacrifices for their families. That's what a strike is."

Mr. Hurley crouched down beside them. "We're picketing the Plank Ridge Saturday. My boy's comin'. Happy to bring Mike with us."

"Can I go?" Mike asked, leaning closer.

Uncle Sean reached for his collar, but winced and fell back into the snow.

Chapter 11
Friday, January 17, 1873

The next morning, Mike got up extra early. He wanted to get to Plank Ridge before anyone else, case the place, make sure there weren't any cops or blacklegs. But when he got downstairs, Uncle Sean was already awake, sitting at the table, with his arms pressed tightly to his sides. His eye was even more swollen than the night before, and his nose hung awkwardly to the side, as if the bones holding it together were gone. His face was one enormous purple bruise.

"Sit down."

Mike grabbed a chair, wondering what his uncle wanted now. But before he could sit down, Sean stood up and smashed his fist on the table. "I've made a decision. You're goin' to work today. We can't afford to go from three incomes to none."

"But if we don't fight, even three incomes won't—."

"Fight?" Uncle Sean stared directly at him. "And wind up dead? Like your old man?"

The words thundered in Mike's ears like a freight train bearing down on him. His body tensed and his hands locked into fists. He wanted to sort out what he'd say before it came gushing out on its own, all wrathy and muddled. But the room was so small and he was so hot that nothing came to him but a string of flailing curses. So, he kicked over a chair.

"I'm joining the strike, ye feckin' blackleg! And you can't stop me!"

Sean's swollen lips pulled back, exposing his yellow teeth. There was spittle in the corners of his mouth. His hands were shaking.

"Ye little shit!"

Mike's heartbeat echoed in his ears. But he was ready. When his uncle lunged, he shoved the table into his guts, causing his body to jackknife and his head to smack onto its surface.

"'Scuse me!"

Disoriented, Mike stumbled to the door and made his way to the street. His head was thumping. The sky was dark and everything felt enclosed, like he was in a narrow valley. He started running as fast as he could, as if his life depended on it, though he had no idea why. Uncle Sean wouldn't chase him. Nobody would. But he knew he had to get as far away as possible. So, he raced across town, the buildings whizzing past him in a gray blur. He didn't stop until he reached the sandlot on Catherine Street. He brushed the snow off the log behind third base and sat down, panting, his muscles trembling and his shirt soaked with sweat.

He leaned back and laughed, wishing Tara was there with him. She would've loved seeing Uncle Sean's eyes bugging out when the table slid into his guts, the helpless grunt as his head slammed down, Mike's sarcastic apology at the end. Everything the worthless scut ever did to them, the violence, the shaming, the mockery, all thrown back in his face.

But nobody was there to share his victory. Nobody was even awake.

He hugged his knees, shivering in the dark gloom of the Kohinoor breaker, which loomed over him from the top of Glover's Hill. He wanted breakfast, but had no idea where he'd eat, let alone where he'd sleep tonight. He certainly couldn't go home. Sean would never let him back. Not in a million years. Worse than that, he wouldn't get to see the twins grow up or taste Aunt Mary's cooking ever again. It would break Mamai's heart. Tara would have to take care of Bill by herself. Da always said to fight with honor, but where was the honor in running away and leaving them at Sean's mercy?

He yanked off his cap and threw it on the ground.

"That wasn't a victory! That was the dumbest thing I ever did!"

Shaking his head, he leaned down and punched the frozen earth. For a moment, his shoulders relaxed and the pain in his temples went away. He did it again, harder and harder, until his knuckles started to burn and bleed. It wasn't enough. He needed to keep going, to punish himself further, but his hand was throbbing and his body quivering.

He reached for his cap, but his fingers wouldn't bend, so he had to use his other hand.

"That was the second dumbest thing I ever did!"

Sucking his wounds, he struggled to think of a solution. As long as the strike continued, he'd have nothing for rent or food. If it ended now, with wages slashed, he wouldn't even have enough to share a room in a boardinghouse.

Across the lot, he could see a light on in Tom's house. He smelled bacon. His stomach twisted in grumbly knots. They'd give him breakfast! Maybe put him up for a night or two.

He got up and dragged his body across the lot, but as he got closer, he noticed someone skulking toward their front door. A man, with a long pointy chin, same as Uncle Sean.

Cringing, he considered going the other way, but before he could turn, the ghoul looked up and started walking briskly toward him.

"Mighael Doyle! Your mother and aunt are sobbing with fright. And your brother's in so much pain he's seeing bats."

Mike reached into his pocket and handed over the medicine the doctor had given him at the infirmary. "I-I meant to give this to him last night."

Uncle Sean held the tiny bottle up to his eye, then smashed it against the wall. "He's gotta take his pain like a man. And he's gotta go back to work."

Raising his hands, Mike stepped backward. "W-why?"

"'Cause your mother and sister don't earn enough to support us. And you've abandoned us."

Mike's neck bent forward. He pulled his arms in to his sides.

"I-I'll come back."

"Like hell ye will!" Sean slammed him against the wall, then let go with a grunt, clutching his ribs.

Tom's door flung open. Mr. Hurley ran out. He slugged Sean in the jaw, sending him staggering backward.

"Ye got some ballocks on ye, Campbell, showin' your face around here."

Wincing, Sean rubbed his chin. "I got a right. He's my ward!"

"Not anymore. Ye just kicked 'im outa your house. Whole neighborhood heard ye. But he's welcome here, long as he wants. He's family to us. Now, get the hell outa here before I bust your jaw. And don't come back, or you're dead!"

Uncle Sean stared vacantly. His Adam's apple bobbed up and down. "Alright," he said after a long pause. "But he best remember his siblings. How they're suffering 'cause of him."

Mr. Hurley waved dismissively, before turning to Mike.

"Hungry? There's grub on the table."

"Starving," Mike replied, but his voice was weak, as if he wasn't really sure.

He followed Mr. Hurley inside, wishing there was a way to undo everything. It was a terrible trap. The Hurleys' generosity was the bait at the center, and now he was stuck, unable to get out, powerless to protect his family or keep them from starving during the strike. His shoulders sagged and his hands went limp.

"Your uncle's wrong," said Mr. Hurley, closing the door behind them. "They ain't suffering 'cause of ye. It's him that's causing their pain. And Heckscher and Gowen. But at least with you out of the house, there oughta be more grub for 'em to eat, not less."

Mike glanced up at Mr. Hurley, whose brows were pulled down, making the scar on his neck lengthen.. Mike knew he was right, at least about the cause of his family's pain. But what about the food? Wouldn't Sean just take more for himself? Or spend the extra money at the tavern?

"Hurry up, Mikey." Tom was already up and wrapping a scarf around his neck. "Don't ye wanna case the place before the others get there?"

"Go ahead," said Mrs. Hurley, wiping her hands on her apron. She cut two slices of bread from a loaf on the counter and handed them to Mike. "Ye can eat these on the way."

"Watch out for the foreman," Mr. Hurley added, as Mike slipped the bread into his coat pocket. "Don't want 'em catching on to our plan."

It was still dark when they got outside, except for the top of the sun, just starting to peek up from behind the crest of Locust Mountain. The air was crisp and stung his nose. Mike wondered what they might find at Plank Ridge. Pinkertons with repeating rifles? Blacklegs with cudgels?

He pulled a slice of bread from his pocket and took a bite.

Tom glanced at him with a hungry look in his eye. "Your sister's a real bun."

Mike struggled to swallow. "Whad'ya mean, *bun?*"

"Um." Tom cleared his throat. "Ye know, a bunny. Cute, twitchy nose. Big, dark eyes."

"You're scared of rodents!" Mike jammed a finger in his chest.

"Am not. I just hate rats. Rabbits are fine."

Mike gave what he hoped was a pitying look.

"They're vicious. Cunning. Chew a man's fingers clean off while he's dead drunk. Every time I see one, reminds me of the cave-in at Rainbow Coll'ry. Came out in hordes, eyes glowing red in the dark, like some kind of living tornado. It was awful."

Mike scratched his jaw. Tara was timid and shrill, but definitely not dumb. Certainly no rabbit or rat. She was way smarter than Tom and deserved better.

"She's not interested in ye."

"Yeh, she is! I saw how she looked at me the other night."

"She called ye useless."

"That was just an act. Girls can't say they like ye in front of their parents. It's part of the game. Makes a feller desperate. Makes us work harder to get 'em. Buy 'em gifts. Promise to be their steady."

Mike turned to walk away, unable to look at his friend, unsure if they could even be friends anymore. But before he could get away, Tom threw an arm around his shoulder. He still had that same lustful grin, but his eyes looked a bit watery, as if he regretted having brought it up.

"I'm glad ye moved in with us, Mikey. It'll be fun. Like having a brother again."

Goosebumps erupted on Mike's arms. Was Tom putting their friendship above his lust?

"Wait, what do you mean, 'again'?"

"Had two older brothers." Tom's voice wavered. "Both died in that cave-in. And a sister who died giving birth."

"Jeez. That's worse than losing a da."

"It's why my motto is: The Devil may care, but I sure as hell don't."

"You don't really believe that. You wouldn't be coming to this picket if you didn't care."

"Important stuff, yeh. But what's the point of doing all the dumb stuff they say ye gotta do? Look, Mikey. Nothing lasts forever. People come and go. Including us. I ain't gonna spend the rest of my life following all the rules in hopes that eventually things'll work out. We could die before that ever happens."

Chapter 12
Friday, January 17, 1873

Standing atop Plank Ridge, beside the breaker, Mike gazed down at the frozen crick bank below, glowing blue in the moonlight like a dead man's lips. An icy breeze rippled through his ragged clothes, sending a shiver up his spine. He wrapped his arms around himself, flinching at the pain in his knuckles. He relaxed his arm, so that his injured hand rested against his side, and scanned the coll'ry for signs of trouble. The place was empty except for two men outside the metal shop, smoking beneath its lamp.

"See any cops?" Tom asked, tightening his scarf.

"Nah, just the foreman and super." His voice was shrill, like Tara's when she was flustered, not confident, as he had intended. He turned and began looking for boonties, baseball-sized rocks for hucking at blacklegs.

Tom started to make his own pile.

They worked in silence, until Mr. Hurley and a stranger arrived. The new feller was clean-shaven, with curly brown hair peeking out from beneath his tweed cap. He was no taller than Mike, with bright, green eyes that appeared surprised, almost astonished, like someone you could really trust.

"This is Ed Coyne," said Mr. Hurley. "The real brains of the union. Only twenty-two, but he knows how to get everyone to play his part. Just like the conductor of a band."

"And ye must be Mike Doyle." Coyne extended a hand. "You've been casing the place, haven't ye? Think we'll shut her down?"

"Sure!" Mike squeezed Coyne's hand. "What's stoppin' us? Nobody here but a dumb super and a foreman!" For once, his voice didn't crack.

"Excellent." Coyne peered around the breaker to see for himself.

"Bet I can hit one of 'em," Tom said, grabbing a boonty.

Coyne grabbed his arm.

"That's the spirit, Tommy. But save it for later. When the blacklegs arrive."

A large group was marching toward the front gate. They were led by a burly miner, a foot taller than everyone else, with a pointy black beard. He wore a long blue Union frock, with shiny brass buttons down the middle; a general leading his troops into battle. He was followed by twenty-one men, waving clubs and spades, and a dozen or so boys, whooping and hollering.

Mr. Hurley's cheek ticked.

"Mike, Tom, run down there and hush 'em up before the super catches on."

"Relax," said Coyne. "Let the lads blow off some steam. We need 'em in a fine fettle."

Mr. Hurley chuckled, jabbing an elbow at Mike. "See? Just like a conductor. Even got *me* playin' my part."

Coyne quirked an eyebrow at Mike and Tom. "An' your part is to get those lads up this hill quick as ye can. You're leadin' the artillery."

Mike pulled in a deep breath. His body seemed to lengthen by a couple inches. He was a strike leader now and it was his job to make sure the other boys played their part. Make sure no blacklegs got through. Easy enough from the top of the hill. Plenty of ammunition behind the breaker. Soon as a wagon came, they'd fire their boonties. With his arm, they couldn't fail.

They hiked down the hill and across the street, toward the culm heap, which looked like a twenty-foot-tall cake, hastily frosted, with patches of chocolate peeking through the snowmelt. It smelled worse than a pack of farting dogs. Back in Avondale, a little girl had died scavenging for coal when the culm heap shifted and buried her alive. Ever since, just being near one made Mike antsy.

They gathered in the empty lot next to the culm heap. Mr. Hurley approached the large feller, taking a look over his shoulder to make sure the super and foreman weren't nearby.

"Koontz, help me set up a line across the road."

Coyne led Mike and Tom to the back of the crowd, where the boys were bobbing side to side. "Listen up, lads. Mike and Tom are your troop leaders. They know the plan."

Mike stepped forward. "How're your arms feeling?"

"Strong as an ox," said a boy who looked no older than eight. Probably the baby in his family, judging by the way his oversized sleeves bunched up around his wrists.

Tom placed his hands on his hips and spat tobacco juice at the boy's feet. "We don't need oxen. We need pitchers. With perfect aim. Can any of ye throw?"

"I can! I can!" called several boys.

"I can do better than that," said a skinny boy with greasy black hair, parted down the middle. He pulled out a slingshot.

"Perfect," Mike said, pointing at the breaker. "Get up there. And start gathering boonties."

The boys raced up the hill, whooping and hollering. Mike and Tom marched after them singing:

I work in the mines where the sun never shines, nor daylight does ever appear;

With my lamp blazing red on the top of my head, in danger I never know fear.

Tom rubbed his hands together. "Think ye can hit 'em from up here?"

Mike eyed the front gate. "Know I can. If I wait till they're close enough."

A wagon rounded the corner of Center and Union. The men locked arms in front of the gate. The road was narrow and lined with boulders. No way it could get around them.

"Out of the road!" the foreman barked, stomping toward the line of men. He was as tall as Koontz, with a vicious edge to his voice. "That wagon's coming through!"

Koontz stepped forward, laughing. "*You* get outa da vay. I move for nobody."

The foreman crossed his arms. "Ye haven't the ballocks!"

The wagon was now only a half-block away, passing the Reading depot.

"Blacklegs!" The boys unleashed a barrage of rocks.

"Stop!" Tom screamed. "You're wasting ammo."

"Let 'em get closer," Mike said. "We need to hit 'em."

The superintendent ran to the base of the hill and shook his fists. He looked like a stern schoolteacher, with his neatly parted hair, gold wire-rimmed spectacles, and long, crooked nose.

"You boys!" His face glistened red. "Come down, now, or else!"

"Or else, what?" Tom said.

"Or else you're fired."

"Did he say fire?" Tom giggled. "Alright, boys. Give 'im what he wants."

The boys hurled rocks at the super, who ran to the metal shop with his arms over his head.

"Huzzah!"

The driver cracked his whip. The wagon was only a few yards away, speeding toward the men like he intended to plow right through them. A dozen blacklegs sat in back with their shoulders scrunched together, their heads bowed low, and their eyes darting anxiously, as if they knew they were gonna die.

"Outa the way," the driver yelled. "This is a public thoroughfare."

"Go home," the strikers hollered back. "This coll'ry's closed!"

The foreman tried to grab one of them and pull him away, but Koontz wrestled him to the ground, yanking his arm behind his back until his eyes bulged out.

"Can we throw?" asked one of the boys.

"Not yet," Mike said. "Still too far."

Tom kept rubbing his face. His da was right in the middle. The wagon was aiming right for him. But at the last second, the men stepped aside, letting the wagon through.

"Now!" Mike hollered.

The boys threw everything they had left. The blacklegs cowered with their arms over their heads as a hailstorm of projectiles rained down on them. The boy with the slingshot hit one in the elbow, who jumped out and ran. But the driver kept going.

"It's now or never," said Tom.

Mike held a boontie in front of his eye, lining it up with the driver's head. He reared back and threw. The rock rasped against his fingers as it left his hand. It rocketed straight for the driver and hit him in the jaw, knocking him from his bench and into the dirt.

"Huzzah!" the boys cried.

"That was fierce," Tom said. "I've never seen a shot that accurate."

The driver got up, rubbing his cheek. "Goddamned sonsofbitches!" He pulled himself back onto the wagon as more blacklegs tried to flee. "Get back in, ye damned cowards!"

Grabbing the reins, he cracked his whip. "Gee! Gee!"

The wagon turned and drove back up Union Street. The boys chased after it for several blocks, cursing, throwing rocks. One curly-headed boy jumped onto the rear bumper screaming, "Go home to your mommies, ye feckin' cocksuckers!"

"Francis Gibbons," Tom whispered, as they hiked down the hill. He scooped up a handful of snow and molded it into a ball.

"John Gibbons's little brother?" Mike's voice went shrill again.

"Yeh. They live down the street from me."

"But he's a Kohinoor Boy. He'll kill us."

"For a snowball? C'mon, Mikey. Everyone does it. Besides, we deserve a little fun. We just shut down a coll'ry! Besides, how ye gonna win their respect if you're always scared of 'em?"

"Let's just go," Mike said, forcing a smile.

"I ain't scared of the Kohinoor boys." Tom waved his hand dismissively and walked toward the crick.

Mike followed, stopping beside him on the bank, where he picked up a stone and chucked it into the ice. "I still wouldn't want to meet any of them in a dark alley. Especially Eddie Lawler. Uncle Sean says he killed a man with his bare hands."

"Ye gotta stop listening to your uncle."

"Well? Did he?"

"Just some Company snitch."

"So, it *is* true!"

"'Course, it is. Everyone knows."

"Then why ain't he in jail?"

"'Cause the coppers couldn't find any witnesses."

Squatting, Mike gazed across the crick at the Reading Railroad yard, where a rusty boxcar with a caved-in side rested precariously on blocks of wood. Same black lettering as nearly every car in Shendo, except this one had a gaping hole in the middle. It reminded him of Sean's house. Sagging ceiling. Rusty stovepipe. Only difference was the Reading just threw stuff away when it got too old, even its employees, which would explain some of Uncle Sean's behavior, his loyalty to the Company and his fear of joining the strike. He was scared of getting thrown away, losing his house, not having enough to eat. But what about his fear of the Kohinoor Boys?

"What ain't ye tellin' me?"

"Um." Tom picked up a stone and threw it into the crick. "Promise not to tell anyone?"

Mike nodded.

"Ye remember that card we found in Sean's pocket?"

"Yeh?"

"Fellers who get coffin notices usually wind up dead. Yet that's his second one."

Mike frowned. "So, why ain't he dead?"

"Good question. And why didn't they kill 'im last time, either?"

"Last time?"

"That's what I was tryin' to tell ye. That guy Eddie Lawler killed was Sean's best friend."

Mike picked up a rock and threw it through the hole in the boxcar. It clanged against the inside. "So, why didn't he kill Sean, too?"

Tom shrugged. "Maybe he paid 'em off."

"Nah. He'd die before doing that."

"What if it's true?"

Mike tilted his head, stroking chin. It did kind of make sense. Why else keep Sean alive? And why else was Sean so desperate to get Mike, Tara, and Mamai's paychecks?

"Alright. Let's say it's true. I still don't wanna make enemies with 'em."

"They won't mess with you, Mikey. It's your uncle they hate. Besides, my da says ye gotta earn their respect. And I know just the way."

Whatever it was, Mike hoped it wouldn't be today.

"Let's go to the tavern? Have a drink with the men."

"You're crazy!"

"Why not? Didn't we drive off those blacklegs?"

"Sure. But your da'll kill us."

"How'll he know?"

"Won't it be obvious? I don't wanna come home staggering and puking."

"Relax. That only happens when you're really soaked. We'll only have a few. Just act normal when ye get home. Let's at least go have a squizz, see if it's worth going in."

Mike tried to keep his expression neutral. It probably would be fun. But acting normal? He had no idea what was normal in the Hurleys' home. But he was pretty sure it didn't include a coupla kids coming home drunk.

Chapter 13
Friday, January 17, 1873

Couch's Saloon was like a circus inside—loud, raucous, and full of laughter. The air was steamy and smelled of beer and tobacco. The ground was covered with peanut shells. Men sat on stools at the long bar and at tables scattered throughout the tavern with mugs of beer, which they clanked and slammed back down so enthusiastically it sounded as though they'd break. They played cards, arm-wrestled, and argued boisterously about the WBA and the Democratic Party.

Tom was bobbing side to side. "This place is amazing!"

Warmth radiated through Mike's body, like he was already part of the crowd. It was the most exciting place he'd ever been. The exact opposite of work or home. He wanted to come back again tomorrow. And the next day. Who was stopping him?

Someone tapped his shoulder. He nearly jumped out of his skin.

"Just me," said Coyne, sitting back down. There were several mugs lined up on his table, as if he was expecting them. "Have a drink, lads. First one's on me."

They grabbed mugs and clanked them together.

"This'll cure what ails ye." Tom took a long swill and wiped his face on his sleeve, grinning like he'd just beaten the devil. "A few more victories like today and we'll win this strike in no time!"

Sucking in his cheeks, Coyne shook his head. "We won a battle, Tommy. Not the war. Plank Ridge was easy. Larger coll'ries'll be tougher. Best not count our chickens before they hatch."

Out of the corner of his eye, Mike saw John Gibbons swaggering toward them with a full mug, sloshing beer with each burly step. He had the square face and ugly grin of a bulldog that's just shaken a cat until it's dead.

"Are the muleboys counting chickens or being chickens?"

"Shut up!" Tom said.

"Watcha gonna do about it?" Gibbons held his mug in front of him like he was going to bash Tom in the face, but then he started swinging it side to side, spilling even more, singing:

Oh, My sweetheart's the mule in the mines,
I drive her without reins or lines,
On the bumper I sit,
Tobacco I spit
All over my sweetheart's behind.

Mike's body tensed. Maybe now was the time to really earn this bastard's respect. He leaned forward in his chair, ready to punch him in the balls, but slumped back when he spotted another Kohinoor Boy walking toward them, the meanest-looking feller he'd ever seen, with squinty little eyes that he could barely keep open beneath the weight of his extraordinarily long and perfectly rectangular brows. There was scruff on his chin and a thin mustache above his lips, which he kept tightly sealed. He removed his coat and scarf and handed them to Tom, who neatly folded them over a seatback and handed him a beer. As he brought the mug to his lips, Mike could see the muscles bulging beneath his shirtsleeves. His fists were like anvils.

"Ye oughta be ashamed of yourself," the new feller said to Gibbons, who sank lower in his chair. "These boys are fuckin' heroes. Right, Coyne?"

"Absolutely! They're the ones that hit the driver and sent them scabs runnin' home. If it weren't for them, we'd still be there now."

Gibbons blew out a noisy breath.

"Ye Doyle?" The bruiser smacked his mug against Mike's.

"Eddie Lawler?"

"That's me."

Tom frowned, then took a long chug of beer.

"How'd ye know about them?" Gibbons asked, his voice rising. "Ye weren't even there."

"I know a lotta things, ye fuckin' jamoke. How'd ye *not* know? You *were* there."

"Enough!" Coyne said. "Both of yiz. Fact is, these two're my artillery command. Doyle has an arm like a cannon, only more accurate. They're exactly the kind of fellers the WBA needs."

Mike peered at his beer, still more than half full. He brought it to his lips and chugged it down, grit and all, then belched so loudly heads turned at the neighboring table.

"I was just messin' around." Gibbons got up. "Anyhow, everyone's lookin' dry. Whadye say I buy the next round?"

Eddie leaned closer to Coyne. "Hear 'bout Colonel Cake? Kicked off the Anthracite Board?"

Coyne's eyes widened. "No, but makes sense. All his men're back on the job at their old wages. Where'd ye hear this, anyway?"

Eddie grinned. "My uncle's on the bargaining committee, remember?"

"Well, boyos," Coyne said, standing up. He fiddled in his pocket for change. "We may not've won the war, but this is certainly grand news. Let's have a whiskey, too!"

Mike turned toward Tom, mouthing the word "Seriously?" His body was already warm and tingly from the first drink. What would two more do to him?

Tom just nodded and grinned.

By the end of the third drink, Mike's head was swimming. Everyone at the table looked handsome and friendly, even Eddie Lawler, who was no longer squinting and whose lips had relaxed into a wiggly smile. Everything seemed funny, too. Gibbons kept patting him on the back, saying what good buddies they were. So, when Eddie got up to buy the next round, promising beer and whiskey, Mike wasn't the slightest bit worried. He already knew what the fourth and fifth drinks would do to him. They'd make him feel great! But as he finished his beer, a thought occurred to him. Was he expected to buy a round, too?

He looked to Tom, who winked and said, "I got the next one."

When it was finally Mike's turn, he took a step toward the bar, but the floor suddenly slipped out beneath him and he fell on his face.

"What's wrong, muleboy?" Gibbons laughed. "Never been soaked before?"

"That's enough!" Coyne helped Mike to his feet. "Time you lads headed home. Slept it off."

Mike's cheeks burned. He pushed Coyne's arm away. "I'm fine!"

He walked toward the exit, taking wide steps, determined to prove he wasn't drunk.

"Let's get outa here!" he called to Tom from the doorway.

The air outside was cold and burned Mike's nose. The midday sun was so bright he had to squint, which only intensified the ache. He leaned against the tavern wall and sighed. "One minute you're on top of the world, buying rounds for the fellers, whooping it up with your buddies. The next you're a weakling who can't hold his liquor."

"Forget it," Tom said. "That was still the most fun we've ever had, right?"

"Sure, but where're we gonna sleep it off? We can't go home."

"Ye worry too much." Tom tried to squeeze out one of his mischievous smiles, but it ended up looking like a suppressed belch. "We only had five or six drinks. No one's gonna know. Just act normal. No staggering or hiccupping."

Mike figured it was at least seven, but each time he added them up he got a different sum.

"And don't get too close to mum or da. They'll smell it on your breath."

"Right." Mike drummed his fingers on his thigh. "No one'll ever know."

"No one," Tom repeated, giggling. He clapped Mike on the back, staggered a bit, then started down Coal Street.

Mike waited a moment, then followed. The ground was soft beneath his feet, like walking on cotton. The buildings swayed as they passed by, blurring together, then trailing away at the edges of his vision. He took slow, deliberate steps, trying not to totter, but it felt unnatural, obvious to anyone watching. He wished he was back in the tavern. Out here it was too bright, too cold, and there was an annoying buzzing in his ears, as if a swarm of muskeetas was following them.

He pulled his cap down over his ears. In a few blocks, they'd be home. Time to muster all his confidence and calm. Mrs. Hurley would be cleaning the kitchen. Maybe they could tell her they were tired and sneak past her to Tom's room to take a nap. But that would only work if Mr. Hurley was out somewhere. He wouldn't believe such bosh.

"Any chance your da won't be there?"

"No." Tom waved his hand dismissively. "But he don't care if I have a drink or two. Sometimes he sends me out for a pail of beer and lets me have a glass."

Mike looked away and muttered, "How 'bout seven or eight glasses?"

Mr. Hurley was waiting at the front door. His eyes were flinty and his lips were pressed flat.

"Look at the two of yiz. Drunk before noon!"

"Patrick," Mrs. Hurley cried. "What about the neighbors?" She stood behind him, with sagging shoulders, her face partially covered by a thick brown lock of hair, as her fingers danced nervously at the hem of her apron.

He yanked them inside by the wrists, then slammed the door.

Mike's stomach roiled, as if he was gonna puke. He clutched his stomach, swallowing hard.

Tom was gaping at his mom, swaying like he might fall.

Her head was lowered and her eyes were moist. She let out a heavy sigh.

"Tom Hurley, what are we gonna do with ye?"

Mr. Hurley's forearm twitched. His muscle tightened. He let out a forceful breath.

"Give 'em a good lickin' and send 'em to bed without supper."

She shook her head. "Got a better idea."

He rubbed his eyebrows. "Ye want 'em doing this again, Ellen?"

She grabbed his arm, without taking her eye away from his. "They won't. Not after spending a Sunday with me and the Knights of Father Matthew."

Mike started to weave in place. Their entire Sunday would be ruined. The meeting would be tedious, full of stiff church ladies.

And what if Aunt Mary or Mamai saw them? A licking would be better: over and done quickly.

"Are ye mad?" Mr. Hurley crossed his arms. "They're worse than Soupers."

"They're Cat'lics, same as us." Her voice was stilted, like she was trying not to curse. "They take a special interest in advancing young men. Exactly what our boys need."

"Those temperance folks are all the same. Bribe ye with gingerbread. Get ye to vote Republican. Tell ye how to live your life. I won't have Republicans living in my house!"

"You'd prefer a coupla fifteen-year-old drunks?"

Mr. Hurley's lips pressed together in a grimace. But then his eyes brightened and his shoulders relaxed. "Ellen, you're right!" He gave her a little hug. "These boys are getting too old for lickings, anyway."

Chapter 14
Sunday, January 19, 1873

Mike stood on the steps of the Church of Anunciation and peered down Cherry Street. He thought he could see Aunt Mary and Mamai rounding the corner, past the Methodist Church, with its two pointy steeples. They were walking hand-in-hand, with Uncle Sean and the twins right behind them, and Tara in the rear, pushing L'il Bill in a wheelbarrow, struggling not to dump him in the snow. As they got closer, he could see that her pretty white church dress was splattered with mud and her face was glistening red with sweat.

"That should be me."

He ran down the steps and into the street, gave Mamai and Aunt Mary each a quick little kiss on the cheek, hugged the twins, ignored Uncle Sean, and hustled to the back.

"I got this," he said, taking the wheelbarrow from Tara, wincing as pain shot through his hand. He lowered the wheelbarrow and brought his throbbing purple knuckles to his mouth. It tasted like a rusty screw.

"It's alright." She shook out her arms, but avoided making eye contact. "I was fine."

"Nah." He lifted the wheelbarrow and pushed it forward. "I shoulda been there this morning. Before ye left the house."

"Damned right!" Uncle Sean blotted his twisted nose with a rag. "But ye weren't. And ye ain't gonna be there when the breaker boss is smackin' him with his switch, either."

Mamai stopped and turned to face him. "You're not sending him back to work?"

"Like hell I'm not. Once this strike's over, we'll need his income more than ever. Besides, ye can't mollycoddle the boy forever."

"Can't I do something else?" Bill pleaded. "Breaker's for boys and old men."

"Ye *are* a boy," Sean said.

"But other boys get to grow up. Drive mules. Work the pit. Have a family before they become infirm and have to work the sorting table."

Mike struggled for a response. He knew Bill was right. No one took a one-legged man seriously, let alone a one-legged boy. "At least the sorting table's easy."

"And safe!" Mamai added.

Bill gave her a sour look.

"Ye got nothing to prove," Mike said. Even without a foot, Bill still wanted to do things the hard way. "We all know ye got grit."

Bill placed his hands on his face and let them slowly slide down his cheeks. "Know that saying, 'Once a man, twice a boy?' I don't wanna be a boy twice without ever getting the chance to be a man."

"Stop your grousing!" Uncle Sean slapped the top of his head. "Being a man means supportin' your family. Doesn't matter what job ye got. If ye ain't workin', you're a leech. That's worse than bein' a tramp!"

"That's quite enough!" Aunt Mary said, reaching down to straighten the lapels of Bill's coat. "It's Sunday. Can everyone please act a little more dignified?"

Aunt Mary loved Sundays. She always said that the Church of the Annunciation was the prettiest in Shendo, with its three arched doorways in front, and the large, round stained-glass window above them, with glowing multicolored rays that looked like the sun. In the morning, spears of light shot through it, catching the swirling wisps of sweet censer smoke and holding them suspended above the aisles as though the Holy Spirit was hovering beside them. There were more stained-glass windows on the sides that depicted biblical stories, and a steeply peaked roof that rose taller than any building in town, making the sanctuary echo as if Father Connolly was preaching inside an enormous cavern.

Mike parked the wheelbarrow next to the rectory. He grasped Bill around the waist, helping him up the steps and into the vestibule, where he deposited him on a bench just inside the front door. He figured the Hurleys had already entered the nave, since they were nowhere to be seen, but the rest of his family was standing near the holy water font. Tara was holding hands with Hannah Lawler, who was wearing a slim blue dress and had a radiant glow about her. He dipped his finger into the font and quickly made the sign of the cross, praying he'd get to sit next to her.

In front of Hannah stood her three younger brothers, one of whom looked like he was Bill's age, and twin sisters about the same age as Deirdre and Johnny. Behind them was a woman in a long woolen dress unlike any he had ever seen. Nothing fancy. A poor woman's dress like Mamai's and Aunt Mary's. But hers rose up to a narrow waist, with a derriere that jutted out. Beneath that dress, he could imagine her frilly white bloomers and her soft, creamy flesh.

His stomach quivered and a pleasant warmth spread throughout his groin. He raised his head slightly. Beautiful round bosoms. Cherry-red lips that were parted just enough to glimpse her sparkling white teeth. Shoulders draped in curly, raven-colored hair. Same as Hannah's.

Mrs. Lawler?

A flush crept across his face. He swallowed hard and abruptly turned away. But now he was looking right at a powerfully built man with slicked-back hair and a neatly trimmed chinstrap beard, a bruiser who could flatten him with a single blow.

It was the same man he had seen walking with Hannah his first day at work. It had to be Michael Lawler, the man he most wanted to meet.

"M-Mr. Lawler?"

"Indeed." He firmly grasped Mike's hand. There was a gleam in his eyes, as if the honor was his. "And you must be Michael Doyle. I've heard lots about ye."

Mike took a step backward. "Ye have?"

Uncle Sean made a slight growl.

Mamai's brows wrinkled, as if she assumed it was something bad.

Mr. Lawler gave an easy nod and came closer. He was nearly a head taller than Uncle Sean.

"Ye should be proud of your nephew, Mr. Campbell. He's the one that drove off the blacklegs at Plank Ridge yesterday."

Uncle Sean's face slackened. He even appeared to smile slightly, the first time Mike had seen him smile for anyone other than Aunt Mary.

Hannah laid a hand over her heart and her eyes seemed to grow bigger, until her mother scowled at her. Then she shuffled closer to her father and clasped his hand.

There was an awkward silence. The bells had stopped tolling.

"It's time!" Aunt Mary whispered. "Inside. Quickly."

Uncle Sean and Aunt Mary sat up front, next to their neighbors the Malones and their boy Jimmy. The pew behind them was empty, so Mamai helped Li'l Bill in and sat down beside him. Deirdre climbed up on her lap. Tara sat on her other side, with Johnny on her knees.

Mike paused to let Hannah go ahead of him, so she could be with Tara. He kneeled, crossed himself, then followed her in, but suddenly stopped when he noticed her smiling at him in a peculiar way. The corners of her mouth were quivering and pulled back slightly, and her shoulders kept scrunching up. It made his hands cold. He could smell his own sweat. He was certain everyone was watching him, waiting to see how he'd react. Was there something he was supposed to do? You couldn't push in a lady's chair in church, or take her coat. There was nowhere to put it. Wait, why was he getting so worked up? She was just one of Tara's friends. Just a girl. But a really pretty girl who wouldn't stop looking at him. She'd probably stare at him for the next two hours and everyone would know it.

He started to turn, but Mrs. Lawler was right behind him, with that same odd smile.

Shit!

Nothing left to do now, except sit down, and keep his eyes on the pulpit. Try not to think about either of them, or anything lusty. Think about God. The meeting of the Knights, later that day. Father Connolly in his ugly cassock, approaching the altar, kissing it, crossing himself.

"In the name of the Father, and of the Son, and of the Holy Spirit."

"Amen," the congregation replied.

"Grace to you," he continued. "And peace from God our Father and the Lord Jesus Christ."

Mrs. Lawler scooted closer. Her hip pressed against his. His legs tingled and his groin started to ache. He tried to focus on what Father Connolly was saying, what the congregants were replying, but even though he had the whole Mass memorized, all he could remember was an endless muddle of *Misereres*, *Domines*, and *Kyrie eleisons*. By the time they were done with the Gloria, his hands were trembling and his knees were ready to buckle. Thank God, Mr. Lawler was all the way at the end of the pew.

When it was time for the First Reading, Mike exhaled deeply. Finally, they'd get to sit down. But his relief was short-lived. Mrs. Lawler had scooted even closer. Their knees, thighs, and buttocks were all touching now, so warm and tight it seemed as though they were naked. He tried to lose himself in the bright colors of the stained-glass windows, making himself part of the story. First panel: apostles weeping as He hung from the cross. Perfect. Nothing less lusty than death. Next panel: apostles removing Him from the cross, gently, lovingly, Mother Mary massaging His bosom, Nicodemus supporting His legs. Last panel: free, but exhausted, His naked body resting on the smooth, round back of Mary Magdalene, her flesh warm and tender, just like Mrs. Lawler's thigh and buttocks.

His penis swelled, pressing against his thighs. Nowhere to go but up.

Shit. What if she notices? Or Hannah? Or Mr. Lawler!

He glanced at his lap. His coat spread across it. His cap on top of that.

Whew!

He looked back at the pulpit, at Father Connolly, but his cheeks continued to burn.

Ignore the females. Just listen to the sermon. Whatever he's saying, it'll calm things down. But the urge was too strong. He turned his head, just for a second, and caught Mrs. Lawler peering at his lap, smiling mischievously.

She knows!

His body shook. He dropped his chin to his chest, closed his eyes, and prayed. *Please God, make it go away. Before the Alleluia. Before I have to march down there for Communion.*

Everyone started to rise. He tried to contain it between his legs, but it sprang loose when he rose, straining against his trousers, poking out like a bell tower. He held his coat in front of himself, unconcerned with how ridiculous it looked. He crossed himself twice, hoping God would come to his rescue. But He didn't. His penis remained as hard as a log throughout the Gospel, homily, Creed, and offertory.

When it was time to receive Communion, his fingers started to tremble. He was sweating so much it oozed right through his shirt. Repeatedly sitting and standing was one thing, especially with his coat to protect him. Quite another thing to walk to the altar with a baseball bat between his legs. Maybe he could stay in the pew. Pretend he was sick? But then he noticed Li'l Bill struggling to get out, and Mamai waiting for him, rocking anxiously, as though she wasn't sure she could get him there. And Uncle Sean glaring at him.

Shit! Bill needs help and he ain't gonna get it from Sean.

Mike stood, dropping his coat and hat on the floor, and shimmied past Hannah and Tara. "I got 'im," he whispered, wrapping an arm around Bill's waist.

Together they limped down the aisle, like a couple of veterans about to receive medals for valor. Each step precise and firm. Chin up. Back straight. Everyone watching.

Oh, shit!

He glanced down at his groin, exhaling when he saw it was flat.

Good God, when did that happen? He hadn't even noticed.

Must've been Uncle Sean's nasty glare.

Maybe that bastard was good for something after all.

Chapter 15
Monday, April 14, 1873

Mike tugged on Tara's arm and tried to get her to follow him down the alley, but the stench of sewage and rotting garbage was overpowering and she refused to comply. It pressed up against them like a powerful wind, as a cold drizzle slapped their cheeks, and swarms of hungry flies buzzed around their ears. It seemed impossible that this cesspool could exist here, right behind Main Street, behind this three-story wall of banks, hotels, and restaurants, all sparkly marble and ornamental up front, with grim backsides of clapboard and brick. But even the rich had to shit, and piss, and stable their horses.

Tom ran past them with a burlap sack, pausing to grin and wave at Tara, before beelining for the garbage pile outside Vandussen's. "C'mon," he called, as he pawed through discarded cabbage rinds and withered carrots, along with a dozen younger kids. "Or we ain't get nothing."

Tara stood there shaking her head, with her arms crossed. "How can he be so haughty?"

"Maybe he's just hungry," Mike said, thinking about last night, Easter dinner at the Hurleys'. No ham or corned beef. Nothing but a potato and a small biscuit with a scrape of lard. Tara said Aunt Mary didn't even have lard. That some days they only got a biscuit to last the entire day. And it showed. Her hair was lank, her complexion sickly, and her legs were twigs.

He fastened his scarf over her face and coaxed her down the alley, past Tom, to the back of Bright's Grocery Store, hoping there'd be less competition, but the crowd was just as thick. A burly, tow-headed boy was yanking kids off the rubbish pile, flinging them into the dirt. In the back of the lot, an emaciated girl in a ripped dress sat on a stack of timbers, knees pressed together, crying into her hands.

A surge of energy coursed through Mike's veins. He grabbed a timber off the ground. With a guttural roar, he charged the bully and hit him across the back. "We're all trying not to starve!"

The boy yelped and collapsed.

Mike tossed the wood and turned toward Tara, but she was gone.

Nothing better've happened to her!

He scanned the lot, spotting her on the wood pile with an arm around the skinny girl's waist, and ran to her side.

"Hannah?"

She looked up, sniffling. Her eyes were red and her face was sallow.

"Her sister died," Tara said. A tear trickled from her eye. "Doc Luks said she had diphtheria. But it was the hunger that killed her."

His hands fumbled near his throat as he buttoned up his coat. What if it had been Deirdre or Johnny? Or Tara, or Bill? He'd gladly return to work to prevent that. Even risk getting beaten by Gibbons and Eddie Lawler. But why was he worrying about himself, and stuff that hadn't even happened, when Hannah Lawler was suffering real grief right in front of him? He could hear her moaning, see her trembling chin. He leaned closer, wishing he could embrace her, rock her gently back and forth, squeeze the sorrow from her tender body.

She wiped her nose and turned abruptly away. "It-it was my fault."

Mike tugged his earlobe. "I thought it was diphtheria."

Tara pressed Hannah's head against her shoulder. "How could it be your fault?"

"It was my job to do the shopping while my daddy was away." Her voice cracked, then broke into a sob. "But I don't earn enough to feed my family. And I couldn't find enough here."

"That's not your fault," Tara said, patting her leg.

"My mom said I could've tried harder."

"She's crazy! Ye did the best ye could. I was with ye, remember? No one was finding much."

Hannah looked up, rubbing her arm. "Really?"

"Of course. Where's your da been, anyway?"

"Traveling with my cousin. Organizing miners." She cleared

her throat. "Wish he would've taken me instead. Eddie would've found enough food. Daddy never takes me anymore." Her head dipped. "I'm no good at anything."

"Don't be silly," Tara said. "Everything ye do, ye do perfectly. Ye got an eye for details. You're better at laundry than me or Mamai. And you're the prettiest girl I know."

"Me?" She wrinkled her nose. "I'm skinny as a sail cat. And look at my dress. Ripped and muddy! I look like a tramp."

Tara grabbed a handful of muddy snow and smeared it across her own cheeks. "No, I'm as ugly as a tramp!"

Hannah's eyes widened and a tiny smile emerged on her lips. She looked like an injured baby bird. Mike wanted to scoop her up and carry her away, to a warm, secure nest, feed her with his own lips and brush away her tears. He wanted to say something tender, but his thoughts were murky and full of doubt. So, he stood there and did nothing.

She reached out, lightly brushing his wrist.

The hair rose up on his arms.

She quickly pulled away.

"We should go," Tara said, pointing at the bully, who was struggling to get up. "Before we get in trouble."

A younger boy kicked him back down, laughing.

"He won't bother us," Mike said. He peered down the alley, where Tom was struggling with three boys, each about half his size, who were trying to wrestle a withered old carrot away from him. "C'mon, Tom. Let 'em have it. We're leaving."

"Ye kidding?" He gave one of the boys a playful nudge. "I worked too hard for this."

"Show-off." Tara snuck another glance back. "Let's go without 'im."

She grabbed Hannah's hand and led them around the corner, down Main Street, past the Stars and Stripes, and the Hotel Immerman. Mike had no idea where they were going. He didn't care, either, he was so transfixed by Hannah's hair bouncing on her shoulders, the soft ridges of her ears, her strange, wonderful smell. His hand periodically grazed hers, sending flashes of warmth through his body. He hoped it would never end. But when Tara stopped at Luks Pharmacy, his heartbeat slackened and his legs began to tremble.

There were two bigwigs in the front window playing cards. Tom Foster, owner of the *Herald,* sitting stiffly with his big, round spectacles, like a grumpy owl, and his companion, a slender man with graying muttonchops and bulging round forehead.

"C'mon." Tara grabbed his wrist. "Don't ye wanna help Li'l Bill?"

He looked around uneasily. Hannah was already halfway to the counter. He couldn't leave now. Besides, they really did have to do something. It had been months since his injury. It was fully healed. Yet he was still keeping Tara up all night groaning in pain, and aggravating Uncle Sean.

He followed them inside. It smelled of bay rum and cigar smoke.

"My men don't read the papers," said Muttonchops, shuffling the deck without looking up. "They don't know what's going on in Paris. Don't care, either."

"They know about Hyde Park." Foster leaned in aggressively. "Breaker burned to the ground. Replacement workers beaten nearly to death. Militias in Scranton. That doesn't worry you?"

"Not at all." Muttonchops laughed. "WBA's requesting arbitration. Know why, Tommy?"

"Of course. Union has no legs to stand on now that the legislature's determined there was no price-fixing. WBA's a sinking ship. Siney wants a quick settlement before it all goes down, along with his fat union salary. But the men won't like it. Could be another riot before it's settled. And you're the logical target. Kohinoor's one of the only collieries still operating."

"With all my little spies?" Muttonchops winked. "I'd know in a heartbeat."

No wonder they hadn't won yet! Mike had to get this information to Mr. Hurley. Find out who these spies were. Have the Kohinoor Boys put the fear of God into them.

Foster's lip curled back like a mule's when it's just smelled something unpleasant. "This one of your boys, Heckscher?"

Mike looked down at his feet.

"No, Tommy, I don't recognize him. Must work at another colliery."

"Who do you work for, son?" Foster asked.

"M-Mr. Thomas." Mike winced at his own voice, disgusted by his lack of confidence.

"Hope the strike kills that cheap bastard!" Heckscher said.

"So you can buy him out?" Foster chuckled.

"Of course. I'm not heartless for no reason. In fact, I'm not even heartless."

He walked over to Mike, placing a hand on his shoulder.

"Those your sisters? Call them over here."

Hesitating, Mike tried not to shrink.

Best to just get it over with.

"Tara, Hannah."

They clutched each other's forearms and started walking toward them, clumsily, bumping into each other. Hannah's eyes were wide and frightened. Tara's were hidden behind her hair.

"Irish," Foster snickered. "Explains a lot."

Heckscher reached into his pocket, jangling with coins. "I can see the strike's been hard on you." He handed them each a penny. "Buy yourselves a treat."

Tara's chin dipped. "Th-thanks," she stammered.

Hannah tugged at her dress, as if trying to disappear inside it.

Mike's vision clouded up. His hands were shaking. He wanted to tip over their card table. Burn down the Kohinoor. The *Herald*, too. Dump both those bastards down a mineshaft. He'd show them they couldn't intimidate him. Another Hyde Park was exactly what was needed!

Pulling in a deep breath, he marched over to Tara and Hannah, squeezed in between them, and grabbed them each by the hand.

"Let's help Li'l Bill."

His muscles were still shaky as they walked to the back of the store, but he held his head up and approached the counter with ease.

Doc Luks was polishing his brass soda fountain. When he noticed them, he stuffed the rag into his pocket, nearly toppling a large jar filled with red syrup. "Michael, Tara, Hannah! How can I help you?" A blond curl dangled above his brows.

"We're here about Bill," Mike said. "Says his foot still hurts."

"But how?" Tara interrupted. "He ain't got one."

"Hmm." Luks rubbed his chin. "Sounds like phantom limb pain."

Tara tilted her head to the side. "Ghosts are causing his pain?"

"Not ghosts," he said, smiling, his gray eyes twinkling. "A vestige, like a phantom is a vestige of a person no longer here. A most peculiar and fascinating phenomenon. First heard about it during the war."

"Can ye fix it?" Mike asked. "He's in agony. No one's getting any sleep."

"You can give him laudanum. Just two drops. And only when the pain's unbearable." He drummed his fingers on the countertop. "I'll give you some on credit."

"Thanks," Mike said, shaking the doctor's hand.

Outside, he gave Tara the medicine.

"Give this to Mamai? Tell her what Doc said?"

"Sure. But where ye going?"

"Tom's house." He led them to the corner of Main and Lloyd. "Tell his da about Heckscher's spies. If we can shut down the Kohinoor, strike's over. We've won!"

"Why don't ye come to *my* house?" Hannah clasped his hand. "Tell *my* da?"

Mike nearly laughed out loud. He'd forgotten that her da was a union leader.

"Sure, but why don't *you* tell him about Heckscher's spies?"

"Me?" Her eyes widened. She started to grin, then flung her arms around him. "Of course! He's always been there for me. Even when Mom's being mean. This would be my chance to help him out for once. Prove I can do something!"

"Best of luck," Tara said, giving her a kiss on the cheek. "Remember, eye for details."

"We'll practice on the way," Hannah said, grabbing Mike by the hand and leading him away.

Chapter 16
Wednesday, April 23, 1873

Mike rushed from the house so quickly he tripped and tumbled into the dirt.

"Goddamn!" he muttered, as he lay on his back, staring into the bright morning sky. A flock of snow geese passed overhead, their hiccupping squawks like drunken laughter. Scrunching up his face, he tried to remain calm. Only two weeks since they visited Luks and Bill was already out of medicine. Uncle Sean would kill Tara when he saw the bill!

He got up and continued to the drug store, praying Luks would keep the secret. But when he turned onto Main Street and saw the crowd in front of Reber's, he choked on his own saliva. It didn't make sense. No one had money for food and Reber had stopped giving credit weeks ago.

His pulse quickened. Maybe they caught a blackleg, or one of Heckscher's spies!

He ran down the street, shoving his way through the crowd, and scrambled up the steps of Schaefer's boardinghouse. Ten men huddled on the balcony, shaking their fists and shouting.

Mike wedged himself between them and gazed into the street. There must've been a hundred people. They completely filled the intersection. Right in the center was Hannah's da, Michael Lawler, standing on a wooden crate and looking very much like a preacher, with his shiny black suit, slicked-back hair, and the trim little beard that barely covered his chin. Mr. Hurley was on his left, and Coyne was on his right, wearing his usual tweed cap tilted slightly to the side.

"Who's still runnin' his mine as if there weren't a strike goin' on?" Lawler yelled.

"Heckscher!" the crowd roared.

"What're we gonna do about it?"

"Shut 'im down!" the men hollered back.

"That's right! Shut him down!"

Mike smiled contentedly. "That's my plan," he said to no one in particular.

"*Your* plan?" said a familiar voice.

Jerking his head up, he realized he had been standing next to Gibbons, who was sneering at him with a cigar dangling from his lips. "Ye think you're the first to come up with that?"

"I heard it was my cousin," said Eddie Lawler, who was on Gibbons's other side, leaning casually over the railing. "I heard she's the one who saved the strike." He started to laugh.

Mike's cheeks flushed. "Well, I'm the one who told your uncle about Heckscher's spies."

His fingers tapped the railing. He wantedto put that cigar out on Eddie's forehead.

Eddie must've noticed his annoyance because he stepped closer and clasped his shoulder.

"Relax, Doyle. I'm just messing with ye."

"Yeh," said Gibbons, blowing a puff of cigar smoke into his face. "Hannah's just a little girl. What's she know about strikes?"

Mike squeezed the balustrade until it started to shake. He wanted to scream that she knew a lot about strikes, maybe even more than Gibbons, but what good would it do? It hadn't helped the other day, when he had walked her home from Luks's and she kept saying her parents didn't think she was good at anything, that her da loved Eddie more than her, that she couldn't even keep her own baby sister alive. He never even got the chance to tell her how much he liked her, he was so busy trying to make her feel better. Never even got the chance to practice what she'd say to her da when they got there. By the time they reached her house, she had forgotten the part about Heckscher's spies, and her da just patted her on the head and said, "Thanks, darling. Already knew about the Kohinoor." And the whole time, her mom had been standing at the top of the stairs, clutching her frying pan as if she had been inside Mike's head and knew exactly what he wanted to do with her daughter.

A ribbon of smoke went up his nose, causing him to sneeze, dispersing the memory like droplets of phlegm. He let go of the banister and stretched his fingers.

Gibbons leaned closer, laughing, waving his cigar at the crowd below. "Get this."

A man with baggy striped trousers was approaching Michael Lawler. Mr. Hurley and Coyne stepped forward to ward him off.

"What about the new Lawler Tax?" the man yelled.

Lawler chuckled, nearly falling off his box. "That what the *Herald*'s callin' it?"

"You think it's funny? Our own union fining us a hundred bucks if we don't return to work? We don't make that in a year!"

"Empty threat," Coyne said. He stood with his chin up and his hands held loosely behind his back, like there was absolutely no doubt in his mind. "Can't squeeze blood from a turnip!"

"Siney!" Gibbons hissed in Mike's ear. "Sonofabitch acts like the bosses' private copper."

Michael Lawler rolled up his sleeves.

"Last week, at arbitration, we demanded three bucks per ton. Woulda brought our wages back to what they were beginning of last year, which was already twenty percent less than they were in '69. But that devil of an umpire decided on two dollars and seventy-five cents, bringing our wages down to ten bucks a week. Think ye can live on that?"

"No!" the crowd boomed.

"Well, your union does. That's why they've called off the strike."

"Feck the WBA!" Eddie hollered.

"Cowards!" said Gibbons.

Michael Lawler's posture loosened. His expression became somber. "We've been fighting for four months now. We've been beaten by yellow dogs. Thrown in jail. And some of us—" His voice cracked. "Have buried our own wee children." He paused to wipe his eye. "Ye ready to give up and let all that sacrifice and suffering be for naught?"

"Hell no!" the crowd bellowed.

"Tomorrow we shut down the Kohinoor. Next week, the rest of

the Reading's coll'ries. Make that bastard, Gowen, feel the pain. Then we can negotiate our own deal. A better deal!"

"Huzzah!" the crowd cheered.

"What about Heckscher's spies?" Mike whispered.

Gibbons raised an eyebrow. "Ye mean the one whose face looks like ground beef?"

"Or the one in the creek?" said Eddie, his chin jutting prominently. "With his throat slit."

Mike's mouth fell open. His arms got cold and clammy. Those men had died because of him!

"C'mon, Doyle." Eddie slung an arm over his shoulder and led him back into the street. "Let's have a drink. You're taking this all the wrong way."

"Yeh!" Gibbons clapped him on the back. "Spies are worse than blacklegs."

Grimacing, Mike rubbed his forehead. A drink sounded awful. His stomach was churning and his throat ached. Besides, Mr. and Mrs. Hurley would both be home. He didn't want to bring more shame on them after all they'd done for him, or risk getting kicked out of their house. And he certainly didn't want to go to another meeting of the Knights of Father Matthew. But how could he say no to these guys? They'd just killed two men. He couldn't risk angering them. Couldn't risk becoming one of them, either.

He wet his lips and tried to relax. "Just one, alright?"

Gibbons slowly shook his head, as if terribly disappointed.

"Um, I gotta get to Luks. For my little brother."

Eddie pulled him into a headlock and knuckled him through his cap. "Anything for a hero."

Chapter 17
Thursday, April 24, 1873

The Kohinoor breaker dominated the neighborhood like a mountain fortress, with its sharply pitched roofs and impenetrable black walls rising abruptly from the craggy hill, and its dozens of tiny windows that resembled gun openings. The slopes rising up to it, scorched from a decade's worth of tailings, were crumbly and unclimbable. The main entrance at the top of Center Street, clearly visible from the Hurleys' front yard, was usually guarded by a C&I or two. Today there were ten, each with a rifle hanging from his shoulder.

The hairs bristled on the back of Mike's neck as they marched in front of the breaker. Even wedged between Tom and his da, with Eddie and Gibbons behind him, and a warm cup of tea in his hands, he was as cold as if he was naked. The sun wasn't even visible yet and the air was already filled with coal and tobacco smoke, and the sound of thunking engines. And several wagons full of shadowy men were parked in front of the breaker, as if it was a normal workday without a strike going on.

"Feckin' blacklegs!" Gibbons said. He struck a lucifer and lit his cigar.

The men in the wagon were restless and jumpy. A fat feller near the front kept wiping his face, as if he'd been working all day in the hot sun. The guy next to him kept standing and sitting back down, like he couldn't decide what to do. No one got out or made a move toward the breaker.

Mr. Hurley shook his head. "Heckscher musta snuck 'em in through the back at two or three this morning. Otherwise we woulda heard the wagons driving past."

"They ain't even from here," Eddie said, flicking his hand in front of his nose.

"Where ye reckon they're from?" said Mr. Hurley.

"New York City. We've been yankin' 'em off wagons all week."

"An' beating 'em to a bloody pulp!" Gibbons added with a grin. He puffed on his stogie.

Tom gave Mike a wink. "That's how ye win a strike!"

Mr. Hurley scratched his head, frowning. "Well, I reckon it doesn't matter where they're from. Right now, they're up there with those yellow dogs, getting ready to crack coal."

Eddie's eyes gleamed. "Then we'll just hafta go up there and stop 'em, won't we?"

Mr. Hurley pulled Mike and Tom closer to him. "That would be suicide!"

"Would be if we were unarmed." Eddie lifted his shirt to reveal a gun tucked into his waistband. Gibbons had one, too.

Mike wanted to look away but couldn't. His field of view had narrowed so much that all he could see was the smooth wooden grip, framed by Eddie's brass suspender hooks, and the lustrous metal cylinder disappearing into his pants. His hands started to shake. What if the C&I saw it?

"You crazy?" Mr. Hurley said. "They've got repeating rifles!"

"They wouldn't dare!" said Gibbons. "There's women and children here. Besides, we'd murder 'em if they did. Look how many of us there are."

Mike peered down Center Street. There was a large crowd marching toward them. Breaker boys and mule drivers, pockets bulging with rocks. Women with rolling pins and broomsticks, sleeves rolled up and ready for battle. And scores of miners and laborers who, according to Eddie, represented every nationality and coll'ry in town.

Mr. Hurley rubbed his cheek, as if adding everything up. "Well, Gibbons has a point. Some of those C&I live right here in town. I don't reckon they'd shoot their own kin."

Mike briefly closed his eyes. He wanted to be still for a moment, let the relief sink in, but Tom was yanking on his sleeve, bobbing up and down like his feet were on fire.

"Look!"

Michael Lawler was marching toward them with Fenton Cooney, who was carrying an American flag on a pole, and Coyne, who was wearing a coat and tie. Big Ned Monaghan and Cosgrove were right behind them, along with Johnny Morris and dozens of others.

Eddie jumped into the street, waving his arms.

"What are yiz waiting for? Let's shut Heckscher down!"

Gibbons tossed his stogie into the dirt and joined him.

Michael Lawler hiked a few yards up the hill, then turned and faced the crowd. His voice was low and steady.

"Brothers, what do we want?"

"Fair wages!"

"And how're we gonna get it?"

"Shut 'em down!"

Lawler had a playful gleam in his eye. "That's right, brothers. Shut 'em down!"

He turned and began marching up the hill, with Cooney and Coyne on either side of him. Eddie, Gibbons, Big Ned, and Johnny Morris were in the next row. Mike joined Tom beside them. He glanced over his shoulder. Mr. Hurley was right behind them with Koontz and a few of his Dutch buddies. Beyond them, the road was completely filled, all the way to Tom's house, with people marching six abreast, shouting, chanting, waving tools in the air.

The back of Mike's scalp sizzled, like a spark running up a fuse. A cozy glow spread throughout his body. He turned and threw an arm around Tom's shoulder. They strutted side by side, chanting and hooting until his voice cracked. The ground was spongy beneath his boots, which grew lighter with each step, even as the road got steeper. He wished Hannah was there. He would've kissed her right on the lips. Who cares what anyone thinks? Heck, he might even kiss her cousin Eddie, the way he was feeling.

Instead, he crashed into Eddie, who had stopped unexpectedly halfway up the hill.

Five yellow dogs blocked their way, rifles aimed directly at them. Another three were posted on the train trestle above them. All were young and slim, except the one in the middle, who was portly, with two silvery spikes of fuzz jutting from his chin, like bolts of lightning.

"Turn around now!" he said. "Don't make us shoot."

"Ye wouldn't dare!" someone yelled.

"Cowards!"

"Bootlickers!"

Coyne and Michael Lawler conferred briefly, but all Mike could make out was Coyne saying it wasn't worth dying for and Lawler saying that if they turned back now, the strike was lost.

Eddie pushed past them, along with Gibbons and Big Ned.

"We ain't stoppin' till we've shut this coll'ry down!"

"Eddie," Coyne pleaded. "Think about what you're doing."

"They don't have the balls to shoot their own neighbors."

"They're scared, Eddie. They don't wanna die at the hands of a mob. Lemme talk to 'em. See if I can settle things down."

"Suit yourself, Coyne, but we ain't turning back."

Coyne raised his hands above his head and approached the cop calmly.

"Look, fellers, I just wanna talk. See if we can settle this without bloodshed. You're from 'round here, ain't ye? Ye know how hard it is to make living."

"Stop where you are!" the older C&I commanded. "We ain't here to fraternize."

Coyne raised his hands higher, took another step.

A cop leapt forward, knocking Coyne to the ground, wrestling him onto his belly.

"Release our buddy!" Eddie hollered.

"We want Heckscher!" his uncle roared. "Bring out Heckscher!"

"Heck-scher! Heck-scher!" the mob chanted.

Just then, Heckscher appeared at the breaker entrance on a large white horse. His chest was so puffed out that the brass buttons of his greatcoat looked ready to pop. There were yellow epaulettes on his shoulders and a sword hanging from his belt. He waved his gun in the air, sneering down at them. "What's all this?"

"Bread or blood!" someone bellowed.

"Bread or blood!" the mob chanted. "Bread or blood!"

"Alright," he roared, aiming his gun at the crowd. "A diet of blood it is! There'll be no commune here."

"Ye can't kill us all!" Gibbons yelled, as he and Ned continued up the hill.

Eddie reached for his gun.

"Shoot!" Heckscher screamed. "Shoot, goddamn it! They're trespassing."

He fired over their heads.

"Run!" Mr. Hurley yelled. "It's gonna be a bloodbath!"

Mike's heart was racing. His skin dripped with sweat. It was like being inside a tiny box without enough air. He tried to run, but the crowd was surging forward. Did they all want to die?

"Fire!" Heckscher shouted. "Fire, you cowards!"

"Please, no," Mike muttered, squeezing his eyes shut. "There's women and children."

A shot rang out. Then another. And another.

He dropped to the ground. Curled into a ball. Prayed he wouldn't get shot. Or trampled. A million thoughts raced through his mind, as people thundered past. How sad Mamai would be without him. How hopeless Tara would feel. How Uncle Sean would snicker and say, "Told him not to go."

His eyes were burning, but the ground had stopped rumbling.

Everything was terribly quiet and still. He sat up, looked around.

Tom was crouched over a body, probably Eddie. But why was he stroking his hair?

Blinking, Mike noticed two more bodies further up the road.

Wait, that's Eddie over there. And Ned. So who's Tom caressing?

He blinked again. This time he noticed the pale blue eyes and the bright red neck scar.

A lump formed in his throat.

Mr. Hurley!

Chapter 18
Saturday, April 26, 1873

For the next day and a half, Mr. Hurley's body sat at the coroner's, while Mrs. Hurley sat at the dining table, sobbing into her arm. She refused to cook, eat, or do anything else. Each time Tom tried to console her, she'd start blubbering and he'd get frustrated and pace the room like a chained dog. It was driving Mike nuts. He was an intruder, snooping in on their grief. He was desperate to escape. But when he tried to leave, Tom snapped at him. "Ye gonna dishonor Da after he invited ye to live with us?"

As soon as he said it, Mike's eyelids got hot and gummy. This whole damned thing was so similar to Avondale. Another long, failed strike. Another dead father. A good one, too. Patient. Understanding. Generous. He made real sacrifices for his family. And now he was gone forever. It was like losing Da all over again.

Mike turned toward the wall and wiped his eyes, remembering how much he missed him. The tickly tip of his long, red beard. The safety and security of his embrace. How nothing ever went wrong when he was around. Now, there was trouble everywhere. In a few days, they'd be back at work, at a fraction of the pay, and Mrs. Hurley would be left at home to grieve by herself.

There were three sharp raps at the door. Neither Tom nor his mom stirred.

Mike slogged to the door, in no mood to greet guests. His clothes were wrinkled, his hair uncombed. He had no idea what he'd say, or if he could say it without exploding.

It was Mrs. Lawler and Mrs. Cooney, in long black dresses, each with a basket of food.

"Morning," they said. Their eyes were dark, their voices emotionless.

"Good morning." Mike reached for their baskets.

Mrs. Cooney proceeded to the table and gave Tom a hug, before planting herself beside his mom and offering a deep sigh.

"We're here for ye, Ellen. Anything ye need."

Mrs. Hurley looked up, with a distant stare, like she didn't recognize her.

Mike placed the baskets at the far end of the table.

Mrs. Lawler kissed Mrs. Hurley's head as she brushed past. "Ye probably ain't hungry right now. But when ye are, we brought plenty of grub."

She started laying out loaves of bread, boiled eggs, cookies. Then she turned toward Mike and gently squeezed his arm. "Time to get the house ready."

A pleasurable shiver ran down his back. He prayed she didn't notice, especially when his thigh started twitching at the thought of those plump round hips, and the sultry scent of her underarms. Even dressed in mourning, she was the most beautiful woman he knew. Not quite as pretty as Hannah, but so much more voluptuous.

"Be a dear," she said, sliding her hand down to his and clasping it. "Open the bedroom window. Close the curtains."

The hair rose up on his arms. His penis throbbed. He started to sweat.

"Y- yes, ma'am."

Cringing at the weakness of his voice, he scrubbed a hand over his face and went to the bedroom. As soon as he entered, he made the sign of the cross and let out a huge breath. His arms and legs, even his head, were suddenly less bulky, easier to move, as if he had just stripped off a soggy coat at the end of a rainy day. When he opened the window, the balmy morning air quivered across the downy hairs on his cheeks. It seemed strange, this custom of opening a window for the dead, as if the soul needed help getting out of the house. If it could escape the body on its own, why couldn't it pass through glass, like light or heat? Or through the cracks in the walls? Or billow up through the chimbly, the way smoke did? And what about men who got buried alive in a mine? Were they consigned to Hell because their souls were trapped in the bowels of the Earth with no windows to escape through?

As he closed the curtains, he could see Michael Lawler and Fenton Cooney approaching in a wagon. Mr. Hurley's corpse and coffin were in the back.

Happy to have another distraction from the grief, and the forbidden temptation of Hannah's mother, he ran outside to help carry in the corpse. When he got there, Cooney was sliding the body out to Mr. Lawler, who held it beneath the shoulders. It smelled like a sack of rotting rats. Didn't look much better, either. His body had swelled and his skin was blueish-green.

Swallowing uncomfortably, Mike sucked in a breath and held it before reaching for a leg. He prayed they'd get him inside quickly, before he had to inhale again. Cooney hopped out and grabbed the other leg. His face was pained. Mr. Lawler wrinkled his nose and began walking backward, with short, clumsy steps.

They carried Mr. Hurley to the bedroom and laid him on the bed. Mrs. Lawler and Mrs. Cooney entered with buckets and rags and made everyone else leave. Washing the corpse and preparing it for the wake would be gruesome. Mike was glad it was done behind closed doors. But things in the front room were hardly more pleasant. Mrs. Hurley was still sobbing uncontrollably. Tom was standing behind her with his hands in the air, as if he had given up.

Cooney sat down beside her and tried to console her.

"Ellen, the AOH has taken care of everything. Ye won't have to pay a penny."

"Nooo!" she screamed, beating her bosom with her fists.

He jerked away from her and swallowed repeatedly. "I-I'm sorry, Ellen."

Tom ran to her side and embraced her, scowling at Cooney, who shrugged helplessly.

"What's the AOH?" Mike whispered to Mr. Lawler.

"Ancient Order of Hibernians," he said, rising slightly on his toes. "True Christian charity to assuage the sufferings of the poor laboring classes."

Mike's eyes narrowed.

"We do good things, Mighael. Like raising funds to help widows and the infirm."

"What about the WBA? I thought they were supposed to help the poor laboring classes?"

Lawler's lips pressed together into a slight grimace. "Let's step outside. Get some fresh air."

The sky was powder blue, with wispy mare's tails curling across it. Beautiful, except for the smell of smoldering rubbish wafting over from Cosgrove's yard, and the sound of donkey engines. Blacklegs were still at it up there, as if nothing had happened.

"Ye saw how they treated us." Lawler spat in disgust. "Gave in to the bosses like whipped curs beggin' for scraps. Then fined us for refusing to roll over. Ye call that helpin' the laborin' classes? Bah!" He spat again. "AOH ain't like that, Mighael. We stick together. Protect our own. And we don't think the laborin' classes oughta stay poor the rest of their lives."

Mike leaned in closer, thinking this might be his ticket out.

"How? Didn't Father Connolly say it was our duty to go back to work?"

"AOH ain't part of the Church, Mighael." He brought a finger to his lips. "The Church disapproves of us. Calls us a secret organization. So keep this quiet. Understand?"

"Sure, but how're we gonna beat Heckscher and Gowen and stop being poor?"

"Politics," he said, with a gleam in his eye. "And pressure from within."

Mike ran his hand through his hair. "Huh?"

"Simple, Mikey. Who're the toughest union paddies in Schuylkill County?"

"The Irish?"

"Exactly. And who represents our interests in the government?"

"Nobody?"

Lawler smiled, nodding. "To be fair, there's a coupla decent Democrats. But we need more. So, we're backing Reilly for district attorney. Same job Gowen had before becoming president of the Reading. Every one of his predecessors was in bed with the coal operators. But Reilly's one of us. He'll see our point of view. Rule for us instead of Gowen and Heckscher. Help us win without even going on strike. Avoid all this hunger and misery and stabbin' each other in the back just to keep our babies alive."

Mike licked his lips. "Is that really possible?"

"Just gotta organize the Irishmen. Make sure they get to the polls. But that ain't all. We haven't had much of a voice in the WBA, with those Hyde Park nanny goats runnin' the show. AOH is gonna change that, too. Get all the Irishmen united. Force the WBA to back our demands. You'll see." He laughed, giving Mike's back a slap. "Now, how 'bout ye head inside and send Cooney out? Gotta return to the infirmary. Check on Eddie and Ned. Coyne gets outa jail today, too. Besides, Tommy needs ye. Don't think Cooney's helpin' matters."

Mike fiddled with the cuffs of his shirt. He wanted to stay and find out more. See if he could be a member, too. Prove his worth. Anything to not let the opportunity slip away. But Tom did need him. Every time Cooney opened his mouth, Mrs. Hurley bawled worse than before. Guess the AOH hadn't taught him how to assuage the suffering of poor widows.

By suppertime, Mr. Hurley's body was ready. He was laid out in a white shroud, festooned with black ribbons, his eyes closed and lips pressed together. Candles burned at each end of the bed. A bucket of hot pine tar sat in the corner, making the room slightly less malodorous, like a week-old deer carcass, half-eaten by vultures and burnt to a crisp in a bonfire.

Tom approached the body first. Tears were trickling down his cheeks. He clasped his father's hands together and wrapped a rosary around them, then kissed his cheek, before slowly backing away. His mother came next, advancing shakily, like a decrepit old woman. When she reached her husband, she collapsed onto his chest, shrieking. Mrs. Lawler and Mrs. Cooney ran to her side, wailing just as loudly. They held her by the elbows, rocking side to side, their voices rising and falling in painful bursts.

The hairs on Mike's neck stood up. His ears rang. They sounded like a flock of screeching loons in a dark and stormy sky. He threw an arm around Tom's shoulder and pulled him toward the door. "Let's get out of here. Come back when things've calmed down."

Tom nodded, rubbing an eye.

They walked across the lot and sat down on the old log behind third base. The Kohinoor breaker cast a gloomy pall over the neighborhood. It seemed like dusk, though it was only four. Sharp gusts rippled down from Glover's Hill, rattling the trees, knocking off their frail pink buds. The dirt was sprinkled with them. It looked as though someone had butchered a pig. Maybe not the best place to take a grieving friend, but better than where they had been, surrounded by anguish and the stench of death. But now he had to come up with something quick or Tom might start bawling too. He tried to remember his own da's death, how he got through it, how inconsolable Mamai had been. But as miserable as she had been, she still managed to toss out a few of her old-fashioned sayings now and then.

What was that one she was always saying? Oh, yeh. *Misery loves a companion.*

"Reckon we're in the same boat, now."

"Yeh," Tom snuffled. "Two fatherless muleboys."

"Things'll get better."

"Ye mean like they did for you? Moving in with Sean Campbell?"

Mike's back stiffened. He wiped his forehead.

Goddamn! He was worse at this than Cooney. Then again, this was exactly how it went for him, and Tara, and Li'l Bill. When Da died, anything anyone said made them feel worse. Time and patience are what did it. And having Tara to complain to.

"You're right. Moving in with Sean has been a nightmare, but eventually I stopped feeling sad. And if it wasn't for his death, we never would've moved here. And I never would've met ye." He gave Tom's shoulder a light punch. "And ye wouldn't't've met Tara."

A tiny smile crept onto Tom's face, but then his eyes scrunched together.

"How'm I gonna support my mom?"

"Um." Mike pressed his fist against his thigh, wondering what would happen if he gave Tom some of his paycheck once they returned to work. Would it be enough? Would he have any left to give to Tara and help his own family? And how would he save anything?

But if he didn't give Tom something, they'd get evicted. Then where would he sleep? Besides, it was the honorable thing to do. He was using their house, wasn't he? Eating their food? If he didn't help, he'd disgrace the memories of both their fathers.

He leaned closer, with a hand on his knee. "I'll help out! Ain't I part of your family, now?"

"But what about getting your own place?"

Mike's fingers fluttered. He stuffed them in his pockets and cleared his throat.

"Guess it'll just take longer."

When they got back, the house was crowded with friends and neighbors. The table was covered with good things: fresh baked breads, roast turkey, shepherd's pie, pails of beer, cakes and cookies. As Mike ate and drank, a pleasant drowsiness overtook him. He couldn't imagine being anywhere else. The house was warm, the food delicious. Everyone was friendly and kind. The exact opposite of Da's death, when the Company whisked him away before they could say goodbye. No friends or family. No piles of grub. No stories about the good old days.

He tipped back his head with half-closed eyes, satisfied with everything. The terrible keening had stopped. Everyone was enjoying themselves. Cosgrove was pouring beers. Coyne was passing around the pipe, making the room smell almost agreeable for the first time today. Tom was calling people over, telling them about his da's accomplishments, looking proud and in charge. Another couple of beers, a glass of whiskey or two, and Mike figured he'd sleep like a baby, even with the house full of people. But then he noticed Hannah walking toward him, biting her lip.

"Mike, can we talk?"

He put down his plate, wondering what new terrible information she was going to share. He led her outside, behind the house, to the same spot where he had chatted with her father. A cool mist lightly sprayed his neck and arms, like the splatter from a nearby waterfall. He tentatively reached out a hand, unsure if it was alright, gradually resting it on her shoulder.

She wrapped both arms around his waist and pulled him closer, her soft hair lightly brushing his cheeks, her pelvis pressed firmly against his, their privates virtually touching. Warmth flooded his groin. It ached in the most pleasant way. Her sweet, resinous scent and shivery breaths were making him drunk.

He clasped his arms around her, squeezing tighter, hoping to draw the pleasure up through the rest of his body. But then she gasped. He flashed on the memory of her on the log pile behind Bright's, frail and helpless, and quickly loosened his grip.

She took a step back, becoming very still.

"What's wrong?"

"Um." She looked up at him with concern. Her voice deepened. "How're you doing? I know he was like a father to ye."

"A-alright, I guess." Mike squeezed his lips tightly together to keep them from trembling. He started to feel cold. He wanted to be alone, but at the same time, he longed for the comfort and warmth of their bodies pressed up against each other again. He reached for her hands. "How're *you* doing? Ye look upset."

She looked down at her feet and spoke in a whisper.

"Your uncle found out Tara had tab at Luks's for Bill's medicine. Beat her black and blue. Said he'd do it again every day till she paid it off."

"That sonofabitch! I'll kill him!"

She jerked away from with her arms crossed.

His hands fell to his sides. What the hell was he thinking? It wasn't her fault.

"I'm sorry."

He reached for her, desperate to fix things, but pulled back, convinced he was unworthy.

She grabbed him by the collar as if she was going to sock him in the nose.

He closed his eyes, more from shame than fear, but instead of a painful jolt to his nose, there was a warm, feathery tickle to his lips.

A kiss!

He parted his lips, hoping for more, but that was it. Just that one.

Lowering his head, he wondered if he'd kissed her wrong, but when he opened his eyes, she was peering up at him with a shining, expectant look.

"Couldn't ye give her a little each week? I'll take it to her. Ye won't even have to see him."

His brows pulled together and he looked down, rubbing his arm. He had just pledged his income to Tom. But if he didn't give money to Tara, too, Uncle Sean might really hurt her. He had to give her something. Besides, it would give him an excuse to see Hannah every week.

"Alright. But I won't get my first paycheck for a while."

"Really?" She clasped his hand to her bosom, bouncing on the balls of her feet. "My daddy could loan you some until then."

Instead of making him warm and tingling, as it did before, her touch was now heavy, uncomfortable. There'd be nothing left for him, with his entire salary going to Tara and Tom. And what were the chances of ever getting a raise? The strike was a disaster. The bosses would never give in now. And with less money, Sean would get even meaner. There'd be no one there to stop him and no way to move everyone out.

"I'm going over there. Punch that bastard in the nose!"

"Please don't." Her hands got clammy and started to shake.

Mike pulled her closer, squeezed her, rocking gently back and forth.

"I'll be fine." He stroked her hair. "It's late. He's drunk, helpless. Be back in no time."

She gave him a pained, watery stare. "What about Tom?"

Grimacing, he bit his lip. Why'd she have to bring that up?

He couldn't abandon his best friend in his time of greatest need. But if he didn't do it, Sean would continue beating them until someone got seriously hurt. And Tom wouldn't like that, especially if it was Tara. On the other hand, one of the last things his da did before he died was clobber Sean and warn him to leave them all alone. It would disgrace his memory if he didn't finish the job for him. Tom wouldn't like that, either.

"Sorry. I gotta do this. For Tara *and* Tom. He'll understand."
He kissed her lightly on the lips and ran off.

The rain was thicker now, plump teardrops slapping at his face.
The road was scattered with puddles, which he ran right straight
through, as if they weren't there. He was completely focused on
his goal, how he'd burst in quickly, wake the bastard up, pop him
in the nose before he had time to react, and tell him not to lay
another finger on any of 'em. Then he'd apologize to Aunt Mary
and run back to Tom's. It was perfectly simple. Easy, too. He was
quicker than Sean. More alert and clear-headed. And he had
righteousness on his side.

When he got there, the door was locked. He had to knock.

"What a pleasant surprise," said Aunt Mary, a little too loudly.

He stepped unsteadily inside, wondering if she had ruined his
plan, but when he saw Mamai and Tara doing dishes, and Uncle
Sean asleep at the table, snoring as if he'd finished an entire bottle
of whiskey, he let out a huge breath. He glanced quickly around
the room. The gray skunk stripe down the middle of Mary's hair
seemed longer than he remembered, and the bags beneath Mamai's
eyes were heavier than ever. Tara continued scrubbing dishes,
without facing him, probably ashamed of her bruises and scabs.

Sean had no right to do that to her! Mike marched right up to
him, grabbed him by the collar, and pulled back his fist.

"Ye hit any of 'em again, you're a dead man."

Sean's eyes popped wide open, but then they suddenly
narrowed. His fist slammed into Mike's chin before he could react.
It had the force of a mule-kick. His head jerked back. Bells rang in
his ears. He almost fell to his knees. But then his arms started
pulsating, as if they were filled with rattlesnakes. He couldn't let it
end this way. That would just encourage the bastard. Make it
worse for everyone.

He snatched the whiskey bottle and broke it over Sean's head.

His uncle stared, blinking rapidly, like he couldn't believe what
had happened.

Mike's fists clenched and unclenched. "Next time, I'll kill ye!"

Sean's eyes rolled back as his torso folded onto the tabletop.

Tara ran to Mike's side and clasped his arm. Even through the bruises, her eyes seemed to brighten.

A gratifying warmth flushed across his achy cheeks. He wanted to enjoy the moment, but Mamai was shaking her head, frowning, and Aunt Mary was stooped over Sean's motionless body with a pained look on her face.

His belly knotted up and his hands fell to his sides. What had he done?

"You need to leave," Mary said, without looking up.

He let out a long, low sigh, then trudged to the door. Best to just slink back to Tom's, before he screwed things up any worse, have a few drinks and go to sleep.

Mamai followed him to the door. He turned to give her a kiss. Her pupils were big and her expression soft. "I'm proud of ye," she whispered. "But next time, find a better way."

It was midnight when he got back to Tom's. Almost everyone had left, except Mrs. Lawler and Mrs. Cooney, who were chatting softly as they did the dishes. Mrs. Hurley was asleep at the table with her head buried in her arms, snoring like a wheezing duck. The floor was sticky with spilt beer and the room smelled of yeast and rotting meat, despite the bedroom door being closed. At the other end of the table, Tom sat in front of a flickering oil lamp with a deck of cards and a bottle of whiskey. He gave Mike a nod, as if to say "Thanks for trying."

Mike sat down and filled a glass. He drank quickly as Tom dealt the cards, then poured another. A comforting warmth surged through his face and neck. But when he looked at his hand, his focus kept drifting and he couldn't tell whether he had two queens of hearts or one. Blinking just made the queens bounce around, which was completely unhelpful. He rolled his neck to loosen the kinks and looked again. This time there were three.

He slapped the cards down on the table. "I'm going to bed."

Just then, the door swung open. Cooney stepped inside, followed by Michael Lawler, and Eddie, with droopy, red-rimmed eyes. His arm was in a sling and he had a peculiar, wobbly grin.

Mike groaned when he staggered toward the table. He'd never get to bed now.

"Took one in the shoulder for yiz," Eddie said, taking a playful swing at Mike with his good arm, but missed and fell to floor with a grunt.

His uncle yanked him back to his feet and pushed him into a chair. "How 'bout takin' it easy a coupla days, like the doctor said?"

"I'm fine." He laughed. "Just a bit slow from the morphine."

Mr. Lawler crossed his arms. "If ye weren't so slow at the coll'ry, maybe one of them yellow dogs would be wearing that sling instead of you."

Tom winced.

"This ain't nothing." Eddie sneered. "Ye should see Gibbons. Don't reckon he'll walk for months."

"Oh, dear!" Mrs. Cooney dropped the pot she was washing. "Who's gonna pay the doctor's bill?"

Eddie's head slumped to the side and he started to snore.

Fenton kissed his wife on the forehead. "Everything's gonna work out. AOH is coverin' the doctor. An' we can put him up till he's able to work again."

"Speakin' of work—" Mr. Lawler gave Mike a wink. "—a little bird told me yiz could use some extra cash."

The blood surged into Mike's head, like a rush of tobacco. He jumped to his feet.

"Yes?"

Tom's face lit up into a grin.

Lawler leaned closer. His hands were clasped behind his back. "Borrowed some money and bought me a tavern. Coupla blocks from here. Corner of Coal and Catherine. Gonna build some coops out back for my gamecocks. Could use some help getting it ready and caring for the birds. Think ye could find time to stop by every day before work?"

Mike licked his lips. This was just what he needed! "Absolutely!"

"Me too!" Tom said.

"Alright." Mr. Lawler gave Tom's shoulder a squeeze. "Stay strong, son."

He pinched Eddie's nose until his head jerked back with a snort.

"Fuck!"

"Time to go."

As Eddie got up, Mr. Lawler cupped a hand to Mike's ear. "That little bird's precious to me. Ye wanna keep your new job, and your fingers, you'd best keep them off her."

Chapter 19
Tuesday, May 19, 1874

Mike awoke piss-proud. He rolled onto his side, hoping Tom wouldn't notice. The room was still dark, but a tiny full moon glimmered suspiciously in the corner of the window, like the white of a darting eye. He crossed his arms over his privates, but that only aroused him more.

Tom sat up, laughing. "My manly legs, eh?"

"Knock it off, Tom. Ye know damned well I was thinking of Hannah. Haven't held her hand since your da's wake."

"Jeez God, Mikey. That was last year." Tom climbed out of bed, lit a candle, and walked to the pisspot. "Forget about her. Time to find a cherry ye can reach." His voice was dampened by the sound of urine tinkling against tin.

One year? Christ, it felt like a hundred!

Mike pulled the covers up to his chin, shivering at the memory of Hannah's warm, moist lips. Sucking in her sweet breath as her taut nipples poked against his chest. The ache in his groin. The certainty that she was the only person in the world who could ever make him feel that way. That he was doomed to spend the rest of his life without ever experiencing any of this again.

"She's the one I want, goddamn it! Forcing me to choose between her and my family? That was a deal with the devil!"

"Ye got it wrong, my friend." Tom grabbed his trousers from the floor and slipped in a leg. "He still wouldn't've let ye near her, even if you'd said no to his deal."

"I know." Mike sighed, then abruptly sat up. "There's gotta be a way to get her."

"And lose your fingers? *That* would be a deal with the devil."

"C'mon, Tom. Ye think he's still gonna hold that over me? We've been sweeping his tavern. Feeding his birds every day. Running 'em through their paces. They've won dozens of fights 'cause of us. That's hundreds of bucks in his pockets. He'd be proud to have me as a son."

"Or suspicious you're gonna rob him blind *and* steal his daughter. Maybe sneak up on 'im when he's asleep, like ye did to Sean."

"But Sean deserved it." Mike chuckled nervously, then lowered his head. A lot of good that had done. Aunt Mary still wouldn't look him in the eye at church. And Tom was right. Hannah's da didn't trust anyone. Not even her. Didn't matter how good you were, it was never good enough for him. Besides, he totally depended on Hannah around the house. He wouldn't just give that up so she could run around town with some yob muleboy.

"Wait!" Tom let out a throaty laugh. "Maybe ye *can* get her. But you'll have to start small. Prove you're trustworthy and strong. We'll start by asking him to get us jobs in the pit. He'd do that for us, right? After all, we *have* won him hundreds of bucks."

Fidgeting, Mike cleared his throat. More money would be good, no question about it. But how would that help get Hannah? How would it even be possible? "Remember what Cooney said yesterday? 'Banks, railroads, coll'ries going under?' No one's gonna hire us right now."

"And remember what Coyne said? 'Coll'ries 'round here are all owned by the Reading. And Gowen owns the legislature. They won't let him fail.' So, what's your worry?" Tom's expression slackened. He rubbed the heel of his palm against his chest and shivered. "I miss my da."

The vigor drained from Mike's body. He stared at his empty hands. It was like he'd lost a girlfriend and two fathers all at once. "They were a lot alike."

"Our das?" Tom offered a small smile. He grabbed Mike's trousers from the clothes hook and tossed them, but they landed on the floor.

"Yeh." Mike lunged, fishing them onto the bed. "Both were WBA. Honest and true."

"Wish I was more like him."

"Ye look like him. Except for the knife scar."

"Ha, ha. I meant the honest and true part. He always played by the rules. That's not me."

"It's what makes ye interesting." Mike smiled and slipped on his pants. "And fun."

"Not to your sister. I think she prefers honest and true."

"Yeh, she's pretty sincere." Mike's stomach gurgled. "Speaking of rules, let's grab some grub and get going before those pit jobs go to someone else."

The air outside was cool and damp, fragrant with the aroma of smoked meat. Mr. Hoffman was sweeping outside his delicatessen in a leather apron and black porkpie hat. Mist twinkled in the lamplight as it fell upon his tulips, like a nest of baby cardinals, with their beaks in the air, awaiting breakfast. Mike could almost hear their faint little tweets. He started to salivate. What he wouldn't give for one of Hoffman's sausages. Ever since the strike ended, breakfast consisted of a warm biscuit or two and a weak cup of tea, maybe an egg on Sundays, hardly enough to get him to lunch.

He let out a shallow sigh.

"Ye know, Tom? When Da was alive, we had meat at least once or twice a week."

"Fish on Fridays?" Tom's eyes brightened.

"Of course. At least when I could get down to the river."

Tom shoved his hands into his pockets and stared across the street, where a boisterous row of men was queueing up outside the tavern.

"Lawler!" Hoffman slammed his broom to the ground. "Sun's not even up and they're already lining up for beer."

Mike's shoulders slumped. Tom was rubbing his neck like he knew their plan was shot. No one ever waited in line for drinks in Shendo, not with six taverns on this side of town and dozens more on the eastside. This had to be the elections. Absolute worst time to ask about jobs.

Tom spat tobacco juice from the corner of his mouth. "We're screwed, ain't we?"

"Disgusting!" Hoffman picked up his broom and waved it at Tom. "Do that in the street."

Ducking, Tom slipped on the icy boardwalk and fell on his butt.

There was laughter from across the street.

He leapt to his feet, nostrils flaring, and marched up to the last feller in line, a curly-headed boy no older than they were.

"Whatcha laughing at, ye big jamoke?"

The boy looked down at his feet. "Big ja-what?"

His trousers hung low, as if they belonged to his grandda, and his boots were so full of holes they looked like they were made for bog sloshing.

Tom exchanged a knowing look with Mike. "Ye ain't from around here, are ye?"

"Nah, I live over the hill. Sweet Li'l Irish town called Mahoney."

"Ye mean Mahanoy City?" Mike laughed. "That's no more Irish than Shendo. Say, what's your name, anyway? I'm Mike. This is Tom."

"Jamie McAllister."

"Probably lives in Little Ireland." Tom elbowed Mike. "Bet he's never seen a Modoc."

"Modoc?" Jamie's voice rose in alarm.

"Yeh," Tom goaded. "Vicious gang of Welshmen. Brutalize honest, hardworking Irishmen just for fun. Got 'em here in Shendo, too, but yours are worse."

Jamie's face turned ashen. "Worse?"

"Much worse," Tom sniggered. "Our Modocs are dumb as a bag of coal. Yours are led by a brute named Bully Bill Thomas. Over six feet tall. Two hundred fifty pounds. Clever as a fox and he never fights clean. Brass knuckles, revolvers, knives. Arrested dozens of times, too, but always out the next day 'cause of his pals in the C&I."

The feller in front of Jamie pulled a pipe from his mouth and blew out a puff of smoke. "'Scuse me for buttin' in, but ain't just C&I protectin' him. He's Burgess Major's main muscle. Makes sure everyone's votin' Republican."

"Wait," Jamie said. "Ye sayin' the government and police are mixed up with criminals?"

"That's right," said the man with the pipe. "But ain't so different here, now, is it, with Mr. Lawler payin' us to vote Democrat?"

"Watch your mouth!" Mike said. "He's no Modoc. Ain't no murderer, either."

Jamie nodded, smiling nervously.

"Right, ye are," agreed the feller with the pipe. "Lawler's for the workingman! Got me a job at the Centennial. Only cost me a month's wages, too."

Mike choked on his own saliva.

"A month's wages?"

They'd never get laborers' jobs now.

"Could be worse." The man sucked on his pipe. "Some of those Welsh foremen'll charge ye two months in advance, but Lawler gave me mine on credit."

"What do *ye* know?" said the man in front of him, a short feller in a black derby. "If the WBA was doin' its duty, we wouldn't have to fight the Welsh for the good jobs!" He pulled a newspaper from his pocket. "Says here the Anthracite Board of Trade and WBA have agreed on wages fixed upon a basis of two dollars and fifty cents per ton, same as the previous two years."

Tom slapped a hand to his face. "Another year without a raise?"

Mike closed his eyes and slowly shook his head. Laborers would be lucky to earn two bucks a day. Mule drivers even less.

"Worse'n that." The man with the derby pointed to the bottom of his paper. "WBA ain't doing anything about it. Siney says the collaboration of labor and management has kept the mines open and the men working. He's happy to say they haven't called a single work stoppage since the strike. And he doesn't intend to change that now."

Mike's jaws ached, he'd been clenching them so hard. He couldn't decide which disgusted him more: another year of declining wages and getting further from his goal, or another year of the union doing nothing. Only sixteen and he'd already lost two strikes. Turning, he spat into the street, nearly hitting Coyne, who was marching toward them with his fists tight at his sides. If anyone could make sense of this, it was him.

"Alright, alright!" Coyne said. "Let's not forget why we're here. We get our lad Kehoe into the assembly, he'll rip up the Reading's monopoly. Then Gowen'll have to fight us fair and square."

"An' if he loses?" said the man with the pipe. "Siney gonna roll over and take it, same as he always does?"

"That's right!" The man in the derby wagged his finger at Coyne. "Siney'd rather cut deals with the operators, protect his cozy union salary, than protect us from starvation!"

"I thought the AOH was gonna pressure the WBA from within," Mike whispered.

Tom shrugged.

Coyne took a deep breath. "Siney ain't the union, fellers. *We're* the union. Things get any worse, we'll strike without 'im!"

"That's the spirit!" said the man with the pipe.

"What about them Welsh bastards?" said the man in the derby. "And the Dutch? Wouldn't be in this mess today if them traitors had stuck with us last time!"

Coyne crossed his arms. "The more we do to build unity with 'em, the better. But don't forget, we already got our lad Reilly into the D.A.'s office. If we get Kehoe in the state assembly, we could win without ever walking off the job. And if push does come to shove, we got the AOH backin' us, now. They've got plenty of ways to hurt the owners."

"See," Tom whispered, leaning closer to Mike.

Mike wanted to know how, but before he could ask, the tavern door swung open and Fenton Cooney stepped out, in his wide-brimmed hat and red and green plaid vest, with a cigar dangling from his mouth. "Alright, ye dumb bastards. Shut up and get inside. Ye sound like a bunch of paid criers out here. Want the whole world to know what we're up to?"

He walked down the line, scooting men along with the back of his hand. His cheeks were blotchy and his nose looked like someone had taken a rasp to it. He stopped when he reached Mike and Tom. "Muff says yiz were 'posed to here thirty minutes ago."

"Oh, shit!"

They ran to the front of the line and squeezed inside. The air was warm and moist, the floor gummy with sawdust and sour-smelling beer. Men were lined up at the bar, where Jimmy McKenna handed them voter cards, scribbled into a ledger, and sent them to the other end of the bar, where Mrs. Lawler gave them a glass of whiskey and a quarter.

Tom wedged through the crowd and leaned across the bar. "Hey, Jimmy." McKenna was short and stocky, with a gold watchchain in his breast pocket. His mustache looked like two door handles reaching up and sliding the spectacles away from his eyes, which always had a peculiar twinkle to them, as if he knew something you didn't and was mighty proud of it. He smiled and poked the glasses back up his nose with his fingertip.

"Watcha two foosterin' around here for? Muff wanted yiz out back ages ago."

"We know," Tom said. "We're on our way."

Mike followed Tom out back, wondering why McKenna's grin had made him feel so guilty. They were a bit late. So what? They hadn't done anything wrong.

The yard smelled of feathers, ground corn, and chicken shit. It pulsed with clucking and the occasional squawk. The sky was beginning to brighten and the birds were anxious for breakfast. They were short-limbed, with eerie puffs of feathers sprouting from their cheeks, like downy muttonchops, typical of the muff breed, the only breed Michael Lawler raised and the reason everyone now called him Muff Lawler.

After watering the birds, Mike brought out Muff's champion, Cú Chulainn, a gray cock with short, muscular legs and sharp, curious eyes, kind of like McKenna, who was also a good fighter, lightning-fast with his fists and his wit. He was the only guy Eddie couldn't lick, and the only feller Muff trusted, which seemed strange considering he'd only been in town three months. But then again, he did have credentials from the Buffalo AOH. Kehoe himself had vouched for him.

Mike kneeled on the training mattress, with one hand on Cú Chulainn's breast and the other at the base of his tail. He tossed the bird forward, as if sending him on his way out of the yard, but Cú Chulainn flew right back, the force of his wing-strokes sending a flurry of leaves and dust into Mike's face. Definitely a champion with strength like that.

He repeated the exercise several times and ran him through some other drills before returning him to his coop. But as he opened the gate, he glanced back at the house and noticed Hannah's silhouette in the upstairs window. The hair rose up on his arms. Somehow, in the past year, she had become even more curvaceous and alluring than her mother. Taking a deep, satisfied breath, he turned so she could see who he was carrying, and that's when Cú Chulainn wriggled free, bolting straight for Tom, who was exercising a bird named Finn.

Tom shielded Finn as best he could, but Cú Chulainn landed with his claws in Tom's arm.

"Fuck!"

Just then, the back gate swung open and Muff walked in, accompanied by Eddie, Gibbons, who was limping slightly, and Ned Monaghan, who was dressed in a blue constable's uniform.

"How're my little pugilists?" Muff asked.

"A bit too game." Tom displayed his bloody arm.

Tucking Cú Chulainn under his arm, Mike skulked back to the coop.

"Good." Muff chuckled.

"Maybe the muleboys should stick to mules," Gibbons sneered.

Tom jumped to his feet and shoved Finn at Gibbons's face. "Maybe you should get the clap!"

Muff pushed them apart. "Sorry to disappoint, Jack. But they're not muleboys anymore."

Mike's breath caught. "We're not?"

"Not if ye get to Plank Ridge before the startin' whistle tomorrow. Real men's work, too. Contract miner named Bevan Johns lost two lads in the cave-in last week. Tragedy for them, but an opportunity for yiz."

"Huzzah!" Mike shouted. Real jobs in the pit and higher wages than he'd ever had. But what he really liked was being called a man. Up until now, he had always been breaker boy, or muleboy, or just plain boy. "Whad'ye think now, Gibbons?"

"I think there's just enough time for yiz to buy us a round before we have to go to work."

"Dirty work." Eddie snickered, flashing a gleaming set of brass knuckles. "But someone's gotta make sure everyone's voting properly."

"And not being disorderly," Ned chuckled, running his hand up and down his club.

"Uh, alright." Mike sidestepped into the tavern without taking his eyes off them. "Um, you'll give us credit, right, Muff?"

"Wait!" Tom interrupted. "How much we owe ye for this job?"

Muff smiled coyly. "How long ye been workin' here?"

"A year."

"Remember what I paid ye those first three months?"

Tom scrunched up his eyebrows. "Hey, ye didn't pay us anything!"

"Well then, consider the debt repaid." Muff patted him on the back. "Now, let's go inside. Have a quick one before ye have to go break the sad news to Miller."

Mike burst out laughing. Sure, why not buy a round? He could afford it now that he'd be making real scratch. He'd finally be able to move his family. Maybe put Tara and the twins in school. Get Bill a wooden leg. But when he got to the bar, a chill flushed through his body. This job wasn't really free, was it? Muff would want something in return. Something bad, like the dirty jobs Eddie and Gibbons did for him. Could he live with that? Did he even have a choice?

Muff raised his glass. "To the newest Kohinoor Boys!"

Eddie sucked his down, grinning as though he hadn't a care in the world. A gold watch chain hung from his shiny new vest. Gibbons was wearing a silk top hat and smoking a fat cigar. Ned was a goddamned cop. None of them was bothered in the least by what they did. They had all the money they needed and no one ever messed with them.

Mike clanked glasses with Tom and tossed back his drink. Of course, this would be good for him. A real Kohinoor Boy, with a job in the pit! More money and respect than he'd ever had. And eventually, full membership in the AOH.

Muff put his arm around their shoulders.

"You fellers are pretty lucky. Johns is a good boss. One of the safest miners I know."

"But watch out for his buddy," said Eddie. "He's the one that caused the cave-in."

"Yeh." Gibbons tossed his cigar butt. "Don't wanna spend Bonfire Night in the infirmary."

Chapter 20
Wednesday, May 20, 1874

Plank Ridge was ten blocks east of Tom's house, an easy walk if Mike hadn't tossed and turned all night between all those dreams of falling. As it was, he could barely keep up with Tom, who kept looking back and rolling his eyes, as men and boys passed by, beneath swirls of sweet tobacco smoke and garbled chatter that sounded as if they were buried under a culm heap. Shoveling coal would be a hundred times harder than mule driving. How was he going to dance all night with Hannah, let alone dodge her father, when he could barely keep his eyes open now?

Coyne was waiting at the front gate with his arms crossed and his cap askew.

"Ye fellers aim to be late on your first day?"

"Ye sound like the boss," Tom said. "I thought ye were real WBA."

"I am, but I'm tryin' to be a good buddy, too. Don't forget, they're layin' fellers off right now. And impertinent micks are the first to go."

"Or wind up dead," Mike muttered, forcing a smile.

Tom wrinkled his nose. "Ye talking 'bout Cosgrove? That was just Gomer James being an asshole, as usual."

Coyne's face tightened. "Ye kidding, Tommy? Cosgrove was murdered two days after he told the boss they'd walk off the job if he kept laying off Irishmen."

Mike's eyes widened. "They killed him for that?"

"Not likely," Tom said, shaking his head. "Cosgrove was tough, but quiet. Always let others take the lead."

Coyne gave him a long, pained look. "The Depression's squeezin' us all, Tommy. Could've reached the end of his rope. Everyone's gotta speak up someday."

Tom got a mischievous gleam in his eye that gave Mike a chill, like he was planning something that would get them both into trouble.

"Don't even think about it," Coyne said. "Wanna end up dead? Or unemployed? Owing Muff a lotta money?"

Squirming, Tom spat against the fence.

"Let the WBA take care of our grievances," Coyne continued. "And the courts take care of Gomer James. Now, let's get to work before we're all fired."

They walked briskly up the dark path toward the headframe, a looming shadow in the distance. The twang of a Jew's harp was just barely audible over the donkey engines. A booming laugh. Pipe smoke. Flickering headlamps. Faces coming into focus. A glowing cigar butt tossed to the ground, squashed beneath a boot. The shrill groan of the pulley as the cage reached the top of the shaft.

Everyone stopped. For a moment it was ghostly quiet. Then they fought to get into the cage first. Maybe there was a good spot that gave a smoother ride. Perhaps they just wanted to be next to their buddies. Didn't matter to Mike. He climbed in last, his heart racing, sweat streaming down his flanks. Slow and steady, he kept telling himself, in a fruitless effort to control his breathing and snuff the panic. Men did this every day of their lives. And how often did the cage fall to the bottom and kill them? Almost never. But almost never meant there was still a tiny possibility, a possibility that Mike couldn't shake from his mind.

He wedged himself between Coyne, and Tom, who smiled as he picked wax out of his ear and rubbed it on his trousers. Coyne just stared at the greasy black floor. It was hot and cramped. No one said a word.

The warning bell clanged. The floor dropped out from under them. They plummeted straight down as if the cable had snapped. Mike's guts flew into his throat and his ears throbbed, as if his brains were being squeezed out through them. He looked at Coyne, hoping for reassurance, but his rattling pupils told him nothing. Tom was frozen in place, his coat rippling like eddies in a river.

Mike closed his eyes and clenched his teeth, his cheeks jiggling uncomfortably.

Then his knees seemed to rise above his ears.

He opened his eyes. It was pitch black, except where men's headlamps shone. Tom's coat was smooth and Coyne's pupils were steady. They had reached the bottom and no one had died. Men casually exited the cage, as if it had been a Christmas sleigh ride. Mike followed them out, feeling relaxed and slightly giddy, victorious. Must get easier each time, he figured.

They climbed into the tiny shoofly, the train that took them to their work sites. Mike sat with his knees pressed against his chin and his back twisted awkwardly against something that bulged out from the rear of the car. It clattered and jerked down the dark tunnel, occasionally passing through gates that were opened and closed by nipper boys.

After what seemed like an hour, Coyne said, "Wake up, lads. Last door before our breasts."

Mike gave Tom a wink. Every time he heard the word "breast" it made him laugh. So profane that Aunt Mary wouldn't even use it to describe the meaty part of a turkey, which she referred to as the bird's bosom. Yet down here it was so commonplace it didn't raise an eyebrow. Breasts were the chambers from which they removed coal. Dark. Jagged. Cold. The least arousing thing imaginable. Men hacked at them with their picks. Exploded them with powder and squibs. Pissed on them when they had to relieve themselves. The complete opposite of bosoms. The name made no sense at all. He was just about to ask Coyne about it when they came to another door. He recognized the nipper.

"Say, ain't that Jimmy Malone?"

"Surely is," said Coyne. "Jimmy the nipper."

The Malones lived next door to Uncle Sean. Aunt Mary loved them. It would be nice working with him so close by, like they were neighbors again.

The shoofly came to a stop in an exceptionally dark chamber. Coyne hopped out.

"How 'bout a wee tour before I go to my breast."

He led them up a narrow tunnel running perpendicular to the gangway, with tiny tracks that seemed built for a toy train.

"Manway," he said, pointing up the tunnel. "Some of 'em so steep they have to use chutes to get the coal down to the shoofly.

We're lucky. Ours are gentle enough for buggy tracks. End of the day, just hop right in and roll back to the gangway." He paused, cupping his ear. "Hear that?"

A scraping sound was coming from the end of their manway. Metal against rock.

"Probably your boss. Bevan Johns. Everyone calls him Barmy Bevan."

Tom's eyebrows drew closer. "Is he?"

"Naw. He's the best miner here. You're lucky to have 'im. Always early, inspecting the face, checking for gases."

Mike inhaled deeply, but all he could smell was shit and piss. No poisonous gases. Barmy Bevan had done his job. Maybe if he was here early, he'd leave early, too, and they'd make it home in time to clean up before Bonfire Night.

"Then why call 'im that?" Tom asked.

"Squints a lot. Like he's confused. Talks in grunts, too. They say a timber clonked him on the noggin, but he's never made a mistake since I've known him. Much more thorough than my boss, Reckless Rhys. I'll introduce ye. Then I better go, make sure Rhys doesn't bring down the overburden on our heads."

A tiny shiver ran across Mike's shoulders. Eddie's warning must've been true.

He shot his eyes down the gangway before following Coyne up the manway.

"Hey, Johns," Coyne called as they got closer. "Looks like you've been at it a while."

The breast was cavernous, at least ten yards across, separated from Coyne's breast by a wall of uncut rock and coal known as a pillar. Another wider pillar was on the other side. The ceiling was braced with fresh timbers and stacks of slate. The working face reflected their headlamps. The coal sparkled like stars on a perfectly clear night. It reminded Mike of Hannah's eyes, the way they twinkled when she wanted to kiss him. If he was lucky, that would happen tonight, maybe more, if they could sneak away from the bonfire, and Muff's protective eyes.

Johns turned, his brows narrowing. "That you, Coyne?" His face was box-shaped, clean-shaven except for a mustache, which hung like a frilled curtain beneath his long, narrow nose.

"And your new lads, Tom Hurley and Mike Doyle."

Johns's cheek twitched as he looked them up and down. "Know what to do down here?"

"Of course," Tom said. "Fill the buggy."

Johns nodded, stone-faced.

"Spades. Over there." He pointed to a pile of tools. "Blasted a good clean face for ye. Enough to fill a couple two-three buggies."

Coyne ducked into the crossheading that connected their two breasts. "Gotta go, lads."

Mike gave him a nod and started shoveling.

Tom snatched a spade and joined him.

It took an hour to shovel up all the coal scattered on the floor. They spent another two hours with picks, removing the loose chunks from the face. Johns watched over them, more suspicious than a prison guard, stopping them only when he wanted to improve their technique. No breaks other than these. Mike's throat was so dry, he didn't think he could speak. Blisters were rising up on his hands. His back ached and his arms trembled with each swing. Sonofabitch might be the safest miner in Shendo, a small consolation if he worked them to death.

"Alright lads," he said. "That's a ton."

"Ye kiddin'?" Tom fumed. "The buggy's full! That's at least a ton and a half!"

"Yeh, if ye count the slate. But you're only paid for the coal."

Mike wanted to kick something.

"No way that's a half-ton of slate!"

"Doesn't matter. Checkweighman always docks ye a third."

Mike staggered back a step. It'd be 8 p.m. before they reached their quota! He wouldn't be able to go home after work. And when he got to the bonfire, Hannah wouldn't want to dance with him because he'd be so filthy and smelly. Or worse, she might be gone.

He'd just have to work harder. Faster. With greater efficiency.

Grabbing the pick, he swung with all his might, wedging it in the face. Placing a boot against the breast, he pried it loose, pulling out a chunk of coal. He swung again, and again, freeing several more lumps. By the time he stopped to wipe his forehead, the ground was scattered with coal and Johns was gone.

"Thank God," he said, letting the pick fall from his hands. His shirt was soaked with sweat and his trousers clung to his thighs. He slumped against the wall. "Thought he'd never go."

Tom laid some slate across two rocks and sat down. "Might as well enjoy it while we can."

Mike squatted on the ground beside him, with his back propped against the wall, the echo of Coyne's pick ringing through their breast. Spitting out his tobacco, he reached into his pocket for a biscuit. It tasted like coal. So dry, he could barely swallow it. He took a sip of water, swished it around, and spat it out, but he could still taste the grit between his teeth.

Three hours to fill one buggy! Three hours for one miserable ton. By quitting time they'd barely have three tons. At fifteen cents per ton, they wouldn't even get a half-dollar each! And Muff said they'd earn at least two dollars a day. What was he talking about? They'd have to load thirteen tons to earn that much! Hell, at a dollar a day, he wouldn't be able to give Tara a penny!

Tom casually picked at the lint on his bread.

"What are ye doing?" Mike shouted. "We gotta get back to work!"

"Calm down," Tom's eyes narrowed. "See the boss anywhere?"

"No, but if we don't work harder, we'll earn less than we did as muleboys."

"Ye heard Coyne. Let the WBA take care of our grievances. I ain't breakin' my back for Johns. Or anyone." He yawned, then took a bite.

"Ye really believe that bosh? WBA hasn't authorized a strike all year. They don't care about us. We should join the AOH. At least they're doin' something."

"Relax, Mikey. It's only our first day. We'll get quicker with time. Anyway, don't ye wanna have some steam left for Hannah?"

Mike stared at his blistered black hands as though they were the enemy. He could work twice as fast and still have energy for Hannah. But without any money, what good would that do?

Chapter 21
Wednesday, May 20, 1874

Even before moving to Shendo, Bonfire Night was Mike's favorite holiday. When he was little, they'd sit around the roaring fire, eating cake, as Da told stories about fairies, and Áine, who could turn into a red mare and bite off a king's ear. Mamai would let 'em stay awake as long as they wanted, because if ye fell asleep on Bonfire Night, the devil might take your soul. When they'd start to doze, she'd gently tickle them awake, but blame it on a friendly grogoch named Timothy. And all night long, this crazy old woman would crawl around the bonfire on her knees, praying for an end to cholera and pox.

In Shendo, it was a festival. There were booths on Line Street, with food and drink and games for the children, and there was usually a big fire, with flames higher than the tallest buildings. Mike couldn't see any flames yet, probably because the sun had barely set, but he could see smoke rising up from the hillside above Main Street and smell the burning pine resin. There were couples dancing in front of the Hotel Immerman, to a flautist and fiddler in matching tan vests, who rocked back and forth like a pair of courting cranes. And in the background, children shrieking and blowing tin whistles.

Squeezing through the crowd, he could now see the bonfire at the top of Main Street, and a crowd of people sitting on the hillside above it. He scampered halfway up the hill before spotting Tara and Li'l Bill on the grass, with the twins jumping up and down, giggling, between them. Tom was on his back a few feet above them, scratching his head with a stick. Hannah was nowhere to be seen.

Mike's head dipped. Had she already given up and left?

"Mike!" Deirdre cried, rushing toward him. "Look at the fire!"

Smiling, he wrapped his arms around her head, pressing it against his thigh. Hannah could wait. This was exactly where he wanted to be right now.

Johnny ran to him, waving Tom's stick. "Can we light it on fire, Mike? Can we? Don't want the devil to get me."

Tom sat up, eyes glinting. "Yeh! Wouldn't want *me* getting 'im in his sleep."

"Ye may be *a* devil," Tara said. "But ye ain't *the* devil."

"Oh, no?"

"No. That's Uncle Sean."

Bill cracked one eye and wiped his dripping nose. "Sorry, Hurley. Devil's already got 'im." His lips smacked as he spoke.

"He hurtin' yiz?" Mike asked.

The twins pressed tighter against his thighs. Tara leaned forward, with a pained expression, her hands draped limply over her knees. Tom stood up, oblivious to the mood change, and tried to plop down between her and Bill, but there wasn't enough room and he landed awkwardly on one of Bill's crutches.

"Hey, watch it, Billy boy."

"That's your own damned fault, Hurley."

Tom pushed him over backward, then grinned at Tara with one eyebrow raised and his jaw drooping slightly, like he was drunk. "So, ye think I'm a devil?"

"Aint' ye? Pickin' on poor, defenseless cripples?"

Bill sat up. "I ain't defenseless."

He clonked Tom on the head with a crutch, causing him to fall over backward.

Tara scowled at Bill, then leaned over Tom, gently lifting his head. "Ye alright, Tommy?"

He squeezed his eyes tight and puckered his lips.

Mike suppressed a gag.

"Ye *are* the devil!"

She yanked her hands away. His head hit the ground with a hollow thud.

"Ha, ha!" Bill laughed.

"Johnny, Deirdre," Mike called. "Let's light some sticks on fire."

"Yay!" They ran past him to the woodpile to look for sticks. He watched from the foot of the hill as orange flames crackled and hissed behind them, but he couldn't get the image of Tom's puckered lips out of his mind. It gave him a sour taste. He spat, but when he looked up again, the twins were sword-fighting with flaming sticks.

Shit! He raced toward them, but Deirdre had already tossed hers into the air. It twirled several times, nearly landing on Johnny Morris's head.

"Who did that!"

Deirdre's chin started to quiver. Johnny's stick dropped to the ground. Mike's arms stiffened.

"That sonofabitch!"

Tara ran to Mike's side. "Lemme take care of this."

She marched right up to Morris, stopping inches from his face. Her fists were balled up at her sides. "That's a wee Doyle you're barking at, Johnny Morris. And I won't stand for it."

Morris took a step back with his head bowed, as if he might turn and run, but instead he held out his hand. "My humblest apologies, Miss Doyle. Might I gain your forgiveness with a dance?"

Tara's eyes widened. She gave him her hand and followed him to the stage.

Mike looked around in confusion.

Tom was clomping toward him, breathing rapidly, his cheeks flushed. "That show-off!"

Mike nodded, but without enthusiasm. Morris *was* a show-off, but so was Tom. Only difference was that Tom lost and now he was jealous. At least he'd get over it and Mike would never again have to imagine his best friend's tongue in his sister's mouth. The bad news was that she let Morris hornswoggle her, and that was bound to end in tragedy. That dog always had two or three girls on the side. When she found out, she'd be heartbroken. Yet, if he told her the truth now, she'd think he was a bastard for killing her joy.

"Goddamn," he muttered, accepting that he'd just have to try and be happy for her.

"I really mucked that up," Tom said, sulking. "Didn't I?"

"Ah, ye got some puss on ye. Let's get a beer."

"Wait," Bill called, tottering unsteadily down the hill. "Bring me one? I'll watch the twins."

On the corner of Line and Jardin, Muff had a stand selling whiskey and beer. Beside it was a table with sweet-smelling cakes and juicy blueberry pies, and Hannah and her mother standing behind it in matching flowered aprons.

"Michael Doyle," said Mrs. Lawler. "Ye look handsome tonight. And Tom Hurley," she added with a clumsy smile.

Tom lifted his cap.

"Thanks." Mike rubbed the back of his head. "Y-ye both look beautiful, as always."

Hannah hid behind her hair, but he could still see one of her eyes peeking back at him.

"Well, uh, I guess you're workin' tonight?" His voice cracked as he spoke.

She shrugged, with a helpless pout, as if to apologize for letting him down, but it just made him want to get as far away from there as possible. It didn't make sense. She wasn't supposed to be working. She would've told him if she had known.

Mrs. Lawler edged closer to Hannah and patted her shoulder, but as she did, her mouth opened wide, as though she was about to devour her; and the whole time she was glaring at Mike.

His heart started to race. She must've figured out they liked each other and now she was undermining their chance to court.

He jammed his hands into his armpits, wondering what to do. Just a matter of time before she told her husband. Then he'd lose his job. And his fingers! He glanced at Muff, who was waving and smiling pleasantly, as he slid a beer to a customer.

"Hurley, Doyle, come have a drink."

Mike pressed a palm to his heart. Of course, Muff didn't know a thing, or he'd have already lost his job. For some reason, her mom was keeping it to herself. At least for now. Maybe as a bargaining chip? Goddamn, she was devious!

Hannah grasped his hand. "See ye at church?"

"Yeh, yeh," he stammered, pulling it back and stuffing it into his pocket.

She gave him a long, pained look.

His toes curled up in his boots. He couldn't look her in the eyes, so he bowed and left. If he couldn't have a kiss, he might as well get drunk with the fellers.

There were two lines. One for beer and another for whiskey, which Fenton Cooney poured from a clay jug. "Step right up," he sang. "Five cents a smile."

"How much for a laugh?" Tom asked, when they reached the front of the line.

"Charge 'im a dollar," Muff said. "That boy drinks like a fish."

"Aw," Tom groaned. "I don't got a dollar."

"How 'bout a giggle?" Cooney sniggered, pushing the jug toward Tom.

Eddie Lawler strode up to the stand.

"How 'bout a barrel of laughs?"

He grabbed the jug, hooked it over his shoulder, and headed up Pig Shit Alley.

Mike and Tom followed him, to the Main Street fork, where Gibbons was leaning against a tree, with a cherry flickering at the end of his stubby cigar. He smelled like burnt toast.

Eddie removed the cork with his teeth and poured a stream into his mouth. Wiping his face with his sleeve, he passed the jug to Gibbons. "Ye fellers hear about McKenna's little quarrel with Linden?"

"Who's Linden?" Mike asked.

"Dontcha know nothing?" Gibbons took a gulp of whiskey. "He's chief of the C&I."

"The boss copper." Eddie chuckled. "My uncle, McKenna, coupla their buddies, hopped a train out to Coughlin's Shebeen, but Linden jumped on around Gilberton. Tried to grab McKenna, who pulled out a pistol and said, 'Back off, copper. Ye got nothing on me.'"

"Did he arrest 'im?" Tom asked. "Beat 'im up?"

"That's the crazy thing. Said if he wanted to arrest 'im, he would've had his gun drawn and brought backup. Said he was just investigating what kind of rabble he was running with. But if half the stories he'd heard were true, he'd get him eventually."

"What kinda stories?" Mike asked.

"Counterfeiting. Bank robbery. Murder."

"So, why's he working at Indian Ridge?" Gibbons asked. "Why not live the easy life?"

"Ye really that thick?" Eddie snatched the jug from him and took a swill. "He'd get pinched in a minute. Think about it. Jobless mick with loads of money?"

He passed the jug to Tom, who took a long swill.

"Tough day?" Eddie asked.

"You've no idea!" Tom spat.

"My sister gave him the mitten." Mike clapped Tom on the back.

"This jamoke went after your sister? Right in front of ye?" Eddie seized the jug from Tom and offered it to Mike. "Here. You're the one that needs it."

Tom lowered his chin. "He got the mitten, too."

"From who?" Gibbons leered.

Mike flashed Tom a cold, stern glare, mouthing the word "no," but Tom answered anyway, his voice quavering, as though he knew it was wrong.

Eddie did a double take. "My little cousin?"

"Please don't tell anyone." Mike's neck was moist with sweat. "Specially your uncle. He'll kill me."

No one responded, but Eddie eventually gave an easy nod.

Licking his lower lip, Mike brought the jug to his mouth and took a drink, but it did little to quench his thirst, or his confusion. Did that nod mean Eddie would keep his secret or use it against him? And what about Gibbons? That guy was a loose cannon.

Chapter 22
Thursday, June 25, 1874

"Two hundred fifty tons!" Tom said, sweeping his hands in front of him to indicate how little coal was left in their breast.

"I don't know," said Coyne. "Two fifty's a lot for a coupla beginners."

Mike sloshed closer, examining the face. Tiny cascades trickled from cracks in the ribs and ceiling. Droplets plunked his head and frigid water seeped into his boots. The musty odor of black powder lingered in the air. One mistake now and they could hit a pocket, flood themselves, bring the overburden down on their heads. He wished they had already moved on to a new breast, far away, and were finished here forever. His old fear of riding the cage seemed absurd, pathetic, in comparison.

"Ye think that little of us?" Tom flexed his biceps. "Feel that? Solid steel!"

"Alright." Coyne laughed. "So ye got some guns on ye. Just keep 'em to yourself or you'll wind up in jail with McKenna. Every time he gets soaked, he nearly kills someone."

"Don't worry." Tom patted his biceps. "We ain't like McKenna. We only use ours for good. Right, Mikey? Ten buggy-loads a day for the past month."

"Psst." Mike grabbed a spade and started shoveling. "Look who's coming."

Rhys emerged from the crossheading, hunched over, his face knotted up as though he was trying not to puke. "Dag blame you, Coyne! How long you been shirking here with the kids?"

"Seconds." Coyne frowned. "Shoofly just left."

"I've already been at it for hours, ye scoundrel. Plenty of coal for you to load. And when you're done, I want you to finish her off."

"Rob the pillars?"

Rhys moved closer, until he was inches from Coyne's face. "Exactly."

Mike dropped his spade. Tom had backed into the face, as if that would save him from the coming disaster.

"You're mad!" Coyne protested. "Side pillars are already too thin. Won't be able to bear the extra weight. It's suicide!"

Rhys pushed even closer to Coyne, until their chests were nearly bumping. "Gotta be done."

Coyne took a step back. "Remember what happened last time? Want two more dead lads on your conscience?"

"Your choice, Coyne. Plenty of men would gladly take your job if you don't want it."

Mike had known this time would come; he just wasn't expecting it so soon. Every day, as they burrowed deeper, the pillars got thinner and they had to add more timbers and props to support the roof. Cutting away a pillar was like removing a wall of a house while still inside, just to recover a few nails. A good miner could sometimes pull it off. Other times there'd be a chain reaction. Neighboring breasts would collapse, crushing everyone in the vicinity. Coyne always said the owners should just abandon the breasts when they reached this point, but they seldom did, especially not in desperate little coll'ries like Plank Ridge, where the process had been on the rise ever since the Depression began.

"Tell ye what," Coyne said. "If *ye* do it, I'll haul the entire load myself. If it collapses on your head, I'll dig ye out first, then load it all up."

"I'll tell *you* what. You can follow orders or leave. But don't bother coming back."

Coyne picked up a spade. Mike thought he was going to bash Rhys over the head, but he just tossed it to him. "Better unemployed than dead."

"Blast it, Coyne!" Rhys threw the spade back at his feet and stomped away.

Coyne leaned closer to Mike and Tom, stone-faced. "Keep your eyes and ears open, lads. If the overburden comes down next door, ye could still get it on the noggin in here."

Mike's fingers were ice cold. He wanted to leave.

"What about Jimmy? He in any danger?"

"Don't think so." Coyne cleared his throat. "But I'll warn him on my way out."

Tom took a chew of tobacco and passed it to Mike. "This don't feel right."

"No, it doesn't." Mike's mouth filled with saliva and he spat. His skin itched with sweat, even though they hadn't started working. He reached for a pick, but knocked all the spades over. "Dammit! Let's just leave. Coyne wouldn't've quit if the risk wasn't serious."

"Ye think we'll still have jobs tomorrow?"

"Probably not."

Mike pulled off his headlamp and cap and ran a jerky hand through his hair. His breakfast was gurgling back up his throat, leaving it sour and burning. Sipping from his canteen, he tried to think of a solution. If they left, they'd lose their jobs and infuriate Muff. They might even get blacklisted. Both their families would starve. If they stayed, they could die, and their families would still starve. But what if Rhys did it right this time? He must've learned something from his last mistake. Even if he didn't, maybe only his breast would collapse.

Mike closed his eyes and quietly exhaled. When he opened them again, he saw a hideous face jutting out from the breast. "Look, there's Franklin Gowen!" Same pointy nose and big, round forehead. He lodged the pick in Gowen's neck, jiggling it until his head rolled to the ground.

"Nice job." Tom grinned fiendishly. "But they'll just replace him. I'm destroying the Anthracite Board of Trade!"

He swung, knocking a larger chunk to the ground.

"Oh, yeh? Here's one for John Siney and the WBA." This time his pick got stuck.

Tom rested his pick against the wall and took another bite of chew. "Ye know, Rhys must have enough sense to not kill himself."

Mike rocked his pick back and forth to dislodge it. "Yeh? If he did, those other two boys'd still be alive and we wouldn't have their jobs."

"Probably." Tom spat.

They worked in silence for the next thirty minutes, until Mike noticed something peculiar out of the corner of his eye. He turned toward the crossheading to get a better view. The floor was churning, like slowly boiling soup. He started to swoon. Grabbing the wall, he wondered if they'd hit a pocket of blackdamp and the fumes were making him dizzy.

Adjusting his headlamp, he looked again.

This time he saw tiny round potatoes springing up from the writhing floor, each with two glowing red eyes. A stampede of rats! Thousands surging toward them, as though they were being chased by an army of cats. Their screeches echoed through the breast, as they bounced against the walls and scampered over Mike and Tom's feet.

Tom stood perfectly motionless, with his arms held rigidly at his sides.

A cold draft rippled through Mike's sleeves. His pulse raced. He could barely breathe.

"Run!" he yelled.

The floor jolted, explosively, knocking them to the ground. The sound echoed, a cannon blast rattling the room. Rocks fell from the roof. Water gushed from the walls. Scrambling to their feet, they bolted down the buggy road, hands over their heads, as stones plunked their arms and neck. The gangway was underwater; the tracks were no longer visible. It smelled of shit.

They scrambled in anyway and splashed down the road, with achingly cold water up to their knees.

"Jimmy!" Mike hollered.

"We're coming," Tom yelled.

The road rose slightly as they approached the door. They pushed it open. Fortunately, no one was there, because water spewed down the other side, a torrent in a storm. But if no one was there, where was Jimmy?

Mike pinched his brows. He must've already fled, but Rhys might still be alive.

"We gotta go back!"

"No, Mike. Too dangerous."

"They'll call us cowards if we don't help him. We'll never work again."

Tom's forehead wrinkled. He expelled an impatient huff. "I'll kill the sonofabitch!"

They started back down the incline, jogging until the water was too deep to run. It was now up to their chests, greasy, disgusting, full of dead rats. They slogged through it anyway, using their hands as paddles, recoiling in disgust each time they touched something. They forced their way up the buggy road, like climbing a waterfall, with debris and rocks smacking into their legs.

"He's probably in the crossheading," Tom said.

It was all gobbed up with rubble.

They dropped to their knees, digging with their bare hands, shoveling dirt and rocks between their legs like dogs chasing a gopher. The air was so dusty Mike could barely breathe. It stung his eyes. His mouth tasted muddy. He was soaked from head to toe. He wanted to go home and bathe, get into some warm clothes, have a beer at Muff's, forget about Rhys, the damned bootlicker. But then he flashed on Da, trapped behind the brattice, alive, but running out of air. Maybe Rhys had kids. They had to keep going.

They dug as fast as they could, tossing aside rocks and splintered timbers. Every few seconds Tom glanced over his shoulder, as if he was expecting another cave-in. His face was pale, damp with sweat.

Mike kept trying to swallow, but his throat was as clogged as the crossheading. His fingers were cold and itchy, almost too stiff to bend. The dirt didn't bother him, but everything else was coarse and revolting. And then he grazed something soft and flaccid. He jerked his hand away and gaped for a moment. A worm, way down here?

No, it had to be a finger.

He burrowed quickly around it until a filthy black palm was visible, and five tiny fingers.

His stomach heaved and his mouth filled with saliva.

"Jimmy?"

He glanced at Tom, whose eyes were like empty holes, his mouth a twisted snarl.

"What's he doing way over here? He woulda been safe at his gate."

Tom slowly shook his head.

"He alright?" someone yelled.

It was Rhys, paddling toward them. He struggled out of the water and hiked up the buggy road, a dripping wet dog. He plopped down beside them and started digging. His arms were slimy and smelled of ammonia.

Mike cringed, then resumed unearthing Jimmy's arm. But then he stopped and sat back on his haunches. They had to do something. It was murder, plain and simple.

Tom must've been thinking the same. He stood up, with his fists shaking at his sides.

"You knew he was here?"

He reached for a spade and raised it over his head.

Rhys leapt to his feet, squinting. "You best think twice, Hurley."

"Or what?" Mike lunged for another spade.

"Or you'll hang. They find me with my head bashed in, who you think they'll blame?"

Mike lowered his spade. "He's right, Tom. Let's just tell the foreman."

"Tell him what?" Rhys's voice hardened. "The boy went in there on his own. You know how kids are. Always wanting to prove they're men. Earn a few extra bucks. Besides, Bradley won't believe a coupla micks over me."

The spade fell from Mike's hands. Sonofabitch was right about that, too.

"C'mon, Tom. Let's get outa here."

"No!" Rhys stood up and blocked his way. "Keep digging. I'll report the accident."

"Fuck you!" said Tom.

Mike placed a hand on his shoulder. "We leave now, we lose our jobs *and* they'll call us chickens. Besides, what would Jimmy's da think if we left him alone with *him*?"

Tom crossed his arms and gave Mike a flat, disgusted look.

Rhys brushed unnecessarily close to them as he left.

"Fucking bastard!" Mike said, as soon as he was gone. "What're we gonna do now?"

"Shoulda killed him." Tom's fists were shaking. "He's always getting away with murder!"

"Maybe not. There's gonna be an inquest. They'll ask us what happened."

"And what?" Tom's eyes narrowed. "Have the Modocs after us for ratting out their buddy?"

"I know!" Mike cocked his head. "Let's tell Jimmy's da what really happened."

"But he'll kill him." Tom's brows drew closer. "Modocs'll blame us for that, too. Might as well've killed him ourselves." He tapped his lip several times. "Gotta keep our mouths shut. Can't tell no one. Not even Jimmy's da."

Mike twisted his earlobe. Saying nothing would be an utter betrayal. Mr. Malone deserved to know what really happened. And what if he figured it out on his own and killed Rhys anyway? Wouldn't the Modocs still blame them?

"Gimme your Barlow knife," Tom said. "My mom's got no one left but me."

He sliced his thumb and handed it back.

Mike drew the blade quickly across his thumb, shuddering at the sharp tickle. Rivulets of blood bubbled up through the black slit. It started to throb.

Tom pressed his bloody thumb against Mike's.

"Swear to keep what ye saw today secret?"

"Uh huh."

"Me, too."

Mike's throat ached. He pulled at his collar, disgusted at his cowardice. But if he broke the oath and went to Mr. Malone, he'd be betraying his best friend. That was even worse.

"Goddamn!" he muttered, crouching back down to continue digging.

"Yeh," Tom said. "A feckin' mess!"

Chapter 23
Thursday, June 25, 1874

Mike smoothed down his clothes and prepared to knock. He hadn't been inside his old house in a year. But Uncle Sean wasn't his biggest concern. It was still early. He could easily tell Aunt Mary about the cave-in and leave before he got home. It was Aunt Mary that worried him. Jimmy was like a son to her. She'd shriek and wail, and fret about how it could've been him. Easier to turn around and spend the rest of the day fishing, or drinking beer. No one would know the difference, at least not until evening. By then, everyone in town would know about the cave-in and everyone would call him a scoundrel for not telling his family he was safe.

Sighing, he slowly shook his head. At least he brought a gift.

Raising the package to his nose, he drew in a deep breath. The metallic odor of raw meat. He closed his eyes and pictured a steaming bowl of Aunt Mary's stew. Sticky chunks of beef melting between his teeth. Sweet, creamy turnips, carrots. Everyone smiling, full and content.

"Be a man," he muttered, forcing himself to knock.

Aunt Mary opened the door. Her hand splayed against her chest.

"Mighael, what a lovely surprise!"

"Brought ye something." He handed her the package.

"How thoughtful." She kissed his forehead, then took a step back, studying him from head to toe, her eyes soft and glistening. "Ye must've worked today. You're covered in soot."

Before he could respond, Deirdre and Johnny staggered up the steps, each with a bucketful of scraps from the culm heap, their hands as dark as his.

"Mike!" They dropped their buckets and ran to embrace him.

"You're breaking me," he joked, squirming loose, hoping they didn't notice his moist eyes. Even though he saw them every

Sunday at church, they seemed taller than he remembered, and so much more responsible.

"Have a cup?" Aunt Mary grabbed the teakettle from the stove.

"Of course," he replied, joining her at the table.

She sat with her chin propped on her fists, gawking as if she couldn't believe it was him.

"How's work? Shut down early today?"

Mike's heart was thumping. He wanted to say "fine," but nothing came out.

Her eyes widened. She reached across the table and grasped his hand.

His back arched. It was now or never.

Placing his other hand over hers, he looked her in the eye. "There was a cave-in."

She was blinking rapidly, frightened, waiting for the rest.

"J-Jimmy Malone was killed."

Her hands flew to her mouth and her shoulders started to quake.

"Not sweet little Jimmy!" She started to cry.

He squeezed her hand tighter.

"His poor da. He's got no one left."

Deirdre and Johnny stared uneasily at each other.

Then Johnny's head pricked up. "He's still got his dog."

"Yeh," said Deirdre. "We help feed her sometimes."

Aunt Mary dabbed her eyes with her apron.

"Then we'll bring him supper. Remember how they brought Billy soup after his accident? It's the least we can do."

Mike shifted in his chair. "Um, where *is* Bill?"

"He ain't feeling well." She returned to the stove, lit it, and placed a chunk of fatback in a pot. "Tara stayed home with him."

Mike nodded, as if he wasn't surprised, but inside his stomach was churning, partly from the smoky, barnyard odor of the crackling fat, and partly out of worry. Bill never got sick enough to need help. And Tara couldn't afford to miss work. Sean would kill her for that. He pictured Bill on the stretcher after his accident, pale, quivering, terrified. What if he was dying?

He jumped to his feet, but then sat back down, pursing his lips in thought. He'd seen Bill just the other day and he was fit as a fiddle. No way he was dying. This was probably just Tara worrying over nothing and Bill taking advantage of her, as usual, getting her to wait on him like he was a plutocrat's son. Goddamn! Didn't she have enough trouble? He had to get up there, pull her away. Maybe offer to sit with Bill so she could earn a few pennies before Sean got home. Tell her something encouraging, like how Morris had been asking about her. That'd buck her up.

"'Scuse me," he said, standing again. "I wanna see 'im."

Halfway up the stairs, the smell of vomit stopped him dead. Saliva filled his mouth. He swallowed it down, took a deep breath, then continued to the sick room.

Bill was sitting up in bed, his face pale, dripping with sweat. His eyes were big, watery, darting back and forth. He was shaking so violently the bucket teetered on his belly ready to topple to the floor. Tara sat beside him, holding it steady.

Mike sucked in more air and stepped inside. "Jeez, Bill, ye look like a goner."

"Feel like it," Bill groaned, before retching into the bucket.

"Hasn't been able to hold down any food." Tara reached for the bucket. "Keep him company while I dump this?"

"Mike?" Bill rasped, shivering. "Can ye go to Luks? Get me some medicine?"

"My God. Your foot's hurtin' too, on top of all this?"

"Nah. All this is 'cause I'm outa medicine."

"How? That's never happened before."

"Sure it has." He sniffled, rocking back and forth, his hair matted with perspiration. "Happens every time I stop taking it."

"But I thought ye stopped last year, when Uncle Sean found out about the lab at Luks?"

"I did, for a while. But Tara's been sneaking me more with the money ye give her."

Shifting about, Mike tugged at his collar.

"Didn't Luks say to take it only when the pain's unbearable?"

"It *has* been unbearable!" He lowered his gaze. "Every day since ye left."

Every day? Mike punched himself in the palm. He never

shoulda let his brother work during the strike. Never shoulda moved out, either. Bill was too impulsive and needed more than just Tara looking after him. Goddamn, what was taking her so long?

Just then, the front door slammed. "Tara Doyle! Where the hell ye think you're going?"

Bill glanced at the door. "Now you're fucked."

Mike took a shaky step toward the stairs. They were all fucked. Especially Aunt Mary, for letting him in. Maybe he could sneak out while his uncle was distracted.

"Cripes almighty!" Sean bellowed so loudly the walls rattled. "I can't believe you'd even think of going back to Luks after the beating I gave ye last time."

Heat flushed through Mike's body. He leapt down the stairs two at a time. No way he'd let him lay another hand on her.

When he reached the best room, Tara was backed against the front door, hands in front of her face. Uncle Sean was staggering toward her like a mad dog, his shoulders curled forward, sweat dripping down his neck. Impossible to stop him with the table in the way, and the twins sitting there with their mouths wide open.

"She's just tryin' to help her brother," Aunt Mary pleaded. It came out as almost a whisper.

Uncle Sean glared in her direction. He still hadn't seen Mike.

"You keep outa this, woman! Billy's gotta take his lumps same as everyone else. Nobody ever died from what he's got. And he's gotta start contributing to this family instead of moping around feelin' sorry for himself. Besides, Tara can't go walkin' 'round town alone no more. Not lookin' like that. Every whoremonger in town would be after her tail."

The spoon fell from Aunt Mary's hand, rattling on the floor. She slowly turned, mouth slack and eyes agape.

"Jeez, Mary. Don't act so naive. Just look at her, all filled out below the neck. One of them Kohinoor Boys already has his eye on her. A John Morris, or something."

Aunt Mary's gaze darted toward Tara, then Mike, then back to Uncle Sean, whose eye twitched, as if he realized someone else was in the room but couldn't look because that would give Mary the upper hand. She ran her fingers through her hair, then lifted her chin decisively.

"Ye got nothin' to be ashamed of, Tara. You're becoming a bonny young woman."

Uncle Sean squeezed his fists tightly at his sides. "Goddamn it, Mary. Shut up!"

Aunt Mary looked as if she was going to crumple to the ground.

"I ain't ashamed!" Tara's cheeks were crimson, moist with tears. She reached for the doorknob. "And I ain't letting Billy suffer no more!"

Uncle Sean lunged and blocked her way, and that's when he noticed Mike.

"Didn't I tell ye not to come into my house anymore? And taking a job from that Molly Maguire. I ought to kill ye!"

"Kill me?" Mike stepped toward him. "You're the one that should die!"

"Stop!" Aunt Mary jumped between them, with both hands out to hold them at bay. "I won't have people I love fighting in my house!"

For a moment, she seemed bigger than Uncle Sean. Completely calm and unshakable. A torrent couldn't have knocked her down.

Mike slowly backed away, with his elbows tucked at his sides, ashamed that he had done this to her. He glanced at the twins, who were wide-eyed and completely still, which made him feel even worse. Even Uncle Sean was moping back to his chair with a hangdog look on his face.

Pulling his cap down low, Mike decided he should leave. He had successfully defended himself, and his sister, without anyone getting hurt. Anything more and who knew what Aunt Mary might do? But once he left, how long would they be safe? And how long could Tara live as cloistered nun?

"I'm sorry," Mike said, pausing at the door. "I think Tara should come with me."

Sean leapt back to his feet. "Absolutely not!"

"She ain't stayin' with you!"

"It-it's alright." Tara squeezed his wrist. "I'll be fine."

Mike turned the handle and released it without opening the door.

"Alright," he said, glancing at his aunt. "But Tara gets to go out on her own, right?"

Aunt Mary, who seemed even taller than before, glared at Sean through the corner of her eye, but did not respond.

Six blocks away, when Mike reached Couch's Saloon, he was still shaking and boiling up inside. He swung the doors open, hoping for some refreshing distraction, but the place was nearly empty. No lively music. No card games. Just Roberta Couch, humming as she dried glasses behind the bar, and two customers, hunched over their beers as if afraid someone might snatch them away.

"What'll ye have?" she called.

The other two fellers turned. It was Eddie, unmistakable, with his narrow eyes and thick, rectangular brows, and Gibbons, with his stony face that looked like he was always on the verge of pummeling someone with his fists.

Licking his lips, Mike hurried to the bar. They'd know what to do about Sean.

"Here comes the hero!" Eddie laughed.

Mike grinned. "Whiskey and a beer, please."

"Hero?" Roberta asked.

"Didn't ye hear?" Eddie took a drink of beer. "Cave-in this morning at Plank Ridge. Nipperboy died, but Doyle here, and Hurley, ran back in. Risked their lives trying to save him."

Roberta's eyes brightened. "Then first one's on the house."

"Really? Thanks!"

He pulled up a stool, as she slid the drinks toward him.

Gibbons grabbed his wrist before he could take a sip. "These ain't free gifts, Doyle. They're an investment."

"Huh?"

"She's countin' on ye makin' it out alive each day. Spendin' your hard-earned cash in here. That whiskey's a debt ye can't repay if you're dead. So, be smart down there."

"That's right," said Eddie. "Ye makin' sure the fire boss has checked for blackdamp?"

"And double-checkin' your timbering?" Gibbons asked.

"Jeez, didn't I make it out alive today?" He stared through the golden liquid in his glass at his grimy fingers. "Believe it or not, I got bigger problems than that."

"Women?" Gibbons snickered. "We can fix that."

Roberta gave him a dirty look.

Gibbons picked up his beer and moved to a table in the back. Eddie and Mike followed.

"Got someone knocked up?" Gibbons asked.

Eddie's boxy brows narrowed into a bushy ribbon. "Not my cousin!"

"N-no, of course, not."

He closed his eyes and took several deep, controlled breaths.

How could she be knocked up? It had only been a few weeks and just that one time, under the willow in Heckscher's Grove, after giving her the money for Tara. That lusty kiss and warm embrace. Her privates throbbing against his. His legs weakening, their bodies tumbling to the ground. That awkward moment with her pinned beneath him. Giggling. Her hand guiding his beneath her dress.

A sudden flush of warmth spread from his groin to his thighs.

He shook his head and exhaled. Not now. Not with these two.

"Well," Gibbons asked. "What is it, then?"

"Um." Mike pinched the skin between his thumb and forefinger, trying to regain his focus. "It-it's my uncle. Gotta get my family away from him. Thought I'd be able to get us our own place. But now I don't think I'll ever save enough. And it's getting worse. First he got Li'l Bill dismembered. Now he's treating Tara like a prisoner. If I wait any longer, someone's gonna die because of him."

Gibbons winked at Eddie. "Always hated that blackleg sonofabitch."

"We'll get 'im outa your hair." Eddie pulled out his watch chain and dangled it back and forth. "Happy to do it, too. Won't be just your skin that's saved by it, either."

"Whadya mean?" Mike's voice sounded like a frog's croak. He

took a gulp of beer. "Doesn't he give you money each week?"

"Not since the strike." Eddie tucked the watch into his pocket. "Worse than that, he's been naming names."

"Uh, what names?"

"Ours." Gibbons spat. "C&I pulled us in for questioning yesterday."

"That scumbag!"

"Exactly. Why, we're happy to help." Eddie placed a hand on Mike's shoulder. It was cold and heavy, like a block of ice. "But there's something ye gotta do for us."

"W-what?"

Mike wished he'd never opened his mouth.

"Nothing, really." Eddie grinned fiendishly. "Just do right by Jimmy."

Taking another large drink of beer, Mike tried not to panic. Accessory to Sean's murder *and* the outright murder of Rhys? He'd hang for sure. Or get killed by Modocs. And how would he even get to Rhys? The guy didn't drink. He couldn't just wait for him outside a tavern. And if he tried it at work, Tom would stop him.

"Wait! How'd ye know it was Rhys's fault?"

"We didn't." Gibbons bit off the end of a cigar and spat. "But we knew he was a coward."

"And his story made no sense," Eddie added. "Especially after talking to Coyne. He said Rhys had tried everything to avoid doing the job himself."

"So?" Gibbons tapped his foot impatiently. "Ye gonna do it?"

Mike reached for his beer and took a sip, spilling most of it down his shirt.

"I don't wanna kill anyone."

"Who said anything about killing?" Eddie laughed. "Just tell Jimmy's da what really happened. Let him have the satisfaction of avenging his son."

Mike flopped back in his chair and closed his eyes. He wasn't gonna hang for murder. At least not Rhys's. But Jimmy's da would certainly kill Rhys and he'd get blamed. If the Modocs didn't kill him, Tom sure would.

"Um, what about the Modocs?"

"What about 'em?" Gibbons lit his cigar, puffing furiously to get it going.

"They'll blame me and Tom. They'll kill us!"

Gibbons spat. "Gonna live your whole life worrying 'bout Modocs?"

"If we thought that way," said Eddie. "Nothing'd ever get done around here. Besides, Kohinoor Boys take care of their own. We'll be lookin' after ye. Now, we got a deal?"

If Mike refused, and one of his brothers or sisters died, it would be his own fault for not stopping Sean when he had the chance. And telling Mr. Malone was perfectly reasonable. They were neighbors, after all. He had an obligation to tell 'im. But there was that stupid oath. Tom would know it was him. Probably never speak to him again. And the rest of his life, always looking over his shoulder for Modocs.

Chapter 24
Friday, June 26, 1874

Mike's head throbbed as if it was inside a big bass drum. His fingers were numb, his legs hollow, and his mouth tasted as if he'd eaten sawdust for breakfast. Even before they'd gone a block, his armpits were slimy with sweat. He smelled like an old dog. If they could just make it to the shoofly, maybe Barmy Bevan would already be gone and they could take it easy for the day. Better yet, maybe they could skip work and go to Coyne's, find out how he was spending his newfound freedom. But the thought of opening his mouth to speak, and letting in more dry air, seemed unbearable at the moment, so he followed Tom silently across the street.

"How'd it go yesterday?" Tom asked, as they passed the tobacconist. "Didn't get a chance to ask ye last night."

"Never better." Mike grimaced, as a tinge of nausea swept over him.

"Really? Ye were tossing and turning all night."

Mike gazed at Indian Ridge. A thin band of sunlight pulsed along its murky crest, searing into his aching head. Looking away, he pressed his thumb and index finger to his eyes.

"Of course not! Bill's leg still hurts *and* he's developed a habit! And Uncle Sean thinks Tara's a slut. Won't even let her outa the house!"

Tom bared his teeth. "I'll kill him myself!"

"You'll have to get in line."

"Huh?" Tom stopped and probed around inside his ear.

"Uh. I might've said something to Eddie and Gibbons."

"Ye sonofabitch." Tom grinned.

"They'll just rough him up, right? Like last time?"

"Ye kidding? He's already gotten two coffin notices, remember? Nobody ever gets a third. Anyways, ye oughta be celebrating. Ain't this the answer to all your troubles?"

Mike stared into the street, his fingers tapping restlessly against a hitching post. More likely, it was the beginning of far worse troubles. But if he tried to stop Eddie and Gibbons, they'd just think he was a chicken and do it anyway. They wanted Sean dead as much as he did. Then, in retaliation, they'd tell Muff about him and Hannah, and that would be a death sentence, too!

"Ye alright Mikey? Ye look sick."

"Goddamn it, Tom! I'm the first one they'll suspect."

"Not if ye shut up and stay calm. Everyone in town wants that cocksucker dead. Now let's get to work, before we're fired."

Mike plodded along after him, trying to keep his expression neutral. Shutting up was the easy part. They'd soon reach the headframe. No point in sharing the plot with everyone at work. But how would he sleep at night, never knowing when it was going to happen? Or stay calm afterward, waiting to be called in for questioning? And then there was Mamai. And Aunt Mary. He'd never be able to look them in the eye. Goddamn, his mouth was dry.

He pretended he was a sponge, absorbing the mist droplets tickling his burning face. That calmed him for a moment. But then he heard a clacking behind him, getting louder by the second. He jumped back, flattening himself against a building, as a police wagon sped by. Then, when he noticed Tom rolling his eyes, he shoved his shaky hands into his pockets and tried to laugh it off. "Um, sounded like it was gonna run us down."

Tom shrugged and continued walking. Mike waited a moment before following, to avoid further teasing. He passed the Washington Hotel, then the Reading depot. The headframe was just ahead. But something wasn't right. Tons of miners standing around, smoking, stroking their chins, yet no one getting into the cage, even though the starting whistle would blow any minute. Nobody was talking, either. So quiet you could hear the breeze rattling the cable against the headframe. It didn't make sense. No other breasts were damaged by the cave-in. They should be down there pumping out water and clearing debris. And why were all those C&I here? And the coroner? Jimmy's body was already at the morgue.

It had to be Rhys! He ducked behind a boxcar. Tom rushed to join him, but then his eyes narrowed.

"What're we doing back here?"

"Look at all those cops," Mike said, mopping his brow.

"So? We haven't done anything."

Squirming, Mike searched for an answer that wouldn't incriminate himself, but all he could think of was how loathsome he was. How stupid it was to have trusted Eddie and Gibbons. How every time he tried to fix things, they just got worse. Yet, if he didn't do something quick, Tom would figure it out. So, he peeked around the side of the boxcar, trying to look natural, hoping he hadn't already given himself away. The C&I and coroner were following the super into the cage. He had no idea how long they'd be down there, but he knew what they'd find. The question was, should he act surprised and try to fool Tom, or should he confess everything right now and risk ruining their friendship forever?

"Mike!" There was a sheen of sweat on Tom's cheeks. "What the heck's going on?"

"I have a bad feeling," Mike said, scraping a hand through his hair. "I-I think it might be Rhys. We should leave before they blame us."

Tom's mouth twisted into a sour expression. "Ye broke our oath!"

Growing flustered, Mike rubbed his nose. "Eddie and Gibbons made me."

"Some friend you are!" He turned away in disgust.

Mike lowered his gaze. His mouth was sour and his armpits smelled of stale beer. And now Tom hated him. He'd probably get kicked out and have to find somewhere else to live. Always looking over his shoulder. Never knowing when the Modocs would get him. Why couldn't he have just kept his big mouth shut?

Maybe there was something he could do to win Tom back. He pulled out his tobacco, bit off a chew, and handed him the rest. "Ye can have it. All of it."

Tom stuffed it in his pocket, then crossed his arms and turned his back to Mike. "Ye think this makes us square?"

"Of course not." Mike grabbed a fistful of his hair. He had to offer more, but what? They were both broke and the only thing he owned, the Barlow knife, was the source of all this strife. Offering that would be an insult. "I screwed up, Tom. I'm sorry. But ye told them about Hannah. Doesn't that make us even?"

"Ye gotta be kidding!" Tom's voice was strangled. He turned, with his hand up, as if to hold Mike back. "That wasn't an oath! Or life and death!"

"It is if Muff finds out."

"I didn't break an oath!"

"I didn't woo your sister!"

"Alright, ye damned blackleg! Ye wanna be square?"

Mike's arms fell to his sides. He nodded, even though he knew he wasn't gonna like it.

"Get me another chance with your sister."

Cringing, Mike turned away. His skin felt like it was crawling with bugs. He wished he was in a warm tub with plenty of soap, scrubbing his skin raw. It was revolting! A new betrayal to erase an old one? It would break Tara's heart. She'd never agree to it. Never speak to him again, either. He couldn't risk that. But he had to win Tom back. He didn't want to move out and he couldn't fight the Modocs alone. Maybe if he told Tara the truth, that it was life or death, she'd understand, agree to play along, at least until Tom was convinced of his loyalty. She wouldn't have to dump Johnny Morris. Wouldn't have to do anything with Tom, either. Just smile at him at church. That'd be enough to drive him crazy. Heck, with Uncle Sean keeping her locked up, she wouldn't be able to see either of them anyway.

"Alright," he sighed, wilting. "I'll talk to her Sunday. But tonight, we talk to Muff, right after the fights. Ask him to make us AOH members. Eddie and Gibbons already promised to watch out for us, but with the rest of the AOH on our team, no Modoc'll ever get near us."

Chapter 25
Friday, June 26, 1874

When they got to Muff's that evening, there were so many men crammed at the bar that the brass footrest wasn't visible through the tangle of legs. And the din of clanking glasses and garbled voices made it sound as if everything was underwater. Mike fondled the bottle of medicine in his pocket and watched Cooney pour whiskey from two bottles at once, while Mrs. Lawler frantically filled beer mugs, spilling great quantities onto the counter and floor. Somehow, he'd have to squeeze in there and convince her to take a break, get the medicine upstairs to Hannah so she could get it to Tara. Otherwise, Bill would have to suffer until tomorrow.

Tom was tapping his foot impatiently. "C'mon, Mike. We're gonna miss the hack fights."

"I'll just be a minute."

"Ye better." Tom glanced at the door to the basement. "If we're late for Cú Chulainn's fight, there's no way Muff'll let us into the AOH."

"Why don't ye find us a good spot? I'll meet ye down there."

Tom scowled, then walked away, muttering about how Mike cared more about his dumb brother's drug habit than their own lives.

Mike moped to the bar and squeezed in between two short fellers, wondering if maybe Tom was right. But when he handed Mrs. Lawler the bottle, and her fingers closed gently around his, he forgot all about Tom, and Bill. His knees weakened. He fumbled with someone's empty shot glass, as his gaze shot downward. He knew he'd be going to hell for killing his uncle. But coveting his girlfriend's mother, too? Was there even a place in hell deep enough for him?

He tried to put down the shot glass, but it slipped and rolled onto the floor. "Um, 'scuse me." He abruptly pulled his hand free of hers. "Muff needs me downstairs. Can ye get this to Hannah?"

Tipping his cap, he scurried toward the staircase. Halfway down, he heard the rumble of drunken spectators and the squawking of chickens, and forgot all about Hannah's mother. With a throaty hoot, he bounded the rest of the way down, two steps at a time, bursting into the basement as if he was the main attraction.

Nobody noticed, at least not that he could tell through the haze of smoke and dust and the whirlwind of feathers. The air was muggy and smelled of chicken shit and blood. The ring, which was made of split beer barrels, bound with baling wire, was swaying with the crowd. He could see McKenna strolling into the center, looking distinguished in his shiny brogues and hat, his mustache waxed and curled to perfection. He had Cú Chulainn locked under his arm like a naughty toddler that was trying to squirm away. Behind him, just outside the ring, Tom was waving his fists and shouting support, with Johnny Morris, beside him, in a black vest and derby.

Mike marched through the crowd, positioning himself between his buddies.

"What took ye so long?" Tom asked, with a cocky smile.

Fidgeting, Mike decided not to respond. No point in adding fuel to that scuttlebutt. Besides, a bald, heavy-set man in baggy trousers and suspenders was entering the other side of the ring. He could barely contain his bird, a fat-necked Hackle with an orange breast, thick yellow legs, and eyes that flashed across the pit at Cú Chulainn, who glared back with equal ferocity.

"Atta boy, Murph!" someone yelled. "Your bird'll kill Lawler's dove!"

Mike shifted uneasily. That bird was twice the size of Cú Chulainn!

"Hey, Muff," someone yelled. "Ye call your bird a champion? Looks more like string bean!"

"Does not," Mike muttered. It was true that Muffs were slim compared to Hackles, but they were sinewy, too. All muscle. Lightning fast. Nearly impossible to kill.

A gangly old man squeezed into the ring and called the two

pitters to the center.

Tom nudged Mike. "Must be the judge."

The pitters approached each other, slowly, stroking their birds as though they were puppies. As they got closer, the birds' feathers stood on end. They beat their wings and tried to wriggle free. McKenna squeezed tighter, the cords in his neck quivering, like he was holding back a battery of coal. Another coupla steps, they'd be face to face.

Murphy's bird crowed. He lunged for Cú Chulainn, snatching his wattle.

"No!" Mike screamed, rocking the fence.

The judge pushed the birds apart. The two men backed away, briefly, but returned almost immediately, this time jabbing the cocks at each other like they were swords. The birds grew more feverish and difficult to contain, shrieking, pecking at each other as viciously as if they were on the ground, free of constraint.

"Place yer bets," Cooney called from behind the bar. "Murphy's giving two to one that Cú Chulainn can't lick his Anthony."

"What kinda name is Cu Cunt?" someone yelled.

Laughter erupted from Murphy's side of the pit.

"It's what ye call a ladybird that can't fight!" someone else hollered, causing even more laughter. "Count me in for ten bucks!"

"I'll wager twenty against Cu Cunt," yelled another. "Anthony'll murder 'im!"

Mike didn't like them shooting off their mouths. He wanted to yell that looks were deceiving, that Cú Chulainn could slaughter Anthony, but that might've changed the odds to Muff's disadvantage.

The judge called the pitters back to their lines and gave the signal. They let go of the birds. Anthony flew at Cú Chulainn with his gaffs pointing out, wings churning like a windmill in a storm. Cú Chulainn leapt, too, but he went straight up, landing on Anthony's back, causing him to stagger a few steps before regaining his composure. Then they faced off again, breasts puffed out, provoking each other with cackles and caws. Anthony sprang, attempting to land his gaff in Cú Chulainn's neck, but Cú Chulainn jumped, too, and neither bird made contact. They pounced again, and again, one right after the other, flapping furiously as they did, like some kind of demented dance. And in the background, the frenzied roar of spectators, their pitch rising and falling with their favorite bird.

It seemed an even match until Anthony stepped back with his neck feathers sticking out perpendicular and his eyes glowing red. He let out the screechiest crow Mike had ever heard, then rocketed straight at Cú Chulainn like a hot cannonball, with his claws and gaffs aimed at his breast. But Cú Chulainn leapt, stabbing Anthony in the neck, knocking him to the ground, jabbing him over and over until he went limp, with blood pooling beneath him.

Cheers rang out from McKenna's side of the ring.

Muff, who was standing in a corner with a cigar dangling from his mouth, shook his fists over his head. "Another win for the Muffs!"

"Cheater!" Murphy cradled his limp bird. "No way that scrawny bird coulda beat my Anthony!"

"Yeh!" screamed his followers.

Eddie and Gibbons stepped into the pit.

"Now, now, friends," Muff calmly replied. "There were no tricks or deceptions. Ye suggestin' it wasn't judged fairly by Mr. Kohler, an outsider chosen by our mutual consent?"

The judge stepped forward. "Just to be clear, friends, when we made the main, Mr. Murphy won the coin toss. He chose the weight class. Many of you were ringside for the weigh-in. You witnessed my inspection. Gaffs were in order, were they not? The fact remains that Lawler's bird weighed considerably less than Murphy's. That gave him greater speed and agility. Now whad'ye say ye throw in the sponge, Murphy? Let us all go home peacefully?"

"He's right, Murph," someone said.

Murphy lowered his fists, but continued glaring.

"C'mon," Tom chaffed. "Ye ain't gonna welsh, are ye?"

"Hey, what kinda thing is that to say to an Irishman?"

"It's what you say when you don't want your Irishman leaving without paying his debts."

There was considerable laughter, mostly from McKenna's side of the room.

"What if he was a Welshman?" someone asked.

"Then I'd say, 'Pay up, taffy, or I'll give your nancy foreman's job to a fuckin' mick!'"

This time the whole room burst into laughter, including Murphy.

"C'mon, Murph," someone said. "Let's have a drink an' get back to Hazleton. It's late."

As the crowd funneled upstairs, Tom collected dirty mugs, lining them up on the counter, and Mike dragged a rake across the floor. There were feathers everywhere, even on the bar. Peanut shells, too. Cigar butts. Puddles of blood. Chicken shit. Broken glass. A truly fine mess. But Cú Chulainn had won and it was all because of their hard work. Muff would be in the perfect mood. Just clean the place up, then get their reward.

Thirty minutes later, the door flung open. Cooney poked his head in. "Muff wants yiz."

"See?" Mike grinned. "Tonight's the night!"

They bolted for the staircase and ran up both flights, straight to Muff's office, which was bright and clean compared with the basement. Moonlight filtered in through the window. An oil lamp on the table cast flickering shadows of Muff and McKenna onto the Jesus painting hanging behind them. The air had a medicinal smell from a coal oil spill, which Cooney was mopping up with a rag. There was a bottle of whiskey on the table, and four glasses.

"How 'bout a drink?" Muff said, with a satisfied grin that tugged on his chinstrap beard and made his round ears pop out, like Hannah's. "Ye did a fine job, lads."

He removed the cork. As he poured the gurgling liquid into the glasses, Mike was filled with the fluttery, light-headed anticipation of his first drink of the evening. This was it! AOH initiations always started with toasts.

"To victory," Muff said, raising his glass.

"To victory," they repeated, clanking their glasses.

"Think they're ready to start pitting the hacks?" Muff asked, before taking a swallow.

"Definitely." McKenna replied. "Ready to learn how to gaff 'em, too."

Gibbons cleared his throat. "What about that other business?"

"Oh yeh." Muff gulped down the rest of his whiskey. "Got a wee job for yiz."

Mike nearly dropped his glass. They weren't getting initiated?

"A final test of your mettle," McKenna added with a wink.

"As ye know," said Muff. "Modocs've been on the warpath for months. That attack in Connor's Patch. The murder of Cosgrove, then Lanahan. And now this business with Rhys."

"His fault!" Tom scoffed, pointing at Mike, who sucked in his cheeks and squinted back.

Muff stood up. "Nonsense, Tommy! Telling Malone the truth was both noble and courageous. Kinda thing the AOH stands for. Aiding our fellow Irishmen in times of need."

"Getting Irishmen thrown in jail is more likely," he muttered.

"That's not fair," said McKenna, wagging his finger. "Malone would've figured it out on his own and he'd still be in jail. And the Modocs would've blamed ye either way."

"That's a fact," said Muff. "So, best we create a distraction. Get 'em off our tails."

"What about *my* tail?" Tom's voice rose in pitch. "They wanna kill *me*!"

Standing, Muff pressed his fingertips onto the table. "Relax, Tommy. We'll be watchin' over yiz. At least till things blow over. But if we distract 'em, get 'em to focus on someone else for a while, you'll have a bit less to worry about."

Tom raised an eyebrow. "How?"

"Tell 'em, Jimmy."

McKenna rubbed his hands together. "Been casin' Evan's Saloon the past coupla weeks. Just got a fresh shipment of booze this mornin'. An' tonight, after closin', you're gonna rob 'im."

Mike's breath caught. "Are you nuts?"

They didn't know how to rob a saloon. They'd get caught for sure, killed by Modocs, or arrested and beaten by the C&I.

Tom had a dazed look on his face, clearly thinking the same thing.

"Nothing to it." McKenna leaned back in his chair, with his hands behind his head. "You'll be there in the wee hours, well after closing. Everyone will be home asleep."

Muff walked to the window. "Take a look, fellers."

Mike struggled to his feet. Tom was even slower getting up.

In front of the barn was a wagon and two beautiful mules, their sleek brown coats glimmering under the nearly full moon. Jonesy and Jack!

For a second Mike stopped breathing. "How'd ye get 'em?"

"Miller owed me a favor," Muff said. "Think ye can handle 'em?"

"Handle 'em?" Tom laughed. "Ain't we the best drivers in Shendo?"

"Wait," Mike said. "Won't they assume it's AOH and come after us even harder?"

"Why would they?" McKenna chuckled, tossing him a billfold. "Take a look."

There was a job card inside. Mike turned it over and over trying to decipher it. It said Thomas Colliery in the upper corner, along with a bunch of words he couldn't make out, just like any job card. But the signature looked awfully familiar to him, the spidery capital "S" and the scrawling letters that followed, like something he'd seen at home.

He shuddered.

"Uh-Uncle Sean?"

McKenna peered over the rims of his glasses. "Perfect, right?"

This wasn't the deal! Eddie and Gibbons were supposed to do it. Not him and Tom. It would be almost the same as killing his uncle himself. There'd be no denying it. No way to claim ignorance or innocence.

"Brilliant!" Tom laughed. "Poetic, too."

Mike vigorously shook his head, but Muff grabbed his chin and held it firm. "Ye don't gotta choice, Mikey. I'm callin' in my chit. Got your jobs at Plank Ridge, thanks to me. And your work here in my tavern. Now I'm countin' on yiz to make a clean job of it."

He walked to the cabinet and pulled out a revolver.

Clasping his knees tightly together, Mike tried to look calm and in control, but his hands were trembling beneath the table. A gun just increased the chances he'd become a murderer.

"Ever use one of these?" Muff slid it across the table.

"Of course," Mike lied, his toes curling within his boots.

He took a deep breath, enough to ease the shaking, but his guts continued to burn. He picked up the gun and balanced it in his hand, as though he'd done it a hundred times, then clenched the grip and aimed at the window, pretending it was Gomer James. His shoulders relaxed. The nausea disappeared. A smile emerged on his lips. No Modoc could hurt them now!

McKenna pulled out another gun and pushed it toward Tom, who slipped it into his trousers.

"Ye got a coupla hours to get ready," Muff said. "Need anything?"

"Yeh," Tom replied. "Got any rags? Grease?"

"Sure. Whadya got in mind?"

"Those wagon axles are noisy as hell. If we grease 'em up, wrap the traces, we can make the quietest mule wagon ever!"

"How 'bout some socks?" Mike asked.

"No more whiskey for him." Muff snatched his glass. "He's drunk."

"Nah, clever," McKenna said, passing his own glass to Mike. "What good's silencing the axles and traces if ye can still hear the mules' clomping?"

They left after two. The air was cool, sweet-smelling, with just a hint of smoke from the coll'ries, and so quiet they could hear an owl hooting all the way from Heckscher's Grove. Not a trace of noise from their wagon. The streets were empty, the houses dark, perfect for pulling off their crime. Yet Mike's stomach churned and his feet bounced restlessly against the footrest, as if they had no plan at all. There were so many things they couldn't account for. What if someone was there, sleeping in the back, or a nosy neighbor spotted them? Or the C&I caught them and turned them over to the Modocs?

Tom peered left and right. "No lights anywhere. Shooting fish in a barrel."

"Yeh." Mike forced a laugh. "Drunk fish."

Tom turned down Cherry Street and stopped at the end of the block. Evan's Saloon looked like a workingman's house, similar to Muff's, without the second story living quarters. A block and a half past that, they could see the belltower of the Catholic Church.

Hopping out, Mike peered inside. "Looks dead."

"Good." Tom approached with a crowbar and wedged it between the door and the jamb, pulling back until there was a loud crack.

Mike pulled out his gun, blinking rapidly, scanning up and down the street. Searching for anything. Sudden movement. The flicker of a candle. Fluttering curtains. Nothing.

Covering his mouth, he let out a huge breath, then slid the gun back into his trousers, shivering as the cold metal touched his skin. He stepped inside the tavern, lit a lucifer, and searched for the till. Tom was already at the bar, rocking a whiskey barrel onto its side. He started rolling it toward the door, but a creaking noise made them freeze.

Mike snuffed the flame. He held his breath, unable to see or hear a thing. Probably just a loose floorboard. He pulled out the lucifers. Prepared to light another, when something scuttled across his foot.

He gasped, jerking it away.

"What?" Tom whispered.

"Rats."

Crossing himself, Mike tried to relax, but his heartbeat was reverberating through his fingers.

Just get the job done, quickly.

He leaned over the till and reached in. He was almost done when he noticed a shadow near the back.

"Tom?"

"What!"

"A man. In the back."

Laughing, Tom struck a lucifer. "Look again, silly."

A coatrack?

"C'mon, Mikey. Help me with this barrel." Tom was already at the door.

Mike wiped his forehead. He staggered outside. Looked around.

The houses were still dark, the street empty. The only noise was their mules' gentle breaths.

He helped Tom hoist it into the wagon. Then they went back for more.

They loaded six barrels total, and a couple dozen bottles. By the time they were done, they were too tired to speak. It wasn't until they passed the Davis Coll'ry that Tom asked about the billfold.

Mike reached back. It was still in his pocket.

"Shit! Wait here."

He jumped off the wagon and ran as fast as he could. As he rounded the corner, his feet skidded out from under him. He leapt back up and dashed to the saloon, his palms burning from the fall. As he got closer, he heard the door knocking against the jamb, as it swung in the breeze. Yanking it open, he skimmed the billfold across the floor. When he turned to leave, a light flickered in a house across the street.

He dropped to the ground and tried to make himself invisible, but the silhouette in the window seemed to be looking right at him. His heart was beating so hard he was sure they could hear it inside the house. Beads of sweat trickled down his cheeks. What if more lights went on? If someone came out? He'd be caught for sure! So he scooted forward on his belly, one inch at a time, as though he was a cat sneaking up on its prey.

The silhouette didn't move. He scooted another coupla inches.

Again nothing. But way too slow. Tom was bound to get worried and come looking for him. Then they'd get caught.

He tried scooting forward a coupla feet.

The door swung open. A man stepped out. "Who's there!"

Shit!

Another light came on. And another.

Mike jumped to his feet. Sprinted to the end of the block. Rounded the corner. Ran another half block. Leapt into the wagon.

"Go! Go!"

Tom slapped the reins. The wagon lurched forward.

"Someone see ye?"

"Yeh." Mike glanced over his shoulder, breathing heavily. "But nobody's following us."

"I'm turnin' anyway, just in case. Don't want 'em seein' where we're going."

Mike collapsed onto his back, laughing.

"We did it! Now we're guaranteed to get into the AOH!"

Chapter 26
Saturday, June 27, 1874

Hot wax splattered Mike's fingers as he paced the dark hallway. He desperately wanted to know what was going on inside, but all he could hear was faint mumbling. Finally, giving up, he handed the candle to Tom and pressed his ear to the door. He could hear something about Saint Patrick, the Glorious Apostle of Ireland, and beseeching our Heavenly Father to protect us. It was Muff's voice, only darker and more mysterious. The meeting was starting!

Rubbing his sweaty hands together, Mike prayed they'd get enough votes.

"First order of business," Muff said. "The admission of Thomas Hurley and Michael Doyle to our Order. Who can vouch for their integrity?"

"I can." The voice was Coyne's. "All of yiz know what happened to Jimmy Malone at the bottom of my pit. Lesser men would've skedaddled. Or given in to bloodlust. But these two kept their wits. They acted with courage an' intelligence."

"Hear! Hear!"

"We're gettin' in!" Mike whispered.

"What about loyalty to their Irish brothers?" Muff asked.

"I vouch for Doyle." It was Eddie's voice this time. "He risked his hide tellin' Malone what happened to his son down there. But Hurley was more concerned with saving his own skin."

Shit. If he got in, but not Tom, it would drive the wedge deeper between them.

"They're still lads," someone said. "They got time to learn."

"Alright," Muff continued. "How 'bout compliance with the duties of the Church?"

"I can vouch for Hurley," said Cooney. "I was at his baptism and confirmation."

"What about Doyle?"

No one spoke up.

Fuck! Blackballed because none of 'em were in Avondale when he was baptized?

He slouched away from the door and plopped down beside Tom, wishing he could leave. What was the point in staying when he already knew the outcome? But he couldn't afford to disrespect Muff and McKenna. So, he closed his eyes and tried to convince himself that Eddie and Gibbons could really keep him alive.

"Whadye hear?" Tom asked.

"Not much. Mostly mumbling."

"Don't worry." Tom leaned back against the wall. "They'll have to let us in after last night. We got over a hundred bucks! Plus, all that booze."

"Yeh, but only Muff and McKenna, know about that. Maybe Eddie and Gibbons. That's only four votes. We need a two-thirds majority. Eight votes each!"

"Everyone knows we trained Cú Chulainn. Everyone saw him slaughter Anthony. That's top-shelf AOH, Mikey. Kind of stuff that McKenna or Eddie does."

"Sure." Mike ran a hand through his hair. "But that doesn't prove we're trustworthy, loyal, or true to God. Doesn't improve the conditions of Irish workingmen, either."

He turned his head toward the door, anticipating the call to enter, but all he saw was the light at the base of the door, swelling and throbbing like the bright band of sunlight on the horizon just before it drops out of sight. Then the candle went out and he couldn't see his own hand. He could hear a dog howling outside, Tom's breath puffing in his ear, the sound of chairs scuffing the floor, footsteps. They must be lining up to vote.

White balls elect, black balls reject. How many black balls would they get?

There was a long silence before the door swung open. McKenna called them in. It smelled of burning tallow from the two large candles on the table, where ten dark figures huddled, motionless, silent, with their hands folded like they were praying. Eddie Lawler, Big Ned Monahan, Gibbons, and Johnny Morris were on the right side, with James Dugan. Across from them sat

Fenton Cooney, Dick Finnen, Dan Kelly, and Coyne. Muff stood at the far end of the table, beneath the Jesus painting, in a white cassock with a green and orange sash, as still as a statue. His expression was grave, as if he had only bad news to share.

"Division Master," he said. "Bring forth the candidates."

Cooney led them back, positioning them in front of Muff, who looked them up and down, as if measuring their worthiness.

"Sirs," Muff said. "You're about to enter an ancient brotherhood, which for centuries has labored to sustain the Catholic Church and preserve the traditions of the Irish race."

The tension drained from Mike's body. They were getting in!

"The motto of our Brotherhood is Friendship, Unity, and Christian Charity. The chosen Counsellors will teach you the wisdom born of the experience of the Irish people. Division Master, would ye instruct the candidates in the meaning of friendship?"

Cooney placed a hand on each of their shoulders.

"Sirs, friendship is a love that grows in intimacy and loyalty, through adversity and affliction, till we regard each other as brothers. In friendship, we sympathize with one another. In misfortune, assist each other in distress, always promoting the welfare, betterment, and happiness of our members. Will yiz embrace such a friendship and remain loyal to its obligations?"

"We will!"

"Well, then," Muff said. "I reckon they're ready for the next pillar. Thank you, Mr. Division Master." He nodded to Cooney, who sat down, then turned toward McKenna. "Mr. Secretary, will ye instruct the candidates in Unity?"

McKenna beckoned for them to approach. He gazed at them over the rims of his glasses. "Unity, sirs, is a bond between brothers. Secure in resolve, resolute in purpose, invincible in battle. Out of weakness it conjures strength. Out of fear it summons courage. Out of despair it brings victory. The Ancient Order of Hibernians unites its members in sentiment, purpose, and action. Will yiz join us in these bonds?"

"We will!"

"Then you're ready for the third and final pillar. Mr.

President?"

They returned to Muff's end of the table and stood side by side, their shoulders knocking against each other.

"Our third pillar is Charity, the Divine Love that fills the universe with inspiration and hope. Charity of thought, action, and speech forms the basis of fraternal love. Will you cultivate charity in your hearts and extend it to Irishmen everywhere?"

"We will!"

"Do yiz swear to defend all AOH brothers, even at the risk of death?"

"We do!"

"Gentlemen, you are in possession of the Knowledge. You are now members of the Ancient Order of Hibernians."

"Huzzah!" everyone cheered.

McKenna pulled a whiskey bottle from the cabinet and started filling glasses.

"A toast to our newest brothers!"

"Hear! Hear!"

Mike sat down and swallowed the liquor in his glass, enjoying the warmth as it spread through his body, the friendly faces, the comradery. Only seventeen and they were AOH! Same as everyone in the room. Real men, with good jobs and someone always watching their backs.

McKenna passed the bottle. Everyone refilled their drinks. Then he raised his glass and said,

To Irishmen everywhere who espouse Erin's cause!
And an Ireland free of vile British laws!

"Hear! Hear!"

For several hours, they drank more toasts, joked, and told stories. By midnight, Johnny Morris and Dick Finnen were fast asleep. Everyone else had slumped so deeply in their chairs it looked as though the lower halves of their bodies had melted away. Mike counted twelve empty whiskey bottles on the table, which was leaning precariously, as if about to topple over.

He blinked and the table righted itself, but now there were six bottles. His shoulders curled forward. He brought a shaky hand to his head. Was he really that drunk?

Next thing he knew, his face had smacked into the table.

McKenna grabbed him by the collar and pulled him back up. "Close one eye, Mikey."

When he tried it, the table stopped swaying and the number of bottles remained convincingly at six. "Goddamn," he giggled. "It actually works!"

Tom leaned clumsily over his shoulder. "Let's go. I'm beat."

Muff walked them downstairs. "G'night, lads. Be safe."

"Thanks," Tom said, as they stumbled out of the tavern.

Mike grabbed the wall for balance and peered drowsily into the misty night, his muscles slack and his mind at ease, content to spend the rest of the night on Muff's boardwalk.

Tom rested an elbow on his shoulder and exhaled. "I guess we did it, Mikey."

"We sure did! Cash. Protection. Buddies again."

"Hold on there, Mikey. Don't ye still owe me a date with your sister?"

Why'd he owe him anything? Hadn't everyone said that telling Malone was the honorable thing to do? Heck, it was probably the main reason they got into the AOH. Just the same, he couldn't risk Tom's friendship, so he offered a weak smile.

"Sure. I'll talk to her tomorrow at church. Maybe even get ye a seat next to her."

Tom threw his cap in the air, but he was so drunk he nearly fell on his face trying to catch it.

"Let's go." Mike rubbed his arms. "Hope we don't run into any Modocs."

"In *our* neighborhood? They'd be crazy to come here after dark."

They walked to the end of the block and turned down Catherine Street.

"But if we *do* see any Modocs," Tom continued, "I'll kill 'em with my bare hands!"

Mike grabbed Tom's shoulder and stopped. Two C&I had just rounded the corner and were walking briskly toward them. One was twirling his club. The other had his hand on his holster.

"Cops!"

They turned to run, but Gomer James and another Modoc, Randall Hughes, were blocking their way.

Hughes gave a quick, disgusted snort. "Planning murder, we were?" He stepped closer, until he was nearly on their toes. There was no way around him, but even if there was, James was right behind him, and he was even bigger, with a foot-long knife hanging from his belt. He had a jagged scar on his solid, square jaw, and dark, lion eyes that gleamed in the moonlight, as if he knew that anything he wanted was his for the taking.

"N-no," Tom said, stepping backward, stumbling into the fat cop, who gave him a quick shove back toward Hughes.

"Drrrunken troublemakers. Arrest 'em, we should."

"Strange," said the other cop. "Evan's was completely dry today. Couldn't even get a beer. Think these fellows had anything to do with it?"

"Doesn't matter if they did," said the fat cop. "They're going to pay for it, they are."

"His uncle already did." James jerked a thumb at Mike.

Mike felt like he'd been kicked in the gut. He tried to look shocked. "W-what do ye mean?"

"Show 'im what ye found at the crime scene," James said.

The fat cop pulled a billfold from his pocket and dangled it in Mike's face. Same one he left at Evan's Saloon. He pretended to study it, as if he'd never seen it before, scrunching his eyes, scratching his head. And as he did, he realized how brilliant the plan really was. There'd be no inquiry, since the Modocs and C&I were in cahoots. If anything, the C&I would cover it up. Call it a drunken accident, a barroom brawl. That meant Mike wouldn't hang. Wouldn't even be interrogated. He'd be able to move back with his family. Take care of 'em properly. No more living in fear. Assuming he survived the beating they were about to get.

He let out a jittery laugh.

"Think it's funny?" said the fat cop.

"N-no."

"Relieved," Tom said. "His uncle was a bastard."

"True," James agreed. "A pleasure to be rid of him. But that doesn't clear the two of you of your crime: Aiding Malone in the murder of John Rhys!"

Mike's hands were shaking. He dragged them down the legs of his trousers. Instead of hanging, he'd get beaten to death. They both would. And it was all his fault. Maybe if he kept 'em talkin', he could think of a way out.

"Rhys was a good man," he stammered. "Tragedy what happened to him."

"Tragedy," Tom repeated, his voice strained.

James's mouth twisted into a crooked grin. "We know you were there and saw everything. We know you were loyal to the Irish boy."

Hughes jabbed a finger in Mike's chest. "Blamed Rhys for his death, you did. Then told his father to kill him."

Mike glanced briefly at Tom, then back at Hughes. It was hopeless; they were gonna get thrashed. Tom would never forgive him. He had to do something. Anything.

"I did it!" he blurted out. "I told Malone. Tom knew nothing about it!"

Soon as he said it, his stomach heaved. An entire week's worth of food came spraying out.

Hughes jumped back. "You disgusting fucking mick!"

Something slammed into his back and he fell to the ground, right into his vomit.

"You fucking Modoc bastards!" Tom screamed.

Then he, too, was on the ground, with James kicking him in the face and Hughes booting him in the ribs. With each kick, his body jerked. Strands of bloody drool dangled from his nose and mouth. A crack opened above his eye. He tried to curl up, but Hughes wouldn't give him the chance. And the cops just stood there watching, laughing, shouting encouragement.

"Brain him! Bust his guts! Break his face open!"

Mike had to stop 'em before they killed him. But there were four of 'em. Each bigger than he was. Armed. Crazed with bloodlust. And his back so sore, he could barely move.

It didn't matter. Real AOH defend their brothers. *Unity makes ye invincible in battle.*

Wincing, he pushed himself onto his feet. He lunged at Hughes, intending to strangle him, but the Modoc was ready and punched him in the nose.

Pain shot straight into his brain. He staggered back, tears streaming from his eyes, and fell to the ground. Blood trickled down his throat. It tasted rusty. He wanted to crawl away, but Hughes jumped onto his chest, knees first, and socked him in the jaw, over and over again.

He couldn't breathe from the weight on his ribs. The pain was too much. He was choking on his own blood. His vision was dimming. Everything was going black.

Next thing he remembered, a familiar voice said, "Up ye go," and someone raised his back.

Squinting, he looked for Tom, but couldn't see much through the darkness with his swollen, crusty eyes. He could make out McKenna's stocky frame kneeling beside him, his glasses and handlebar mustache. Hughes lay just past him, motionless, along with two other bodies that had to be Gomer James and Tom. Eddie Lawler stood over them, his brass knuckles gleaming in the moonlight. And beyond him, Big Ned Monohan and Gibbons. Each had a metal pipe. And at their feet, the two cops, also unconscious.

Eddie slipped the brass knuckles into his pockets. "Someone help me with Hurley. He's in bad shape. Gibbons, get Doc Luks!"

Gibbons threw his pipe at the two unconscious cops and ran toward Main Street.

McKenna helped Mike to his feet. "Throw an arm over my shoulder. We gotta go."

The skin on Mike's face was stretched tight from the swelling. Each step, his jaw spasmed painfully. He watched Tom, hanging flaccidly in Eddie and Big Ned's arms, his breathing weak and shallow.

"Please don't let 'im die."

"He ain't gonna die," McKenna promised. "Just some broken ribs and a cracked skull. Luks'll fix 'im up."

Mike wiped his forehead. "I gotta get home."

McKenna gripped him tighter. "How 'bout lettin' Doc look ye

over. Have a nice long nap before ye run off?"

"But…"

Eddie flashed him a disapproving look. Mike knew exactly what he was thinking: *How can ye possibly know your uncle's been killed unless ye had something to do with it? It happened in the middle of the night, all the way across town. Wait till tomorrow. Act natural till then. And when ye finally do hear about it, ye best be horrified.*

Chapter 27
Sunday, June 28, 1874

The walk to Uncle Sean's was brutal. Every bone in Mike's body ached. His face was a ripe plum, ready to burst, throbbing and stinging all at once. His eyes ached from the bright midday sun, but squinting made it worse. Even swallowing hurt. And his legs were so wobbly he had to concentrate so they didn't crumple beneath him. Women in church clothes gaped with their hands over their mouths. Children pointed and stared. Even the dogs seemed horrified, sniffing at his boots, then skulking away, whimpering. Yet none of this compared with his anguish over what he would say when he got there. How he'd be able to look Aunt Mary in the eye and tell her everything was gonna be fine, when he was the cause of her suffering.

By the time he got there, he was completely drained. He wanted to curl up and go back to sleep, wait for everything to work itself out, but he knew it wouldn't. If he didn't get in there and put on a good show, it would look suspicious, and that would be even worse. They could never know he had anything to do with it.

He let out a dejected sigh and lifted his fist to knock.

Tara opened the door. "Oh my God! What happened?"

"Nothing." He tried not to grimace. "Just a little fight. How're ye holding up?"

"Awful," she sobbed.

He wrapped his arms around her, rocking gently back and forth, with his cheek resting against her soft hair, which still smelled clean from her Saturday night bath.

"I think he's gonna die," she said, with a shudder.

His hands fell to his sides. How could he still be alive?

She pulled away and shook her head, frowning.

Clutching himself, he glanced inside, past Li'l Bill, who was playing on the floor with the twins. Uncle Sean was sprawled on the dining table. Doc Luks stood over him with a needle and thread, his mustache twitching beneath his grave eyes. Aunt Mary was sitting beside him, caressing his hand, sobbing, while Mamai rubbed her back. Even from the doorway, it was obvious his throat had been slit, probably by that terrible knife that hung from Gomer James's belt. His neck had more stitches than a baseball.

Tara grabbed his arm. "Mike, I'm scared."

"Don't be. They got 'im, 'cause he's a blackleg. They ain't interested in ye."

"It's not that." Her voice was so soft he could barely hear it. "What if he survives? I'll have to care for him. Help him recover so he can torment us more. I couldn't stand that. I *want* him to die! And I'm goin' to Hell for it."

"You and me both."

But it wasn't the biblical Hell that worried him. It was the living hell of having to come up with enough money to pay for both Sean and Tom's medical care, and support both families by himself. That would mean late nights in the tavern after long days in the pit. And lots more dirty jobs, each with the risk of jail or death.

Tara's face sagged like she was a hundred years old. "Ready to go inside?"

As soon as he entered, he had to stop and swallow several times. The air was stale and tense, a strange mixture of blood and despair. Perspiration. The leathery odor of carbolic. Aunt Mary's soft whimpers. Sean's slow, wheezy breaths. His deathly green skin.

Mike closed his eyes and crossed himself. No way that bastard was gonna live.

"*Buíochas le Dia!*" Mamai cried. "What happened to ye?"

Aunt Mary looked up, her eyes puffy and red. "Were ye there, too? Did ye see who did it?"

Shaking his head, he couldn't meet her gaze. Somehow, despite the way Uncle Sean mistreated her, she still loved him, or at least cared about his suffering. And her loneliness when he died, her despair, would be entirely Mike's fault.

"Completely unrelated," Doc Luks said. "Modocs got Michael. I was at the Hurley's stitching him up, and his friend Thomas, before I heard about your husband. But that's only because he'd been dumped on the railroad tracks behind Donahue's Tavern. They didn't find him until hours later. I'm sure he was attacked earlier in the evening. Probably a bar fight."

"Jeez God!" Mamai let go of Aunt Mary. "What's this town coming to?"

"Just a particularly rough evening," Luks replied, his voice deepening. He tied a knot in Sean's stitches, then tilted his head toward Mamai with a concerned look. "And your son's going to be fine. Minor injuries. Michael got the least of it. Thomas was nearly brained."

Tara squeezed Mike's hand. "Poor Tommy."

"It's Sean I'm worried about." Luks stroked his goatee. "Took me hours to sew him up. I've no idea how much blood he lost before I got there. A fellow was holding him together with a rag."

Aunt Mary buried her face in her hands and wept.

"If anyone can save 'im, it's Doc Luks." Mamai patted her back, then glanced at Bill, who was sitting up with his eyes closed and a bit of drool hanging from the corner of his mouth.

"Tara, honey, check on the twins?"

Luks slowly shook his head, as if he was fed up with Bill's monkeyshines. Mike certainly was. More than a year since the accident and he was still sitting around the house pretending to be infirm, dependent on Tara for everything. His medicine. Bathing. Protection from Uncle Sean. And look at him now, head slumped to the side when he was supposed to be watching the twins. Maybe Uncle Sean was right. Maybe he would be better off without his medicine. But if Uncle Sean was right about that, did that mean he actually cared about Bill and the rest of them? That he was trying to be a good father?

Mike glanced at his aunt, whose eyebrows were drawn together, as though she knew he was unlikely to survive.

"Aunt Mary? Uncle Sean's got more fight in 'im than all the coal bosses put together."

The hair rose on the back of his neck as the truth of the statement hit him. Anyone but Sean would already be dead from a wound that bad. It was pure orneriness that kept him alive. He'd never let anyone get one over on him, not even Death. He'd fight back till he regained his strength and could return to work, even in the middle of a strike.

And there was nothing Mike could do about it.

Chapter 28
October 31, 1874

Tara lilted down the steps, humming merrily, her blue hair ribbon bobbing against the back of her wool coat. She smelled festive, too, oranges and rosemary. It matched the fiery swirl of yellow and red in the sky above them.

"I can't believe he's letting ye go to Mahanoy," Mike said, hooking his arm through hers.

"Uncle Sean?" She blew out a burst of air that rattled her lips. "What's *he* gonna do about it? Still so weak he can barely shake a fist. And when he talks, he sounds like an old toad. Aunt Mary's the only one that can understand him."

"Serious?" Mike scratched his jaw. "It's been four months."

"Gets better than that." She waved her hand dismissively. "Other day, he tried giving Deirdre a licking, but fell over. Couldn't get up again. Didn't even make her cry. But later, he tried kicking a ball around with her and Johnny. At least until the pain got to him."

"Damn, wish I was there!"

"Me too. Say, ye comin' with us tonight? The O'Donnells have the best parties!"

"Wish I could." He lowered his head. "But Muff ain't gonna let me run off with Hannah. Besides, I'm s'posed to go mumming with him, remember?"

They turned down Main Street, passing several stands selling candy and cider. It smelled of cinnamon and cloves. One stand had apples hanging from strings and a tiny blindfolded boy on his tiptoes was trying unsuccessfully to take bites out of them.

Tara grabbed Mike's arm and gazed up at him with a watery look in her eyes.

"Ye any closer to movin' us out?"

"I'm sorry." He scrubbed a hand over his face. "Been working ten hours a day in the pit. Another six at the tavern. Still haven't saved a penny!"

She clutched his arm tighter. "Even with Li'l Bill and Tom back at work?"

"Bill's at the sorting table, getting breaker boy pay. And Tom didn't work most of July. When he finally came back, he only got half-pay 'cause he was so slow and clumsy. And then there's the doctor's bills." He glanced at his feet. The only thing keeping 'em from starving was the small allowance the AOH was giving Mrs. Hurley each week.

"W-we'll be alright. And Bill's doing better. Still struggles with the crutches. And the pain. But no medicine in weeks." She twisted a lock of hair. "Um, one of Sean's buddies visited. Asked why the Modocs attacked him. They aren't going to come back and hurt us, are they?"

Mike's hand flew to his chest. "What'd he say?"

"Got angry." Her eyebrows squished together. "Said it was the Kohinoor Boys that did it. Strange, right?"

"Not really," Mike said, relieved that his secret would stay safe. "Kohinoor Boys have been after him for years."

A slow smile built up on Tara's face. "Hey, I might know how ye can come with us tonight."

"Really?"

"Sure. Ye can chaperone us. Muff won't let me and Hannah walk all that way alone."

"Brilliant!" He rubbed his hands. "Ye should be teaching school, not doing laundry."

"Maybe I will," she said, bouncing slightly on her toes.

The Lawlers' kitchen smelled deliciously of spiced barmbrack dough, which Mrs. Lawler had just placed in the oven. Mary McAndrew was at the table with Lizzie Cooney, cracking nuts. Hannah stood near the window, her dark curls gleaming in the soft orange warmth of late afternoon sun.

"Tara! Mike!" she cried, running to greet them.

As the girls embraced, Mike hoped he'd be next. But when her mother scowled at him, he quickly looked down, murmured a lackluster "Afternoon," and joined the ladies at the table.

Mrs. Cooney pushed the bowl of nuts toward him. "Goin' to the O'Donnells' party?"

"Wish I could." His shoulders drooped, but he promptly hitched them back up again.

"Please," Hannah begged.

"Sounds fun, but—"

"He's goin' mumming," her mother interrupted. "With the grown-ups."

Hannah's lip protruded in a pout.

"Wait." He swallowed several times, then looked right at Mrs. Lawler. "Mannoy's a long ways away. They could use an escort."

"He's right," said Mrs. McAndrew. "Day after payday? Halloween? Could be trouble."

"It's already arranged," Mrs. Lawler countered. "John Morris will accompany them."

Mike glanced around the room. Hannah was gripping her elbows with a pained look. Tara was blinking rapidly, as if confused. And Mrs. Lawler was marching straight toward him, squinting, with her chin poking out. She had a heavy burlap sack, which she dropped in his lap, right in the nethers! He tried not to grunt.

"Take these turnips to the office. Have the lads carve 'em."

For the first time since he'd known her, she looked repulsive to him, a vulture, with her long nose and mean little eyes. He imagined her getting kicked by a mule, or stumbling into a ditch; anything to prevent her from interfering with their Halloween. But he had no control over that. All he could do was leave and try not to let her know she had vexed him.

He got up and walked to the door, with his eyes directed at Hannah, who was standing behind her mother, with her hands on her hips and her tongue sticking out. He tried not to laugh, but it was too much to bear, and it came out as a snort.

"Have fun at the party, girls."

Muff's office smelled like beer, cigar smoke, and sweat. Manly and free. The exact opposite of the kitchen. Probably a lot more fun, too. Gambling with the boys. A night of mumming. Plenty of whiskey. Well, maybe not as nice as being with Hannah, but at least her mother wasn't there.

Mike placed the sack on the floor and sat next to Tom, who was clacking faro chips on the tabletop. Gibbons and Coyne sat across from them, each with a glass of beer. There was a pitcher in the middle of the table. McKenna was at the near end of the table, dealing.

"Goddamn it, McKenna!" Coyne slammed his cards down on the table. "Cheating again!"

"'Course he is," said Gibbons, chewing on his stogie. "Ain't that how he made his living in Buffalo?"

McKenna peeked over the top of his glasses. "Ye crybabies done whining?"

Tom stacked five fifty-cent chips in front of him. "Gonna deal the last three cards?"

"Wanna call 'em?"

"Ace, four, ten, boyo!"

Gibbons slapped his last two chips on the ten. Coyne put his on the four.

McKenna pulled a card from the shoe. An ace.

Tom licked his lips. Still in the running.

Everyone leaned closer for the next card. A four.

Coyne punched the air. "Yes!"

Tom leapt to his feet. "Pay up, McKenna. That's ten bucks!"

"Goddamn it!" Gibbons stomped so hard that beer sloshed from their glasses. "That was a month's worth of dirty tricks, a broken rib, and a weekend in jail."

The door swung open.

"Muff!" everyone cheered, except Gibbons, who slumped in his chair.

"How was Harrisburg?" asked Coyne.

"Interesting." He dropped his satchel beside the cabinet and poured himself a drink. Then he peeked into the burlap sack and gave Mike a playful punch. "How 'bout ye fellers start carvin' these jack-o'-lanterns, an' I'll tell yiz all about it?"

Mike bit his lip to keep from smiling. They were still buddies! Mrs. Lawler still hadn't told him anything about him and Hannah.

Muff turned a chair around and sat with his elbows on the backrest. "First off, Siney's out."

"Yes!" Gibbons raised his glass and finished it in one gulp.

"That's good, right?" Mike asked, pouring himself a glass of beer.

"Depends." Muff's forehead wrinkled. "Started a new union, the MNA. Took most of the Welsh and Dutch with him."

"Huzzah!" Tom cheered.

Coyne grimaced. "There goes our unity."

"Replaced by a feller named Walsh," Muff continued. "Same ilk as Siney. Rather sleep with the bosses than fight 'em."

Gibbons jumped to his feet. "Goddamn, Muff! Is there any good in all this?"

"Actually, yes. Both unions say we should start stockpiling weapons, considering all the violence these past few months."

McKenna scooted his chair closer to Muff, his voice hushed and excited. "I'll start a mayhem committee. Raise funds for the weapons!"

"I've got some sources," Gibbons added.

Muff gave them each a nod. "Good."

Coyne took a hard, obvious swallow. "Didn't ye just say 'both unions'?"

Muff's face tightened. "So?"

"Well, if the Welsh are in the new union, and most of the violence is being committed by Modocs, ain't this just gonna make it easier for 'em to kill us?"

"Yeh," Gibbons scoffed. "They're in with the C&I. Already got lots of guns. At least this'll give us a fighting chance."

Tom edged closer to the table. "I'm with Gibbons."

Mike offered a half-hearted shrug. He'd never felt safer than the night of the robbery, with that revolver tucked in his waistband. But if everyone was armed, it would escalate tensions. Give the C&I and Modocs justification for killing them.

"There's more," Muff said, refilling his glass. "Both unions are supporting Reilly for Congress."

Coyne cleared his throat and stood up, slowly shaking his head.

"Shit!" snapped McKenna. "Got a problem with Reilly, too?"

"Course not. He's for the workin' paddy, ain't he?" He paused, twisting a shirt button. "It's just we've got more urgent problems that neither guns nor Reilly can solve."

"Like what?"

"The owners're preparing to squeeze us."

"What're ye blathering about?" said Gibbons. "We've had more hours past coupla months than the past coupla years combined! Even *you're* working again."

"Ever consider why? More importantly, ye savin' any of it?"

Another strike? Mike's throat dried up like hot brick. He sipped his beer, but it burned as soon as it hit his stomach.

"Ye suggestin' they're stockpilin' coal?" said Muff.

"Know they are. Gotta friend in Philly. Says the Reading's got a score of wharves at Port Richmond, all overflowin' with coal. Can store a quarter-million tons. I think they're gonna provoke a strike, right as we head into winter."

McKenna yanked off his glasses. "If they want a strike, we'll give 'em a strike! We don't need the feckin' WBA. Or the MNA. Don't need those damned taffies, either! Any a ye happy with your current wages?"

"Not me!" Gibbons threw his cigar butt at the spittoon. "McKenna's right. I'll strike, with or without the Welsh."

"Better off without 'em!" Tom said, spitting in disgust.

"Yeh!" Mike cleared his throat. "Too many of 'em work for the C&I."

Coyne weaved slightly, as though he'd just taken a punch to the jaw, but then he pulled back his shoulders and said, "We're stronger with 'em than without 'em. But either way, we need to get the word out. The men gotta start savin' up while there's still work to be had. Otherwise, we won't last a month."

"Agreed." Muff raised his glass. "We'll start tonight."

Chapter 29
October 31, 1874

After supper, they got into their costumes. Muff wore his white cassock, with a tall conical mask of plaited straw that completely covered his face and came to a point two feet above his head. Cooney, who played King Coal, dressed similarly, but with a necktie outside his robe. McKenna wore a C&I helmet and a sword. Everyone else, including Tara and Hannah, smeared their faces with soot, then threw on coarse tunics, cinched with musty straw belts that crackled when they moved.

They marched down Center Street, each carrying a jack-o'-lantern with a chunk of burning coal inside, stopping at houses along the way. Mike and Tom would bang on the door and Muff would jump out, singing:

Here I am, Captain Mummer, and all o' me boys
With our whistles and drums, we make lots of noise
Give us room to play and sing our rhymes
We'll give you diversion these Halloween times
And if you don't believe what I say
Come out Old King Coal and clear the way. . .

Cooney would follow, singing:
Here I am, the miserly Old King Coal
I'll eat your time and I'll eat your soul
It's money I want an' money I crave
An' profits you'll give me till you're in your grave
All summer I gave you plenty of toil
And juicy fat paychecks that made ye feel royal,
But now that me stores are all filled to the brim
I can fire ye all, and not let ye back in
An' if ye don't believe what I say. . .

The other mummers came out in turn until the finale, when Big

Ned Monaghan appeared in a bright green corset, frilly white petticoats, and his constable's hat.

Here I am, the innocent, darling Miss Funny
With me gunnysack for ye to toss in your money
Or Halloween treats or bottles of whiskey
If you've nothing to give, you'll just have to kiss me

Since nobody wanted to be kissed by a six-and-a-half-foot tall copper dressed as an adventuress, his gunnysack quickly filled with cakes and cookies and even a few bottles of whiskey, while Coyne made pleas for everyone to start saving up for the coming strike.

At Main Street, Hannah and Tara ran to the front. "Can we go over the hill, now?"

"We'll be headin' there soon enough," Muff said, taking a quick peek up the road.

"But we'll miss all the fun, Daddy."

"Ain't safe," McKenna protested. "Too many drunks out. And Modocs lookin' for mischief."

Muff removed his mask and scanned the group. "Where's Morris?"

"Probably with another girl," Tom muttered under his breath.

"Quiet," Mike hissed. "That's no way to get Tara to like ye."

"He's already there," said Gibbons. "Helped deliver the keg."

Tara's chin dipped.

Hannah gently bit her lip. "Couldn't Mike accompany us?" She cast a quick glance at him, but her soft expression suddenly hardened as her mother pushed her way forward.

"Ye go with 'em," Mrs. Lawler said to Gibbons, who stared back with a blank look.

"Lemme do it," Mike said. "I'll protect her like she's my own sister!"

Mrs. Lawler glowered at him.

Muff squeezed her shoulder. "Annie, a young man oughta protect his own sister."

A comfortable warmth flooded Mike's face, as the tension drained from his shoulders. They'd have an hour together, unchaperoned, before the others got there. Maybe longer if they hurried. "Ye won't regret it." Then, turning to the girls, he made an exaggerated bow. "Ladies?"

Giggling, they positioned themselves on either side of him and marched away.

"Keep to Center Street," McKenna called. "And watch out for trouble."

As soon as they turned the corner, they linked arms and skipped to the Creek Street Bridge, with their jack-o'-lanterns flickering like fireflies. Gentlemen at the Mansion House tipped their hats as they passed. Everyone must've thought he was the luckiest feller in Shendo to be with two such pretty girls.

He was still smiling an hour later, as they descended the hill into Mahanoy City, which looked like a giant carnival, with all the lanterns and bonfires. The cool air was permeated with the smell of warm butter and sugar. Stands selling boxty cakes and spiced-apple fadge. Clove-scented penny candies. Peppermint. Apple cider. Tiny witches, ghosts, and Egyptian princesses running up and down the street, squealing with delight.

There was a band at the corner of Main and Centre, and couples dancing in front of the Grand Central Hotel. Hannah clasped Mike's hand and pulled him closer. Her eyes closed and her lips parted. But as he leaned down to kiss her, Tara stuck her elbow into his ribs.

"We goin' to the party, or what?"

Grimacing, he jerked away. That's when he saw Jamie McAllister, in a dress and bonnet, walking toward them. If that bumpkin started talking to 'em now, they'd never get there.

Mike tugged the girls' hands. "Let's go."

But Jamie stopped right in front of them, clapping his hands together.

"Mike Doyle, right?"

"Um, we're kinda in a hurry."

"On Halloween?"

"We're goin' to a party," Hannah said, her voice bubbling with excitement.

"Oh, that's rich." Jamie chuckled. "There's a party at *my* house."

"Really?" Tara asked. "Where ye live?"

"Maggie O'Donnell's place."

Hannah slapped a hand against her cheek. "Why, that's where we're go—"

She was interrupted by the echoing crack of a gunshot.

Mike looked at the girls. They were clutching each other, shaking.

Three more gunshots.

"Run!"

They sprinted down Water Street, sloshing through the crick, stumbling, jumping back up and stumbling again. Two blocks they ran before Jamie finally stopped, gasping for air.

"We safe?"

Mike listened for danger. His stomach was rock-hard, his legs jittery and cold from his soggy trousers and socks. It smelled of manure, damp wood, and rotting food. It was so dark he couldn't see a thing. The only sound was their own panting. He licked the salt from his lip.

"Think so."

He took a cautious step forward, but his foot hit a soft lump and he fell.

"Ow!" the lump cried.

"Ye alright?" Hannah asked.

Mike figured she must've thought it was him. But before he could reply, the lump said, "I ain't dead."

Jamie crouched closer. "McCann?"

"Jamie?"

"Ye know each other?" Mike asked, sitting up, calmed by the realization it wasn't a corpse.

"Know each other?" Jamie hooted. "McCann rooms with me at the O'Donnells'."

"Probably not after tonight." McCann chuckled nervously.

Mike started to get up, but his hand grazed against something odd. He ran his fingers along the object. It was cold, smooth, and hard. A gun? Shit, Muff would really kill him now!

He jumped to his feet, placing his body squarely between the girls and McCann.

"Who'd ye shoot?"

"It-it was an accident." McCann's voice cracked.

"McCann," Jamie pleaded. "Tell us who."

There was a long pause.

"Um, George Major."

"The burgess?" Hannah said, her voice trembling.

Mike's ears pounded. He wiped the sweat from the back of his neck, wondering how it was possible. McCann would be hanged. And the C&I would crack down hard on the AOH. Blame them for everything. Modoc attacks would escalate on both sides of the hill. They wouldn't be satisfied with McCann's neck. Major was their leader. They wouldn't rest till they'd killed dozens of Irishmen!

Rolling up his sleeves, Mike stepped toward McCann. "Are ye crazy?"

"Wasn't my fault. He was drunk. Waving his gun. Screaming, 'Order in my town! Order!' I told 'im to go home. Sleep it off. But he started shooting. Hit a dog and fell over backward."

Tara balled up her fists. "He deserved to get shot!"

"Thought I was safe at that point." McCann cleared his throat. "But then he got up. Took another shot. Got me in the thigh."

"Ye kill 'im?" Jamie asked.

"Doesn't matter," Mike said. "He'll hang either way. Ye gotta get 'im outa here."

"Me? Ain't ye gonna help?"

"Gotta get the girls home. Cops'll be everywhere."

"What about Johnny?" Tara cried.

"Help me get 'im home," Jamie pleaded. "It's only a coupla blocks."

"The O'Donnells have a wagon," said McCann. "They can drive me to Cooney's. His wife's my cousin."

Mike tapped an index finger against his lip. If he didn't get the girls home safely, Muff would kill him. But if this guy was related to Cooney, he must be AOH. That meant he had an obligation to help him. If he didn't, he'd get kicked out of the AOH and left to the wolves.

He shuffled closer to Tara and Hannah, grabbed their hands, and squeezed. "Can ye run ahead to the O'Donnells'? Have 'em get the wagon ready? I'll be there quick as I can."

Hannah pushed the hair out her eyes and glanced at Tara to see what she thought.

Tara nodded. "Of course we can."

It was well after one when they finally left the O'Donnells'. The air was chilly and cloudless, illuminated by a silvery half-moon. The road was strangely quiet, considering how hectic it had been earlier. Just a hooting owl and a couple of night watchmen patrolling the coll'ries on Molasses Hill. No one else until they reached Shendo, where they saw a cop outside the Union Street Station. They turned up Bridge Street to avoid him and walked behind the Lehigh Valley Railroad bridge. Two more blocks from there to Uncle Sean's, where they dropped Tara off.

It was another seven blocks to Muff's. Hannah held Mike's hand the entire way, squeezing so tightly it started to tingle. They made it there without any trouble, but her mom was waiting in the doorway with her arms crossed.

Mike quickly released Hannah's hand, as his own fell to his sides.

"Young lady, go straight to your room!"

Hannah's shoulders curled forward. She moped up the steps without even glancing at Mike.

"And ye, Mike Doyle! Muff's office, now!"

Mike could hardly breathe as he dragged himself through the dark tavern. Muff would rip him limb from limb. Mrs. Lawler probably told him everything, the spiteful biddy. The fact that he got Hannah home safely *and* helped a fellow Hibernian escape a lynching would mean nothing in light of that. Yet, as much as he wanted to turn around and leave, he had to tell Muff about the killing, give him a chance to warn the others. When the C&I swept through town looking for McCann, everyone in the AOH would be at risk.

He opened the door and walked in. Muff was slumped at the table, with a half-finished bottle of whiskey and a glazed, distant look in his eyes. Not the look of an angry man.

"Ye alright, Muff?"

"Eddie's dead."

Mike felt a cold, stinging pain, like a snowball had burst inside him. He grabbed the back of a chair to stop himself from falling. "H-how?"

"Gomer James."

Mike squeezed the chair tighter. "We'll kill him!"

Hanging his head, Muff stared dully at the bottle of whiskey, before pouring a glass.

"Sit down, Mikey. Have a drink. It'll help ye see more clearly."

"See what?"

"Any minute now, streets'll be crawling with C&I. They'll drag every one of us in for questioning. Modocs'll be on heightened alert. Think ye can get near James amidst all that? You're crazier than a bedbug." He drained his glass and threw it against the wall. "And that's just the beginning of our troubles. They'll use the murder to disrupt our organizing. Divide our unity. Provoke a sectarian war. Strike'll end before it even starts. Lot of good men'll die."

This was worse than Mike had thought. He rubbed his wrist, wondering how they could win a strike if they were constantly getting arrested and shot.

"Hey, how'd ye know about Major?"

"News travels fast." Muff snorted. "Especially by wagon. O'Donnell left here half an hour ago. McKenna's already on his way to Philly with McCann. Have 'im on a boat to Ireland by tomorrow. Lucky sonofabitch. Danny Daugherty ain't so lucky. He's been arrested for the murder."

"Jeez God! Why?"

Muff tugged pensively on his goatee. "Cops found 'im a block away from Major with a bullet in his noggin."

"But if Major's bullet hit McCann, who shot Dougherty?"

"Question for the ages, Mikey. A Modoc? Husband of one of the women he's been screwin'. These're dangerous times. Lot of ways for a feller to get hurt. Ye best be mighty careful goin' home tonight."

Chapter 30
Wednesday, February 3, 1875

Johnny Morris grunted as he edged the barrel of flour off the wagon, staggering slightly from the weight, almost losing his black derby in the process. He put the barrel down long enough to straighten his jacket, then lugged it to Muff's shed with tiny, cautious steps to avoid slipping on the ice. His back arched so much he looked as though he'd fall over backward. Mike wanted to follow behind him to help keep him balanced, but Tom was already dragging the next cask to the rear of the wagon. It was almost his turn.

"Feels familiar, don't it?" Tom asked, resting his elbows on top of the barrel.

"Guess so."

Mike glanced up at Hannah's window and sighed. No enticing silhouette today. Not a light on in the house. The yard was completely still except for the warm, nasal mule breaths and Morris's boots crunching on the ice. Even Cú Chulainn and the other birds were still asleep. Maybe Muff would come out and invite them in to thaw their frozen fingers over the potbelly stove and have an early breakfast, with Hannah flashing glossy-eyed glances at him. More likely, her mother would be there, and he'd just stare at his food, praying for it to end quickly.

He wrapped his arms around the cask. It smelled strongly of salted herring. His mouth filled with saliva at the thought of a flaming pan of crisp, poteen-soaked fish fillets. Shit, only one month into the strike and he was already acting like a bear waking early from its winter nap.

At least the AOH was looking after them. Or, more accurately, *they* were looking after the AOH. This was their third robbery in as many weeks, each haul feeding a dozen families. But this wasn't at all like their first dirty job, when they spent hours muffling the wheels and hooves, and they could barely contain their excitement and fear, and there was hope that the deed would rid him of both Uncle Sean and the looming threat of Gomer James. Now that both men had recovered and everyone was suffering from hunger and cold, these burglaries just seemed desperate, a never-ending chore.

"Gotta do something different." He lugged the fish barrel to the shed and deposited it next to the flour. "We'll never beat Gowen this way."

Morris scrubbed a hand over his face. "Ye mean picketing and marching, while the Welsh and Dutch continue working? Or getting clubbed and shot at by goons and Pinkertons?"

"Both." Mike fiddled with his scarf. "We're getting nowhere."

"At least you get to see your girlfriend. Mine's imprisoned by your uncle."

"Why don't you do something about it!"

"Like what?"

"Like not being such a big crybaby!" Tom said from the bed of the wagon.

Morris grabbed a stick. "I'll kill you, Hurley!"

Mike lunged, hoping to knock the stick out of his hand, but missed, accidentally tripping Morris, whose head smacked against the wagon.

"Oh, shit." Tom tittered nervously. "I think ye killed him!"

"No, I didn't." Mike took a step backward, without taking his eyes off the body on the ground. Muff would be furious if he knew what happened. "Probably just knocked out."

A light went on.

"Quick," Mike said. "Let's drag him to the barn."

The back door creaked open. Footsteps.

"Wrap him up with blankets. I'll distract Muff."

Mike walked briskly toward the house, sweating beneath his coat.

"Hey, Muff. W-we didn't wake ye, did we?"

"Nah." He leaned back and yawned, stretching so wide his coat opened up, revealing his night shirt. "I never sleep well till I know a job's done and everyone's safe. How'd it go?"

"Perfect. Um, there's a crate of bacon in the wagon. And tons of eggs."

"Great." Muff rubbed his hands together. "Why don't ye hand 'em down to me and then finish unloading? I'll fix breakfast."

By the time they finished unloading the wagon, the first rays of sunlight were melting through the jagged orange clouds. The cocks were beginning to forage and crow. Morris was still unconscious, curled up on a pile of hay, beneath several horse blankets. Mike tried shaking him, but he didn't even twitch.

"Let's just leave 'im," Tom said. "He won't freeze with all those blankets."

"I don't know." Mike looked Morris up and down, wondering how long he'd stay that way, or if he'd have any sense when he awoke. What if he wandered around in a daze and got attacked by Modocs? "He could lose a finger from the cold."

"Don't have a choice, do we? Muff'll kill us."

"No, he won't." Mike squatted down, wedging a shoulder under Morris's left arm. "Get the other side. Help me carry him in. I've got a plan."

They dragged him into the tavern and propped him in a chair. The table was sticky with spilt beer and smelled of old smoke, but flames were crackling in the stove and the room was warm. Cooney and McKenna were at the bar, beneath the lamp, drinking tea and sharing a pipe, like they'd been there all night.

"Have some?" McKenna filled two cups without waiting for a response.

Cooney waved his dudeen toward Morris, whose face had flopped onto the table.

"What's with him?"

"Drunk." Mike scraped a hand through his hair. "And we haven't slept all night."

The upstairs door opened, and Muff appeared with a large, steaming tray of food. As he proceeded down the stairs, a sweet smokiness wafted toward them.

"Mm, bacon!" said McKenna.

Tom gave a dramatic bow. "Thank to us!"

"There's crates for each of yiz to take home," Muff added, placing the tray on the bar.

Mike ran to the counter and started filling his plate. Tom was right behind him.

As they ate, other AOH members trickled in and lined up for grub. First Paddy Dolan and Dan Kelly. Then Coyne, Dick Fennin, and Cooney, followed shortly by Gibbons and Ned.

At first, everyone was too busy shoveling food into their mouths to speak. But eventually Dolan spoke, as he mopped up the last of his egg yolk with a piece of toast. He was as tall as Big Ned and fat as a hog, with a voice like a slowly creaking door.

"Fellers, we oughta give up on blockades and picketing. Ain't doing any good and we're just sitting ducks for yellow dogs and goons."

"Ain't that the truth," said Gibbons. "Four weeks into the strike. Instead of negotiating, the owners slashed wages again. We're better off dumping coal-carts in the night."

Everyone in the room nodded, except Coyne, who wrinkled his nose as if the idea was pure shit. Good old Coyne. He'd talk sense into them. He knew how to win a strike.

Every day he'd been at one of the coll'ries, leading pickets and blockades. Most of the time, Mike and Tom had been with him. Small groups of Irishmen, ten to fifteen strong, marching back and forth with signs and flags, a drummer bringing up the rear, occasionally enough to stop the blacklegs from getting through. Yet every time they went to the Centennial, West Shendo, or Kohinoor, yellow dogs would show up, or masked goons smelling of whiskey and sweat. They'd call 'em Papists and Communists, and clobber 'em with truncheons. One time they forced 'em through a gauntlet of drunken Modocs, who shot at their feet like they were gophers. Luckily, only three men were hit. But Dolan had a point. There had to be another way.

"'Tis true," Coyne said, forming a steeple with his fingertips. "We ain't making progress. But that's 'cause neither union's joined the strike and the Northern Districts are still on the job."

"Hyde Park taffies!" Tom scoffed.

"Well," Coyne continued. "They'll soon have no choice. This second wage cut brings our pay down to half what what it was five years ago. Besides, public's on our side. Hate Gowen and the

Reading as much as we do. Damned monopoly's driven every small-timer outa business. But if we start behaving like thugs, we'll lose their support. And any chance for unity. Anyhow, weather's perfect for picketing. Sun's out. Sky's clear. Spring's a-comin' early, boyos!"

"He's right about unity." Muff walked to the window and opened the blinds. It was as bright as a summer day, despite the icicles hanging from the eaves. "Northern Districts'll join us by the end of the week. But he's wrong about spring."

"Wrong?" Coyne raised a brow. "How d'ye know?"

"'My neighbor, Bach, has a groundhog in his yard. Came outa its burrow yesterday. Sniffed around. Ran back inside. Dutch say that's a sure sign winter'll last another six weeks."

"Blast it!" said Cooney. "We're already down to spuds and biscuits."

"That'll change," Coyne argued. "Soon as the unions join us, and the Northern Districts, we'll win back the minimum wage and sliding scale. Maybe even a raise!"

"And let's not forget," Muff added. "With Reilly in Congress, he'll bust the monopoly!"

Mike sucked on a slice of bacon, amazed at how quickly he had shifted from despair to hope. All it took was a little common sense from Coyne and Muff, a reminder that this past month they had their hands tied behind their backs. Things would really change now. Instead of ten men at a picket, they'd have thirty or forty. And Modocs wouldn't shoot if there were Welshmen there.

"What if he don't?" Paddy Dolan rolled up his sleeves as though he was preparing to fight. "What if Gowen buys 'im off, just like every other politician? What if Siney and Walsh hold out? Or the taffies refuse to join us? With this damned depression, there's no shortage of blacklegs."

"There's a shortage of beer."

Everyone turned toward Morris, who was sitting upright with a dazed look on his face.

"My head's killing me!"

"Of course," said McKenna, laughing. He walked behind the bar and filled a glass. "There's plenty we can't be sure about. But one thing's for certain: we're wasting our time at pickets. Let the blacklegs work. They're so inept, they're slowin' down production for us. Besides, the Reading's still got a huge surplus. We're better off focusing on distribution. Make sure none of it gets to market. I'm with Gibbons. Mayhem in the night!"

"How 'bout blacklegs in the night?" Kelly said, chuckling. "Like that explosion at Hauser's Hotel? Reckon no more blacklegs'll be stayin' there."

"And what about Mantzinger's?" said Gibbons. "Day after the headframe burned down, all the Welsh and Dutch walked off the job. Proves mayhem's *more* effective than picketing."

Tom shared a mischievous wink with Mike, who leaned back with an arm hooked over his chair, content for the moment with his buddy's glee. Tom had no conscience. No common sense, either. He didn't care what the public thought, or the Welsh and Dutch. Mayhem in the night appealed to his sense of creativity. It was an opportunity to show Gibbons and McKenna he was just as clever and bold as them. It was a way to get back at all the petty foremen and superintendents who had abused them at work. At the C&I for all the AOH men they arrested. At the Modocs for all their beatings and murders. So what if Danny Daugherty was still in jail? So what if McCann had to flee the country? So what if Mr. Hurley, himself, would've sided with Coyne? Tom could no more resist his urges than a cat could resist killing a mouse.

"Enough!" Muff barked. "Ye know Pinkerton has spies everywhere. Maybe even here. Ain't just his uniformed boys in the C&I. Men're gettin' plucked off the streets, beaten, just 'cause they're AOH. How ye think they know who to nab?"

"I ain't scared." Morris spat on the floor.

"Me neither," said Gibbons.

Mike wiped his hands on his pants. "There *is* a spy among us."

McKenna jerked around. "Who?"

"Don't know who. Just know we got one."

Muff's expression tightened. "Got proof?"

"Yeh!" Mike stood up, with his shoulders back and his legs spread wide. "My sister works for Mrs. McGill. Her husband's C&I. Yesterday, she overheard him say they got a spy in our lodge."

"That's right," Muff said. "Hannah used to work there, too. Think I remember her saying something about Mr. McGill being C&I."

"Sounds like we got our little own spy." Cooney laughed. "Guess that makes us even."

Coyne's expression remained stern. "We still gotta keep quiet 'bout this stuff. Remember, they wanna destroy us. Mischief doesn't just put ye at risk. It brings unrestrained police violence on all of us. Justification to arrest us. Disrupt our actions. Remember Halloween? Twenty-five good organizers thrown in jail. Two of us murdered by Modocs. Three more in the infirmary. Besides, only way to get the union to support us is through peaceful actions. Only way to get Hyde Park, too."

"Fuck Hyde Park!" Tom said. "Fuck Gomer James!"

"Fuck Hyde Park," Coyne repeated, jabbing a finger for emphasis. "Don't trust 'em any more than ye do. But there's a lot of 'em. And whatever they do, the rest of the taffies follow. Ye think we can win this with a couple of overturned hopper cars and coal wagons? A few burnt headframes? A bunch of us in jail? Or dead? We need unity. And that means pickets, marches, blockades. That's why a bunch of us are going to Plank Ridge tomorrow. Who's with me?"

Gibbons started for the door. "Too late, Coyne. We've already got unrestrained police violence. Modoc violence, too. I ain't gonna be a sittin' duck anymore."

Dolan gave a dismissive nod. "Ain't ye tired of gettin' beat up, Coyne? Sleepin' in jail?"

Coyne shrugged. "Sure, but it's how ye win a strike."

Mike trusted Coyne about these things. Unity and public support were critical. But McKenna and Gibbons also made sense. Halting distribution *and* production would really put the squeeze on Gowen. If he couldn't sell any coal, he'd go bankrupt. He'd have to negotiate. Give in to their demands. "Ye can count me in."

Tom looked like he was going to leave in protest.

Mike leaned over and whispered in his ear. "We can do both."

"Fine. I'll be there, too."

Chapter 31
Thursday, February 4, 1875

The LV&M clacked slowly across Cherry Street, a black cloud spewing from its smokestack, a tornado swirling against the frozen daybreak sky. The thin air stung Mike's cheeks, yet for a moment, his body warmed to the smell of coal smoke, as if he was standing in front of a hot stove. But then the brakes screeched and gave off a chilling odor, like a long, continuous spark. Shivering, he buried his hands in his underarms and tapped his foot. Goddamn, it was slow!

Ten cars. Fifteen. Twenty. At this rate, they'd get there after the blacklegs.

Tom seemed indifferent, his eyelids drooping as he packed his lip with tobacco.

Coyne fiddled with the buttons of his coat, as a pig rooted around in the snow, then pulled his tweed cap over his ears, as if to dampen the noise. "We'll be doin' those blacklegs a favor," he said loudly, pausing when the train whistle shrieked. "That is, if we ever get past this beast."

"Favor?" Mike asked.

"Sure. At least one of 'em dies every week, right? Another half-dozen hurt so badly they can't come back. Poorly trained, clumsy, stupid. Shutting down the coll'ry will save their lives."

"Yeh," Tom laughed. "We're providing a public service." He spat a brown wad at the train.

"Should be easy." Mike stepped across the tracks. "Only one entrance to block."

He rushed down Cherry Street, along the edge of the frozen crick, pausing for the others at the bridge. They continued to the front gate, where a group of miners was marching, led by Dan Kelly, in his knee-high boots, and Paddy Dolan, who was waving a green flag with a golden harp on it. Several Welsh miners were there, too, including Barmy Bevan, who looked like he was at a funeral, with his neatly pressed suit and somber expression. Just inside the gate, behind them, Foreman Bradley conferred with two C&I, trying to appear unconcerned, but he kept shooting glances at the strikers, as if he expected trouble.

Sure enough, within minutes, a wagonful of blacklegs approached. Dolan stepped into the road. "Alright, fellers. Form a wall."

He turned toward the wagon, menacing the mules with his flag, as the men linked arms behind him, and Tom scurried up to the driver.

"We're the Committee for Public Safety. Turn 'round now and no one gets hurt!"

Bradley stomped through the shrubs to get around their wall. "You threatening our men?"

"Just stating a fact," Coyne said. "Your men are dying like flies. They're poorly trained, inexperienced, and overworked. We're protectin' 'em from the hazards of the job."

"That so?" Bradley leaned back with his arms crossed, his sandy little mustache twitching beneath his pointy nose. "How 'bout you come in and show 'em how it's done?"

"At our old wages?"

"You know I can't do that."

"Then we can't let 'em in. They could die."

Bradley's feet shifted. He patted his pockets like he'd lost something.

"You rat! You're the one that could die, talking that way."

"Nonetheless," Coyne said, raising his chin with a haughty smile. "We ain't lettin' 'em through. Right, boyos?"

"Right!" the men shouted.

Dolan pressed closer on Mike's left and Tom squeezed in on his right, between him and Coyne. No way those scabs would get through with the fourteen of them hooked together like the links of a chain. The yellow dogs would have to pry them loose, one by one, then cart 'em off to jail. That would take an hour or more and seriously disrupt production. Best of all, it was completely peaceful. No way they could be accused of thuggery. If any violence erupted, it would be the C&I attacking them.

Mike could hear their boots crunching in the ice behind him, getting closer, causing goosebumps to erupt on his arms.

"Off the road!" one of 'em yelled.

"We ain't budgin'," Coyne replied, without turning. "This is a public street."

"You're a public nuisance," said the other C&I, who was right behind them, his voice as sharp as a pick. "Disperse or else!"

Mike could smell the coffee on their breaths. He slowly turned his head. One of 'em had a bandolier across his chest, covering his badge. The cop pulled back his truncheon and swung it into the back of Coyne's knees.

There was a pop. Coyne yelled and fell to the ground, writhing, groaning. The C&I with the bandolier forced him onto his belly, cuffed him, and yanked him to his feet.

"It's the hoosegow for you. And anyone else who doesn't leave!"

Coyne fell back down with a grunt. "We ain't budging!"

"We'll see about that!"

A truncheon whizzed past Mike's ear. An uncontrollable shudder swept through his body. But there was no nauseating crack. No bells in his ears. Just a heavy thump on the arm. Tingling fingertips. Pain shooting up to his elbow, shoulder, neck! His entire limb, a sack of bricks.

He tried to hold on, but his fingers wouldn't work and his hand fell lifelessly to his side.

Dolan reached for his shoulder, but never made it. A truncheon crashed into his noggin. He fell like a tree, pulling Mike down with him.

Cold dirt filled Mike's nose and mouth. He tried to spit, but couldn't lift his head. There was a yellow dog on his back, gouging his wrists with the handcuffs. Dolan lay beside him, motionless, blood trickling from his head.

"Up you go."

The cop heaved Mike up by the cuffs, wrenching his injured arm. It brought tears to his eyes. He tried to anticipate what his captor would do next, so he could comply and minimize the pain. A Black Maria was parked behind the blacklegs. It had red wheels and rusty iron bars. There were two C&I on the driver's bench. The one holding the reins wore long, tan gloves, and a bell-shaped hat strapped beneath his lip, as if his chin was too long to accommodate it. The one beside him had a shotgun and was so fat that his long wool coat bulged out like he was hiding another cop inside it. Two more jumped down from the rear bumper. One of 'em pulled the rifle from his shoulder and approached Bradley.

"This the one?"

"Yup." Bradley had his arm around Coyne's waist to keep him upright.

"Here's how we treat agitators."

He thrust his gunstock into Coyne's head, knocking him to the ground. It sounded like a watermelon thrown against a rock. Blood gurgled from the hole.

Mike's ears pounded. Everything went blurry, except for his buddies, who oddly became more vivid. Dolan's mottled skin. Kelley's muscles straining against his neck. Tom's hands clenching and unclenching. The entire crowd pulsing as though it was going to explode.

"On your bellies! Now!"

The yellow dogs ran at them, guns drawn.

Everyone dropped to the ground, including Mike, who screamed in pain when he hit.

One by one they were crammed into the Black Maria. Mike couldn't move his knees. His arm throbbed. His fingers were numb. The cuffs were cutting into his wrists. He tried rotating his hands, but that made it worse. Tom sat across from him with his chin pressed against his knees. No one spoke. It was a goddamned failure! They were cleared off the road in less than thirty minutes. The blacklegs were probably already in the pit, marching to their doom.

That night, Mike slept restlessly. The cell was freezing. Every time he shivered, his throbbing arm would awaken him. Then he'd lay there, staring at the flickering shadows on the ceiling, unable to doze because of his comrades' farting and snoring, and the jailers' mindless banter, and the reek of the overflowing slop bucket. He finally gave up when he noticed the spears of light coming in through the bars on the window.

Sitting up, he looked around the cell, hoping they'd get out soon and he could get a bite to eat somewhere far away from this awful stench. Kelly was already awake, pacing the cell, muttering to himself. Tom was still asleep, his shoulder rising and falling with each breath. Dolan was lying on his back next to him, with one eye open, the other swollen shut, his hair matted with dried blood, as though he'd been beaten a second time and dumped there in the middle of the night.

"What happened to you?" Mike tried to sound calm.

"Linden." Dolan sat up, grimacing. "Brought me in for questioning. Don't think he liked my answers."

Cringing, Mike tried not to laugh. "Muff always said ye knew how to talk to coppers."

"Yup, me an' the coppers have a mutual understanding."

Tom opened one eye, then the other, smiling as if he'd been listening the whole time.

Dolan's gaze bounced around the cell. "Say, any of yiz seen Coyne?"

Mike shifted uneasily, trying to remember when he saw him last. *Blacklegs. Yellow dogs. Gunstock to the head.* And then it hit him.

"Bradley got him."

"Impossible!"

"'Fraid so," said Kelly. "Saw 'im draggin' 'im into the machine shop."

"We gotta get outa here! That bastard's gonna kill 'im."

"Probably already has," Kelly said with a dejected sigh, as he clung to the bars.

"Hey, Driscoll," Dolan called. "When we gettin' out?"

"Soon as you sonsofbitches shut up! Sheriff doesn't want to feed and house a bunch of Molly Maguires. Unless you're dumb enough to get arrested again. Then you'll get a week on bread and water!"

It was snowing when they were released. The entire town was

silvery gray, like a daguerreotype. The Black Maria was in front of the jail, with both horses harnessed. The one closest to the building nickered loudly, swishing its tail, a pile of fresh dung steaming beneath it.

Tom inhaled deeply. "Ahh, the smell of freedom!"

"Thank God!" said Kelly.

Mike stood rigidly with his hands on his hips. "We gonna save Coyne?"

When no one moved, he bolted down the street, past McDermott's and Lessig's, his lungs stinging from the frigid air. Turning down Cherry Street, he could hear someone breathing behind him, but didn't look. Tom was the only one fast enough. Dolan would be slowed by his injuries and Kelly was probably heading home, convinced Coyne was already dead. But Bradley wouldn't have killed him outright. Not with so many witnesses. Beat him to a bloody pulp, maybe, and left him to die.

Tightening his fists, Mike pumped harder, ignoring the pain in his arm, the stitch in his side, the sandpaper in his throat. He ran like a deer, with long, loping strides, his chin up, so he didn't miss a thing. The Williams Hotel. Main Street. Brennan's. Half a block more to Coyne's boardinghouse.

"That him?" Tom asked, panting, slowing to a walk.

There was a small crowd near the LV&M tracks. Dazed housewives. A grocer in a white apron. A constable. Probably nothing. It was Friday, after all, nearly noon. Most likely, just folks out doing their usual business. Except the constable was backing away from something with his mouth wide open. They were too far away to see what it was, but someone was crouched on the tracks examining it.

Mike raced toward the tracks, his mind scrambling for an alternative explanation. A train accident. A mad dog. An injured child. But as he got closer, he could see it was Tully, Coyne's roommate and best friend, hovering over a body. Coyne's body. His face was mangled, his lips blackened with blood, his eyes bulging green, like old, boiled egg yolks. And the letters R-A-T carved into his forehead, right above the truncheon gash.

"Goddamn." Mike kneeled beside Coyne's corpse. "What'd

they to do ye?”

“He was a good paddy,” said Tully.

He *was* a good paddy. Honest. Loyal. Always fighting for the working man. Willing to go to jail. Able to get each man to play his part. Even the Welsh. Heck, they were all good paddies: Da, Mr. Hurley, even Eddie, in his own perverse way. Every one of ’em had risked his life for Mike. Each of ’em had more grit than a dozen blacklegs. So, why’d they all have to die and Sean got to live?

Mike shook his head. It wasn’t fair!

Coyne died playing by the rules. Da and Mr. Hurley, too. But what was the point when the unions weren’t even supporting the strike? When Modocs could just grab a feller off the street and kill ’im, and yellow dogs could beat ye up and throw ye in jail?

McKenna and Gibbons were right. This war had to be fought in the dark of night.

Muff’s tavern was packed that night, despite being closed to the public, a jumble of yammering voices, clanking glasses, and crackling flames. Nearly every AOH member in Shendo was there, plus a few from Mahanoy, Gilberton, and Girardville. Everyone looked orange and shadowy from the candles, Halloween demons, with hollow black eyes and demented grins. But it was warm and smelled pleasantly of beer and tobacco. It reminded Mike of his first time in Couch’s Saloon, when he was just a kid, and for a moment he forgot how angry he was.

“I need a big whiskey,” Tom said, wedging his way toward the bar, where Cooney and Mrs. Lawler were both too busy pouring drinks to notice them.

Gibbons, who was sitting at the end of the counter, reached over and grabbed a bottle.

“Here, this’ll get the bitterness outa your throats.”

Tom leaned back and poured a stream into his mouth, then handed it to Mike.

“Quiet!” Muff yelled, clanging a spoon against his glass. “Attention!”

He stood midway up the stairs, waiting for everyone to calm

down. His posture was loose and unfriendly. His eyes were dark. Big Ned Monaghan was at the foot of the stairs, in his constable's uniform, with McKenna and Dolan.

"Coyne was one of the best," Muff said, pausing to weigh his words. The room was so quiet you could hear the windows rattling from the Kohinoor's engines. "A giant among men!"

"Justice for Coyne!" someone yelled.

"Justice!" the others echoed.

Muff peered downward. "Ned, how's the investigation going?"

Ned went stone-faced.

"Tell 'em," Gibbons hissed.

"They won't let me near it." He slowly shook his head. "They say I was too close to 'im."

Dolan crossed and uncrossed his arms. "Ye musta heard something."

"They're sayin' he died from a police truncheon. That it was justifiable use of force."

"Outrageous!" Dolan hollered. "How's it justifiable when his legs were already busted? He couldn't even stand up."

"What about Bradley?" Kelly screamed. "Coyne was still alive when he dragged him into the shop. That's cold-blooded murder!"

"Yeh!" Mike tugged off his scarf and threw it on the floor. "He'd been threatening Coyne for weeks. Ever since Rhys died!"

"Even called 'im a rat," Tom said. "Everyone heard 'im."

"All true," Ned agreed. "But they still aren't gonna charge 'im."

Gibbons jumped to his feet. "What a load of crap!"

"'Tis," Muff nodded. "But what'd ye expect? Bradley's a feckin' foreman."

"And an Englishman," McKenna added with a disgusted snort.

Gibbons jabbed his knife into the counter. "Then we'll get justice ourselves!"

"Calm yourselves!" Dolan raised his hands high. "We'll figure this out."

"I've got it figured out!" Gibbons's eyes flashed with hatred. "First, we get Bradley. Then Gomer James, like we shoulda done a long time ago."

"Yeh," said Tom. "That bastard's been nothing but trouble for us."

"Especially for ye." McKenna glanced down. "Would've killed ye if we hadn't shown up."

"All the more reason to kill 'im! Count me in."

"That's a terrible reason," Muff argued. "You'd be the first one they'd suspect. Besides, we can't go murderin' folks in our own backyard. Too many witnesses could identify us."

"You'd be lucky to make it to jail," said McKenna. "Modocs'd lynch ye."

"Modocs don't exercise restraint!" Gibbons screamed. "Why should we?"

"I'll tell ye why." Muff crossed his arms. "Coyne would be outraged to hear us talkin' like this. Ain't even buried and here we are defiling everything he stood for. He'd want us right back on the picket line, fightin' the bosses, not the Welsh. Heck, there's still plenty of 'em fightin' side by side with us. With a little unity, we can still win this thing." He grinned playfully. "And Coyne's gonna help us."

"What?" Kelly cried. "Are ye drunk?"

"Sober as a judge." Muff leaned back with his hands on his hips. "If they find Bradley guilty, it'll make the coal companies look like the murderin' thugs they are. That means more public support for us. And if they don't, Coyne will still be a martyr. Everyone knows what kind of man he was. When we carry his coffin through town, thousands'll show up. It'll be inspirational! Even the Welsh and Dutch will march with us."

"Hear, hear!" Dolan cheered.

McKenna walked to the bar and grabbed the whiskey bottle from Mike.

"Don't worry," he whispered. "We'll get our justice. Once things've cooled off a bit."

Chapter 32
Mahanoy City
Wednesday, March 17, 1875

Muff looked presidential in his stovepipe hat and frockcoat, waving to the crowd from the Opera House balcony, flanked on either side by marble columns that glistened in the morning sun. The temperature was close to freezing, but Mike was warm, packed snugly between Tom and Johnny Morris, with McKenna in front of them, and hundreds of other Hibernians, adorned in green, swaying like the blades of fresh spring grass sprouting from the moist, earthy-smelling hills. They completely filled Main Street from Centre to Pine, blocking the entrance to Knapp's market, and clogging the boardwalk in front of the Grand Central Hotel. Most remarkable of all was the shiny black hearse parked beneath the balcony, with its white curtains pulled back, and the bright red lettering on the casket.

"What's it say?" Mike asked, edging closer to peek inside.

McKenna removed his cap and lowered his head. "Monopoly. Rest in Peace."

"Good riddance!" Tom laughed.

Morris feigned a pout. "Have some respect for the dead."

Mike shoved his hands into his pockets, wishing it were true. The Reading now owned nearly every coll'ry in Schuylkill County. They controlled transport for the entire state. A year and a half into the depression, with hundreds of failed coll'ries and railroads, the Reading had somehow managed to expand, gobbling up its competitors, waiting calmly as the strike idled half its mines. And Gowen, worth millions, unwilling to pay 'em a measly buck twenty-five a day.

A trumpet blared. Muff raised his hands above his head, waiting for the cheering to subside.

"Friends and fellow Hibernians. Each year, on March 17, we march through Mahanoy City to honor the life of our patron Saint

Patrick, kidnapped by pirates and brought to Ireland as a slave, where he fought bitterly for his freedom, and for the rights and dignity of all people everywhere. His life is an inspiration to all of us here today, fighting for our own rights and dignity."

"Huzzah!"

"Risking martyrdom, he traveled the land, spreading his message of peace and love. In so doing, he drove the snakes from Ireland. Just last month, many of yiz were at the wake of another martyr, Edward Coyne, who also spread a message of peace and love. But his snakes are still here. Relaxing in leather armchairs, smoking fat cigars within the halls of the Anthracite Board of Trade. It was *they* who snuffed his life. And *they* who must pay!"

"Boo!" the crowd roared, rattling the windows of the Opera House. On the blackened hillside behind it, the smokestacks of Hill's breaker seemed to sputter in agreement.

"But his death was not in vain," Muff continued, lifting his hands like a priest, though he resembled Abe Lincoln, with his chinstrap beard and deep, honest eyes. "Within a week of his passing, Hyde Park joined the strike."

"That's right!" someone yelled.

"Then both unions agreed to support us."

"Long live Coyne!" McKenna hollered.

"Huzzah! Huzzah!"

"Thanks to Coyne, and your hard work," Muff continued. "Nearly every miner in Pennsylvania has joined the strike. Most of Reading's railroad employees have joined us, too! They're runnin' outa coal! Steel mills are shuttin' down!"

The crowd erupted in cheers. They waved little green flags. Trumpets blew. Pipes trilled. Snare drums rattled. Mike's body quivered with energy. He glanced down the street, where stores and restaurants gave way to fancy homes, at families huddled nervously on their balconies as if expecting a riot.

"There's more!" Muff gripped the banister and nodded to the crowd. "As many of you know, I've just returned from the Anti-Monopoly Convention in Harrisburg, where miners joined with other tradesmen. Grangers, too. And small, independent coal operators who want nothing to do with Franklin Benjamin Gowen and his corrupt combination. We've formed a new party to represent the interests of workingmen, the Greenback Party, which supports an eight-hour workday and opposes the use of troops to put down strikes."

"Huzzah!"

"But most relevant to us, the independent mine operators are uniting with us to pressure the legislature to end the Reading's monopolization of the coalfields. Governor Hartranft's already received our demands. He's convening a commission to investigate the Reading."

There was another explosion of cheers, this time so loud and prolonged it rattled Mike's bones. He got so giddy he teetered into McKenna, whose solid frame kept him on his feet.

"And now, I want to introduce a young man I met at the convention. Mr. Jack O'Brien, from Tamaqua. A true anti-monopolist, if ever there was one."

Applause reverberated down the street. The bells in the Humane's firehouse clanged. Two men waved from its tower, which poked up behind the Opera House like a witch's hat.

O'Brien pushed up his sleeves as he surveyed the crowd. He was stocky, shorter than Muff, with wavy hair that swirled like fiery orange clouds at sunset.

"Whatta we want?"

"'Seventy-four wages!" the crowd hollered back.

"When do we want it?"

"Now!"

"That's right, brothers. We got Gowen against the ropes and the governor on our side!"

"Huzzah!"

"I heard someone's been derailing coal trains." He spoke like a father to a naughty child, stone-faced, stern. "Dumping hopper cars, too."

"Damned right!" McKenna shouted.

Tom gave Mike a shove. "See?"

Mike's pulse sped up. He pictured them up at Fowler's Station, spragging the tracks above Yatesville. It had been so easy. Back in bed with an alibi before the train even got there.

"That's the spirit!" O'Brien grinned mischievously. "Make the Reading bleed!"

"Hell yeh!"

"Now, before we march, I'd like to recite my poem, 'Strike Against Monopoly!'"

You sons of liberty awake,
Your hearths and altars are at stake;
Arise, arise, for freedom's sake,
And strike against monopoly!

What soul but scorns the coward slave;
But liberty is for the brave;
Our cry be union or the grave,
And down with usurping monopoly!

Bowing, he stepped back, yielding to Muff, who waited for the applause to die down.

"Brothers," Muff said. "Father McFadden and the city authorities fear we'll be violent. They've called us Molly Maguires. Communists. Every name in the book. But we aim to show 'em that we're clean, upstanding citizens, honoring our Holy Saint Patrick, as we've done for hundreds of years. So, anyone who gets drunk or unruly will be stripped of his membership in our hallowed organization. Also, remember that Main Street divides the city. There'll likely be hecklers. You must resist the urge to engage in sectarian shenanigans. I know you're angry about all the Modoc violence against us, but we must stand up to the mark like men, and not act like boys."

"Follow me," said McKenna, climbing up the Opera House steps. "We'll get a head count, then join the parade. No point rushing. Shendo's the caboose of this train."

The Saint Clair drum and fife band led the march up Main Street, past the Grand Central Hotel, where onlookers waved green ribbons from the balcony. The hearse was right behind them, followed by row upon row of Hibernians marching ten abreast. First the Mannoy division. Then Gilberton, Girardville, and Hazleton. Tamaqua. Tuscarora. Delano. And finally Shenandoah,

with their own marching band and choir singing:
Come all you jolly colliers, wherever you may be,
I pray you will attention give and listen unto me,
I have a doleful tale, and to relate it I will strive—
About the great suspension in eighteen seventy-five.

Now two long months are nearly o'er—that no one can deny,
And for to stand another month we are willing for to try,
Our wages shall not be reduced, tho' poverty do reign,
We'll have the seventy-four basis, boys, before we'll work again.

"Fifteen hundred!" Morris proclaimed, as the procession passed the First National Bank, where three C&I stood guard.

"You're crazy!" Tom spat tobacco at his feet. "There's at least two thousand of 'em."

McKenna clapped him on the back. "Seventeen hundred and thirty-seven, to be precise."

"Who cares?" Mike said, tapping his foot. "Parade's gettin' away from us."

Gibbons and Ned, who were at the end of the procession, had just tipped their caps at the yellow dogs, mockingly, and were turning the corner. Mike chased after them, catching up near the alley. The chimbly of the gasworks was visible behind the houses. Two blocks ahead, the front of the march was already turning down Catawissa.

"Where's everyone else?" Gibbons asked him.

Mike glanced over his shoulder nearly smacking heads with Tom.

"Right here," said McKenna, panting, cross-eyed, a few steps behind them.

"Ye drunk?" Ned asked.

"Nah. Just winded. Say, ye pick up Gomer James yet?"

"Yeh. But he had an alibi. Had to let 'im go."

"Ye kidding?" Mike said, his voice rising in volume. "Sonofabitch shot Tully right in jail!"

"Said he was gonna kill us next!" Tom added, rubbing his temples.

Ned shrugged. "He's been sayin' that forever."

"Nearly succeeded, remember? I couldn't work months!"

"Shoulda killed 'im long ago!" Gibbons growled. "For Eddie!"

"For Coyne!" Mike added.

"And you'd all be hanging from the gallows," said McKenna.

Gibbons balled up his fists. "We're just gonna let 'im kill all our buddies, one by one?"

"We'll get 'im," McKenna whispered. "When the time's right."

"Psst," Morris hissed, as they came to the church. Father McFadden stood outside, with his arms crossed and brows wrinkled.

They marched past him silently, all the way to Mahanoy Street, when Morris finally broke the silence. "So, why'd he shoot him? Wasn't Tully already in jail for stabbing Bradley?"

Tom punched him in the arm. "'Cause he's an asshole, ye big jamoke!"

"He was sending us a message," said Gibbons. "Modocs can get ye anywhere. Even jail."

McKenna offered a deep sigh. "It was dumb what Tully did. Right in the open, too. Poor sonofabitch knew Coyne longer 'n any of us."

Gibbons started to speak, but was interrupted by a chorus of boos. Dozens of men were leaning from the windows of the clapboard rooming houses that lined the street, shaking their fists and spitting onto the parade. A crowd of Welshmen stood outside Davies Tavern, beside the Citizens' fire engine, screaming epithets.

"Spud niggers!"

"Donkeys!"

"Go back to Shendo, you filthy micks!"

Hulking over them was Bully Bill Thomas, a big clumsy bear, with his square face and narrow squinty eyes, and trousers drooping despite his leather suspenders. He snorted, then hawked up a tremendous wad of snot, flinging it into the middle of the parade.

Gibbons took a step toward him, but McKenna grabbed his shoulder.

"Remember what Muff said?"

"We can't let 'im get away with that."

"We won't." McKenna flashed a hard smile. "He's the one's gonna pay for Coyne's life."

Mike glanced at Tom, then Morris and Gibbons. They all looked stunned.

"He ain't the one that killed Coyne! He ain't the one threatening us!"

McKenna raised a brow.

"Was it justice when he shot Danny Daugherty, day after the judge acquitted 'im? Or when he killed James Dugan for daring to walk on the Southside? Or sapping Mickey Clarke and leavin' 'im for dead? Cocksucker's worse than Gomer James. But easier to get. He ain't expectin' us. And we're less likely to be recognized over here."

Tom kept swallowing, running his hand through his hair.

"How's that help us? James'll just come after us even harder!"

"Not likely." McKenna chuckled. "He'll be dead."

"Huh? How?"

"Mannoy boys, of course. We solve their Modoc problem for them. They solve ours for us."

Morris pressed his lips into a fine line and slowly shook his head. Gibbons nodded, but with a rigidity, as though he was not fully committed. Tom looked like he was trying not to have the runs.

Mike glanced at Bully Bill, who was playing with the nozzle of the firehose, holding it to his eye like a little boy with a toy gun. At the moment, he seemed far less dangerous than McKenna, whose plan was completely deranged.

"What's this?" Gibbons hollered. "They think they can extinguish the flames of our passion?" He picked up a rock and headed toward the engine.

McKenna grabbed his collar. "Later, Jack. When he's not expecting it. When there ain't witnesses. When we have alibis."

The Citizens pumped the brake handles. Bully Bill tightened his grip on the nozzle.

"Here's how we deal with rats, like Coyne!"

Water burst from the hose, knocking marchers off their feet.

"I'll kill 'im!" yelled a toad-faced miner with a shoe-brush chin beard, breaking free from his buddies who had been restraining him. He bolted toward Bully Bill. A bunch of Welshmen tried to block his way, but he kept going, like he intended to plow right through.

Bully Bill handed off the hose. Pulled out a gun. Fired.

The man fell, as the shot echoed through the narrow street.

For a moment, no one moved, as if they were all weighing Muff's warning with what had just happened. Surely, they'd be justified. They outnumbered the Modocs a hundred to one. But before they could react, the doors of Davies Tavern swung open and ten C&I spilled out. Each had a rifle with a bayonet.

"What's going on?" barked the captain.

"He threatened to kill me," Bully Bill pleaded. "Everyone heard him."

Mike stared in disbelief. The sonofabitch was gonna get away with it! Suddenly, McKenna's demented plan seemed reasonable. Necessary. Bully Bill *was* worse than Gomer James. Someone had to stop him.

Gibbons's hands were twitching as though they needed someone to strangle. He gave McKenna an intense, fevered stare. "Count me in!"

"Me, too," said Mike.

"Me, too," said Morris and Tom.

All the way home, Mike couldn't stop rubbing his hands. He'd really done it, now. Backed himself into another stupid corner he couldn't get out of. When the WBA said to arm themselves, it was for self-defense. This would be cold-blooded murder. Bully Bill never threatened any of them. But Gomer James had already tried to kill them *and* threatened to finish the job. Doing him would be self-defense. Even God could forgive that. But sneaking up on a man who didn't even know them, gunning him down in the middle of the night? That was cowardly. They'd know it was AOH, even if they didn't know which ones. Everyone would come down harder on them. Mannoy Modocs. Shendo Modocs. C&I.

Pinkertons.

"What's wrong?" Tom asked.

"McKenna's plan is shit!"

"C'mon, Mikey. He's no chancer. Every place we've robbed, every coll'ry we've vandalized, every caper planned out perfectly. Always cases the place, learns their routine, considers every possibility. What can go wrong?"

"Plenty!" Mike cleared his throat. "We could get shot. Or caught and hanged. But even if we succeed, Gomer James'll still be free. No guarantee the Mannoy boys'll get him before he gets us. If they get him at all."

"That's what worries me," Tom replied. "Let's give 'em a week. If he ain't dead by then, we'll do it ourselves."

"Alright." Mike figured they had no choice. If they didn't get James, he'd certainly get them.

"Promise?"

"Yes!"

"Remember what happened last time?"

"That was different. I never wanted to make that oath. It was wrong. This time's different. We have no choice. We don't get him, we're dead!"

Tom grasped Mike's shoulder. "Hibernian oath? Swear to cut off your right hand and lay it at the hoosegow door if you betray this pact?"

"Yes, goddamn it! Yes."

Chapter 33
Sunday, March 21, 1875

They left at three in the morning. Tom drove. Mike, Gibbons, and Morris huddled in the back beneath a wet horse blanket. The air was steamy from their breaths and smelled of rotten cheese. The only sounds were the mules clomping through the mud and the raindrops pelting their heads.

Morris peeked out from under the blanket. "What a miserable night!"

"Quit whining!" Gibbons snapped. "Conditions couldn't be better. Nothing's open. Lights're out. Everyone's home, asleep. Especially Bully Bill. Probably started drinking at noon, soon as he got outa jail. Dead drunk. Easy target."

"S-sure," Mike said, his teeth chattering. "Perfect conditions. Plenty of water to jam our guns. Mud to slip on. What more could we want?"

"Nothing," Gibbons replied. "Clouds. Raindrops. Flappin' trees. It'll cover our noise. Reduce visibility. Anyone comes out, they'll be under capes and eaves. Less likely to see us."

"I guess that makes sense," Morris said. "But there's something I gotta know." He leaned closer to Mike. "Can I marry your sister?"

"Shut up!" Gibbons hissed. "We're about to commit murder! Ye need to concentrate!"

"I-I will," Morris sputtered. "Once I know he's alright with it. Was gonna ask her today. After church. Wanna free her from Sean. Once and for all."

Mike stared in disbelief. He was the one who should be saving her from Sean, not some weasel in a fancy hat. But it would make her happy. Probably the best thing for her, actually. And he'd still get to see her. Make it easier to free the rest of his family, too. He'd only have four to move out, instead of five.

"Alright."

Morris let out a huge breath. "Really?"

"Only if you promise to give up other girls."

"Of course."

"And protect her with your life."

"Absolutely!"

"That means succeeding tonight. Ye focused?"

"Never more so!"

"Prove it," Gibbons demanded. "Repeat the plan."

"Easy." Morris sat up straighter. "I'll be on the right. Mike on the left. Guns drawn. You slide the barndoor open. Then *blam*!"

"No! No! Start shootin' *as* I'm slidin' the door."

"Th-that's what I meant."

A gust of wind rippled through the blanket. Trembling, Mike hugged his knees together, convinced they'd never pull this off.

When they arrived in Shoemaker's Patch, all ten houses were dark. Tom remained in the driver's seat for a quick getaway. Everyone else climbed out and headed toward the stable, where Bully Bill lived, taking slow, deliberate steps through gloppy mud that smelled like a latrine. The wind whistled through the trees, as raindrops pinged their cheeks. A chorus of frogs chirped from an invisible pond.

Mike took another step. A twig snapped beneath his boot. He froze until the frogs started chirping again. Then he proceeded even more cautiously, testing the ground with his toe before applying his full weight. Hearing nothing but the squeak of mud and his own heavy breathing, he continued toward the stable.

Gibbons waited at the door. Morris pulled out his weapon and crept beside him.

Mike gripped his gun and moved stiffly into position. His heart was racing and his hands shook so much he doubted he could hit a bear from three feet away.

With his fingers on the doorhandle, Gibbons raised his gun.

One.

They cocked their revolvers.

Two.

Took aim.

Three!

Shots rang out before it was halfway open.

Mike ducked to the side, firing blindly into the barn.

There was a thud. He hit something, but couldn't tell what.

Gibbons pressed himself against the door, peeked inside, then beckoned.

Mike couldn't move. His throat seared. He pictured Uncle Sean with his neck slashed. A stranger holding him together with a rag.

Reaching up, shakily, he touched his throat. It was wet. Blood!

He got dizzy and nearly collapsed. This was not how he was supposed to die!

"C'mon," Gibbons growled, stepping inside.

C'mon? With a bullet in his throat?

Morris gave him a pitying look.

Mike licked his finger. It tasted salty, not bloody. Just sweat and raindrops.

Shuddering, he forced the saliva down his throat and peered around the corner.

A dead mule. Bill's head, peeking up behind it. A gun barrel propped on its back.

CRACK!

Gibbons jumped.

Mike fired.

Bully Bill's head jerked back.

Vomit exploded from Mike's mouth.

"Let's go!" Morris cried, tugging at his sleeve.

Shaking his head, Mike brushed his hand away. Took a few deep breaths. Then started to run. Tom was already pulling away, the mules braying in protest. Lights came on. Men ran out. Gibbons jumped into the wagon. Then Morris.

"Hey, you!" someone shouted. "Stop!"

Mike tried to speed up, but his boots were heavy with mud. He pulled at the air like it was palpable. He reached for the tailboard. Heaved himself in. Right on top of Morris.

"Quicker!" Gibbons huffed.

Tom slapped the mules' haunches with the reins. "Sounded like a battlefield back there."

No one spoke. It smelled like mud and sweat.

"Well?" Tom asked. "Was it a clean job?"

"Shut up and drive!" Gibbons snapped.

Morris peered over the back of the wagon. "I think we lost 'im." His voice was shaky.

"Good," Mike groaned, clutching himself, rocking side to side.

It hardly seemed important now. He'd just killed a man! A mule, too. Even if they didn't get caught, he'd have to live with that the rest of his life. But how could they *not* get caught? So many loose ends. Maybe no one saw their faces, but they must've noticed their wagon. Knew there were four of 'em. Saw they were driving toward Shendo. Could've guessed they were AOH. And they still had three miles to go. Plenty of time to be caught. Even if their alibi with Muff satisfied the cops, there'd still be the Modocs. Gomer James would know it was them.

Mike sat up. They were approaching Robinson's Patch. It was completely dark. No one was stirring. Maybe they wouldn't get caught.

"Well?" Tom asked, peering back at them.

"We got away, didn't we?" Gibbons laughed, clapping Mike on the back. "And muleboy, here, saved my life."

"Mule killer," Mike muttered, his voice cracking.

No one seemed to hear.

"He shot back?" Tom asked.

"Shot first," said Morris. "Like he was expecting us."

"Someone warn him?" Tom laughed nervously.

"Impossible," said Gibbons. "Nobody knew about it except us. And Muff and McKenna. None of yiz mentioned it to anyone, did ye?"

"Nah," Tom replied. "Musta heard ye outside. Bastard probably sleeps with a gun by his head. Been shot a dozen times, hasn't he?"

"Guy's inhuman," Gibbons agreed.

"So?" Tom said. "He walkin' away this time?"

"Nah." Mike stared at his hands, clasped in his lap. Bastard would never walk again, thanks to him. Then again, he'd shot first. Deserved it. "I got 'im right between the eyes!"

"Must be dead," Gibbons said. "Mannoy boys sure will be happy."

"Not as happy as I'll be," Tom said. "Once they take care of their end of the bargain."

"*If* they do," Morris corrected.

Chapter 34
Wednesday, March 31, 1875

Mike relaxed into the cushioned backrest and kicked out his legs, enjoying the vibrations as they rattled down the tracks. It resembled a millionaire's coach, with its shiny brass lamps hanging goosenecked from the wood paneling and the green curtains tied back with gold sashes. Red carpet ran down the aisle. It smelled of clean leather and pipe smoke. McKenna sat on his right, sucking a pipe. Tom was on his left, pretending to doze, uncharacteristically quiet ever since Morris proposed to Tara. Li'l Bill sat across from them, next to Gibbons, gripping the bench with both hands, his face as white as a sheet. He probably thought the train would jump the tracks and tumble down the mountainside, it was jerking and rocking so much. How could he know it always did that? He'd never been on a train before.

McKenna leaned forward and patted his knee. "Just a few more minutes till Mannoy."

"And Black Diamond's the best line in the country," Gibbons added, in an uncharacteristically soothing tone.

Bill's eyes hardened. "I ain't scared."

"Me neither." Gibbons chuckled. "We've been through much worse, right?"

Fortunately, Bill had no idea what Gibbons was talking about and Gibbons was smart enough not to elaborate. First the gunshot at the Kohinoor picket, and then nearly getting shot again by Bully Bill. But that was nothing compared with Bully Bill's luck. Only ten days since they supposedly killed the brute and he was already out of the infirmary. What a waste of time that had been.

McKenna pulled out a pouch of tobacco and filled his bowl. "By the way, the governor's approved some of our anti-monopoly resolutions."

"Yes!" Tom pumped his fist. "Crush the monopoly and the strike's over!"

"Noo," Bill groaned.

"What's wrong?" Mike asked. "Don't ye wanna start eatin' again?"

"Sure, but fighting the bosses is funner!"

Mike chuckled. "It's nice havin' ye on the picket line with us. Nice ye ain't droopy-eyed no more, too!"

Shrugging, Bill leaned back and closed his eyes. He looked calm and relaxed. The color had returned to his face, which, for the first time Mike could remember, was clean, and free of scabs and scratches.

Gibbons got up and staggered to the window.

McKenna leaned closer to Mike. "Mannoy's called off the deal."

Tom licked his lips as if he'd just been offered the last piece of pie. He'd wanted to kill Gomer James from the start. Now they had permission.

Mike wasn't so happy. Bully Bill's survival meant he was no longer a murderer. Killing James would turn him right back into one. Not killing him would put him in James's crosshairs. Either way, he was doomed.

"Almost there," Gibbons called, barely audible over the screeching wheels. "There's Mannoy Station. Coupla passengers beneath the awning. Shit, two yellow dogs!"

Mike tried to get up to see for himself, but stumbled as the train decelerated. He crawled to Gibbons's seat. "Bill, stay here till we've disarmed 'em."

"I can take care of myself!"

The train let out a long, throaty whistle.

"Fine! Take care of yourself. *After* we've disarmed 'em."

"It's alright," said McKenna. "We need a decoy. Billy, can ye fake a fall?"

"Sure!"

Mike sat straight up. Bill was *his* brother. *He* was the one who should be making this decision. Not the crazy sonofabitch who nearly got them killed at Shoemaker's Patch. Using his brother as cop bait was pure madness. He was a damned cripple who never followed directions. And he certainly couldn't run away if things went wrong. Yet the more McKenna talked, the more Bill's body perked up and confidence gleamed in his eye. He actually seemed to be paying attention for once. Mike relaxed back into his seat, smiling. This was exactly why he had brought Bill along in the first place, to prove that a feller didn't need two legs to make a difference, to be a man.

Scooting closer, he laughed and threw an arm over Bill's shoulder.

"You'll be perfect! You're great at falling."

Before Bill could respond, the train stopped moving. McKenna gave him a little kick.

"It's time."

The two of them moved into position at the door. Mike and the others rushed to the windows. The C&I were beneath the awning, chatting, while people bought tickets and snacks, and porters loaded their trunks. There was a sausage wagon near the tracks, but all Mike could smell was the burnt-metal odor of the brakes, and a hint of creosote.

"It ain't gonna work," he muttered. "They ain't looking."

McKenna stuck his thumb and finger between his lips, let out a shrill whistle, then ducked back inside the train.

A lady in a flowery dress pointed at Bill, who was leaning on his crutches in the doorway, teetering like a decrepit old man. One of the cops took a tiny step toward him, then stopped and glanced around, as if looking for a porter, but they were all helping other passengers.

Bill cautiously lowered one of his crutches to the next step. He planted the other beside it and slowly swung his leg down, pausing to steady himself. He took another wobbly step, but his arms started to shake.

The cop grabbed a stool from a cart and ran to the train, placing it at the bottom stair.

Mike pulled out his gun.

A crutch slipped from Bill's hand. He started to fall.

The cop lunged.

McKenna leapt from the train, knocking the cop to the ground.

"Quick, someone get his gun!"

Tom jumped down and removed the revolver from his holster.

The other cop ran over. His gun was pointed at Tom.

"Nobody move!"

McKenna looked up, smiling. "I think you're outnumbered."

The cop squinted at the train car. Six men with guns aimed at him, including Mike.

"Drop your weapon," said Gibbons, stepping off the train.

The gun fell to the ground.

"Kick it to me."

Gibbons picked it up and jabbed it in the cop's back. "March!"

"Ye, too!" McKenna yanked his yellow dog to his feet, shoving him toward the awning.

Mike climbed down and helped Bill up. He brushed the dust from his brother's torso and handed him a crutch. "Ye alright?"

"Never better!" He beamed like a cat with a mouse dangling from his teeth.

Porters and passengers stared as they cuffed the cops to a pillar near the ticket window.

Miners filed off the train jeering.

"Yellow dogs!"

"Scum!"

"Throw 'em down a mineshaft!"

"Calm yourselves!" Mike yelled. "We ain't murderers."

"They're feckin' yellow dogs!" cried a man with a pick. "They're starvin' our children!"

"They kill miners!" screamed his buddy, waving a pistol. "Killin' dogs ain't murder!"

Several broke free from the crowd and headed toward the pillar, nearly knocking Bill over. Mike's hand shot out to catch his brother, who looked away, as if embarrassed to know him.

Damned fool was all grit and no common sense. Killing a C&I would be a disaster. It would bring in the militia. Every AOH man in Schuylkill County would get arrested. The strike would end at the barrel of a cannon.

"Wait!" Mike screamed. "Gowen's the one starvin' us! "Killin' yellow dogs won't change that. We gotta shut down Gowen's coll'ries."

"Shut 'em down!" someone hollered back.

"Let's go," yelled a porter, dropping his bags at the feet of a trembling old woman with curly white hair and a funny-looking dog with matching fur. "Hill's Coll'ry's right around the corner."

The man with the pick shrugged and followed, singing:
Blackleg scum are worse than bums
Wherever they may be
Traitors to us, a disgrace to their race
And the rest of society

"Follow me," said Gibbons.

He led them through a door behind the ticket counter, which let them out across the street from the coll'ry. The hillside was crawling with men. Every pump and engine had been shut off. Not a single swirl of smoke in the air, which was fragrant with wild onions and mint, and harmonious with cheerful banter and singing. Five boys were hucking rocks at the breaker's windows, while two men with hatchets chipped away at the headframe.

Jamie McAllister stood on a fencepost in front, scanning the crowd. Despite his precarious position, he looked confident and relaxed. "Hello, Schuylkill!"

The crowd cheered.

"Looks like five thousand of ye out there!"

"Ten!" someone yelled.

"Even better. We appreciate the support."

"Tomorrow, Hazleton!" hollered a man in a stovepipe hat.

"Sure," Jamie said. "But today we're doin' Mannoy. Southside's where you're needed."

"What about Bowman's?" McKenna called out. "Shoemaker's? Ellengowen?"

"Already shut down! Mannoy lads got this entire hillside covered. Got a coupla coppers locked up in the storage shed, too."

Bill's eyes lit up.

"Alright!" McKenna yelled. "To the Hartford!"

"Quick," Gibbons said. "Back through the station."

They rushed back in and came out the other side, near the front of the march, on Main Street, which was eerily quiet. The First

National Bank had all its blinds shut, even on the second floor. The Grand Central Hotel had none of the usual carriages out front. Across the street, Knapp was frantically boarding up the windows to his grocery store.

They marched past City Hall and Pine Street, which was barricaded on one side by the Citizens' fire engine, and on the other by the Humane's. Both fire crews stood proudly beside their rigs, waving their helmets over their heads. The crowd erupted into a long, noisy cheer that rattled windows. Mike felt a rejuvenating contentment surging through him, as though it was a dream in which he could fly. He bumped shoulders with Bill and Tom, who staggered like drunks. This burg was theirs! If they could pull this off in a few more places—Shendo, Hazleton, Tamaqua—they'd force Gowen's hand. Even if he wanted to hold out, the bankers and businessmen would never let him. They'd all go broke. They'd make him cut a deal.

Rising up on his tiptoes, Mike could see the Hartford breaker. Two C&I at the top window, rifles aimed at the marchers. Another near the smokestack and one more in front of the engine room. Others were scattered about the hillside above the breaker. And Captain Linden, with a long brass pipe, the size of a fire nozzle, held to his mouth.

"Men!" His voice boomed, like a gunshot in a canyon. "Turn around now and disperse!"

McKenna pulled out his gun. "I'm gonna get that Pinkerton sonofabitch!"

Gibbons started to reach for his, too, but then froze, as if having second thoughts.

Mike's toes curled inside his boots. The C&I were protected by buildings. Their rifles had longer range. The two in the breaker would be impossible to hit. They could continue sniping till every one of 'em was dead. He had to do something.

He charged forward and grabbed McKenna's wrist.

McKenna yanked his arm back. The gun went off. Everything froze.

No sound. No movement.

Nothing but the ringing in Mike's ears. The sulfurous smoke, curling from the gun barrel. The spots, pulsing before him. An overwhelming sense of dread. And then gunshots!

He turned and fled. Zigzagging past fallen men. Wild energy coursing through his veins.

Tom and Gibbons were scurrying Bill away. Toward the alley behind Saint Paul's. The only sensible move. At least they'd have buildings protecting them. Everyone else was pushing up Main Street, a herd of cattle funneling through a chute to the slaughter.

When he caught up, Bill was leaning against a wall, mouth agape. Tom was sitting on the steps, soaked with sweat. Gibbons was crouching, hands on his thighs, panting like a dog. Mike plopped down beside Tom, equally winded, the pounding in his ears even louder than before. Fortunately, none of them had been shot. At least not yet. But C&I could be roving the streets, chasing men down, looking for ringleaders. Especially him.

He jumped back to his feet. "We gotta go!"

"He's right," Gibbons said. "To the depot. Get Billy on a train back to Shendo."

"That's ten blocks!" Tom said. "Let's hide in Saint Canicus. It's right around the corner. Head back when things calm down?"

Gibbons let out a hard sigh. "Things ain't calmin' down. Silliman Guards're probably already sweeping through town. Besides, Father McFadden won't let us in. He thinks we're all Molly Maguires."

"I can make it to the depot," Bill said. "Ye saw how quick I am."

"What about McKenna?" Tom asked. "We can't just leave 'im. He'll get shot, or arrested."

"Wanna get shot, too?" Gibbons replied. "Or arrested?"

"No."

"McKenna'll survive. Always does."

Mike peered around the corner. Soldiers were marching toward them.

"We gotta hide!"

They ducked back behind the church and waited. No one spoke. They hardly moved. But their breathing still seemed dangerously loud, like they had brass speaking horns at their lips.

After ten or fifteen minutes, Gibbons took another peek, but immediately pulled his body back in, indicating with hand gestures that there were still two clusters of soldiers on the street.

They waited another hour before it seemed safe to sneak out. They took South Alley to First. Both streets were narrow. Houses close together. Hard for anyone to see 'em. But when they had to cross Pine, Gibbons motioned them to stop.

"Could be trouble. Billy, ye hobble out first. Innocent and feeble. Like back at the depot. See if the coast is clear."

Bill took one step out, then froze. "It's McKenna!"

"Where?" Tom said.

"Across the street. In the schoolyard. Talkin' to that cop from the breaker."

Mike sidestepped around Bill to look. He rubbed his eyes, as he tried to make sense of it. McKenna hated Linden, yet here they were, talking as if they were buddies.

"It can't be! Wasn't he just trying to kill 'im?"

Gibbons grabbed his shoulder, pulling him back into the alley.

"Quiet! Everyone!"

He glanced at the school, then ducked back into the alley.

"Other way, fellers. We'll take our chances on Catawissa."

"We can't leave 'im with that butcher!" Tom said. "We gotta help 'im!"

Gibbons gave him a long, pained stare. "He's beyond our help, Tommy."

"Beyond our help?"

Mike had the urge to slap Tom to wake him up.

"He's a spy, goddamn it!"

Bill was leaning on his crutches, blinking rapidly.

Tom's eyes squished together. "McKenna?"

"Think about it," Mike said. "Who else coulda tipped off Bully —?"

"Gotta go," Gibbons interrupted. "Without 'im seeing us. Get back to Shendo. Figure out a plan before we're all arrested."

Gibbons's words rang in Mike's ears. He could barely move. His first few steps were like walking on sponges. What kind of plan could save them now? That Judas knew every detail of every crime they'd committed. Hell, the sonofabitch planned most of 'em himself. It'd be worse than a confession!

"Faster," Gibbons hissed. "Help me with your brother."

They each shimmied under one of Bill's shoulders and started to jog, a giant insect dangling helplessly between them. Tom ran ahead of them with the crutches. The cool breeze against Mike's sweaty arms, the slap of earth against his soles, was like waking from a dream. Everything suddenly became clear. They'd have to kill McKenna, and that wouldn't be easy with the Silliman Guards mustered, and the C&I looking for vengeance. But they had no choice. If he testified against them, they'd hang for sure.

Without warning, Tom stopped. They barreled right into him.

"Don't move!" came a gruff voice.

Two soldiers stepped around the corner and stood over them, rifles out, bayonets pointing at their faces. They wore the gray uniforms and frying pan caps of the Silliman Guards. One of 'em had a pencil-thin mustache. The other had smooth, baby-pink skin.

Mike closed his eyes and groaned. This was it. The beginning of the end. Jail today. The gallows tomorrow. Bill, too, the poor helpless bastard.

Another soldier appeared behind them. He had mop-like epaulets on his shoulders and matching mutton chops on his cheeks. Probably a captain or something.

"On your bellies!" he commanded.

Mike dropped onto his hands and knees, then flattened himself. One of the soldiers confiscated his gun. Another disarmed Tom.

"Rioters," the captain snorted.

"Actually," said Gibbons. "We were heading home. Didn't want any trouble on account of the boy's leg."

"Where's home?" the captain asked, his voice easing.

"Shenandoah," Mike mumbled.

"Long walk for a cripple," snickered one of the younger soldiers.

"Enough!" the captain barked.

"I can handle it," Bill said. "I got grit!"

"I'm sure you do," the captain laughed. "Got any weapons on you?"

"Just my crutches."

The captain searched him anyway. "Promise not to use 'em for anything but walking?"

Mike prayed Bill wouldn't get smart.

"Promise, sir. I just wanna go home."

"Alright, then. Smith? Hobbs?"

"Yes, sir?"

"March 'em to the edge of town. Make sure they leave. Any trouble along the way, shoot first. Jail any survivors. The Easton Grays're on their way. Every one of 'em's killed plenty of savages and Confederates. Won't have any scruples shooting a few rioters."

Chapter 35
Wednesday, March 31, 1875

The entire walk back, everything was a dismal blur. The hillside. The houses. The other folks on the road, if there were any. Mike couldn't remember. Moving was better than standing still. Destroying something would've been even better. McKenna! But how? That sonofabitch was wily. And a cop. Who knew how many other spies he had working for him? How much he'd already told Linden? Mike wanted to ask Gibbons if he had a plan, but no one had spoken for the past two miles. Tom was staring at the ground. Gibbons straight ahead. The only sound was Li'l Bill, hobbling behind them, whimpering with fatigue.

Finally, Mike stopped and turned, waiting for him to catch up.

"Hop on my back. Tom'll carry your crutches."

Bill complied, but he sure didn't like it.

"Why're we running away? We should go back and kill 'im!"

Gibbons turned his head sharply. "Pipe down! Ye know the hills have ears."

Bill became very still, except for his Adam's apple, which bobbed against Mike's neck.

"Sonofabitch lied to us. Pretended to be our friend. You're all goin' to jail 'cause of him."

"We'll be fine." Gibbons's tone softened. "Just gotta get to Muff before he does."

"How?" Mike stopped to readjust Bill. "Those soldiers held us forever. He's probably already there. Filling Muff with lies."

Tom picked up a stone and threw it against a tree. "Fuck!"

"Even if he beats us there," Gibbons said, speaking to the air. "We'll convince Muff otherwise. The evidence is overwhelming."

Sweat dripped down Mike's flanks. He staggered under the weight, which seemed a hundred times more than just Bill, as though he was carrying a house that was crumbling apart, trying to keep his family from tumbling out. How long would it take to get arrested? How long until they were hanged? Shit, with what McKenna knew, even Johnny Morris would go to prison. Tara would lose her brother *and* her husband-to-be. Hannah would lose her boyfriend *and* her father! So many lives ruined. And for what? Gomer James and Bully Bill were still alive. Uncle Sean was still alive. Franklin Gowen had won. Anyone who wasn't arrested would have to return to work at wages half what they were a year ago, and their babies would still starve.

Gibbons stopped. "Lemme take a turn. You look fagged."

They made it to Uncle Sean's by dusk, but dropping Bill off gave Mike little relief. The heavy twilight sky pressed down on him like a giant boot squishing a bug. His limbs were too heavy to move. He kept falling behind.

"Just a few more blocks," Gibbons said. "Muff'll know what to do."

Of course he would. He had even more to lose than they did, with all the dirt McKenna had on him. Plus, he knew McKenna better than anyone, including his weak spots.

But as they got closer, Mike saw that something wasn't right. The tavern was dark. No one was lingering outside. No raucous voices or clanking glass.

Mrs. Lawler let them in. She was holding a candle. Her eyes were dead, her lips were trembling, and her hair looked as though it hadn't been brushed in days.

Mike reached for her hands. "Wh- what's wrong?"

"He's been shot."

"Jeez, God. Is he. . .?"

"Clinging to life." Her voice cracked. "In his office, with Doc Luks. And Jimmy."

Gibbons ran for the stairs. Mike wanted to go with him, find out where they stood, help manage the threat, but Mrs. Lawler was sobbing so miserably he couldn't bear to leave her alone, especially with Tom, who looked as if he was ready to break something.

"Tom, go with him. I'll be up in a minute."

He reached for her shoulder, but hesitated, glimpsing Tom's narrowing eyes.

"Who did it?" Tom said.

Her head jerked back, smacking Mike in the lip.

"Ow!" they both cried.

"Ah, hell!" Tom stomped away in a huff.

She immediately buried her face against Mike's shoulder and wept. Her breathing was slow and heavy. His arms hung limply at his sides, his knuckles brushing against her warm hips, burning as if he'd just come in from the snow. Her neck smelled lemony. The odor of her armpits made him hard. He knew he should embrace her, whisper something soothing, but he was afraid he'd get even more aroused. She squeezed him closer. Her hands rubbed circles in his back. Their heartbeats thumped in unison. He wanted to feel her naked. The hard tips of her nipples. Her inner thighs. But what if Hannah walked in? She'd never speak to him again. His chin started to tremble. His thoughts were unforgivable. He wanted to pull away, find Hannah, apologize.

Where was she, anyway? She didn't get shot too, did she?

"W- what about Hannah?"

Mrs. Lawler shoved him away with an ugly laugh. "She knows nothing."

Mike wanted to lash out, tell her she was wrong, that Hannah knew a lot more than she realized and was capable of remarkable things. But then he considered the other meaning of her statement. If Hannah knew nothing, that meant she wasn't there and couldn't have been shot.

Relieved, he struggled to say something. But what could he say? He tugged on his sleeve and eyed the staircase. The silence was killing him.

"Um, I'm goin' up."

When she didn't respond, he shuffled away quickly, then bounded up the steps two at a time.

The office was hot and stuffy, with a strong smell of chemicals. Muff lay on the table with his eyes closed, motionless, like he was dead, except for a faint gurgling coming from his throat. Doc Luks, in a bloody frock, was bandaging his abdomen, while McKenna and Gibbons held him steady. Tom sat slumped in a chair, looking green.

"Anyone know who did it?" Mike asked.

"Gomer James," McKenna replied, without looking up.

Mike grabbed the top of a chair for balance. So, they *had* talked. But what could he have said? That *they* were the turncoats? That Linden was really an AOH, spying on the C&I for 'em? Nah, Muff'd never believe that bosh! And there'd be no reason to say it. He didn't know they saw him talking to Linden. Did he?

"He'll be alright." Luks wiped his hands on his frock. "Didn't hit any organs. Probably be up and about in a week. Should rest easy, now, with all that morphine in him."

Mike flopped into the chair. "When can we talk to 'im?"

"Later," Luks whispered, heading for the door. "Right now, he needs rest."

McKenna followed Luks into the hallway, flashing a dirty half-grin that made Mike shudder.

If that sonofabitch knew they were onto him, it'd be impossible to kill 'im. But how could he know? He couldn't have seen them. They were too well hidden. Maybe that crooked smile was just him being haughty. So, what was it this time? Beating up five yellow dogs single-handedly, then flying back here on the back of an eagle?

Mike chased McKenna into the hall, with Tom and Gibbons right behind him.

"How'd ye get back here so quickly?"

"Yeh!" Tom said. "How come ye ain't in jail? Or dead?"

"No thanks to either of yiz!"

"Quiet!" Gibbons hissed, spurring them toward the stairs. "Ye heard Doc. Take it into the tavern. Let Muff have a rest."

McKenna waved his hand dismissively and strutted past.

Mike aimed a finger at his back and pretended to shoot. Nodding, Tom gave the thumbs-up.

"If ye must know," McKenna said, when they reached the tavern. "Linden tried to arrest me, the feckin' Prod! But a coupla boyos pulled 'im off. We ran, of course. One of 'em got shot, but the other feller and I got away. Sheer luck. Probably half a dozen corpses back there. Another two, three dozen in the infirmary, or jail, I reckon."

"Goddamn!" Gibbons chuckled, throwing an arm over McKenna's shoulder. "You are one lucky sonofabitch." He winked at Mike and Tom. "But ain't that what I told ye fellers back in Mannoy? Jimmy always comes out on top?"

"Yeh." Tom said. "Good old McKenna. Never loses a fight."

Mike backed away slowly, as if one false step would bring in the C&I. He sat down at a table and tried to relax, waiting for Tom to return with a bottle of whiskey. Cooney was behind the bar, whistling. The pimples on his nose glistened beet red in the lamplight. Mrs. Lawler, who had been scrubbing tables with something that smelled like coal oil, stopped to smooth down her dress, as if to show everyone she was fine.

McKenna sidled up to her and whispered something into her ear that caused her to hug him and run upstairs. Then, he intercepted Tom, grabbed the bottle, and took a long swig.

"Hell of a day, eh boyos?"

Mike spat. He couldn't wait to put a bullet in that cocksucker.

Tom snatched the bottle. "Why don't ye use a glass, like a civilized person?"

"'Cause I'm a beast, Tommy." He twisted the ends of his mustache and smiled coyly. "Besides, I'm in a rush."

Gibbons cupped a hand to Mike's ear. "Courtin' Kerrigan's sister in-law."

The taste of bile filled Mike's mouth. He spat again.

McKenna tapped his visor and left.

"Must be a pretty dumb lamb," Mike muttered. "To go with that wolf."

"She's young." Gibbons chuckled. "Maybe a little naïve. But he's always had a way with the colleens."

Tom sat down, poured two glasses, and slid one toward Mike. He took a sip, then slammed his glass on the table. "I bet Kerrigan's a spy, too! Crazy sonofabitch acts just like McKenna. Always showing off. Getting into brawls. Drinking more than everyone else."

Mike reached for his whiskey and took a sip. McKenna had probably already turned Muff against them. His wife, too. Didn't he just tell her a secret? He put down his glass and stood up. "Let's go back up. Find out what Muff knows."

Tom corked the bottle. "Guess we're all beasts."

When they got back to Muff's office, Mrs. Lawler was leaning over him, whispering into his ear. He was propped against pillows, nodding, with an unfocused stare. Neither of them noticed they had visitors.

Gibbons cleared his throat.

Mrs. Lawler raised her head and looked directly at Mike, as if everything was his fault.

He walked to the window to avoid her glare, opened it, took a deep breath. Horse shit and coal smoke, but better than the nasty smell of Muff's wounds.

"How's he doin'?" Gibbons asked.

"Um." She gave Muff's hand a squeeze. "Better, I guess."

"I'm fine." Muff's voice was weak. "Is that whiskey, Tommy?"

Tom hurried to his side. "Best medicine in town!"

Mrs. Lawler cringed as he took a swallow.

"Annie, can I have a moment alone with the fellers?"

Gibbons closed the door after her.

"We're killin' 'im tonight!" Tom said. "Right?"

"Yes." Muff's eyes were half-closed, with a satisfied look on his face. "But not tonight."

"He's right." Gibbons was pacing the length of the table. "We need time to plan. Get alibis. Make sure there's no witnesses."

"Wait." Mike blocked his way. "Don't we have more urgent problems?"

Muff's eyes widened. "What could be more urgent than Gomer James?"

"McKenna." Gibbons's voice cracked as he said it.

"McKenna?"

"He's a copper," Tom said.

"Can't be. He's as dirty as us."

"Saw 'im talkin' to Linden," Gibbons said. "During the riot. They were lurkin' in the schoolyard."

"Think about it," Mike added. "How else would Bully Bill've known we were comin'?"

"Does he know ye know?"

"Not a chance," said Tom. "We were completely hidden."

"Good! Then he's *not* as urgent as James."

"Not as urgent?" Mike's voice went shrill. "He'll get us all arrested!"

"Sure," Muff agreed. "But when and how we do it makes all the difference in the world. What do ye think'll happen once the Pinkertons find out he's dead?"

Gibbons snapped his fingers. "By God, this place'll be crawlin' with coppers. Every one of us'll be nabbed. No way to kill James from jail."

"Yeh," Tom mocked. "James'll just shoot us like ducks in a pond. Same as Tully."

"But if we kill James," Mike argued, "McKenna'll know it was us. Instead of jail, we'll get the gallows!"

"No!" Tom cried. "We ain't lettin' 'em both get away!"

"Take a drink, lads," Muff said. "And stop acting like little girls. If McKenna ain't already wise to ye, we can deal with him later. But we gotta get rid of James now or we're all dead meat. Besides, last AOH meeting, the district's bodymasters put a five-hundred-dollar bounty on his head. Ye want someone else to get that prize?"

Tom's eyes sparkled, as if he was already figuring how to spend it.

Mike opened his mouth, then closed it again. What could he say? Five hundred bucks was a lot of scratch, even split two ways. More than enough to solve all his problems. But if they didn't take care of McKenna, he'd be jailed, or hanged, useless to his family.

"I know just the time and place," Muff continued. "Heckscher's Grove, Saturday after next. Welsh Firemen's picnic. He's tending bar."

"Ye crazy?" Tom said. "There'll be a hundred people there! We'll never get away with it!"

"'Course ye will. Do it after midnight, when everyone's drunk and visibility's poor. It's feckin' brilliant! They'll be so confused they won't remember a thing."

Muff continued talking, but it was completely garbled after that. All Mike could hear was the dull thud of his heartbeat, the jailor's baton rattling against the prison bars, the gallows pulley creaking in the wind. He grabbed a chair, sat down, then suddenly stood up again.

"Wait! If we're caught, can ye guarantee our families'll get the bounty?"

Chapter 36
Saturday, April 10, 1875

The tavern was as quiet as a church, with Muff gone and the doors closed to customers. It seemed almost holy, too, the way the light reflected off the mirror behind the bar, giving Cooney a saintly halo. The only sound was the faint swoosh of cards being dealt at the back of the room, where Gibbons sat beneath a cloud of cigar smoke with Johnny Morris and Big Ned Monaghan. But spiritual was not what Mike wanted at the moment.

"Wanna drink?" Cooney filled a beer glass.

Gibbons glanced over his shoulder, smiling. "It'll steady the nerves."

Mike pulled a plug of tobacco from his pocket, bit off a chew, and handed it to Tom, who pushed it away and swaggered to the bar.

"My nerves are fine. But I'll take a beer. I'm dry as hell."

Mike sat down at an empty table, savoring the smoky sweet saliva trickling onto his tongue. But rather than relaxing him, as it usually did, his headache only worsened, as did his shakiness and gloom. How could Tom be so calm when they were about to kill a man, right in front of his friends? When they were about to throw away their lives? When McKenna knew everything and could have them arrested at any moment? Nothing in the past week and a half had changed his viewpoint on the matter, not even the knowledge that his family would be looked after if they were caught or killed. And here it was, only eight. What were they gonna do for the next four hours? Get drunk and play cards?

Tom placed two beers on the table and plopped down beside him.

"Have a drink, Mikey. Gibbons is right. You'll feel better."

"I'll feel better knowing we aren't gonna hang!"

"How can ye know that?"

"By killing McKenna."

"Ye know we can't." Tom sipped his beer. "Cops would flood into town. Then how'd we get Gomer James?"

"We wouldn't." Mike spat a brown bullet onto the floor. "Not right away. But maybe all those extra cops'd keep 'im from killing us. Buy us a little time."

"C'mon, Mikey. James first." Tom grinned like a guilty little boy caught in a lie. "It's an easier job. Good warmup for McKenna. Put us in a better mood, too. The bounty! Sweet revenge! No more having to look over our shoulders!"

"What?" Mike coughed so hard he nearly lost his chew. "We'll always be looking over our shoulders! Every Modoc in Schuylkill County will be after us. Assuming McKenna doesn't get us first. By the way, where is McKenna?"

"Girardville," said Cooney. "Went to Kehoe's with Muff. Poor bastard's still too weak to carry his own luggage."

"Perfect alibi, though." Gibbons leaned back and blew a cloud of smoke.

"Just as well," said Tom. "If McKenna was here, I'd shoot 'im between the eyes."

Cooney brought over two shots of whiskey. "You fellers are gonna be fine. Just do the job. Get back here quickly. Like we planned. Cops ask, you were with us all night."

"What about Hannah?" Mike asked. "And the rest of her family?"

"Mannoy. At the O'Donnells'."

Mike relaxed back in his chair. At least she'd be safe there. Maybe he'd even get to see her again. Spend some of that bounty on her! Start living like a human! It would be dark, after all. Everyone would be drunk. How hard would it be to fire off a shot or two and disappear into the woods? They'd have masks on. They were young. Quick.

"To freedom." Tom raised his glass, nodded, and tossed back the whiskey.

Mike spit out his chew, shrugged, and swallowed his shot, too. It tasted sour after the tobacco, but more calming. The first drink always went straight to his knees, a hollow, pleasant lightness, spreading into his neck and face. His shoulders loosened. He cracked his neck. At least they had a solid alibi. "So, what happened at the rally, today? What'd Walsh have to say?"

Gibbons shook his head. "Nothing but horseshit!"

"What'd ye expect?" said Ned. "Hyde Park already back at work? Militias in Mannoy and Hazleton? Ye think he was gonna tell us to take up arms?"

"That scrawny weasel didn't even have the balls to get on stage without two bodyguards."

"He looked like a mangy dog," Ned added. "Wrinkled gray suit. Sagging eyes."

"'Men, we are beaten,'" Morris said, climbing up on a chair. He stood stoop-shouldered, with his trousers hanging low and his palms up, as if pleading for mercy. His eyes were vacant. His Adam's apple bobbed. He teetered like he was going to fall.

"That's him!" Ned laughed. "To a T!"

"'We've been forced by the desperate cries of our wives and children to accept terms we told the Coal Exchange we could never accept. Terms not much better than starvation.'" Slouching further, his chin started to tremble. "'The judge has declared us a criminal conspiracy. Our secretary got a year just for doin' our books. Never even set foot on a picket line!'"

"Fuck the WBA!" yelled Gibbons. "Let the AOH lead the strike!"

"'Be reasonable,'" Morris pleaded, in Walsh's thick, strangled voice. "'A third of Schuylkill County's under the control of the state militia. You wanna go up against Gatling guns?'"

"Better to starve free," Ned said, "than as their slaves!"

"'Ye won't starve free.'" Morris waggled his finger. "'Ye'll starve in prison, whilst your wives and children starve alone. You've all been declared criminals.'"

The chair started to wobble. Morris crashed to the floor.

Cooney's eyes widened. Everyone else broke into laughter.

Tom slapped his knee. "That was hilarious!"

"You're a genius!" Mike said, clapping.

"Yeh," said Gibbons. "If only it weren't so damned bleak."

Cooney held a glass up to the light, rubbed it with his sleeve. "At least you'll be getting a paycheck again."

"Half what we were earning before." Gibbons snorted. He glanced over his shoulder at Mike and Tom. "At least yiz two will have that bounty."

They left around midnight, sneaking out Muff's back door. They took Catherine Street to the sandlot behind Tom's house and crossed Springhouse Run, which was ankle-deep and icy cold. The sky was dark, the moonlight blunted by fog, but Heckscher's Grove was visible ahead, a fuzzy black mound of oak trees, pulsing with flickering torchlight. As they got closer, they could hear thrumming banjo music and smell grilled meat.

"Ye keep watch," Tom whispered. "I'll do the shooting. I wanna see his face when he dies."

Mike tried to look confident, but his hands were so shaky he had to press his elbows to his sides. He took a few rigid steps through the trees, peeked through the opening, and nearly fainted. The bar was all the way across the glade, past several tables full of partiers. They'd never get away with it.

Tom tied his bandana around his face and strode calmly ahead.

The bar was built against a tree, sheltered, not far from the creek. Several empty kegs and whiskey bottles were scattered on the ground. The two men at the closest table were fast asleep. The musicians were at the opposite end of the clearing and most of the revelers were facing them as they danced and drank.

Mike tied his bandana and followed, feeling slightly more confident. Nearly everyone was facing the other way. Maybe they could escape out the back without getting caught.

Tom pulled out his gun and approached the bar. Mike positioned himself in front of the tables to obscure the view.

Gomer James was filling a mug with his back to them. His sleeves were rolled up and he wore a dirty apron, and that horrible, long knife hung from his belt.

"I'll take that beer." Tom aimed the gun at his face.

James turned, his eyes widening as he realized what was happening.

Tom pulled the trigger and the Welshman crumpled to the ground. The gun's echo was still ringing in Mike's ears when Tom leaned over the counter and shot again.

The drunks awoke, rattled their heads in confusion. Others ran to the bar.

Tom had already disappeared.

The glade was shrinking, the trees moving closer. Mike edged toward an opening.

"Hey!"

Someone grabbed his wrist. Fingernails, like the jaws of a wrench biting into his arm.

Ignoring the pain, he yanked it away. His other fist, a cannonball in the man's nose.

"Yeoww!"

Mike turned and ran. Ears pounding. Throat burning.

Through the trees. Across the creek. Sweating. Suffocating.

He reached for his mask. Tried to pull it down. It wasn't there. Fuck!

Did he lose it in the struggle? Had he been recognized?

"No. No," he whimpered. "This isn't happening."

He darted down an alley. Over a fence. Through someone's yard. Away from Muff's.

If he'd been identified, that's exactly where they'd look.

He ran down Chestnut. Over another fence. Through another yard. Impossible to get enough air. Shards of glass slicing his lungs. No idea if he'd lost 'em. Looking would slow him down. Can't take the chance. Must keep going. Another alley. One more block to Muff's.

He glanced over his shoulder. No one.

Breathless, he flung open the gate. Jumped inside. Locked it shut. Fell to his knees.

Chapter 37
Sunday, April 12, 1875

Mike opened the back door and slipped inside the tavern. But instead of relief at having made it back alive, he felt dizzy and faint, with the same sense of dread he had the first few times he rode the cage down into the pit. It was completely dark inside, silent, as if everyone had given up and gone home. His alibi was shot, and Tom was probably lying by the river, dead. Just a matter of time before they got him, too.

He locked the door and floundered to the bar, bumping into tables and chairs, thinking he might be able to drink himself to death before they caught him. But as he got closer, a dark shape rose up from behind the bar and he realized they were going to deny him even this small pleasure.

Fine, if that's what God wanted, he was ready. He inhaled deeply, waited for the bang.

Instead, there was a scratch and a sizzle. A tiny flash. A hint of sulfur. Gibbons's silhouette coming into focus, lighting a candle. Big Ned. Tom! And twenty sparkling shot glasses lined up on the counter. Ned pushed one toward him.

"That took grit, marching into the middle of a Modoc party!"

Mike smiled, then broke into a laugh. He grabbed the whiskey, downed it in a gulp.

Tom quickly drained two shots.

"Whatcha gonna do with your reward?" Ned asked.

"Drink myself silly," Tom said, with a cross-eyed grin.

Gibbons scoffed. "We all know what Doyle's doing with his."

"Yeh." Mike grabbed a stool and sat down. "But—"

"You alright, Doyle?" Gibbons poked him in the shoulder.

"We're going to jail!"

"No, you're not."

"Like hell. That party was crowded. We must've been identified."

Ned laughed so hard he knocked over his whiskey.

"How could yiz've killed anyone? Ye were here with us all night. Remember?"

"Sure." Tom tapped his fingers on the counter. "Your word against theirs."

"Have another drink." Gibbons passed him a shot. "Relax. Ned's a feckin' cop. Think a jury's gonna believe a coupla drunk taffies over him?"

Ned pulled out a deck of cards and started dealing stud. "How 'bout wagerin' some of that bounty? Might help take your mind off things."

Mike didn't need any convincing. No way he was sleeping tonight. He quickly tossed down two more drinks. He immediately started to relax, but when he examined his cards, all he could see was a swirl of color, and a two-headed killer stabbing himself over and over again.

"Doyle, ye gonna bet?"

Gibbons was waving his cigar at Mike. It made him sneeze. He was about to do it again, when the door flung open. Johnny Morris burst inside, slammed it shut, and ran to the bar. His face was flushed. His eyes looked crazed.

"Muh-muh-muh," he spluttered.

"Jeez God," said Ned. "What's with you?"

"T-Tara's in jail."

Mike leapt to his feet, grabbed him by the shoulders, and shook him.

"What the hell?"

When Morris didn't respond, he pushed him away and turned toward the door, but Gibbons grabbed him by the shirt before he had gone more than two steps.

"Ye nuts? They'll arrest ye if ye go near that jail."

"I'll go," said Ned. "They all know me there."

"Ye can't," Morris said. "There's Modocs everywhere."

Gibbons released Mike's shirt and grabbed Morris by the collar.

"What the hell're ye talkin' bout!"

Poor guy looked like he was gonna crap his pants. His lips kept wiggling, but nothing came out.

Ned pushed the two apart. "C'mon, Jack. Let the feller speak."

"They've taken over Shendo! They killed Dick Finnan! Thrashed Couch's Saloon. Beat up Roberta bad. She sent me for help. Every few blocks I had to dodge another gang of Modocs. They're marching with clubs. Torches. Shootin' off their pistols. Beating anyone they can."

"I'll kill 'em!" Gibbons stomped to the bar, probably to retrieve Muff's rifle.

Ned blocked his way. "Wait."

"What about Tara!" Mike cried. "What happened?"

Morris started pacing. "The C&I were at your old place. I figured Sean finally did something stupid enough to get arrested. So, I stopped to enjoy the show. But instead of dragging him out kicking and screaming, they had Tara by the hair. 'She knows!' Sean yelled. 'She knows where he's hiding! Knows everything!'"

Mike collapsed back into his chair. This meant they'd been identified. Tara would do time because of him. And he would hang!

Tom jumped to his feet. "My mom!"

Ned gripped his shoulder so he couldn't leave

"Um." Morris cleared his throat. "Th-there's more."

Mike dragged his hands down his pants legs. How could there be more?

"Your brother's been shot."

"What!"

"He called Sean a blackleg. Attacked him with his crutch. C&I shot 'im dead."

Jumping back to his feet, Mike kicked his stool across the room. Raised another over his head and smashed it on the floor. "I'll kill 'im!"

He pulled out his revolver, figuring he'd shoot a few Modocs along the way. He was almost to the door when there was a gunshot and shattering glass.

"Get down!" Gibbons snuffed the candle.

Mike was already on the floor, crawling away from the door, sweaty, faint, disoriented. The others must've been behind the bar.

He couldn't see a thing. Nothing but a shadowy head peeking up from behind the counter. The faint shimmer of metal. Muff's rifle.

Squinting, he scooted closer. Maybe they could get to a window. Fire back.

But then came another bullet. And another. Then dozens more.

He flattened himself on the floor, unable to move. Unable to think, with all the exploding bottles, cracking wood, and flying debris. Liquid splattered the floor. It smelled of whiskey. Sweat. Musty, sulfurous smoke. If the bullets didn't kill him, the air would. But how could the bullets not kill him? They were coming from every direction. Without letup. Like the entire cavalry was attacking.

"Kill Hurley!" the mob screamed. "Kill Doyle!"

He covered his ears with his hands. This can't be happening.

"Assassins!"

Another barrage of gunfire. Heavier than before.

A bullet ricocheted off the spittoon, inches from Mike's face. He jerked away. Dove for the bar. The echo still ringing in his ears. His pulse racing. A stampede inside his skull.

"Follow me!" Gibbons ran for the staircase.

Mike clambered up after him, like a drunken weasel fleeing a pack of dogs. He flung himself into the hallway and sprawled on the floor. It sounded as if they all made it, though he couldn't be sure with the heavy breathing and gunfire. It was pitch black, until Gibbons lit a lucifer. He was sitting against the wall, visibly tense, gripping the rifle in his lap.

"Let's wait here," Ned whispered, scanning the hallway, making sure everyone was alright.

"You nuts?" Gibbons lit another lucifer. His eyes were glowing red. "Gotta get to a window. Fire back. We're AOH, goddamn it!"

Tom and Morris were nodding.

Big Ned drew himself up to full height and gazed down at them, disappointed.

"And have 'em start shooting again?"

Tipping his head to the side, Mike could hear faint voices, crickets, but no gunshots.

"Right now, they probably think they've killed everyone in

here three times over. Probably leave if we keep quiet a bit longer. Convinced Mike and Tom are dead. That they got their justice. Give us a chance to get these fellers outa town."

The voices outside grew louder. They were arguing about what to do next. Must've been an hour before they faded away, and the crickets became audible again. And then there was the cry of a whip-poor-will.

"That's gotta be Cooney!" said Gibbons.

He ran into Muff's office to peek out the window, then returned to the hallway.

"Wait here."

Seconds later, he returned with a lantern and a visibly shaken Cooney.

"You fellers're lucky to be alive!" He swallowed several times. "There's at least two different Welsh mobs runnin' 'round town. Hollerin' for Mike and Tommy's hides. Blamin' 'em for everything. From Gomer James to the wage cut."

"We gotta get outa here," Mike said.

Cooney shook his head. "They'll catch ye for sure."

"But it's suicide to stay. Everyone knows they can find us here."

"Safest place in the world right now. They musta put a hundred bullets in the tavern. Plenty up here, too. Far as they're concerned, you're already dead. They ain't comin' back."

"Isn't that what I told yiz?" Ned stood with his hands on his hips. "Now, stay away from the windows. Keep the lights out. Pack as much food as ye can. We'll let ye know when it's safe."

"I can't leave town," Mike said. "What about Tara? Li'l Bill?"

"Me neither!" Tom's eyes darted back and forth. "I gotta see my mom!"

Cooney sliced his hand through the air. "Keep your wits, lads. You can't see your families. If yiz don't leave town, you're dead meat. That ain't gonna do them any good."

"Don't worry," said Ned. "We'll make sure they're taken care of."

Tom groaned. "What about our bounty?"

Cooney slowly shook his head. "I reckon we can ask."

"Hell, yeh, we will!" Gibbons bit off the end of a cigar. "They earned it."

"And I'll get Tara outa jail," Morris added. "Get her away from that cocksucker Sean, too!"

Mike tried to look appreciative, but try as he might, he couldn't shake the sensation that the sky had broken open and dumped the entirety of its bleak contents onto his head. He started pacing the hallway, but it felt like his legs had shrunk down to the size of an insect's.

"You're gonna be fine," said Gibbons, as he headed to the stairs. "We'll get you out."

Sure. These guys could sneak an elephant outa town. That wasn't the problem. Leaving made sense. Staying wouldn't help his family. They had enough grief and misery without having to watch him swinging from the gallows. But he couldn't just run away, either. He had to see Mamai before he left. And the twins. Give 'em one last hug.. But most of all, he had to deal with Sean.

He headed briskly down the hallway and opened the kitchen door.

"What're ye doin'?" Tom asked.

"The Pennsy leaves at six. We'll need a coupla day's food."

"Ye nuts? It'll be daylight. They'll see us."

"Ye wanna stay here all day, sitting ducks, waitin' for night to come around again? Besides, I ain't waiting till six. Gonna kill Sean. Be back by four-thirty. Maybe five. Meet ye behind the West Shendo Coll'ry. The Pennsy comes right past. We'll catch it on the fly."

"Oh yeh?" Tom said with a huff. "Then I'm checkin' on my mom."

"Fine. But don't stay long. We need provisions. Food. Whiskey. Cash from the till. I'll be back in an hour. Maybe less. Sonofabitch is either asleep or drunk. It'll be quick."

"Better, 'cause I'm getting on that train. With or without you."

Chapter 38
Sunday, April 11, 1875

Mike ran up the steps, pulled out his gun, and burst inside with a guttural roar, but his finger froze on the trigger when he saw Li'l Bill curled up on the floor in a pool of blood, and the twins kneeling beside him. Mamai was cradling his head and Aunt Mary was crouched beside her. Everyone was weeping and the room smelled of blood, puke, and urine. He squinted through the hazy light, expecting Sean to say something scathing like, "So, the killer returns." But he said nothing. He was doubled over the table, with his face resting in his own vomit.

Mamai glanced up at Mike, at his revolver.

"Put it away, Mighael. Ye don't need it anymore."

"He's d- dead?"

"About an hour," Mary said, turning away from him.

Mike fumbled with his gun as he tried to slip it back into his waistband.

"Ye sure?"

"Deirdre, Johnny." Mamai stood up and gave them each a kiss. "Say goodnight to Mighael and go to bed. We'll plan Billy's wake tomorrow."

"I love you," Mike said, as he hugged them, blinking rapidly and trying not to cry.

As they trudged upstairs, Mamai glanced at Sean's corpse, then turned to Mike.

"I couldn't bear the thought of any more dead Doyles. Or any more in jail."

"We did it together." Mary squeezed Mamai's hand. "After the C&I left."

"Might even say Billy helped." A tiny smile emerged on Mamai's lips. "With his old medicine."

"Poured the whole damned bottle right into his whiskey glass."

Mike gazed at his aunt without blinking, as if her skin had

cracked open to reveal an entirely different person hiding inside. The true Aunt Mary. Da's big sister. A real Doyle, same as him. There to protect and defend them, just as Da would have. And Mamai. He had no idea she had it in her. All his life, telling him not to make waves. All her life, so terrified of risks, of having to flee again, like Avondale, or Tipperary. Yet, here she had taken the biggest risk imaginable and solved all her problems at once. No more dead Doyles. And nobody would ever suspect her!

"The twins are in good hands." He swiped at his tears.

Mamai grasped his wrist. "But what about Tara?"

"They can't keep her long." His voice deepened. He placed his other hand on top of hers. "My friend Ned's a constable. He'll look after her."

"Ye would've been proud of her, Mighael. Didn't tell those yellow dogs a thing! Told 'em Sean was lying. Even refused to go with 'em when they asked."

"Ye gotta talk to Fenton Cooney," he said. "There's money coming my way. They promised they'd get it to you. Enough for the wake and plenty more."

She flashed him a yearning smile.

"H-how soon ye leaving? Ye staying for Billy's wake?"

He glanced at the window. He knew he should leave now, before they came looking for him.

She covered her face with her hands and sobbed.

Mary went to the cupboard and returned with a basketful of biscuits.

"Take these. For your trip."

As she handed him the basket, Mike thought he heard clomping hooves outside and the squeal of wagon axels slowing to a stop. He considered jumping out the back window, fleeing through the coll'ry, hiding on Locust Mountain, but the cops were probably already surrounding the place. He'd just end up getting shot and dying in front of Mamai. She didn't deserve to go through that twice in one night.

He sat down and waited, determined to give them no reason to shoot. He squeezed Mamai's hand and watched, as the doorknob turned without a knock. The door swung open and Hannah stepped inside.

Bouncing back to his feet, he laughed out loud.

She ran into his arms. "Thank God, you're safe!"

Her neck smelled of sweet lavender. The ruffle of her bonnet tickled his scalp.

He struggled to speak.

"I-I thought ye were supposed to be at the O'Donnells', away from all this madness."

"I was." She pressed a finger to his lips. "We don't have much time. I borrowed their wagon. Tom's hiding in back. We need to go."

He knew she was right, but he wanted to press closer, to brush his fingers against her silky skin, to draw in her calming warmth one last time. Collect enough of it to last the rest of his life. God knows, he would need it.

He let go of Hannah and embraced Mamai.

"I'm so sorry," he said.

"Nothing to be sorry for." Her teardrops burned against his neck. "Just promise you'll be safe. That someday, we'll be together again."

He wanted to promise, but he couldn't imagine how and he couldn't bring himself to lie.

"I love ye, Mamai."

"C'mon," Hannah growled. "Ye wanna get caught?" She pried his hand away from Mamai and pulled him toward her. "I'm sorry, Mrs. Doyle. Tell Tara I love her?"

"Me, too," Mike said.

Aunt Mary stood by the door, holding the basket of biscuits in front of her, like she did with his lunch pail on his first day as a muleboy, only this time she reminded him more of a lion than a mouse. "You look just like your da. Only more confident."

Chapter 39
Sunday, April 11, 1875

Mike didn't realize he'd been asleep until Hannah pulled off the blanket and the bright midday sun seared through his lids. Using his hand as a visor, he slowly opened his eyes, sat up, and looked around, his back aching from the hours curled up on the hard bed of the wagon with Tom's knee in his spine. He quietly observed the station's blue roof and witch's hat cupola, and decided they must be at Mount Carmel Station. Gibbons said it was the best place to catch a train west to Pittsburgh. From there you could switch roads to anywhere in the country. Mike figured it would only take 'em a few days to reach Saint Louis, where they'd change their names, become invisible, and start new lives. Safe from Modocs, cops, and the gallows.

He climbed out of the wagon.

Hannah looked so beautiful, standing before him with the breeze rippling through her dress and her eyes sparkling in the sunlight. He pulled her into his arms, desperate to smell her neck and feel her heartbeat against his chest. Taste her lips. Feel her fingertips in the small of his back.

In another life, they'd get married, share these feelings forever.

"I'm gonna miss ye," he murmured, his voice cracking.

"Miss me?" Her hands fell to her sides. "I'm coming with ye!"

"Wait!" Tom hopped out of the wagon. "That wasn't part of the plan. She'll slow us down. Get us caught. We can't risk it."

"Really? Who got ye this far?"

He opened his mouth, but instead of responding, he became sullen and grim.

"If it wasn't for me, you'd both be in jail by now! And ye know why I did it? Why I risked my own freedom? Destroyed any hope of ever returning home?"

"Um, 'cause ye love me?" Mike said.

Her expression momentarily slackened, but then it turned

wrathy again.

"My parents thought I was frail and helpless, too. Turns out, they were the weak ones. Da was so scared of the gallows that he set you both up to take his place. And I'm the one that stopped it! So, who's the helpless one now?"

Mike grabbed the rim of the wagon bed for support. "Muff set us up?"

"Overheard him talking to my mom. McKenna said he'd hang if he didn't cooperate. Help catch some Mollies. Not just you, either. He's setting up Gibbons. Morris. Mr. Kehoe. Bunch of the Mannoy boys, too."

"That double-crosser!" Tom kicked the wagon. "He knows we're not Mollies!"

Mike still couldn't believe it was true, not after all they'd been through together. But if Muff was a traitor, everyone they knew would go to prison. Or hang. Including Morris and Ned. Then what would happen to Tara? Mamai would be devastated. The twins would grow up with no siblings. He truly wouldn't be able to come home again. Never.

His throat ached, like he was going to start sobbing. But he didn't want to cry. He wanted to destroy something. Hit somebody. Get revenge! It was precisely because of traitors, like Muff and McKenna, that he was in this mess. Kohinoor Boys had everything. Money. Respect. Decent jobs. They seemed powerful, invincible, but it was all just an illusion. A house of cards. They had no integrity. Their loyalty could be bought and sold, same as job cards and ballots. And what did it get them in the end? They lost the strike and most of 'em would wind up in jail or hanging by their necks.

He reached into the wagon, for their bindle, figuring a drink of whiskey would clear his head. But by the time he had the bindle, he forgot why he wanted it and was thinking about what Hannah had just said. She really had saved their hides. She had done more to protect him in the past few hours than Gibbons, or McKenna, or even her da, had done in the past few years. And she did it without harming anyone. Without any chicanery or threats. There'd be no retaliation by Modocs. No more tit for tat.

A light warmth washed over him, like a gentle, summer breeze at the end of a long and gratifying day. He slung the bindle casually over his shoulder and returned to Hannah's side, humming: *There's a Good Time Coming, Boys, A Good Time Coming.*

She smiled confidently, taking sleek, relaxed strides. She knew she had won.

He flashed her a knowing grin. "The O'Donnells are gonna miss their wagon."

"That all ye got to say?" Tom huffed, hustling to catch up. "We're running away from everything we know and love. Poorer than ever. Betrayed by everyone we ever trusted. We'll never see our families again. Our friends are gonna hang! And we'll still be looking over our shoulders the rest of our goddamned lives!"

Mike squeezed Hannah's hand. "We beat Muff and McKenna, didn't we?"

"Um." Tom smiled nervously. "Dumb luck."

"We beat the Modocs and C&I, too. Even Uncle Sean."

"Wait, didn't your mom and aunt kill him?" Tom rubbed his chin, pensively, then suddenly threw back his head and laughed. "Alright, maybe we do need to rely on others sometimes. And Hannah's a goddamned genius!"

Exactly, Mike thought. And now they were about to hop a train together, poor but free, without any debts or asshole bosses. Finally getting to see a bit of the country. Like real tramps.

Chapter 40
Pittsburgh
Monday, April 12, 1875

Mike ran for the hopper car, reaching for the ladder. Hannah was already up, scrambling over the rim of the car, onto the pile of coal inside it. Tom was on the car ahead of them.

Speeding up, Mike tried not to slip, ignoring the pain as rocks jabbed into his soles. Glassworks and steel mills blurred in his periphery. Straight ahead, the rusty iron truss of the Pittsburgh, Cincinnati & Saint Louis Bridge. Forty feet below, the frothy brown water of the Monongahela.

It was now or never.

Running faster, he caught the side of the ladder. Grasping the cold metal, he pulled himself onto the first step, and exhaled so deeply he nearly fell off.

Hannah was peering down at him, her hand clasped over her mouth. He wanted to hold her in his arms, tell her everything was alright, celebrate their victory. But he was still too jittery to move. He glanced over his shoulder, happy to be leaving Pittsburgh. Smokestacks sprouting everywhere, a forest of brick trees with black plumes for leaves. Air so filthy you couldn't see the end of the block at noon, even with the street lights on. The entire city, like living inside a coal breaker.

The train whistle hooted three times, like some strange metallic bird.

They were almost to the bridge. He had to climb up now, hoist himself over the rim into the pile of coal with Hannah. But when he looked up, there was a man in a blue uniform standing beside her, glaring at him with a long stick in his leather-gloved hand.

The shack!

He started backing down, with no plan in mind.

The brakeman leaned down and swung, cracking him across the knuckles.

Pain shot up his arm.

He refused to let go.

"No!" Hannah screamed, grabbing the brakeman's neck. She tried to pull him down.

His cap flew off and drifted past Mike, like an autumn leaf drifting to the ground. He swung his elbow into her ear, knocking her back into the coal.

"Hannah!"

Mike scampered back up the ladder.

The last thing he remembered was a flash of white light, his head throbbing, his body rolling down the embankment, rocks and sticks jabbing him in the arms and legs. And Hannah's voice trailing off. "I love you, Mike."

It was dark when he awoke. He was shivering cold and his head still hurt from the brakeman's bat. All he could think was that he had to hop the next freight, catch up with 'em in the next town. They'd surely be waiting. But when he tried to stand up, he fell back to the ground, screaming in pain.

He clutched his thigh and tried to hold it steady. The muscles in his shin kept twitching; each spasm like being kicked by a mule. Closing his eyes, he tried to coax his leg to calm down and relax. But all he could picture was his best friend and his best girl getting further and further away. His hopes and dreams, fading like mist on the horizon. The tragic irony of having simultaneously won the struggles that did not really matter in the end and losing the one that really did.

At some point, the contractions began to subside. He wasn't sure when, or why, but it was then that he settled in with the thought that it would be a long time, if ever, before he'd be able to hop another freight, and that he'd be living in the Big Smoke for the foreseeable future. That the future was really all he had left. And that when one has lost everything, including their hopes and dreams, maybe the future, with all its uncertainty, excitement, and potential, wasn't such a bad thing, after all.

THE END

If you enjoyed this novel, reviews are appreciated.

Acknowledgements

I would like to thank Suzaynn Schick and Sammy Dunn, for all their encouragement and patience, for reading my early drafts and never getting bored, and for all their suggestions on how to make it better. I want to thank Vida Pavesich for all her editing help in the final stages. And both of my developmental editors, Michael Mohr and David Aretha, for helping me to see the problems I could not see on my own. And Irv Schick, for his help with historical firefighting methods. And Michael and Pam Rosenthal, for their superb copy editing, and for helping me to appreciate the value of creating behavioral surprises in my characters. And James Tracy, for all his support and encouragement, for connecting me with indie publishers, and for his excellent blurb. And my old friend Russ Castronovo, for his outstanding blurb. And George Matiasz and Bill Meyers, for showing me the ropes of publishing.

After the Long Strike

This song-poem was written shortly after the Long Strike of 1875 and its final line is the basis for the title of my book, *Anywhere But Schuylkill*. The strike effectively destroyed the Workingmen's Benevolent Association (WBA), one of the largest industrial unions of its era. Many strikers were falsely convicted of murder and imprisoned or executed. Many others were blacklisted and had to leave Schuylkill County to find work. There would be no effecive union representing miners for another fifteen years, when the United Mine Workers formed in 1890.

Well, we've been beaten, beaten all to smash,
And now, sir, we've begun to feel the lash,
As wielded by a gigantic corporation,
Which runs the commonwealth and ruins the nation.
Our "Union" lamp, friend John, no longer shineth;
It's gone up where the gentle woodbine twineth;
A great man demonstrated beyond a doubt
The miners would better fare without
Any such thing; trade unions were a curse
Upon God's fair creation, nothing worse.
It died, because the miners did neglect it;
And he declares they shall not resurrect it.
And thus the matter stands. We do not dare
To look a boss in the face and whisper "Bah,"
Unless we wish to join the mighty train
Of miners wandering o'er the earth like Cain.
And, should you wish to start upon a tramp,
O'er hillock, mountain, valley, plain and swamp,
Or travel as the pilgrim of John Bunyan,
One talismanic word will do it, "Union."
Just murmur that, and all the laws of state
Or Congress will not save you from your fate;
They'll drive you out, forfeit your goods, degrade you,
Just as the British did in old Acadia.

Our wages, John, grow beautifully less,
And, if they keep on growing thus, I guess
We'll have to put on magnifying specs,
To see the little figures on our checks.

The sliding scale which once some comfort sent us
Is now declared to be non compos mentis.
To curse it dreadfully we are incited,
Because, somehow, it works so darned one-sided.
It suffers from a bad disease, "decline,"
And pines away right down to twenty-nine.

It's nothing strange to find on seeing the docket
We've worked a month and still are out of pocket.
It makes a man feel dirty cheap, you bet,
To work a month and then come out in debt.
And now, friend John, in fewer words I'll state
What I've been trying to communicate;
Lest anything herein you misconstrue,
In Anglo-Saxon plain I'll say to you—
If in exchange for the labor of a day
You wish to have an honest fair day's pay;
If you do wish to have just rights among
Those of freedom of action, speech and tongue,
If you do wish to have a fair supply
Of wholesome food, be buried when you die
With decent rites—by this I mean at least
Sufficient to distinguish man from beast,
Stay where you are, or, if you must go hence,
Go East, go North, go South, no consequence.
Take any direction; you'll be blest
Sooner with what you seek than coming West.
In short, if you wish to enjoy God's bounty,
Go anywhere but Schuylkill County.

Glossary

According to Hoyle: doing things strictly by the book, or according to the rules. It refers to Edmond Hoyle (1671-1769), a British barrister and writer who was the first to codify the rules for numerous games, including backgammon. He was most famous for his book, "A Short Treatise on the Game of Whist," from 1742.

AOH: acronym for the Ancient Order of Hibernians, America's oldest Catholic Irish fraternal organization. Founded in New York and in Pennsylvania in 1836, the AOH played a prominent role in supporting coal strikes in the 1870s, particularly the Long Strike of 1875, when the WBA (miners' union) was waning. As a result, the mine owners saw the AOH as an enormous threat and accused them of being a front for the Molly Maguires.

Black Damp: is one of the numerous dangerous gases that threatened miners' lives. Black damp is a mixture of carbon dioxide and nitrogen gas. It is heavier than air and, therefore, found near the floor of mines. It was also called Choke Damp because it could suffocate the miners. (See fire damp, below)

Black Maria: (pronounced "Black Ma-RYE-a") a horse drawn police wagon for rounding up striking miners, or an ambulance for taking them to the hospital after a mining accident. Some authorities believe the word was first used in New England in the early 1800s, but the term probably goes back much further, because there are similar terms in Norwegian (Maja, or Svarte Maja), Icelandic (Svarta Maria) and Serbo-Croatian (marica). The Clash referenced it in their song *Guns of Brixton*.

Bobtail Check: a paycheck in which the miner owed the Company more than he earned. Because the Company docked miners for tools, food, coal and medical expenses, some miners worked years without bringing home a penny. Take home pay was typically only 60-70% of a miner's salary, but only if he was frugal. In 1875, a contract miner earned only $3 per day and his laborers earned only $2. Additionally, mines often shut down for days at a time to regulate production and prices, leaving miners with expenses, but without any income. In 1875, the average miner worked only 132 days. Merle Travis refers to the bobtail check in his classic song: *Sixteen Tons* (You load 16 tons and what do you get? Another day older and deeper in debt).

Bony: (also known as "bone" or "cocko") is slang for slate and other impurities. "Gobbing the bone" meant cleaning the bony, or impurities, from the coal (or gob). However, gob also referred to the fine coal refuse left on the floor of the breaker or the mine pit.

Breaker: is a large building where coal was broken up and sorted into smaller, commercially practical chunks (e.g., chestnut was 0.875 to 0.9375 inches, whereas pea was 0.5 to 0.625 inches). Conveyor belts delivered the raw anthracite coal to the top of the breaker. From there, it went to the crusher, made of two cast iron rollers (one with teeth, one with holes to accept the teeth), before rolling down a chute to the cylindrical sorting screen. Finally, it traveled down long chutes to the breaker boys, who removed impurities, like slate and ash. Footmen loaded the cleaned coal into hopper cars for shipment to wholesalers and storage facilities.

Breaker Boys: boys who worked in the breaker, removing impurities from the coal after it was crushed and sorted. The boys (usually 10-12 years old, but sometimes as young as 6) sat on wooden planks above the chutes, kicking their feet in and out of the rushing coal to slow it down. They reached in with their bare hands to remove the impurities, sometimes slicing themselves because the slate could be sharp as glass. They weren't allowed to wear gloves because it impaired their dexterity. Consequently, their hands and knuckles would crack and bleed from the acidity of the coal (see Red Tip, below). Many lost limbs unclogging the belts or died from injuries. And the breaker boss hit them when they weren't working fast enough. Sometimes the boys exacted revenge by throwing coal at him, or by walking out en masse.

Breasts: are the rooms (or stopes) where mining occurred. Breasts resembled rectangular dark halls. Pillars were thick blocks or veins of coal between breasts. Wagon breasts (less than 6°) were large, shallow breasts that were big enough for wagons to carry away coal. Buggy breasts (6-12°) were steeper and required a buggy, not a wagon, to carry away coal. And Chute Breasts (12-90°) were so steep that coal had to be fed down a chute to reach the Gang Way.

Checkweighman: weighed the coal and determined what the miner earned. The miner was paid by the ton of coal he extracted. However, a ton was never really a ton, because it was presumed that a large percentage of it was actually slate, bone and rock. The checkweighman never properly examined the coal to see what percentage of it was actually anthracite, but the miner was docked the same every time, regardless, oftentimes by as much as 33%.

Clachan: a small settlement of clustered homes in Ireland. They were inhabited by renters who were usually members of the same extended family. There were no stores, schools or churches. Just the houses and the agricultural lands, which were held under the Rundale system, where absentee landlords took most of what was produced as rent, leaving the tenants with tiny, poor-quality plots for growing their own food. In *Anywhere But Schuylkill*, Mike Doyle's father, William Doyle, grew up on Drumnakeel Clachan, in Glenshesk glen, on the eastern side of Knocklayde Mountain, near Ballycastle, on the Antrim coast of Ireland.

Coal and Iron Police: a private police force, first established in Schuylkill County, PA, in 1865, by the Pinkerton Detective Agency. They were also known as the C&I or Yellowdogs. In the late 1800s or early 1900s, immigrant Slovak miners started calling them Cossacks. The Coal Operators used them to brutally suppress strikes, undermine union organizing and intimidate the miners. In 1897, they fired into a crowd of peacefully marching strikers at Lattimer Mine, killing 19 and injuring 32 others, in what became known as the Lattimer massacre. Their brutality was depicted in Dos Passos's "U.S.A Trilogy" and in Sherlock Holmes's novel, "The Valley of Fear."

Coll'ry: is a coal mine and its associated buildings and structures (e.g., headframe, mine shaft, breaker, stable). The correct spelling is "colliery," and the correct pronunciation is "call-yer-ee." However, according to CoalSpeak, the "official" coal region dictionary, the Schuylkill pronunciation is "call-ree."

Contract miner: a skilled miner who worked with explosives and tools to extract coal from a breast. He usually hired one or more laborers to help him shovel up the coal and load it into wagons, carts or buggies. Contract miners were paid by the amount of coal that they extracted, and then paid their laborers a fraction of that amount.

Coupla or Couple two three: some number between two and six, according to the Coal Speak Dictionary.

Cú Chulainn: or "Culann's Hound," was an Irish mythological demigod who appears in the stories of the Ulster Cycle. It is also the name of the prize gamecock in *Anywhere But Schuylkill*. The mythological Cú Chulainn was originally named Setanta. He got his new name as a child, after killing Culann's guard dog in self-defense and offering to take its place until a replacement could be found. He trained as a warrior in Scotland, under the mystical female warrior Scathach. As a youth, he performed superhuman feats, similar to those of Achilles. At 17, he single-handedly defeated an entire army. He was the champion of the Irish Kingdom of Ulster and unmatched as a killing machine. He had love affairs with warrior queens and fairies. But he was ultimately defeated at the age of 27, by another hero, Lugaid mac Con Roi, through sorcery and treachery.

Culm Heap: the waste pile found near mines and collieries. They were composed of slate, ash, clay and soil, along with fine bits of coal, and could grow as large as a hill. They smelled like rotten eggs from the hydrogen sulfide gas they emitted. Children often scavenged in them, looking for usable grains of coal they could bring home for their family's stove. The C&I arrested or harassed anyone who tried to take any. Sometimes the mounds shifted or collapsed, killing the children. They also caught fire and sometimes exploded, emitting a pale blue flame that was visible at night.

Fire Damp: highly explosive hydrocarbon gas. It was lighter than air and found near the roof of the breast (see black damp, above).

Gangway: the main road in and out of the mine, running from the shaft to the working breasts. They often had tracks for the shoofly (small gauge train). Manways were roads that ran perpendicular from the gangway to the breast, allowing men to get the coal from the breast to the shoofly. Monkey headings were airways, or ventilation tunnels, running parallel to the gangway. The gangway and airway met at the breasts. There was usually a furnace at the bottom of the shaft to maintain air circulation.

Grogoch: a half-human fairy, three to four feet tall, covered in coarse, red hair. They came originally from Scotland, but settled in northern Ireland. They had the power of invisibility, but could make themselves visible to trusted humans. Considered very sociable, they sometimes did chores for humans, especially in exchange for cream. They wore no clothing, just twigs and dirt that collected in their fur. There are no stories of female grogochs.

Headframe: (also known as a gallows frame, winding tower, hoist frame) is the framework above an underground mine shaft that enables the hoisting of machinery, personnel, or materials into the mine pit. Modern headframes are built out of steel or concrete. In the 1800s they were made of wood and resembled a giant gallows. The cage was the elevator that took the men and boys down the shaft to the bottom of the pit.

Jamoke: slang for a dimwitted fellow, (see Coalspeak dictionary). Many believe the word derives from "Java" and "Mocha, conveying that the person lacks the intelligence of a cup of coffee. However, there are other explanations. In the Martin Scorsese film, "Mean Streets," they use the epithet "moke," which may have been a bastardization of "jamoke." Or, "jamoke" might actually derive from "moke," which was used in the early 1800s, in Britain, as a term for donkey or mule. This derivation makes sense, considering how important mules were in nineteenth century mining, and how many miners came from the UK.

Molly Maguires: Irish terrorists who threatened and murdered mine bosses and scabs in the Pennsylvania coal fields. They supposedly infiltrated and dominated the WBA (miners' union, see below). However, the only evidence for such a terrorist conspiracy comes from the testimony of agent provocateur, James McParlan, and his boss, Allan Pinkerton, hired by the coal companies to destroy the WBA. Franklyn Gowen, president of the Reading Railroad, led the legal prosecution, resulting in the conviction of dozens of union activists. Twenty of them were executed on June 21, 1877. According to Irish World (June 30, 1877), the Mollies were "a fiction created in the course of a fierce class battle. . . No where. . . have we found. . . a single authentic document which showed the existence of a group or organization calling itself the MM."

Mumming: a type of itinerant play. The actors, known as mumers, or guisers, marched from house to house at Christmas and other holidays, performing their comical, allegorical plays. Common characters included: Captain Mummer, Beelzebub, the Fool, and Dr. Quack. Mumming was popular throughout much of Europe going back to the Middle Ages, and was brought to America by immigrants. It is still performed in some parts of the U.S., including Pennsylvania, where *Anywhere But Schuylkill* takes place. In some countries, including Ireland, mummers wore tall, conical wicker masks. To modern viewers, this might conjure images of the Ku Klux Klan, but masks in this shape have a long tradition in Catholicism, like the purple capriotes worn in processions during Spain's Semana Santa. To learn more about traditional Irish mumming, see Henry Glassie's, "All Silver and No Brass."

Nipper: errand boy. The nipper opened and closed the gates along the tracks, allowing the shoofly train to pass through. He helped control air flow in the mines by keeping the gates closed when not in use. Nippers spent 10-12 hours a day sitting alone in the dark. Many devised amusements to keep themselves preoccupied, like whittling and rat-killing competitions.

Once a man, twice a boy: When miners became too old and frail to work in the pits, lost limbs, or developed "miner's asthma" (black lung), they often went back to the breaker to work at the sorting tables. Since working in the breaker was considered boys' work, those who went back were "boys" a second time, but without the vigor and exuberance

Paid Criers: professional keeners or mourners. They were almost always female.

Payday Gait: to walk fast, as if in a hurry to pick up your paycheck.

Pluck Me: the Company Store. Everything was more expensive and lower quality than at a public store, but for miners living in remote patch towns, it was often the only choice available. Furthermore, the miners were paid in scrip and had no legal currency; therefore, the Pluck Me was the only place they could shop. So, the Company plucked them once with low wages and again when they sold them their overpriced merchandise. Merle Travis refers to this in his classic Sixteen Tons: *Saint Peter don't you call me, 'cause I can't go. I owe my soul to the Company store.*

Red Tip: a skin condition that afflicted breaker boys' hands. It resulted from exposure to sulfuric acid, which formed when the coal was washed to remove impurities.

Robbing the Pillars: the treacherous job of cutting coal from the pillars (walls supporting the roof). Miners would start with the last pillar at end of gangway, so they could retreat toward the shaft if the overburden started to collapse. Many men died robbing the pillars, when the overburden collapsed on their heads. At the Coal Region History Chronicles (online), you can read the harrowing story of 16 men, trapped when a huge chasm opened up after they robbed the pillars.

Scrapple: a loaf of cooked hog offal, thickened with cornmeal or buckwheat, and spiced with sage and pepper. German immigrants (the Pennsylvania Dutch) brought the dish to Pennsylvania. They called it *panhas* or *pannhaas*, meaning "pan rabbit."

Shoofly: slang for the small-gauge train that took miners from the shaft to their breasts. It also delivered coal from their breasts back to the shaft. It ran along tracks on the gangway. Shoofly is also the name of a molasses pie, popular among the Pennsylvania Dutch.

Sidedoor Pullman: hobo slang for boxcar.

Sprag: a wooden stick, stuck into the wheels of a coal car to slow it down (like a brake). Spraggers were boys who slowed down the coal cars by spragging their wheels. This prevented coal cars from picking up too much speed and derailing. Spraggers sometimes lost fingers or hands when a sprag got caught.

Van Diemen's Land: early British name for Tasmania, where the British had a penal colony. From the early 1800s to the 1853 abolition of penal transportation, some 73,000 convicts were transported to Van Diemen's Land, including many Irish revolutionaries. In *Anywhere But Schuylkill*, Mamai tells the story of how her family fled Ireland to avoid having her father arrested and sent to Van Diemen's Land for his role in the Famine Rebellion, in Tipperary, also known as the Battle of Ballingary. The song, Van Diemen's Land, by U2, is about John Boyle O'Reilly, poet and revolutionary Fenian, who was sent to the penal colony in Tasmania for treason. He later escaped to Boston.

WBA: John Siney founded the Workingmen's Benevolent Association in 1868, in Schuylkill County, PA. The WBA fought for higher wages, safer working conditions and sickness and death benefits. In 1868, they struck for enforcement of Pennsylvania's new 8-hour workday. By 1869, they had organized 32,000 out of the 36,000 miners in Pennsylvania's anthracite coalfields. The WBA was one of the nation's first industrial unions, organizing all workers within the industry into a single union (in contrast to craft unions, which were organized by job title).

About the Author

Michael Dunn writes Working-Class Fiction from the Not So Gilded Age. *Anywhere But Schuylkill* is the first in his Great Upheaval trilogy. A lifelong union activist, he has always been drawn to stories of the past, particularly those of regular working people, struggling to make a better life for themselves and their families. Stories most people do not know, or have forgotten, because history is written by the victors, the robber barons and plutocrats, not the workers and immigrants. Yet their stories are among the most compelling in America. They resonate today because they are the stories of our own ancestors, because their passions and desires, struggles and tragedies, were so similar to our own.

When Michael Dunn is not writing historical fiction, he teaches high school, and writes about labor history and culture. His labor history has been published in several online and print magazines. He also enjoys reading. Some of his favorite writers are: Flannery O'Connor, Toni Morrison, John Dos Passos, Victor Serge, B. Traven and John Steinbeck, as well as contemporary writers like Jess Walter, Wiley Cash, Wu Ming, Roberto Bolano, Arundhati Roy and Isabel Allende.

To learn more about Michael Dunn, the world of his characters, or to read his labor history blog and social media posts, please visit:

https://michaeldunnauthor.com/
https://www.facebook.com/Michael.Dunn.Fiction
https://twitter.com/MikeDunnAuthor
https://www.instagram.com/michaeldunnauthor/
https://kolektiva.social/@MikeDunnAuthor
https://www.thehistoricalfictioncompany.com/hp-authors/michael-dunn

www.historiumpress.com